FIVE   1/197   T. NEWTON SCHULTZ

ASANAS
AND OTHER STORIES
By
David Martin Wood

Drawings by Ted Schultz, a lifer, a friend.

ETERNAL WANDERER PRESS
P. O. Box 55452
St. Petersburg, FL 33732
dmw.13@netzero.net
pawsore@netzero.net
eiryu113144@yahoo.com
huntertrilogy@yahoo.com

Dedicated to Douglas Voak,

A lifer, a friend,

A man who is ready to come home.

PREFACE

I've been writing since I was ten, poems, stories, anything I could, living the frustrations of a young writer, and equally frustrating was trying to get my stuff into print, because like most people, I was afraid of rejection. I am still afraid of rejection, but I managed to get a few of my short stories published over the long haul. These pieces are probably reflections of me, or more likely, different facets of a large, tarnished jewel. I tried to be serious sometimes, sometimes sad, and sometimes I was terribly melodramatic.

I got my first story, "The Gift," published in **The Obelisk, 1977,** the St. Petersburg Junior College literary magazine, when I was the editor, which was the only way, I believed, I could get an editor to accept one of my pieces. When I landed myself in prison in 1987, I thought I would never get anything published again. But I bought legal tablets and kept writing and, in my opinion, improved in what I wrote. I eventually started sending them out to literary markets, more specifically those thin chapbook things published in someone's garage with all the blood and marrow of someone who believed in the importance of writing and being read. None of my stuff was great literature, but someone liked it, and through that means, I began to like my stories as well. I was being rescued by a lot of editors who were spending their own time and money to get me and other writers out where someone could read them.

These stories are not bastions of wisdom or miracles of style, just little pieces I wrote. I have included all the stories I published so far, some humorous, some dark, some thoughtful. I ended with prison stories, because having spent so much time in prison, it marks a turning point in my life, a point where I certified how terrible a person I could be, and how much of a survivor I had to become.

In 1987, I sexually molested my twelve year old stepdaughter five times. I am terribly ashamed of what I did, and I wish I could come up with some mitigating factor or reasonable excuse for my crimes, but there is none. I wish I could go back in time and undo all that I did wrong, but time only goes in one direction. There is the knowledge that, right now, I am the same person who did these things back then, though now I cringe at what I did then, and there is the knowing that somewhere out there someone is carrying the scars of my actions. The pain I feel, the pain I caused, is not reflected in these pages, and I hope someday I will be good enough and brave enough to put words to them. For now, though, all I have is this collection of short stories.

Though my stories are all fiction with made up names, they carry little shards of my life, even the silliest ones, reflecting times I laughed or cried or simply hurt. Sometimes I wonder how I made it this far, and in the end I know the answer, people, family, friends and strangers, all of whom gave me a nudge in the right direction when I was lost or fallen or wounded. I have tried to return those favors, helping out others when I could not help those who helped me, but in the end one is in a constant barter with the world, returning loans and receiving gifts. Some of my friends tell me to never look back, but I believe by looking back you can sometimes get the feeling of where you are actually going. Perhaps that is why I wrote these stories.

Someone once said, we might be through with the past, but the past is not through with us. I believe it.

I haven't written a decent short story in a decade. I wanted to put these ones out there as a reminder, more to me than to you, of what I could do, and what I wanted to do again sometime soon. These stories are about the wilderness, prison, family, friends, good people acting bad, or maybe acting good. Some are over-written and some under-written. But, once, they moved me deeply, and, I think, they moved other people as well. I want them to move me and others again. I hope you enjoy them, dear reader, and see where they lead you to.

--David

Polonius: What do you read, my lord?
Hamlet: Words, words, words.
(Hamlet, Act II, Scene 2, Lines 194 & 195)

CONTENTS

FIVE   1/'97   T. NEWTON SCHULTZ

ASANAS
AND OTHER STORIES
By
David M. Wood

BOOTS'S STORY ABOUT PRINCESS

". . . and so Cinderella and the Prince lived happily ever after."

"Tell me another story, huh, Mom?"

"Not tonight Hon, it's time for you to go to sleep."

"Awww, Mom . . . ."

"Now you remember what I said, Tracy. Just one story tonight, and then you get to sleep."

Tracy frowned, but her mother couldn't see it in the dark. "Oh, all right," she mumbled, lying back in bed and pulling the covers up to her chin.

Her mother kissed her forehead and went to the door. "See you in the morning, Tracy."

"Nite, Mom."

A beam of light from the hallway momentarily came through the door as Tracy's mother left the room. Tracy blinked and buried her head under the warm blankets. Two green eyes under the bed reflected the hall light, but her mother didn't see them. When the bedroom door closed, and it was dark again, a small tenor voice announced, "She's finally gone."

"Hush!" Tracy's head came out of the covers. "She'll hear you if you're too loud."

"Don't worry, kid," the tabby cat said, crawling out from under the bed. "I hear her footsteps. She's walking away." The tabby leaped onto Tracy's bed and touched his nose against hers. "I'm just concerned that your mother might find that hole in the cellar window screen. If she does, the only other way out of the cellar is the furnace chimney."

Tracy sat up in bed and put her chin in her hands. "I guess you're pretty smart, huh?" The cat purred in agreement, licking one of his hind legs. "Are all cats as smart as you?"

"Kid," the tabby said, "if all cats were as smart as me, you wouldn't see any lying by the side of the road with tire marks on them."

"I guess I got the smartest cat around, huh?"

"Sure, kid," the tabby purred. "And I got the smartest little girl."

"Yeah, but you're real special, Boots," Tracy said, hugging the cat. "And I love you." Now Boots was a very private kind of cat, and enjoyed being hugged and cuddled almost as much as he liked huddling on the roof during a freezing rainstorm. But this was Tracy, and with her, he always endured it. What else could he do? He loved her back.

When Tracy released her grip, Boots leaped to the foot of the bed, where he stretched his body, his paws extended and his claws unsheathed. He always made it a point to do this away from Tracy so he wouldn't hurt her. Once, late at night, he forgot himself, and he stretched under the covers. He accidentally scratched Tracy, and she woke with a yell. He just barely got under the bed before her mother came in, thinking she was having a bad nightmare. Tracy scolded him about it later, and he was much more careful after that.

"So what do you want to do tonight?" Boots asked, making himself comfortable.

"Hear another story," Tracy said without hesitation.

"All right," Boots purred. "You talked me into it. Besides I felt like telling a story tonight." Actually he was in no mood for telling stories, but he enjoyed making

Tracy happy. That's also why he never complained about his name, which he detested more than hairballs. He would've preferred a name with some machismo, like Napoleon or Rocky, or even Rambo, but Boots was his fate. "So what story do you want to hear tonight?"

"Well . . ." Tracy pondered. "I heard 'Puss 'N Boots' last night . . ." Boots once explained that Puss 'N Boots was a real cat from cat history, though his real name was Henry 'N Steeltoes . . . " . . . and I'm tired of hearing how Morris became a star . . ." Though Morris was before her time, Boots told her the story of how Morris bribed his way to the top. " . . . and you said you'd tell me the story of Felix-Le-Lobo on Friday night, when I didn't have to go to school in the morning . . ." This was a long folk-tale known only to cats about their legendary cat-hero. " . . . so I guess I'd like to hear about Princess tonight."

"That's a good choice," Boots remarked. It was one of the stories he hadn't told her yet. He cleared his throat and began, "Now as you know, cats can speak any language that they please, though they prefer not to, because human language is so tedious . . ."

"I know that," Tracy moaned. "Get back to the story!"

"In any case," Boots continued, "the story about Princess the Cat is one that mama cats tell their kittens before they teach them English . . ."

"What if they live in China?" Tracy asked.

" . . . or Chinese . . ."

"How about France?"

"Do you want to hear this story or not?" Boots hissed. Tracy giggled and hugged him, and he continued. "As you know, a cat is extremely careful about the person he or she chooses to talk to. If a cat is not careful who he talks to, disaster could follow. And this is what happened to Princess.

"Once upon a time in the mythical city of New York, there lived a little old lady named Mrs. Walgrove, a widow who was a recluse, living near a small market who . . ."

"What's that?" Tracy asked.

"What's what?" Boots sighed after mentally counting to ten.

"What's a re-cluse?"

"A recluse is a person who lives alone and doesn't really have any friends," Boots explained, examining his right paw. "Mrs. Walgrove was a recluse. She had no real contact with anybody around her. But she did have company of a sort, a cat named Princess.

"Mrs. Walgrove and Princess were very close, and neither one had any real friends outside their little apartment. Maybe that is why Princess decided to talk to her one day. You see, cats almost always talk to children because children usually keep it a secret. And even if they didn't, well, Mom and Dad would just say the kid had a terrific imagination. However, some cats talk with older people, retired grandparents or such, because old people are often loving and trusting.

"I guess that was the case with Princess.

"One day, as Mrs. Walgrove set a bowl of cat food with beef gravy down on her kitchen linoleum floor, she called Princess in, and as the cat sniffed the bowl of food and Mrs. Walgrove left the kitchen, she heard, 'Thank you, Ma'am.'

"Mrs. Walgrove turned and looked at her cat, who was peacefully eating her food. She checked her hearing aid, glanced around as though expecting somebody else to be there, then glanced back at Princess. She laughed, feeling silly, then said, 'You're so very welcome, my little friend.'

"Princess looked up from her bowl and licked her lips. 'Yes, Ma'am, I know, and I appreciate it.'

"Mrs. Walgrove swooned all the way to the bathroom where she located her salts. Panicked, Princess followed her in. 'Are you all right?' she asked.

"The old woman screamed and clutched at her heart, then leaped onto the toilet. 'Get away from me!' she shouted, and Princess dashed back to the kitchen.

"Hours later, when Mrs. Walgrove went to see her cat, broom in hand, Princess sat on the kitchen floor, expecting her. 'It's all right,' the cat said, 'I'm just a friend. I won't hurt you. You're not going nuts, Missus.' Slowly Mrs. Walgrove put the broom down and sat on the floor across from her cat. She listened as Princess talked about life in the alley before she came to live in the apartment, and in a week they were both talking to each other without a second thought. Mrs. Walgrove was thrilled. It just warmed her heart to have someone to talk to, and Princess felt the same way.

"From then on, they did everything together, the way old friends would. They'd sit on the couch, side by side, watching soap operas, listening to the radio, or maybe talking about their old memories. Mrs. Walgrove taught Princess how to play two-handed solitaire and checkers, and Princess taught her to play Meowser, a highly complicated game in which one tried to score points by rolling and unraveling a ball of yarn while lying on the floor. The two went for strolls in Central Park, and Mrs. Walgrove no longer had any problems with muggers, who were afraid to rob anybody who talked that much to a cat.

In the evenings, Mrs. Walgrove would read the newspaper to Princess who couldn't read herself (Yes! Yes, Tracy, I remember that you taught me to read from your second-grade reader!), but liked hearing everything on the sports page and the comics.

"Everything went well until one day, when Mrs. Walgrove was standing in a checkout line. She heard the woman in front of her bragging about her mastiff, 'Old Bellow comes when called, and he brings the paper, and guards the house . . .' A Mastiff! They slobber and fart and have runny noses and the brains of gnats! '. . . and Bellows won a lot of ribbons. He stands on his hind legs at command, and . . .'

"'Big deal,' Mrs. Walgrove mumbled, probably tired (and who can blame her?) Of hearing about that stupid dog. 'I have a cat named Princess who talks.'

"The mastiff-lady turned around, snooty-like, and asked, 'So, what does Princess say? Meow?'

"'She does that, too,' Mrs. Walgrove said, 'when she isn't speaking English.' The mastiff-lady laughed, which kept the argument going, until Mrs. Walgrove finally invited her over to the apartment with a few of her friends for dinner and a cat conversation. The lady agreed.

"But Princess didn't like the idea at all, and clammed up from the moment Mrs. Walgrove told her. The old woman didn't take the hint, and when the dinner guests arrived and later when dinner was over with, she brought Princess in. Despite her prodding and pleading, Princess wouldn't talk and the guests including the mastiff-lady, were really feeling uncomfortable watching Mrs. Walgrove on all fours begging a cat.'

"Finally, Mrs. Walgrove began crying, and taking the cat's paw in her hand, said, 'If you're really my friend, please show these people you can talk. If you don't, they'll think I'm crazy.'

"This is what broke that poor cat's heart. Right then and there, going against her better judgment, Princess cried out, 'Please don't cry, Missus. I'll talk for you!'

"Several teacups dropped to the floor. One dinner guest passed out. Hands shook like palsy, and eyes were wide. The cat really could talk! Once they all calmed down, they began talking to Princess, and she began answering. It wasn't a trick, and Mrs. Walgrove wasn't throwing her voice. The cat's lips were actually moving, they all saw it. Now they believed and Mrs. Walgrove was proud of her cat.

"When the guests were finally gone, Princess thought that this was the end of it, but she was wrong; it was only the beginning. More people came to hear her speak, and still more. She had her photograph in the New York Times and the New Yorker, and the A.P. and U.P.I. wire services picked up the story, and Princess graced the front pages of newspapers across the country, then across the globe.

"Scientists came to test Princess, to see if she could really talk, and why she could talk. Government officials came to see if she was a security threat, and if she had any way to teach Socks how to speak. Newsmen from **Times**, **People**, **Newsweek**, and **Life** wanted to do pictorial exposes.

"From then on, Mrs. Walgrove and Princess never had a moment's peace, and they longed for the quieter days before the world found out about the talking cat. Princess appeared on 'Oprah,' 'Dr. Phil,' 'Jerry Springer,' 'Saturday Night Live' as guest host, 'Meet the Press' and dozens of other television shows where she told her life story and talked about many different things that no cat in the world ever cared about before or since.

"In time Princess acquired a manager and a lawyer to keep track of business. She made a fortune doing commercial spots for cat food, tires, antiperspirant, cigarettes, feminine products, and furriers. She joined the Actor's Guild and got bit parts in various soaps and prime time sit-coms. She became a star in a full-length Disney action movie about a cat trying to make its way home after accidentally being stranded in Siberia.

"Mrs. Walgrove and Princess eventually moved from their tenement apartment into a penthouse overlooking Central Park where they used to stroll together. They had a live-in maid and a secretary. Princess had to sign her documents with her pawprint and Mrs. Walgrove was kept busy as her cat's personal manager. They hardly had time to talk to each other anymore. Neither one was happy.

"Princess eventually became so nervous with her busy schedule that she developed an ulcer. Then she began to drink and smoke to calm her nerves, and Mrs. Walgrove, just as nervous, began taking Valiums like they were M & M's. They threw penthouse parties attended only by alley cats and octogenarians, with tubs of catnip and Geritol for endless consumption. There were many times when Princess and Mrs. Walgrove, once best friends, would fight bitterly, with Mrs. Walgrove yelling and throwing couch pillows and Princess hissing and shredding furniture legs. Their fights and general unhappiness became terrible. All that was left was a diamond-studded cat bowl to the old cat toys, memories of a simpler past.

"But Princess was never seen or heard from again. The police, F.B.I., or C.I.A. found neither pawprint nor hair of her. Mrs. Walgrove neither heard news, nor rumor of what became of her cat, and she spent the rest of her life in lonely misery. She regretted ever telling another soul that her cat could talk." Here, Boots went silent, yawning and smacking his lips.

Tracy, whose eyelids were growing heavy, had to ask, "But what ever happened to Princess?"

"Nobody knows," Boots said. "Some say that perhaps the cat nappers let her go, or maybe she escaped, and wanders around filthy alleyways looking for a happy past among the debris and garbage cans. Some say that she's the only cat on Skid Row who tells her life story to any drunk who will listen. Some say that she was killed, and some say that she fell into the hands of some unscrupulous taxidermist and is now posed forever on his fireplace mantle."

There was a sad silence that settled like a stage curtain over the girl and tabby. "Boots," Tracy whispered, "Please tell me . . . did this story really happen?"

"No, dear Tracy, no," Boots answered. "It's just a story that mama cats tell their young. It never really happened, and it never will happen . . . unless you tell somebody that I talk, you sneaky girl!" And with that, Boots playfully nipped Tracy's ear.

"Hee-hee-hee . . . cut that out!" Tracy cheerfully laughed, catching Boots and holding him in the air. "You know I'd never tell anyone in the whole world about you!" She hugged her small friend. "I love you too much!"

"Now, now," Boots said. "It's time to get some sleep. I have to wake up early tomorrow and sneak back to the cellar before your mom comes up. And you have to go to school tomorrow. Did you study for your spelling test tomorrow?"

"Yup! You wanna hear it?"

"Not tonight . . . we both need our rest." Boots snuggled closer to Tracy, purring.

"G'night Boots."

"Goodnight kid" In the dark, two friend closed their eyes and snuggled together. It wasn't long before there was the sound of a child's relaxed breathing. The covers stirred and from beneath their warmth, a small, tenor voice said, "And I love you too, kid."

THE NIGHT OF MENAPEDE

Michelle Jessica Varley screamed when she saw the body dangling in front of her bathroom door, its arms and legs hanging limp, its head in a noose tied to the hall light. Then she recognized the Richard Nixon mask. She squeezed an arm, noticing how soft and light it was — nothing more than clothes stuffed with newspapers. "Peed!" Michelle fumed, pulling her bathrobe tighter.

The phone rang and she dashed to her bedroom to answer it. "Hello?" she said. "Menapede? Yeah, you bet you heard me scream, dammit! Yes, I found your scarecrow!" Michelle pulled the towel off her dark-blond hair and rubbed it over her head a few more times. "Yes, that was a pretty stupid idea, Peed! There's a rapist loose in the city, and your dummy scared the tar outta me! Yes, really!"

A black cat with white facial markings came in and rubbed its back against Michelle's legs. "I know you didn't mean any harm, Peed, but . . . What do you mean fear is good for my heart?" She bent down and scratched behind the cat's ears. It closed its eyes and purred contentedly. "Well, I'll accept your apology, but please don't come into my house any more tonight. There's a reason all the doors are locked, you know."

Michelle listened for a moment, her impatience visible on her face. "What reason are the doors locked? To keep **you** out, Peed," Michelle fumed. "Yeah, okay, I'll talk to you tomorrow. Goodbye." She hung up the phone, sighed, and picked up her cat. "Hello, Marcel Marceau," she chortled. "You haven't been watching the house very well, have you? That girl got in again. I hope you hid from her. She does terrible, terrible things to cats!" Michelle held her tolerant pet up as though to examine it.

The phone rang again, and Marcel leaped form Michelle's clutches as she answered it. "Hello?" she said, brushing her hair with her free hand. "Anne? Anne Hilton? Anne! I haven't heard from you since graduation. What's it like at Michigan State?" Michelle listened intently, her hairbrush pausing in midstroke. "Uh huh. Uh huh. You heard about that? Yeah, the story about that rapist has been in the news for a week. The guy raped six women so far. They call him the Screwdriver Stalker because he always carries a screwdriver with him when he breaks into a house. No other tools, no weapons, no clothes, just him and a screwdriver. It really gives me the creeps. Yeah, I bet you're glad to be in Michigan these days!

"No, I'm at the community college this year. I'm majoring in English, but I don't have any plans . . ." She stopped talking. A short, skinny girl with black, tangled hair and dirty cheeks was standing in the doorway. Her bright eyes and mischievous grin was a cross between cute and feral, and but for her modern, dirty clothes, she might have been mistaken for a lost child from a prehistoric tribe. "Excuse me," Michelle said, then put her hand over the mouthpiece. "Menapede, what are you doing here?"

Menapede looked down at her bare feet as she rocked from heel to toe. She wore threadbare blue jeans, a filthy Grateful Dead t-shirt, and a necklace made out of chicken bone sections. Her hair was so long and tangled that it didn't grow on her head — Michelle thought to herself — it just happened there, about the same way an iceberg happened to the Titanic. "Well," Menapede said in her high-pitched, raspy voice. "I sorta thought maybe I oughta warn you about the other scarecrow." She looked up, her grin even wider.

"Well, you can take both your dummies home," Michelle said. "And please stop picking the lock on the front door."

"I won't," Menapede said. "I broke my skeleton key in it just now, and it doesn't open anymore."

"Peed!" Michelle shouted.

"But you know what?" Menapede went on. "If you get me a hammer, I can fix it!"

"No, you won't, Peed! Just go home!"

"But the front door won't open."

"Go out the back door, or go out a window, but just go."

"But, Michelle . . . "

"Menapede!" Michelle stood firm. Menapede frowned, turned and padded out. "Good riddance," Michelle muttered, uncovering the receiver.

"Anne, you still there? I'm sorry about the interruption. It was just the neighbor's kid. A real pest, a female Dennis the Menace. Her name is Menapede Priscilla Jones. Everyone calls her Peed for short. Yeah, a real 'cute' kid. She's about ten years old, going on forty. She was over here to talk about her 'scarecrows.' No, they aren't real scarecrows, they're life-sized dummies she makes out of her father's clothes and stuffed with old newspapers or old rags. She hung one outside my bathroom door while I took a shower, and when I stepped out, I almost crapped myself."

Michelle listened to her friend as she examined an ingrown toenail. The red nail polish was all but worn off. She had been so busy in her studies she hadn't noticed until now. "What?" she asked. "Yeah, I lock my doors, but she knows how to pick locks. No, Anne, this is not a normal kid!

"Her family moved in next door about three months ago. Her mother and father seemed okay, but Menapede could have been a refugee from the Addams's Family. I know how some girls are just tomboys, I was once myself, but this kid is more like a Sasquatch. Sometimes she gets so filthy when she's playing that I wonder if the bathtub doesn't shudder as she gets in. And her hair is such a mess that I'd like to introduce her to a hairbrush someday."

Michelle listened again before continuing. "I know her so well because she's always around. From the first day she showed up, she started hanging around me. She'd be over every day after my classes to see what I was up to. And you know that seven-foot-high fence around my yard? She took a section of fence down between my yard and hers so she could visit me in my backyard as well. Yes, she . . ."

"Michelle . . ." Menapede said in a singsong voice. She was standing at the bedroom door, a plate of brownies in her hands.

"Wait a minute, Anne," Michelle said, covering the mouthpiece again. "Isn't it past your bedtime, Peed?"

"I wanted to bring you these," Menapede said, ignoring the annoyance in Michelle's voice. "And I'm bored." She smiled and picked her nose.

Michelle nibbled her lower lip. "Put them on my dresser," she said. "Thank you. They're very nice, but I'm busy. Go home and talk to Jack."

"Jack's busy sharpening his knives. Can I play with Marcel?"

"No!" Michelle shouted. "Stay away from Marcel! Now go home! I mean it!" Menapede frowned, put the plate of brownies down, and left. Michelle glanced around until she saw her cat safe under a chair, then lifted her hand off the mouthpiece.

"Anne? Yeah, it was her again. It must be the night of Menapede! Sometimes I wish she'd just move away and get out of my life. I don't know why she doesn't play with kids her own age. She's always annoying me, and always doing strange things.

"Like, just now, for instance. She brought me a plate of brownies." Michelle paused and listened, picking at a tooth with a fingernail. "Yeah, I know that was nice of her. She made the brownies herself. She was trying to make up to me because I was mad about her scarecrow. No, I'm not going to eat them! Why? Because she likes to add potato chips and bacon bits to the recipe to make them crunchy."

Michelle paused and listened, sighing as she glanced at the ceiling. "I am not being mean, Anne. And I do try to be nice. The other day I even visited her. Her backyard was completely bare of grass, but there's an old oak tree in the middle of the yard, and she built a tree house in its branches. She also built herself a swing set, completely made of two-by-fours, nails and ropes. She also built this large plywood thing, eight foot by eight foot square, out of four-by-fours and one large plywood sheet. It's braced against an extended oak branch and looks like an unused billboard.

"I didn't see her at first, but I heard her voice. When I got around that billboard thing, I found her talking to herself in this deep hole. Actually, she was talking to her imaginary friend, Jack the Ripper. What was she digging? A tiger trap, that's what she said. It was certainly deep enough. She used a ladder to get in and out. But I think she filled it in, at least for now.

"Anyhow, she was glad to see me, and offered me the grand tour of her bedroom. You know how kids are. I asked if she collected dolls, and she said yes, and showed me. I nearly fainted. They all had needles in them. They were voodoo dolls!"

"Then I had to ask if she had any pets. She said yes, and showed me this large aquarium with a screen over it. At first I thought she was raising snakes — she's the kind of girl who would. But I never expected to see what I saw when I looked closer. The aquarium was buzzing with house flies, and she said she planned to breed them in captivity if they ever became an endangered species. She even showed me her fly cemetery in the back yard.

"But what really got me upset was her collection of cat skins on the walls. Yes, cat skins. No, I don't know where she got them, but I keep an eye on Marcel Marceau whenever she visits. I don't care if she's just a kid, I think . . ." Michelle paused, glancing at her bedroom window. "Anne? I'm sorry, I thought I saw something outside. No, my parents are out tonight, and so are Menapede's. I guess her scarecrow gave me the creeps worse than I thought. Yeah, and . . ."

*   *   *   *   *

Arthur Middleton preferred to think of it as his own way of coping with his mid-life crisis. In his own community, he was known as the Energetic Electrician. In other communities, he was known as the Screwdriver Stalker. He grinned as he looked through Michelle's window again. "Girl, you don't know it yet, but tonight's your lucky night!" He started humming as he took his clothes off. Finally naked, he drew a comb and hand mirror out of his gym bag and diligently straightened his hair. "Arthur Middleton always goes in style," he said.

He got the coconut oil out and liberally covered himself. Finally done, he admired his gleaming body in the moonlight. "Superb!" he said. "And now . . ." He began groping through his gym bag. "Is it Regular and Phillip tonight?" He tossed hygiene products around while rummaging through the bag, and his confidence began fading as he realized that the screwdrivers were missing. "Damn!" he fumed, slapping his forehead. "I left them on the kitchen counter! How could I be so stupid! I need a screwdriver! It's my trademark!"

He calmed down, sighed, and shook his head. "Well, the show must go on," he muttered. "The kitchen window is open. I'll just have to work acapella." He squirted Binaca in his mouth, cleared his throat, and picked up the wire cutters

*   *   *   *   *

"Now I know you're crazy, Anne," Michelle laughed. "I was never like that when I was her age! Nobody was that way at her age. But I . . . Hello? Anne? Hello?"

The phone had gone dead. Michelle grumbled to herself and put her bunny slippers on. There was another phone in the kitchen. On her way, she stopped long enough to unhang the "scarecrow" and put it in the bathroom, propping it on the toilet and wondering if she should leave it there until her parents got home. She went to the kitchen and tried the wall phone. "Dead," she muttered.

She was just out of the kitchen when she stopped. What had she just seen? She poked her head back in the kitchen and saw a large, naked man, his skin glistening, his eyes glaring, his grin so wide it was ridiculous. "Oh, Menapede!" she fumed, starting for her bedroom. Then she laughed. It was the most ridiculous dummy Menapede had made. And she did say she put a second "scarecrow" in the house, didn't she? The girl was perpetually bizarre.

"Wait a minute!" Michelle said when she got back to her bedroom, a chill running down her spine. "Wait a minute! That dummy was naked!"

* * * * *

Arthur was almost in tears. "She called me Menapede!" he lamented. "She called me Menapede! And then she laughed!" He clenched his fists, his body shivering with fury. "I knew she wouldn't recognize me without my screwdriver! But I'll give her something to remember me by!"

He began rummaging through the kitchen drawers until he came to the cutlery, then pulled out the largest butcher knife he could find. He headed down the hall until he spotted the noose dangling from the hall light. He stopped and examined it, but from the corner of his eye, he noticed someone sitting in the dark on the bathroom toilet. In one quick motion, he leaped into the bathroom, grabbing hair and holding the knife ready to strike. "Nixon!" he growled as the wig came off in his hand. "What the hell is this?"

He went down the hall to Michelle's room, but didn't see her inside. "All right," he said, squatting and looking under the bed, seeing nothing but dust-balls and a black cat with white facial markings, watching him intently. "You know I'm here, and I know you're here! If you come out of hiding, it'll make things easy for both of us. You know you can't escape!"

He glanced about, then saw the closet door. "I don't see why you're hiding," he said. "I'm a celebrity, you know. I read about myself in the newspapers every day! Ha-ha!"

*   *   *   *   *

This is stupid! Michelle thought to herself, hiding behind her window drapes, knowing her feet were visible. This is really stupid! That's the Screwdriver Stalker! He's going to find me! I'm done for! This will never work!

"Come out, come out, wherever you are!" the Stalker sang. "Ollie Ollie outs-in free!" Michelle peeked around the curtain. Arthur, his knife raised, was slowly turning the closet doorknob. "Ah-ha!" he shouted, flinging the door open.

A dummy looking like Freddy Krueger, complete with rubber mask, hat, orange shirt and bladed glove, fell on Arthur. He screamed and fell backwards from the shock. Michelle, seeing her chance, leaped over the man and "scarecrow," followed by Marcel, heading out the door and down the hall. "This is a crazy house!" Arthur screamed. "This is a crazy house!"

Michelle got to the front door, but couldn't unlock the deadbolt lock. "Oh, Menapede!' she shined, remembering who broke it. She turned around and ducked just in time as Arthur swung his knife, jamming it into the door. As he tried to pull the knife out, Michelle pushed past him, heading for the kitchen door.

Arthur finally pulled the knife out, breaking the point off in the process. "This would never have happened with a screwdriver," he growled, following his victim.

Outside, Michelle lost a bunny slipper leaping from her back porch and running to Menapede's back door. She pounded with both fists, gasping, "Peed! Open up! Call the police! Can you hear me? Peed! Peed!"

"Oh, Lord!" Arthur gasped, stepping outside. "I scared her so bad she peed herself. You don't see that happen every day."

Michelle stood back, noticing that all the lights in the house were off. "Peed! Are you home? Answer me!" Then she turned and saw the Stalker approaching. "Oh my God!" she whined, backing to the far fence, then sliding along it, watching the rapist approach. Arthur grinned, the moonlight making his face appear hideous. Michelle kept moving until she got to the fence corner. "Oh, God," she whispered, trapped.

Arthur walked closer, the knife lowered. He knew he had her now. He walked under the swing set, past the oak tree with the tree house in it, and was walking past the large eight-foot-square plywood structure. "Now," he said, and that was it. He suddenly vanished from sight, as though he was swallowed up by the earth. Michelle blinked. She heard a deep, creaking sound as the plywood "billboard" bowed forward and collapsed in a plume of dust over the hole Arthur inadvertently discovered.

"Hey!" Arthur screamed. "It's dark down here! Let me out! I'm claustrophobic!"

"I caught a tiger!" Menapede sang from her back door, holding another plate of brownies in her hand. "I caught a tiger!"

"Peed!" Michelle shouted. "Call the police!"

"I already did, silly," Menapede said, taking a bite of one of her brownies. "You know what? Jack told me you were in trouble, so I called the police."

Michelle, tears of relief in her eyes, rushed over and hugged the girl. "Thank God you were here!" she said. "Thank God you were here!"

"Does this mean you'll let me borrow your chainsaw?" Menapede asked. "I want to learn to juggle. I saw them do it on TV. You know what? You're shaking. You'd better have a brownie."

"Sure I will," Michelle laughed, taking one.

"Let me out!" Arthur screamed from beneath the plywood. "I'm diabetic! I need my insulin shot!" He pushed and pounded, but the four-by-fours nailed to the plywood made it heavy.

Michelle heard the distant call of sirens. "Menapede," she said. "You're really all right. And your brownies aren't bad either."

"I know," Menapede said. "I used a new recipe. I got tired of raising flies."

"You what?" Michelle choked, realizing the implications.

"Let me out!" Arthur screamed. "I should have known it was bad luck to leave my screwdriver behind!"

THE GIFT

The little girl sat up in bed, her eyes twinkling from the moonlight coming in through the window. Although she usually was a sound sleeper, she was too excited to sleep tonight. Tomorrow would be her eighth birthday, a day of partying and gift-getting; her favorite day, next to Christmas.

She removed her blanket and put her feet over the side of the bed. Once she was afraid of the darkness and imagined that there were strange creatures under her bed that would bite off her toes should she dare to put her foot down there, but that was when she was a little kid. Now she was more grown up, a smarter and braver little girl.

She looked around the room, her eyes adjusting to the moonlit surroundings. She could make out her features in the dresser mirror across the room. She took her long hair in her small hands and held it up, giggling at the funny sight of herself in the mirror. She let her hair float back into position, thinking of how a peacock did much the same thing with its tail feathers.

On the corner of the mirror there was a photograph her father took of her on her sixth birthday. On the dresser, with her clutter of dolls, toy makeup kit, hairbrush and comb, was a red, handmade jewelry box with her name, Cindy, printed in gold letters on the side. Her mother had made it in a crafts club for her Christmas present. Among all her belongings, these two were her most precious ones.

She heard a car motor outside, and realized the car was pulling into the driveway. Her mother and father were home! She quickly hopped off the bed and shuffled over to the window, where she watched the car park on the snow-covered driveway. Then she went to her dresser and quietly opened it with one hand.

She heard the front door open downstairs and felt a chilly draft from outside. "Hi, Mr. Wilson, Mrs. Wilson," Ann the baby sitter said, "Isn't the party over a little early tonight?"

Cindy left her door wide open, letting a little light in from downstairs. Then she took her box back to the dresser, set it down, and lifted the lid.

She could vaguely hear her mother speaking. "It wasn't a very good party. Did Cyn get to sleep?" Cindy looked inside her box. The interior was padded with blue velvet, which was spongy to the touch.

"Cindy was no trouble at all," Ann said downstairs. "I put her to bed a half-hour ago. Um, I hate to bother you with this, Mr. Wilson, but do I still get paid for four hours?" Cindy paid no attention to the conversation downstairs. She carefully reached into her jewelry box and brought something out. It was her special treasure, the only thing she kept in the box.

Her treasure was the most beautiful thing she had ever seen. She found it one morning on the sidewalk, standing out like a gleaming gem. She was surprised no one else had found and taken it first. It was a little worn, a little tattered, but it still was very colorful, and very, very pretty.

She was careful in handling her treasure for fear of it crumbling in her grasp. She even controlled her breathing to keep it from falling apart and blowing away like a dried leaf.

Cupping her hands together to protect it, she carried the fragile treasure with her out the door. Her bare feet stepped quietly on the shag rug as she moved like a kitten down the hall. She stopped and sat at the top of the stairs, waiting for Ann to leave so she could see her parents and give her treasure — her gift of love — to them.

"Good night, Mr. and Mrs. Wilson," Ann said, "and if you ever need a babysitter again, well, I'm always available on week nights."

"We'll remember that, dear," Mrs. Wilson said as the front door squeaked shut. Cindy opened her cupped hands and admired her treasure again, although it was too dark to enjoy the colors.

"Well, John," Mrs. Wilson said harshly, "I hope you're satisfied." Cindy looked up from her hands and glanced down the steps. She saw someone's shadow brush against the wall at the bottom.

"Will you lay off, Irene?" her father, John, said. "Didn't you ruin the night for me already?" Cindy sat still and listened.

"If I ruined your night, then we're even," Irene said. Cindy now realized a hostility in her mother's voice. "At least you can't say you didn't enjoy yourself at the party. You guzzled enough booze for the both of us."

"So I drank a little. So what? I drove home safely, didn't I?"

"Listen to the real he-man, who thinks booze'll put hair on his chest. What kind of man are you if you can't control your drinking? You're an alcoholic, John, an al-co-hol-ic!"

"For Chrissake, Irene, I was just trying to enjoy the party! You're the one who dragged me to that goddam place anyway. I just can't understand you. I thought you were enjoying yourself, the way you spread gossip with other women like you were reporting for the *Enquirer* or something."

Cindy didn't like the sound of the conversation downstairs. She closed her hands around her treasure, being careful not to crush it. She sat still, while a feeling of uneasiness grew inside her. She didn't want to hear any more, she wanted to return to her bedroom, but she just couldn't move from that spot.

"Don't make jokes, John! Sure I expected you to enjoy yourself at the party, but not by making a spectacle of yourself. You acted like a damn animal; I should have brought you to the party on a leash!"

"Get off my back, Irene. I'm tired. I wanna get to bed. We can finish this . . . discussion tomorrow."

"Don't you dare go! I 'm not done talking with you! I still have a few things to say about your behavior!"

"Say them tomorrow. Say them to the wall. I don't care, just let me get some sleep!"

"I saw you sitting with Roberta tonight!"

There was an uneasy silence, then John spoke: "Who?"

"Roberta," Irene said, almost straining the name. "Roberta Collins."

In the following silence, Cindy bent over her treasure in a fetal position, while one of her feet protectively covered the other. She had been hoping that they would stop yelling, but now that there was quiet, she felt more uncomfortable than ever.

Finally her father spoke, "What about it?" he asked. "We were just talking."

"Flirting, you mean," Irene said coldly. "You two looked like teenagers on a date!"

"Flirting my ass!" John yelled. Upstairs Cindy was gritting her teeth. Her feet were rubbing over each other as though she was trying to keep her toes warm. She felt a strange, uncomfortable sensation in her skin, a cold goose-pimply feeling. "You're making a big thing out of nothing! Besides, if it bothered you so much, why didn't you say something?"

"This isn't the first time this has happened, John. I've seen you flirting and carrying on at other parties! And don't tell me it was just talking!"

"Irene . . ."

"I've seen you more than once holding another woman's hand, or . . . or with your hand on her knee or around her shoulder, while you laughed like it was a big joke!"

"Irene . . ."

"And I'm not the only one who's seen you flirting! I hear people talking behind my back. . ."

"Irene, will you please shut up? The neighbors will hear!" Cindy rocked nervously back and forth, her small body shaking like a frightened rabbit's. She kept her eyes closed tight, as though it might make the yelling go away.

There was near silence downstairs; the only sound was that of somebody weeping. "I . . . I . . ." Irene sobbed. She cleared her throat and tried again. "I'm tired of pretending. I know you've been . . . getting involved with other women."

"It's just your imagination, Irene. For Chrissake, you're getting worked up over nothing!"

"What about all those nights you worked late, and all those Wednesday nights you went bowling with George? I found out some time ago that George was ill with his rheumatism half those nights."

"I bowled by myself those nights. I coulda explained it to you if you would of asked me, but instead you wanted to fill your lurid imagination with lurid pictures of me having an affair with my secretary or . . .or somebody else!"

For a moment there was again quiet. Was it over? Cindy opened her eyes. She could see light at the foot of the stairs, but she felt the darkness surround her from behind. She held still and listened. Nothing. She was about to stand when she heard her mother speak:

"John, I want a divorce."

Again there was silence, but this time it came with a strange, static feeling in the air.

"Irene, you can't be serious," John said, "You have no grounds except for your circumstantial evidence."

"I want a divorce, and I'll get it somehow!"

"Get out of this nonsense, god dammit!" John yelled. "You're acting crazy!" Cindy shut her eyes tight. She lowered her head until it almost disappeared between her shoulders. Her hands shook and her fingers tensed around each other. She felt her flesh crawl and her heart choke.

"I was crazy the day I married you. I've never been more sane than I am today."

"I'm tired, Irene. I'm damn tired. You can scream all you want to, but I'm not going to be around to listen to you. I'm going to bed."

"Like hell you are!" Irene yelled in a squeaky, hoarse voice. "Don't you dare leave now. Listen to me! Stop!" There was a crash, fragile and loud, the sound of glass cracking, coming apart violently. Cindy covered her ears with her small fists. In the process she had dropped her frail treasure, which now lay on the step, mutilated and crushed. Now a wetness ran down her cheeks, partly because of the yelling, partly because of the loss of her treasure, the irreplaceable gift she would have given . . .

"Irene, you're crazy! Stop it!" There was more breaking, more crashing. "That's it!" John yelled. "I'm not going to sleep in the same house with a mad woman!"

There was one more crash, then silence, then, "Wait!" The front door slammed shut, then more silence.

Cindy's stomach pained. Her usually cute face now seemed scarred and distorted. She felt a great heaving within her, like a powerful, angry scream trying to get out. She stood up and looked around. All was threatening darkness around her; mean, terrible, loud darkness. She whimpered a little, sobbed once, then ran back to her room, stubbing her toe on the way. When she got to her room, she closed the door on the outside world.

Downstairs a woman cried because of a horrible mistake she and her husband made. Upstairs a little girl cried because of the same mistake. Somewhere in between, on the shag rug on the steps, there were the remains of a butterfly's body, now crumbled and crushed, never to be put back together again. It was once a beautiful, colorful treasure. It might have been a beautiful gift.

BICYCLE RIDE IN THE SKY

One night, nine-year-old Charly Starr heard his name called. This time he was ready. It was raining outside his window, but he knew that he was called. He hopped out of bed, put his slippers on, and threw his coat over his pajamas. In the cellar, he grabbed his hammer, the one with the paint-stained handle. Then he hopped onto his bike. Through the garage walls, he could hear the thunder shouting its challenge.

"Here I am!" Charly shouted. "Here I am!"

Suddenly the garage door opened by itself. A thunderbolt came through the black rain and struck in front of the door. It sent sparks into the air and smoke into the garage. "You can't stop me!" Charly shouted to the wind. He pedaled his Schwinn dirt bike into the night, swinging his hammer in the air.

He raced down the driveway and then down the street, splashing water as he pedaled. The street got steeper, and Charly couldn't pedal as fast as his bicycle was going. The water sprayed off his wheels and soaked his pajama pants. The spray grew so thick and strong that the bicycle and the boy were soon lifted off the pavement and sent flying in the air. Now the winds came, and Charly was tossed back and forth, gripping his hammer and holding onto his bike. The ground was far below him. First it was below his feet, then it was above his head. He was upside down, right-side up, holding on tight as he went around. But Charly Starr didn't become dizzy, no sir, not Charly Starr! He looked into the blackness of the storm and said, "Here I am, Storm, here I am! You can't make me barf or make me sick!"

He felt a thump and knew that he was now pedaling on the clouds. The ride was bumpy. When he looked up, he saw his neighborhood where the clouds used to be. With his hammer in his hand, he waved to his house. And then a black hole opened up underneath him, and he got sucked in like a dust ball into a vacuum cleaner. There was nothing but blackness and movement but Charly Starr wasn't afraid.

Then, like groceries through a wet paper sack, he suddenly tore through the darkness. Now he was amidst spinning colored star and flying comets. He directed his bike carefully so as not to hit flying rocks and sparks of light. The Universe hummed loudly and the colored flares continued moving in a circle. Charly shook off the last drops of rain from his body and continued with his task. The humming was like a loud washing machine now and the bike and boy were flying faster than ever.

Suddenly, there was a blackness among the colors, and Charly recognized the enemy. He had often seen the tentacles reaching out from beneath his bed in the darkness of his room. Now it was all in front of him. There were the claws, the teeth, and the big eyeball, with veins popping out all over.

'I'll get you!" Charly shouted. "I'll get you good. Yes sir, I will!" A tentacle reached out to grab him, but he squished it with his hammer. The Thing growled, and he swung his hammer again. Here he broke a claw, and there a tooth. But he kept heading for that eyeball, the same one that used to watch him from the dark of his dream.

"You don't scare me!" Charly yelled at the eyeball, and it squinted back in anger. Black tentacles reached at him but only grabbed air. Now he was so close that his spokes were whistling and throwing off sparks. He swung his hammer madly, threatening the Thing like an angry Viking or a neighbor whose lawn he had bicycled over. Closer and closer he came. Then he threw his hammer with all his might. It sang through the air and hit the eye, which blinked shut in pain. The tentacles fell back and disappeared into the eye. Then, with one humongous roar, the Thing exploded into tiny, shapeless bits.

Boy and bike were thrown through space and time until Charly felt the wind and the dizzy feeling of falling. The quiet whistling was comforting, and he felt like sleeping. Then he saw the ground coming up. He concentrated on steering his dirt bike to a safe landing on his driveway. As his wheels touched ground and he rode into the garage, he heard a thump as his hammer lit the lawn.

The rain stopped and the air was refreshing as Charly recovered his paint-stained hammer. He looked at the sky and noticed that the clouds were breaking apart. Now the stars were beginning to shine through. He sighed, went back into the garage, and closed the door.

Before he returned to his room, he stopped in the kitchen for a snack. "I gotta keep my strength, yes sir," he said as he poured a glass of milk. He grabbed some cookies and ate by the light of the kitchen clock. He didn't hear the footsteps behind him.

"Up a little late, aren't we?" his mother said.

Charly shrugged. "I got the munchies, Mom."

His mother smiled. "You always have the munchies. You're a bottomless pit, aren't you?" Charly shrugged. "Did you notice that the storm stopped?"

"Yeah," Charly said, disinterested.

"I remember when you used to be scared of storms. You used to crawl in bed with Dad and me."

"Aw, Mom," Charly moaned. "That was a long time ago."

His mother laughed. "Go and get some sleep. Remember that you have to help your father build our new fence. And I hope you haven't lost your hammer again."

"Jeez, Mom," Charly whined. She patted his shoulder and went back to bed. Charly finished off his last cookie and went back to his room. He took off his raincoat and crawled back into bed. As he closed his eyes, he heard his name whispered by the stars and didn't feel scared at all.

THE BOY WHO WAS AND WOULD BE

"So you say you're Jesus Christ," Dr. Paula Cook, the Child Psychologist, asked the boy.

"Not Jesus Christ," the boy corrected. "Jesus *the* Christ. Jesus is a very common name."

"*Was* a very common name," Paula corrected, noticing a spider on the ceiling of her office. She recalled reading about a general named Jesus in the writings of Flavius Josephus, then recalled that the name was still used. Hay-zoose, or something like it, was spelled Jesus. It was the name of a son of Maria Concerta, her once-a-week cleaning lady.

"Jesus is still a common name,' the boy said, as though reading her mind.

Paula stubbed out her cigarette and looked at the boy. Albert Watson was short for eight years old, but his attention span and patience belonged to an adult. "Okay," Paula sighed. "What's your favorite book of the Bible?"

"The Confessions of Judas," the tow-haired boy answered. "It's full of human suffering - but it was destroyed in the Second Century. Of the books that survived, I like Revelations."

Minutes later, as Dr. Cook consulted Dr. Gary Mobley on the other side of the two-way mirror, she couldn't help thinking that Albert could see her through the glass. "He seems to have done his research," she said. "He knows more about the Bible than I do."

Dr. Mobley smiled. "Dr. Cook, an awful lot of people in this world have learned to play their roles well.

Mental institutions are full of Oscar nominee performances."

"But he's not acting," Paula said, lighting another cigarette. "He believes every word he says."

"I'm sure he does," Dr. Mobley said, cleaning his glasses. "He's being someone different, not merely acting. But he has researched his new person in depth, as though he was preparing to write his doctoral dissertation."

"But he's only eight!" Paula puffed her cigarette.

"Surely," Dr. Mobley said, "you know about child prodigies and idiot savants. Dr. Cook, the mind is a miracle. The possibilities are numberless, and . . ."

But Paula wasn't listening. Her eyes were focusing on the boy in the other room. He appeared to be talking to his hand, flattered horizontally. Then she saw the spider on his hand, somehow saw most every detail, every hair, as it remained virtually still, only its two most forward legs alternately rising and lowering.

As though it were answering.

* * * * *

It was the second life in which he was a carpenter's child. Sort of.

Sam Watson, cabinetmaker, team bowler, Pittsburgh Steeler fan, loving husband and father, always took eight-year-old Albert for a walk in the park every Saturday. It was one such day that Albert suddenly gained total awareness, watching the geese in the pond, the autumn leaves floating in the dark water.

It was not one of those revelations accompanied by a blinding light, angels and trumpets - although he had at least a dozen of those in various past lives - but this time, he was simply looking at the ripples in the water, and it all came to him, and with it, an infinite calmness. "Dad," he said, "did you know we are all connected by a warm, loving force that makes us all God?"

"What!" Sam mumbled, tossing dried bread out of a bag to the geese. He brushed a dried leaf off his sweater.

"I said," Albert tried again, "did you know . . . Oh, never mind." He sighed, placing his spindly hand in Sam's beefy paw as they strolled back to the car. He would never understand, Albert realized.

On the ride home, Albert calmly paged through the far-reaching wisdom that he had suddenly accumulated. He recalled past lives as a beggar, a slave, a mother of seven children, a warlord, a leper, a king, a countess - so many faces, all his. He dimly visualized the web that connected every person to another, and he saw lines upon lines of past lives of everyone, lines reaching out in two dimensions, three, even four, a finite number of souls, if you could consider trillions as finite.

But something about his past lives kept bothering him. It came out a week later in Sunday school as his mind continued to take information and cross-reference it. Mrs. Huntley, the teacher, was telling the story of when Jesus threw the money-changers out of the temple, and how this, next to the miracles of healing, was His greatest act.

"Nuh-uh!" Albert said, snapping out of his quiet state. "His greatest act was washing people's feet! He wanted to teach us that we were all servants for each other! The miracles He did were to show us what we could do if we only tried! And when He threw the money-changers out of the temple, He just lost His temper, and He wasn't happy that anybody wrote about it either!"

"Albert!" Mrs. Huntley fumed. "This is blasphemy! You can't say such things! You know nothing about Jesus . . ."

"I know everything about Jesus!" Albert boomed. "I *am* Jesus!" It was only then that he realized how true his words were. Mrs. Huntley went silent in shock. The other children laughed, and one of them dared Albert to walk on water. He wanted to tell them that he could, that they could, but he felt as though he had said plenty enough.

Mrs. Huntley talked to Pastor Gordon, who talked to Albert's parents, who talked to the school counselor, who contacted a psychiatrist. Albert talked to all of them, not wanting to lie, and he ended up in an institution where half the children were heavily sedated and restrained and the other half were lethargic and incontinent.

"Are you comfortable, Albert?" Dr. Paula Cook asked, fascinated by the short eight-year-old. Albert ignored the toys that littered the carpeted floor of Paula's office.

"Yes, ma'am," Albert said. His mind worked on two levels now; the one focusing on the conversation, the other exploring his past lives. He was amazed at the famous names from history who were all once him. Harry Houdini, Edgar Allen Poe, Galileo, Buddha . . . And there were others who, having acquired only part of the knowledge he had now, went insane.

"Now you seem to think that you are Jesus," Paula said. "Jesus the Christ. Is this because you like Jesus a lot?"

"Please don't patronize me," Albert said. "You're playing games with me to get answers when I am perfectly willing to tell you everything I know. What's more, you don't seem to believe me, when, deep down inside, you really want to. You really want to know that what I say is true, but your upbringing holds you back."

"We're here to talk about you, not me," Paula said, lighting another cigarette with a shaky hand. "We're here because your parents are worried about you, worried about your future."

"My future is in the Book of Revelations," Albert said.

"Now you're playing games," Paula said, drawing on the cigarette. "No puzzles, Albert."

"What I mean," Albert tried again, "is that my future is just fine. I have a pretty good idea of how my life will be going. It has already been planned."

Paula's glance betrayed her confusion, and Albert understood. As Jesus, he was surprised by his own execution, yet he had been subconsciously telling everyone about it all along. Neither was he aware that he had been Buddha in a previous incarnation, though he knew that John the Baptist had once been Elijah. Even now, aware of the turns his gift would take in the coming years, he was still confused by the strange concept of good and evil being one and the same thing. Evil, he thought . . .

Three months passed in the children's home. Albert patiently waited. Although he could have healed every child in the home of their various afflictions with just a thought, he knew it wasn't the right time. He recalled the sudden, total awareness of all that seized him at the pond months ago, and in other lives, under a tree, at a carpenter's shop, riding in a carriage, standing naked in a thunderstorm . . .

One day he overheard the nurse talking about drugs and cranial operations planned for a child in the home, and he suddenly realized they were talking about him. He realized that unplanned events couldn't stop the future from occurring, but they could slow things down. Albert decided on something drastic. He asked to see Dr. Cook. "It's time for me to go home," he said to her, his tennis-shoed feet dangling above the floor.

"What you mean is you feel homesick," Paula said.

"No," Albert said, smiling. "You can attest to my sudden recovery. Your signature can set me free."

Paula was used to hearing this eight-year-old talk like an adult, but to hear what sounded like a bribe in the making shook her up. "What are you talking about?" she asked, lighting up a cigarette.

"You want proof," Albert said. "You still won't understand, but you want proof. You want to believe me. Yesterday, your old tomcat, Chevy, was hit by a truck."

Paula gagged, dropping her cigarette. "How did you know that?" she asked. "How could you know?"

The child stared at her gravely. "I just know," he said. "Your cat has a funny question-mark scar from an operation. Right?" Paula nodded, stunned, almost a zombie. "You know he was killed. You buried him in the backyard, wrapped in a T-shirt because you couldn't bear to look at his crushed head."

By now Paula was sheet-white. "If," Albert said, "if Chevy comes home, his head healed, dirt on his fur, and an empty hole where you buried him, will you sign the paper?" Paula was silent. "Will you?"

Paula nodded.

*   *   *   *   *

One week later he was home. Christmas was long past, but his ninth birthday was coming up. On that day his friends came over for chocolate cake and ice cream. "I was beginning to worry," Sam told his sister, Florence, who flew down for Albert's birthday. "I thought we'd never see him out of that place."

"What was it?" Flo asked. "Schizophrenia?"

"Worse," Sam answered. "They were about to resort to drug therapy, maybe even surgery."

"Well, praise the Lord, he's better," Flo said.

Albert overheard them and smiled. He considered the irony as the final facts and information filtered into his thinking. It was hard enough for anybody to believe that he was once Jesus. Dr. Cook who probably wanted to believe, was still taking it hard, and probably didn't know what to make of it now that the ill children at the institution were leaving, three or four a day, perfectly healthy in mind and body.

Albert glanced at Aunt Flo as he thought about the Book of Revelations. Aunt Flo, the family fundamentalist. He smiled. Wouldn't she be surprised? Yes, it was said that Jesus was coming again, and there was talk of Armageddon and the Apocalypse and the Antichrist, all these things beginning with A, as in Albert. Good and evil are one and the same, he thought. What a concept.

GRANDFATHER CARP

The slag from the old Pennsylvania coal mines dammed up the creek, creating the deep, dark lake. Tall grasses, blackberries and maple trees were reclaiming most of the black moonscape, but the air still stank of slate, coal dust, and tar. Larry Johnson, CPA, clumsily put a hook and two lead sinkers onto the end of his fishing line while eyeing the black water of the lake.

Larry Johnson, CPA, was the sort of man Rod Serling might have referred to at the beginning of every episode of "The Twilight Zone," an ordinary man living an ordinary life in which nothing exciting ever happened. One day, walking his daschund, "Dependent," down a dirt road and along a well-worn path through the woods, he found the small lake. It was small as lakes go, and deserted, but for a solitary fisherman in waders who already hooked four rainbow trout that morning. It was from the fisherman that he heard the story of Grandfather Carp, a fish so large he had to be older than the lake itself.

Larry Johnson, CPA, wasn't a fisherman by any stretch of the imagination, but he was a dreamer. He could see Grandfather Carp stuffed and mounted over his fireplace mantle, next to the bowling trophy he won ten years ago. There was a general store/post office/hardware store at the beginning of the road, so Larry and Dependent walked the two miles back to it. There, Larry bought the largest fishing pole he could find.

"It'll break if you hook Grandfather Carp," Mrs. Weatherbee, the proprietor, said, after Larry mentioned his plans. "But take this. Grandfather Carp will come for you." She handed him a dog whistle wrapped in plastic.

"You're crazy," Larry said, but bought it anyway. "If this fishing rod isn't strong enough, what should I use?"

"A harpoon," Mrs. Weatherbee said, adjusting her prince-nez glasses and tending to the next customer.

The fisherman was gone when Larry got back to the lake. Larry prepared his rod and waded waist-deep into the water. He cast his line out, then pulled the dog whistle from his pocket, blowing a silent note. Dependent, resting on the grassy shore, raised his head, but nothing else happened. Larry blew again.

The water churned less than fifty feet from shore. With the fishing rod gripped in one trembling hand, Larry blew a third time. "Here we go . . ." he said, just as a large fish head broke from the water. Grandfather Carp leaped, twisting in the air, snapping his massive jaws shut, rising again, with two legs kicking frantically from his mouth as he fell back into the dark, churning water. Larry Johnson, CPA, was gone.

Dependent watched for another minute, then laid his head back on his paws. The dog whistle had been irritating, and he was grateful that it was now silent. He dozed, basking in the early afternoon sun.

LISTING

It's the Canaga Curse, you know. I talked to my mother about it the other day. Like me, she collects house fans, hotel towels, restaurant ashtrays, National Geographics, unmatched socks (we each have a large, cardboard box of them), placemats from fast food places, old newspapers, Reader's Digest, radios we plan to fix someday, postcards, souvenirs from every state, t-shirts with messages on them, TV Guides . . . We categorize our things, listing them, my mother in her old mobile home, me in my crowded apartment.

Listing is our fate. Our homes are full to overflowing. We have paths through out rooms, paths like the Colorado River cutting through the Grand Canyon, with canyon walls of books and old magazines and cardboard boxes. The Canaga Curse.

One day Grandma Canaga fell and broke her hip in her house. If she had broken her hip on the way to the grocery, or hitchhiking to Los Angeles, or even crossing an arctic glacier, she would have had a much better chance of survival. As it was, she starved to death. She didn't have the strength to drag her way along the path through the yellowed newspapers, dusty boxes and stacks of photo albums to the telephone. The postman later reported looking through the windows, but he couldn't see beyond the stacks and boxes.

Of course, Mom and I inherited the Canaga Curse long before Grandma died, but when we inherited her boxes, stacks and brown paper bags as well, we were both overwhelmed. It was confusing at first, but after we divided Grandma's things between us, made our lists, and put everything in its proper stack or pile, things pretty much got back to normal.

I was discussing all this with my mother by phone the other day, just hours before fire destroyed her mobile home and everything inside it. The loss of all those precious things would surely have killed Mother, had not the fire gotten to her first. She wanted to be cremated anyway, and she would have appreciated the romantic touch of taking her things with her.

Naturally I became despondent about losing my grandmother and mother in the same month. I wandered the paths through my apartment for weeks on end, touching my stacks and revising my lists. My friends sent their condolences in cards and letters, and I put them all safely away in a cardboard box. I tried categorizing my friends, listing them, but they couldn't be stacked, boxed or stored.

When the police came, I had lost sixty pounds. I'd been meaning to go on a diet for years. After a few months at the hospital, I got a new apartment. My friends still worry about me, since most of my stuff was taken to the dump by the health department during my absence. But there's nothing to worry about. I collect stamps and coins now. And antiques. And books. And minerals. And postcards.

It's the Canaga Curse, you know.

CALLING

The Willamette Valley with her trees and hills and houses and people and Rachel and the baby we were going to have and the Willamette River running through it all called to me like a distant white bird, and after three months I answered the call. I came. In Eugene, Oregon, Rachel told me once, the rains last ten months out of the year like a special season.

They were gentle rains, sacred rains that Eugenians walk and bicycle through with no more than a passing thought as autumn leaves turn color and the smelled of the coming winter permeate the air with woodstove smoke, decaying vegetable gardens, damp leaves, mud and spicy kitchen smells. I breathed deep, feeling the cold air inflate my lungs and reach through my veins. I'd just hitched a ride from the Southern Oregon border, the fifth ride since Southern California two days ago, where the peach harvesting left me with a wad of money in my pocket. I could've taken a Trailways up Highway 101 along the coast to Florence then headed inland, but I had to answer the call on my own terms.

The truck driver dropped me off near the Ferry Street Bridge and drove off in a gust of diesel while I walked over the Willamette River to Skinner's Butts in the Oregon autumn night. What with the misty rain and the closed storefronts and the chimneys smoking and the houselights watching, I felt lonely and enchanted. I walked along the bicycle trail near the river, listening to the distant murmurs of highway traffic and the heartbeat rumble of an unseen freight train. Stopping under a street lamp I held my wet face up to see the raindrops coming down at me like a gift of scattered gleaming stars.

Fifteen minutes later I came to the Millhouse Pub, a large refurbished building on the river that vibrated with jazz and smell of beer and greasy fried potato skins, and I stepped through the door, stopped and shook some of the wetness off. The saxophone plowed its magic through smoky air while men and women sat at tables sharing pitchers of beer. Billiard balls clicked and the dart board announced the next point with a thock as the music hummed the room in saintly rhythms.

I took an empty booth in back and ordered a large bottle of Tooth Sheath Ale and a basket of fried mushrooms with a bowl of vinegar. I restlessly ate a few as I watched the stage. Rachel was up there under the red lights, perched forward on the stool as though she might topple over but still defied gravity. Her long black hair cascaded over her shoulders and forehead, hiding her face. Her feet danced on the stool leg brace to the rhythm as she held her microphone to her lips and sang wordless sounds, "...do-wop-de-diddy-do-do-unhuh-do..." a clear voice in tandem with the ensembles of drums, sax, bass and piano, rumbling static and prophetic through the dark room.

When they finished their set, I ordered another Tooth Sheath and a Hamm's beer. Rachel dismounted, leaving her mike on the stool. She was tall and thin, with small breasts beneath a folksy silk blouse and an intricate blue Tibetan vest. A cotton Andes skirt covered her legs, and she wore Birkenstocks on her bare feet. Large brown eyes gazed at me from behind round wire-rimmed glasses. Her small mouth and upturned nose gave her a little girl look.

She fingered her hair back from her face before she sat next to me. Her body smelled of sweat and rainwater and frankincense. She smiled, her arms went around me and mine around her. We kissed long, softly, gentle, and then we looked at each other, refamiliarizing ourselves. "Howdy, Sailor Man," she said. "Metta."

"Namaste," I answered, adding "Jazz Girl." I held her hands in mine. Only her hands revealed she was in her mid-thirties. "You sound great tonight.'"

"Why didn't you tell me you were coming back?" she asked, a smile dimpling her cheeks. "I almost lost it on stage when I saw you sitting here."

"I sent a postcard a week ago. A picture of the California coast. I even wrote a haiku on the side," I recited it from memory.

Long slow road through life.
Mountain spirits whisper cloud.
Passing sleepy towns.

"Didn't you get it?" I asked kissing her fingers. "So what's going on?"

A shadowy dark bird crossed her face. I felt winter brush my back. Wrinkles appeared around her eyes and she looked away. Her hand tightened on mine as shoulders trembled. "The baby's gone. I wrote you a letter last week. I guess you didn't get it."

I couldn't find an answer; it wasn't in my repertoire. It was only three months ago I began adjusting to the idea of being a father. I pulled her closer, rested my hand on her belly as though my touch could heal whatever was wrong. "Oh, Rachel, I'm so sorry."

"Just be with me," she said.

I rocked her against me wondering if it would have been a boy or a girl. She told me how it happened while she was shopping at the Kiva grocery story. She picked up a bag of brown rice and a bunch of celery when the woman behind her began pointing and shouting in Spanish. Blood dripped on the linoleum and she suddenly felt sick and terribly ashamed. I told her I wished I was there, but that's not what I felt.

She played one more set, then at two a.m. as she helped the band pack up, I got her knapsack and alpaca sweater. In the rain we walked past the University of Oregon where "Animal House" was filmed in the '70's - we'd seen it a dozen times - I reminded her of the first film we'd seen together at the Bijou Theater; "Choose Me," with Keith Carradine and Rae Dawn Chong.

I was amazed at my own weariness as we walked through dark streets, shiny and slick with rainwater like black obsidian. I held Rachel's hand as she talked about meeting Dizzy Gillespie once before he died, how his cheeks puffed out like a bullfrog's throat would when he played his horn.

Her apartment was sleeping dog warm when we got there. She put on a Charlie Parker C.D. Minutes later we were in her tub, touching and kissing and soaking in the steamy light of dozens of candles, holding long-stemmed wine glasses, and eating crackers and cheese from a stool by the tub. "Remember the first time we did this?" she asked.

"You put on Ravel's 'Bolero' and I knocked the whole plate of crackers into the water."

"And then you had to help me out of the tub because I got a cramp in my leg!" she laughed and I was glad she remembered. I rubbed my nose in her wet hair, smelling shampoo and the essence of her being.

Later we made love, breaking a sweat against every tomorrow to come, and later when it was over we touched each other, our fingers sliding along wet skin. "Are you sorry?" she asked. "Are you sorry I lost the baby?"

"I don't know," I replied, cupping her breast. The aureoles were like dark wild strawberries. "How can you feel sorry about something you can't control?"

"I was afraid you wouldn't come back this time."

"But I did," I said. "How do you feel about . . . what happened?" I couldn't say it just then. It didn't feel right.

"Empty," she murmured. Then she held me tight against something so ominous in the darkness I did not yet see. I held her close. We were slick as San Francisco seals smelling like the sea. Tears poured from my eyes, salty tears I wouldn't let her see. When Rachel was finally asleep I carefully untangled myself, silently put my clothes on and slipped out.

I walked the streets of Eugene, putting my collar up against the chill and rain and neon lights of stores that would be opening in a few hours. I was weighed down by weariness and sorrow, but something inside needed to keep moving. I walked through alleys, stomped through puddles. Somewhere wind chimes tinkled thoughtfully.

I found myself back at the river where I squatted on the muddy bank. The Willamette nodded at me like an old friend passing by, and the roaring waters drowned out my feelings. My clothes were saturated. Not even a Eugenian would be here at this hour, I realized. I sighed, then stood. The river pulled at me, called to me with a desperate urgency as I reached into my pocket and felt the wad of bills. Rachel knew me better than I knew myself. I had to make a decision soon, and this time I did not feel up to it.

PLANTING

As the crummy barreled along the precariously narrow logging road through the Oregon Cascade Range like a bobcat with stinging nettles up its ass, meandering through the steep tree stump and blackberry vine landscapes, nobody was aware that Old Bill Mulligan, leaning against the back heater, was deader than a Willamette River rock. For all we knew, Old Bill could've passed into his next Karmic life any time during the three hour drive from Eugene.

We arrived at seven a.m. near the clearcut timber line on the eastern slope, and though Old Bill was pretty ripe by the time we stopped, we chalked it up to his usual personal hygiene habits and assumed he was asleep. We left him behind to snooze as we filed out into the icy drizzle, one by one, picked up our tree packs with fifty pounds of ten-inch-long Douglas firs and started our planting lines, swinging hoedads over our heads into the mud, putting in a tree and moving on.

We worked ten feet apart, up and down from each other along the mountain side, our lines of trees parallel to each other as our hoedads cut arcs over our heads and packs became lighter, one tree at a time. By the end of the morning we waded up the muddy slope with empty packs and big appetites.

At lunch break we noticed Old Bill wasn't eating, and he looked a little more scraggly than usual. "Goddam, Bill," Crooked River Pete Buchannon said, puffing on a joint between bites of his peanut butter and bologna on rye. "You can't play possum all day, Zeb'll catch on!"

Luke Hargreaves, sitting next to him, gave him a shove, and Old Bill toppled over like a sack of rutabagas. The stench hit us good, like cabbage fermenting into sauerkraut. Appetites evaporated like rubbing alcohol on a California tan as we realized why he'd been so quiet all morning, but Luke still checked for a pulse, then held his coke mirror beneath Bill's nostrils; then he looked up at the rest of us, eyes big as saucers, like he just figured out what the rest of us already knew.

"Holy shit," he whispered.

Lester Johnson looked out the crummy window at the gray sky. The rain was coming down harder, going from a drizzle to something more like a cow pissing on a rock. "Well, you gotta hand it to him," Lester said. "Old Bill sure picked a prime day to permanently sleep in."

"So what do you want to do with him?" I asked. "Prop him up and hope Zeb don't notice?"

"Seems only fitting we leave him here," Crooked River said. "He has no family to claim him, and it wouldn't take long to bury him in this mud." Several heads nodded approval.

"What'll we do for a grave marker?" Luke asked. "A boulder for a headstone?"

"Leave that to me," I said.

Lester wandered outside long enough to make sure Zeb Walton, the crew boss, and Henry Longfellow, a state inspector, were still busy checking the first lines of trees. Then we carried old Bill on a blanket down the mountain in the opposite direction. We trudged carefully through the steep mud down the tree stump moonscape, stepping over rocks and deadfall past patches of snow and muddy streamlets. The air was so cold it could snap like a cucumber and it smelled salty like Pacific Ocean seaweed and tidal pools.

"This is good enough," Crooked River said, eyeing the spot where we stopped. We propped Old Bill up against a log and started on the grave, swinging hoedads in unison as the hole got bigger. Zeb was back at the crummy, hollering for us to quit cluster fucking and get back to work, but we still had twenty minutes on our lunch break, and we figured Zeb was being a pissant because he couldn't see us beyond the ridge.

We finally had a few good feet into the soil, smelling rich and mushroomy like humus and semen, and we rolled Old Bill in. Soon he was completely buried.

Then I did the last necessary thing. Swinging my hoedad hard, I parted the soil and Old Bill's rib cage clean to the ground beneath his back. You could hear the bones and cartilage cracking beneath the soil.

"Jee-zus!" Crooked River croaked.

"Calm down," I said. "You don't hear Old Bill complaining now, do you?" I widened the opening, picked up some long-rooted Douglas firs and planted them in Old Bill's heart. I had to reach down into that human flesh to make sure the trees didn't j-root; they were firm inside him, clean through, taproots protruding out his back, branches reaching up from his chest. There were five trees in all, and in time they would grow together into one massive tree.

The guys helped me brace a few rocks around the trees to give them a fighting chance, then we headed back up to the crummy, break over, picked up our packs - we already had hoedads in hand - and started back on our treelines.

All day I worked, and I dreamed a walking dream of how the great primeval stumps paid tribute to Old Bill as the forest we were planting row after row grew thick and strong, and salmon and trout splashed in the brooks, spotted owls nested in the branches, timber wolves howled and hunted in the shadows of the trees, ferns and moss and amanita muscaria and wayside asters and the wild Oregon grape and brackett fungi thrived, and as the five trees grew into one big granddaddy tree, Old Bill and his substance became a part of it, and deep down inside, I hoped and prayed that chainsaws and lumber jacks would never again work this part of the mountains, because you hate to see a good friend cut down like that, especially when he put his heart into his work.

FIVE   1/ˑ97   T.NEWTON SCHULTZ

MUSTARD SEED

A blizzard meaner than God's rage batters Pittsburgh all night, but Shelly Burton is oblivious to everything outside her hospital window, her breasts full and painful, her arms empty, the near darkness of her room wrapping around her like a thorn bush blanket, and all she can think about is a mustard seed.

Her eyes are dry, swollen and red-rimmed. Reggie sat by her bed until midnight, holding her hand, but he had to drive the Lenwood Dairy truck early the next day, had to get some sleep. Together that morning they named the baby Chelsea, and they went downstairs to the morgue with the hospital chaplain to baptize her, the chaplain reluctant but Reggie was ungiving, determined that this should be done because Shelley wanted it.

Now she is alone, wrapped in her robe on her bed, one rail down, a radio somewhere playing "Deck the Halls with Boughs of Holly." Her lower lip is quivering. Snowflakes big as cotton bales pelt the window, the wind howls, shadows came into her room from outside like unwanted guests. But the mustard seed . . . .

Jesus compared faith and the moving of a mountain to a mustard seed, but she is thinking of the mustard seed Buddha asked for when the young woman brought her dead child in her arms to him, begging him to restore its life. Buddha said he would, if only she would bring him a mustard seed.

A fair trade, Shelley thinks as she pads out of her room, and though the nurses look up from their paperwork at their station, she smiles and nods, a smile she doesn't mean. They smile back and return to their charts. She reaches the elevator doors, shiny sterile chrome mirrors, and steps in. A few minutes later she steps out in the basement hallway as she pulls her hospital housecoat tighter, her nipples leaving milk stains on her nightgown. No one is there to see her and send her back, her luck is holding out.

She knows her way to the morgue, finds her way in through the double doors. She watched the orderly do it, and the stainless steel tray rolls out easily on oiled bearings as arctic air issues from the dark depths. She shivers with cold and fear of being caught, but her plan is set in motion; there is no going back.

Chelsea is naked and small beneath the white sheet, small fingers, tiny nostrils and eyelids, and when Shelley picks her up she expects her to be stiff, but she isn't. She carefully warms Chelsea against her body, then quietly she makes her way up, using the stairwell this time.

There were several accidents that night, and the emergency room is full and buzzing with rushing interns and nurses. "Silent Night" is barely audible over the clamor. She manages to glide through the chaos, the gurneys and curtains, the unconscious and the awake and bleeding, the talking, the moaning; she is invisible to all of them.

She is almost there, almost free, when a doctor suddenly spots her, begins walking towards her. She is panicked, afraid she will be sent back, but she swallows the fear, smiles, puts a finger to her lips; she's asleep, she implies, and it's almost the truth. The doctor nods and stalks off, needed elsewhere. She feels a flood of relief, and once again she is invisible, a sad ghost walking among the wounded with her cherished one cradled in her arms, then out the double glass doors, and as if by magic nobody sees her leave.

The cold pierces her, the wind batters her, and at first she is afraid, wants to go back in, but she knows she must be strong for her baby. You must go back to town . . . she remembers. You must find a mustard seed, one mustard seed, from a home . . . . Her face stings, she is shivering already, stumbling, her slippers are soaked, but she remembers Clarence, her older brother, a Buddhist, telling her the story back when she was a child. The wind whips her hair into her eyes, her episiotomy stitches throb, but she is determined she will be a good mother, leaning hard against the blowing snow like a sailor in a gale.

The darkness becomes complete, no house lights to be seen, only the halogen lamps blazing overhead like errant angels as "Jingle Bells" fades in the storm's wail, and she holds Chelsea tighter, protecting her, though there is no feeling in her fingers or feet.

She is tired, weak, fighting it, but she sits in a snowdrift rocking her child. Rest, just for a moment, suddenly feeling mercifully warm as Jesus and Buddha approach side by side in streaks of red and blue light, and Buddha tells her to find a mustard seed in a home that has never known suffering or death, and tears of frustration freeze to her cheeks as someone holds onto her arm and gently helps her rise.

Reggie is there when she wakes up, and despite her own pain, her hands and feet in bandages, she can clearly see his hurt for the first time, suffering as deep as hers, as deep as the injured in E.R., and she realizes he needs her as much as she needs him. Outside the storm rages, but Shelley grips her husband with all the love and strength she can muster, bracing herself to say goodbye, and bury, her child.

TUESDAY'S SCENARIO

Mickey Stouthead stood naked and shivering at the foot of the double bed. Gloria Radcliffe, with the bedclothes just covering her ample breasts, smiled mischievously at him, beckoning him to her side. Over 20 years his senior, Gloria was absolutely sensual; none of the college girls in his sophomore classes held a candle to her. As Mickey stepped to the side of the bed, eager to fulfill his "Mrs. Robinson" fantasy, Gloria gestured for him to wait. "Let's turn these lights off first, shall we?"

"The lights?" Mickey said, surprised. "Yeah. The lights. Sure." He reached over and flicked the switch, throwing the room into darkness. Gloria's modesty was annoying. She had made him undress in the bathroom while she crawled under the covers. Then again, they'd been dating every Tuesday night for three months before she finally invited him to her one-story home. But Mickey didn't care how eccentric she was. He groped in the darkness until he found the covers, anticipating her body next to his. As he lifted the sheets, he heard the front door open.

"Uh-oh," Gloria said.

"What was that?" Mickey asked.

"My husband," Gloria answered.

"Holy shit!" Mickey gasped as he flipped the lights back on. "Where's the back door?"

"Left and down the hall," Gloria said.

Mickey opened the bedroom door and dashed out, then rushed back in. "My clothes!" he shouted, rushing into the bathroom. He returned with his bundle and sat on the foot of the bed as he pulled his socks on.

"Arthur!" Gloria gasped.

"Gloria!"

Mickey dropped his tennis shoe. Arthur, Gloria's husband, stood stiff and red-faced in the bedroom doorway. With a gray crew cut, thin jowls, and sunken eyes, Arthur looked like the Grim Reaper might look in a three-piece suit. "Ohhh . . ." Mickey groaned.

"Gloria, what's the meaning of this?"

"Arthur, don't get mad, I . . ."

"I'm getting my gun!" Arthur shouted. "Where's my gun?"

That was all Mickey had to hear. He gripped his bundle of clothes to his chest and shoved past Arthur. "Scuse me," he said and ran down the hall. In the kitchen, he found the back screen door jammed shut. He heard a blast behind him and the window next to him splintered apart. Arthur had found his gun.

Without waiting for the next shot, Mickey leaped through the screen door and ran down the sidewalk.

Mickey was going his fastest while keeping his head low. He heard two more shots and suddenly remembered a childhood prayer. He raised his head and glanced back to see if Arthur had stopped. He had, at least long enough to aim. Mickey leaped to the left as he heard another shot.

The streets were deserted at that time of night, but Mickey saw people through the back door of the Frisky Lady Nightclub. He rushed through the door without looking back.

The doorman would have asked for identification but he was too surprised that Mickey wore nothing but socks. Mickey rushed along the back walkway behind the crowd, thankful that the lights were low. The patrons were preoccupied by the band, "The Decapitated Rhinos." The drummer spotted Mickey and froze in mid-beat.

Rushing out the front door and back on the street, Mickey kept running, rushing from the glare of one street light and another. He stopped at the corner and glanced around. Somebody yelled something obscene from a passing car. Mickey gasped for breath and tried balancing on one leg as he pulled on his pants. He heard another shot behind him. "Holy shit!" he gasped, dropping all but his pants and running across the street.

At the next intersection, he spotted a red Mustang waiting for the traffic light to change. "Stuart!" he shouted and ran to the car. Stuart Weaver leaned over and rolled down the passenger side window. Mickey grabbed the car door. "Stuart, you gotta help me!"

"Hey, Michael," Stuart said, raising an eyebrow.

"Stuart, there's a killer following me!"

"Well, you'd better put some clothes on, Mickey," Stuart said, noticing the pants in Mickey's hand.

Mickey tried the door, but it wouldn't open. He looked back and saw Arthur, who had just finished reloading his gun and was now taking a Clint Eastwood stance as he aimed. Mickey leaped head first into the window, getting stuck halfway. "Drive," he shouted, trying to get his dangling legs pulled in. "Drive, dammit!"

"Hey, man, it's a red light!"

"Just drive!" Mickey shouted as he tumbled into the car.

"Hey, Mickey, would you put your pants on, man?" Stuart said.

Suddenly the rear window exploded inwards, spitting glass against their heads and shoulders. "Jee-zus!"

Stuart screamed, flooring the gas pedal. The Mustang leaped forward, darting in front of a Peterbilt 18-wheeler. The Peterbilt swerved into another lane to avoid hitting the Mustang, but its load refused to change lanes and dozens of apple crates went crashing to the pavement.

Mickey glanced through the back window, watching the figure of Gloria's husband disappear in the distance. He turned to Stuart, whose knuckles were turning white on the steering wheel. "Hey, thanks for the lift, Stu." He forced a smile.

Stuart quickly glanced at him without moving his head, then glanced back at the road. "No problem, man," he said. "Long time no see, huh?"

"Yeah," Mickey said, pulling his pants on. "You got some heat in this car?"

"Not when the back window's blown out, man," Stuart said. "But the radio still works." He had finally slowed down to the speed limit before stopping at the next red light and looking over his shoulder. "Who's your friend?"

Mickey zipped up his pants. "You remember that lady I've been dating every Tuesday night?"

"Oh, yeah, man," Stuart grinned. "She's a fox."

"Well, that's her husband."

"Oh," Stuart said, driving on when the light turned green. "I didn't know you went out with married woman."

"Neither did I," Mickey sighed. "I was wondering why she would see me only on Tuesday nights. She'd always call me, but I couldn't call her, you know? I should've figured she was married or something, Stu. I need a beer."

"So do I," Stuart nodded. "We can earn a couple good hangovers tonight, man. What with no morning classes, we've got it made."

"Yeah, I need to get drunk tonight! And you can bet I'll never see that Gloria again. No, wait, I can't."

"Can't stop seeing Gloria?"

"Can't get drunk," Mickey slapped his forehead. "I have a meeting tomorrow at eight. I signed on as a subject for a psychological profile. Somebody wants to study stress on college students who face unusual situations."

"Well, hell," Stuart said, offering Mickey a cigarette. "What's so unusual about your life?"

"Who knows?" Mickey lit the cigarette. "But they paid me $500 when I signed up some time ago, so why ask. I would've forgotten about tomorrow's meeting, but the secretary called me up this morning."

"You could still use a couple of pitchers," Stuart said. "By the way, did you and Gloria ... ?"

"Nah," Mickey shook his head. "Tonight would have been the first time. Only her husband walked in on us. Talk about bad timing!"

*   *   *   *   *

"Talk about great timing!" Gloria said. "You walked in just in time. Mickey was about ready to jump all over me."

Arthur was wheezing, leaning against the bedroom wall, his clothes wet from the rain. "He'll jump tomorrow when he sees me at his psychological profile." He grinned. "The experiment went well. Tomorrow ..." he puffed, "tomorrow we'll have the results." He admired his wife, who smiled back at him, then took a drag on her cigarette. The one-piece strapless bathing suit she wore was perfect for the illusion of being naked under the covers. "He gave me a run for my money," Arthur wheezed, "but it was worth it."

"But did you have to use real bullets?"

"It was more dramatic that way," Arthur said. "Better for research." He opened a dresser drawer and put his gun away. "Besides, I'm a marksman and nobody got hurt."

"Just be sure you use blanks tomorrow night." Arthur thought about it. "I think you're right," he said, pulling a folded piece of paper out of his shirt pocket. "Let's see. Monday's scenario: husband comes home, finds wife and wife's lover, and has a heart attack. Tuesday's scenario: husband comes home, finds wife and wife's lover, and tries to shoot the lover. Wednesday's scenario: husband comes home, finds wife and wife's lover, and shoots wife . . .Yes, blanks it is!"

THE MAN WHO LIVED IN THE CELLAR

When I first met Peter Monk, I thought he was the perfect resident for the cellar apartment. His clothes were like ancient drapes or Salvation Army counter rejects; his hair was a lawn gone to weed; his glasses were a jigsaw puzzle of cracked lenses and frame held together by super glue and masking tape. Like the cellar, he was a collection of flotsam and jetsam.

But what really brought him to my attention was his accusation that Mrs. Hedley, our landlady, came from another planet.

One could locate Peter's room by way of a path that went from the cellar steps to his door, then arched back through the storage boxes to the washer and dryer. My apartment was on the third floor, but I got to know him on my laundry days. To Peter, the cellar was like a horn of plenty. He was always inventing marvelous appliances from the cellar junk

"Lookit this," he would say, holding up an ancient toaster that suddenly played music. "Couldn't get it to toast anymore, so I made it into a radio."

"Nice," I would say, giving him an odd look. There were plenty of broken radios in the cellar he could have repaired, but I guessed he was saving them to make toasters.

Nonetheless, I was really amazed at his mechanical and electrical abilities, and sometimes, I was even thankful for them. For instance, not only did he soup-up my old Volkswagen "Bug," he also built a "fuzz-buster" radar detector out of an electrical toothbrush and parts of a microwave oven. I made some classical runs in the old Bug after that, with no fear of being caught speeding!

One morning he woke me from a pleasant dream. He was in a near-panic. He was standing in my bedroom, holding my clothes. "You have to help me," he insisted. "C'mon, get dressed."

"How did you get in?" I asked, shading my eyes.

"I picked the lock, but that's not important." He adjusted his glasses, which were sagging at the bridge. "There has been an intergalactic crisis on the planet Zen-Thombe, and I have to make contact with a fleet of starships as they pass Earth!"

I blinked my eyes. "Would you kindly repeat that, but slower?"

"Trust me," he insisted. "Zen-Thombe has been attacked, and some other planet will soon be invaded. We have to find out which planet, and stop the invasion."

Still not quite awake, I moved my face closer to his and sniffed his breath. If he was on anything, he must have snorted it. "Look," I said, "everybody's entitled to their own beliefs and persuasions, but enough is enough." I flopped back on my pillow. "And please lock the door on your way out."

"Please!" Peter moaned, flapping his arms. "I really need your help! You can't let me down!"

I opened one eye. I knew I wasn't going to get rid of him. "All right," I said, opening the other eye and taking my clothes. "What do I have to do?"

The supermarket wasn't open that early, but there were several grocery carts in the parking lot. We confiscated two of them, then headed across town with the cartwheels squeaking all the way. As we headed through a park, Peter pointed to a grassy mound. It was six feet high, and thirty feet in diameter, near a set of swings. "Mrs. Hedley's spaceship is buried under there," Pete told me.

I frowned and mumbled, "Don't press your luck, Pete."

We arrived at the Sony shop by ten, bringing the carts in with us. Peter immediately began dragging the salesclerk around, buying television sets, radios, video sets, stereos and satellite parts. He produced a MasterCard, complete with identification for Mr. John Grenthrew, whose driver license photo looked remarkably like Pete.

We filled the carts, but made several more stops on the way home. With other credit cards, and with other names, Peter bought two user-friendly computers, copper plumbing pipe, a thousand feet of thick cable, a kitchen sink disposal unit, and two arcade video games. Arranging for most of it to be delivered within the hour, we pushed the carts back, and unpacked at the cellar door.

That afternoon was hectic. We were putting strange things together. We lodged two television sets in the antlers of a moose head, one control panel set on several stacks of books; flashing lights and screens peered from boxes and crates; speakers hung from every wall.

My sole job was to hold things in place while Peter secured them and quickly connected them electronically to something else. Soon wire cobwebbed the ceiling, and spare parts littered the floor. Peter finally carried the power cable onto the roof and connected it to the power lines. I waited in the basement and watched, feeling an odd sense of accomplishment. Suddenly sparks jumped from the moose antlers, lights went on, televisions brightened, and speakers cackled to life. A minute later,

Peter rushed down the steps and glanced around. "It's working!" he shouted.

"That's great," I said. "Now, what's it supposed to do?" The cellar now seemed like nothing more than a motley version of NASA's control center. The musty air of the cellar mixed with the sparky smell of ozone.

"You'll see," Peter said, and we continued working. That evening, we had take-out Chinese food as we sat in front of our control panels. I promised myself that I would never spend another day off like this again.

"So what will all this accomplish?" I asked through a mouthful of Bok Choy.

"We're listening for invaders," Peter answered. He was constantly monitoring the screens. Every now and then, he would shout an order to me regarding my panel; "Press that red button! No, not that one! The other one! The one in the corner! Yeh, yeh, good!" And then he would go back to his own controls, running his fingers over them like the world's fastest typist.

"By the way," I asked, "how do those video games figure in all this?" I pointed at the two full-sized arcade games, Pac-Man and Donkey Kong.

"I got them for you in case you got bored," he said.

After two more hours, I started putting quarters into the video games. Peter reassured me that he could get them out later. When my quarters ran out, I put my head on an old desk and dozed. Peter nudged me awake hours later. "You're going to have to take over," he whispered.

I rubbed my eyes. "What time is it?"

"Four A.M.," he said. "I need your help. It's an emergency. You'll have to take over."

I perked up. "What happened?" I asked.

"I'm hungry," he said. "I'm going to get some pizza from the 24-hour place down the block. You'll have to watch the screens while I'm gone. Here . . ." He handed me a switch that was hooked up to the controls.

"What's this?" I asked.

"It's hooked to a device that will convert any language to English. I made it for you while you slept."

"Made if for me?" I asked, still groggy. "Don't you need it, too?"

"I'm multilingual," he said. "Besides, you might not need it after all. The antenna box is on the fritz. I might have to fix it when I get back. By the way, do you like anchovies?"

I was left alone at the controls, not daring to touch any of the buttons. I kept on thinking about Peter, wondering what he was really about, why he was so smart, why he was living out this bizarre fantasy, and why in hell I was living it out with him, especially at four in the morning.

Suddenly I heard footsteps, but instead of Peter and the pizza, it was another tenant, Sophie Winkenwerber from the fourth floor. She had her laundry.

She glanced at the electrical equipment, then shrugged. I wasn't sure if Peter wanted to keep his operation a secret, but it was too late to do anything now. The antenna box was on the washing machine. Sophie moved it while she loaded the washer. On her way out, she stopped by the Donkey Kong game, put in a quarter, and started playing.

The washing machine was vibrating frantically, and the antenna box on its lid began sparking. I was about to move it when the speakers hissed to life. Surprised by the noise, I turned around.

There was the same hideous face on every screen, something between a Klingon from the film, "Star Trek," and the back side of a baboon. I glanced from one screen to the next, listening to the speakers, hearing a voice that sounded like a hippo with gastritis. I felt my Bok Choy coming up.

Sophie glanced up from her game. "I see Peter got hisself hooked up to the cable. He done it for just about everyone else in the building. It's about time he got it, too." She blew a bubble, popped it, and continued chewing.

"Yeah," I said, watching the screens, grateful that Sophie had come up with her own explanation to cover the reality, and wondering why "Petey" never hooked me up to cable!

"What's on? A sci-fi from Japan?" Sophie asked. "You'd think they'd have subtitles for what cable costs these days, even at this hour."

"Yeah," I said, "but you're not paying for cable, remember? 'Petey' hooked you up." Sophie ignored the sarcasm. I eyed the switch Peter made for me, impatiently waiting for Sophie to leave. When the game was over, she went up the stairs, and as soon as I heard the cellar door close above, I threw the switch.

The speakers cackled, and then I heard the voice in English: ". . . and we lost two ships, but we're in shape to attack."

The voice matched the mandible movement of the face, and then another voice came on, belonging to a face off-screen: "How many fleets will you have for your next attack?"

"Fourteen," the Klingon/baboon face answered. "But after we conquer Earth, we'll pick up six more on the trip back."

My neck hairs prickled when I heard "Earth." He couldn't mean here, could he? How would he know this planet's name? Or maybe, I hoped, there was another Earth somewhere. I desperately hoped Peter would come back soon!

"Do you plan to take any prisoners?" the off-screen alien asked.

"No reason to," the face answered, "except to fill our meat lockers. We're running desperately low on hamburger. Listen, I gotta sign off. It's time for my favorite soap opera."

"Later . . ."

Then all sound and images disappeared. I anxiously glanced at the big screen in front of me, then at the smaller ones in the antlers. Nothing!

I was suddenly afraid Peter wouldn't believe me. When I heard footsteps, I turned around. Peter was coming down the stairs with a large pizza box in his hands. "I hope you like mushrooms," he said. "The pizza place goofed big time!"

"Peter," I yelled. "They're coming! I heard them! I saw them! They're coming!" I gripped his sleeves, snaking the pizza box between us.

Peter glanced at me, his mouth open, but before he could say anything, a voice, but no face this time, came on, "Listen, buddy, I have some good Hookpeth for sale cheap!"

"Well, I don't know . . ." answered another voice.

"It'll make an interplanetary invasion more fun, keep you going for days, won't give you a hangover, and it can't be detected in a urine test. Furthermore . . ." Peter threw the translator switch, and the English was replaced by garbled rumblings.

"Holy cow!" Peter gasped, then, glancing at the antenna box on the shaking washing machine, he said, "You fixed it! How about that?"

"But you don't understand," I said. "They're coming here!"

"Who?" Peter asked.

I pointed at a blank screen. "Them!"

Peter's eyebrows rose so fast that his glasses snapped in half at the bridge. He twisted and caught them in his hands. "No kidding," he whispered, awed. "I could use some Hookpeth myself!" He blinked in astonishment, then shoved the pizza box at me. "Here. Take this. Eat it before it gets cold. We got work to do." He picked a lock on the Pac-Man machine, and quarters poured onto the floor as he started rearranging wires.

'How can you mess with that now?" I shouted. "We're being invaded!"

"Here! Take these quarters and keep the washing machine going," he ordered. "I don't want to lose contact with the invaders. And hand me a slice of pizza."

Eventually, Peter hooked the video game to his complicated communications system. Suddenly, the game appeared on all the sets. He quickly sat down at the keyboard console and began typing into the computer like a maniac.

"Now what's happening?" I asked.

"I'm blocking their ship-to-ship communications with the image of the video game," he said. "That way, they can't talk to each other."

"Ah," I said, feeling some relief. "And you're setting it to their wavelength with your computer?"

"No," he replied. "That's already taken care of. I'm typing in the directions in their language just in case any of them wants to play. That'll keep them distracted." He typed a little more, then threw a switch. "Done! Toss me your auto keys. I'm going to need your car." I held out the keys to the Bug and watched him dash up the stairs.

"When this is over with," I shouted after him, "I'd like to have a little word with you about cable!" But I don't think he heard me. The door slammed above. I felt reassured that Peter had everything under control. My body was a bundle of nerves. I put a few more quarters into the washing machine, then headed upstairs to my apartment for some coffee.

I was walking along the first floor to the stairs at the back of the hall when Mrs. Hedley stuck her head out of her apartment. She was in a tattered bathrobe and a frizzled nightgown, with dirty, wooly slippers on her feet. She stood all of four and a half feet tall. Without her wig, she was virtually bald. "You're up too," she said as I passed. "Everyone's up early this morning."

"Yes, Ma'am," I said, trying to walk on.

"Do you know what Peter told me?" Mrs. Hedley asked. I stopped and turned around. "He said that we're being invaded by people from outer space!" She emphasized the last two words with her finger in the air. "Now, what do you think of that?"

I thought it was crazy that Peter would breach the secrecy of such an important project with Mrs. Hedley. What if she really was from another planet? But after spending the night watching Peter work, I decided that he must know what he was going. "He's right," I finally confessed.

Mrs. Hedley squinted her eyes. "I see," she finally said. "You both must have gone to the same party."

"No, Mrs. Hedley, I'm serious."

She looked down at the floor and made a "Tch, tch, tch," sound.

"Look," I said, "if you don't believe me, let me show you."

"Oh, I believe you, dear," she said, patronizingly.

"No," I insisted, "I can show you. Really."

"You don't have to show me any people from outer space," Mrs. Hedley said. "It's a little early in the morning for them anyway, I'm sure."

"Just come and see," I said.

Mrs. Hedley sighed. "All right," she said.

Once in the cellar, I presented the entire setup to her. "It's a communications system," I said. "We were in contact with attacking starships."

"Starships," Mrs. Hedley said. She held a delicate porcelain cup and saucer, and she sipped some tea. "All I see is Pac-Man."

"We're using that to block their communications," I said. "That way, they will be in confusion until we can . . ." I gestured frantically. "Well, whatever Peter has in mind."

"You don't say," she remarked, her eyes sparkling.

"Yes," I said. "Do you believe me?"

Mrs. Hedley turned to me and smiled. "Sure, I believe you," she said. "You're a good tenant. You wouldn't lie. Hold this." She handed me her cup and saucer.

Before I knew what was happening, she reached into the robe and brought out what looked like a gun — a very strange gun, silver, with knobs and wires and tiny lights flashing.

Holding the gun with both hands, she took careful aim at the Pac-Man game and pulled the trigger. A succession of four blue sparks shot from the gun and hit the machine, blasting it into a pile of smoke, glass and wires.

My heart leaped into my throat. I glanced around. All the television screens were empty, and a flood of alien voices mixed with the sound of shorting wires. I turned angrily to Mrs. Hedley. "Do you know what you just did?" I shrieked.

She turned and pointed the gun at me. "I'm truly sorry it had to end this way," she said. "You're such a good tenant, but business is business."

"Mrs. Hedley, you wouldn't!" I gasped.

"I thought Peter was up to something," she said, gesturing with the gun. "I thought that if I made you think Peter told me about it, you would show me what was going on." She took careful aim at my chest.

"Drop it!" I heard from behind me.

Before I had a chance to look back, Mrs. Hedley grabbed me around the waist and twisted me in front of her. She was pretty strong for her age. I felt the gun at my ribs, and I heard her say, "Don't try anything or he gets it!"

There was Peter Monk, standing at the top of the cellar stairs. His hair was worse than normal, and his glasses were missing altogether. He had a laser gun in one hand and a gold badge in the other. "Intergalactic police!" he shouted. "You're under arrest!"

"YOU'LL HAVE TO SHOOT THROUGH HIM TO GET ME!" Mrs. Hedley shouted.

"I'll do what I have to do," Peter replied.

"Peter!" I screamed.

Peter gave me a sad glance. "Sorry," he said, "but business is business, you know." I felt my muscles tense. I closed my eyes. The teacup in my hands rattled in the saucer. I was aware of the sounds of humming machinery, and the sizzling, sparking, defunct video game. When Mrs. Hedley released her grip, I felt myself swoon with relief. My legs were jello, and it was all I could do to keep from passing out.

When I opened my eyes, I saw Peter putting handcuffs on Mrs. Hedley. They conversed in a language I never heard before. Then Peter directed her towards the stairs, and she started up by herself. I felt for a chair and sat down.

"Won't she get away?" I asked.

"If she tries," Peter said, "the cuffs will electrocute her."

"Who is she?" I asked.

"Didn't I tell you that she came from another planet?" Peter inquired. "She's an intergalactic spy, that's who she is."

I felt my stomach knot at his remark. "But what about the invasion?"

"A piece of cake!" Peter replied with enthusiasm. "I'm surprised I never thought of it before! I'll just have Mrs. Hedley send false information to the invaders. Let them think we have a plague here, and they'll panic and head back where they came from with their tails between their legs!"

Peter somehow paid off the equipment bills and ended up giving away most of the things he bought as he disassembled his "control room." He kept Donkey Kong, though, and was making scores in the zillions. When he finally got bored with the game, he turned it into a giant body massage and pizza-microwave.

As for me, Peter finally installed my cable. I made a habit of picking up lady hitchhikers, who weren't too impressed with my Bug until they saw how fast it went, and when they asked about the vibrating toothbrush on the dashboard, I'd tell them about this inventor friend of mine, and how one day we teamed up together and saved the world from an intergalactic invasion. It became one of my most successful lines.

BEAVER ATTACK

The evidence was right in front of her: a severely-gnawed kitchen table leg, just barely strong enough to support its share of the weight. Alice Vodwell set down the plate she was drying and bent over for a better view. "My God," she gasped, touching the tooth-marks with an arthritic finger.

She stood up and looked around. Past experience enabled her to spot the signs immediately: wood chips near the seldom-used cupboard beneath the sink. She opened the cupboard doors and reached into the damp storage area. This time she found three short, chewed-up lengths of what had once been a broomstick. "It's happening," she whispered to herself. "It's happening again!"

"Alice," Frank Vodwell called from upstairs. "How much longer will the roast be in the oven? The kids will be here in an hour, and the grandkids will be more than ready to eat."

Alice, her apron flapping, tromped into the hallway and stopped at the foot of the stairs. "Frank," she shouted, "come down here. We have to talk." She brushed a strand of gray hair from a wrinkled, chubby cheek, and felt something wet — a tear? — as she waited for her husband. She recalled the last time it happened, the last night of compounded horrors . . .

She stepped into the dining room, touching the tablecloth and looking at the table settings as her mind raced. "What is it, honey?" Frank asked as he came into the dining room. He wore dark brown pants and a white, long-sleeved shirt. Although his hair was black, compliments of Grecian Formula 16, his moustache retained enough gray to add distinction to his features. He smiled at his wife as he lit his pipe. "Dear, would you like . . ." His mouth dropped open. Alice, gazing into his face, held the broom handle pieces in her hand where he could see them.

"Frank," Alice said, "you said you quit the last time this happened." She put the pieces on the table next to a plate. "Now it's beginning again, isn't it?"

Frank quickly regained his composure. "Nonsense, Alice," he said, puffing on his pipe. "I'm cured, and you know it."

Alice pointed at the wooden pieces. "I know what I see," she said.

"Dry rot," Frank said, averting his gaze.

"And what about that?" Alice shouted, pointing into the kitchen. The gnawed table leg stood out like a sore thumb.

"A bad case of rats," Frank said without looking at it. "It's been that way for a long time. You just haven't noticed it."

Alice's face turned beet-red. She reached down her blouse and brought out a rusty skeleton key tied around her neck with a dirty length of twine. Holding the key between thumb and forefinger, she shook it close to his eyes. "I still have the key!" she said. "Tomorrow, I'm going to burn the suit!"

The pipe fell from Frank's lips. Tobacco and ash peppered the carpet. "No, Alice," he said. "You can't. Not the Beaver Suit! You promised!"

"And you promised not to give in to these . . . urges!" Alice gestured with her hands. "Frank, you need help. I'm not going to stand back and watch you become a victim to your sickness again!" She stuffed the key back down her blouse. "I'm calling Beavers Anonymous tomorrow."

"But . . . Susan and Jim . . ."

"We'll have dinner as planned," Alice said. "Just behave yourself. I don't want Susan and her husband driving home on chewed-up tires." She picked up the pieces of broomstick, gave Frank a look that meant she was dead-serious, and headed back to the kitchen.

Not taking his eyes off his wife, Frank picked up his pipe and backed towards the stairs. When he was sure that Alice was busy drying the silverware for the evening's meal, he quickly tiptoed upstairs. Slipping into the guestroom and closing the door behind him, he went to the closet. Just as Alice had warned, the closet door was locked tight, and she had the only key. But Alice didn't know that the hinges had been chewed off the doorframe.

Frank went to the double bed and reached beneath the mattress. He found the screwdriver that he hid the last time he thought about getting the suit. He shoved it between the doorframe and the door. Using the screwdriver as a lever, he pulled. The old wood groaned, but nothing gave way. Feeling a spasm of panic, he held his breath and pulled harder. The door screeched like an animal in a leghold trap. The hinges popped, sending the door crashing against the old oak dresser.

Frank fell backwards onto the floor, hitting his head on the foot of the bed. His ears rang and his vision blurred, but he pulled himself up and looked into the closet. There was nothing but dust, a few stray wooden hangers, and the Beaver Suit, seeming to stand in wait for its next mission. The suit hung from an ancient coat-hanger, empty, calling to Frank to be filled.

The fur was dark brown and gray, and the suit was tailor-made to Frank's body. The feet were complete with webbing and claws, and the humongous Beaver Tail could fan-cool a room on a hot afternoon. With shaking hands, Frank grasped the Beaver Head and examined it for damage from age. The whiskers were brittle, but the black nose still gleamed. The eyes were like two-way mirrors, with the outsides gloss black and the insides transparent. The teeth were like white, giant chisels, and the ears, by way of string controls, could wiggle.

Frank put the head on the bed and carefully brought the suit out of the closet. It felt heavy, as though it had gained weight in its old age. He held it against his chest and stroked it, coughing as dust floated off the suit.

"Frank!" Alice shouted, throwing open the bedroom door and standing in the doorway. "Don't you even think about it! You know what happens when you put the suit on."

Frank tightened his grip on the suit, which puffed dust like a broken vacuum cleaner bag. "No, Alice," he said. "I can't let you destroy it! I can't!" He began fumbling with the zipper.

"Stop!" Alice shouted. "Don't put it on! I'll let you keep it, if you'll just put it back! I'll even let you touch it once a month!"

"It won't work, Alice. You're just trying to trick me until you get a chance to burn it." Frank's eyes blazed with the urgency of a junkie grasping at his fix. With a shaking hand, he pulled the zipper halfway down until it stuck. "Damned Beaver Hair!" he groaned.

"Frank!" Alice pleaded. "Get this crazy idea out of your head! You're not a Beaver!" She grasped the suit, trying to get it out of his hands. Dust flew everywhere.

"Alice, you tore the armpit!" Frank shouted. "Alice, cut that out!" They fought and pulled at the suit.

*   *   *   *   *

Jim and Susan Andrews and their two children strolled up the walk to the front door. "Now remember," Susan said to Bobby and Tammy, "any trouble from you tonight and you go to bed early tomorrow night."

"And let's remember to leave early tonight," Jim said. "I still have to finish the Governor's speech for tomorrow."

"You should have had that speech finished last night," Susan said, gathering her children before her. She pulled a brush from her purse and began brushing Tammy's hair.

"Ow!" Tammy cried.

"Quiet," Susan said. "You'd better shape up, Jim. If you cause one more problem for the Governor, you may end up pounding the sidewalk for another job."

Jim raised an eyebrow as he ran a comb through his dark-blond hair. "Just because I got one of his speeches mixed up with your letter to Aunt Mildred doesn't mean I'm doomed." He smiled and straightened his tie. "Besides, he caught on when he got to the part about Mrs. Filbert's hysterectomy, and from there, he winged it pretty well."

Susan went over Bobby's hair with the brush, then did her own. "Well, we can leave early tonight, but be sure to act nice to my folks. They helped us out a few times, remember?"

"Okay, okay," Jim said, adjusting his jacket. "But your father sure is strange sometimes."

He raised a fist to knock on the door, but before he placed the first knock, the door flew open wide. Jim's jaw dropped open. Standing before him was the biggest Beaver he ever saw! For that matter, he had only seen beavers in nature magazines, and he never imagined that they could grow so big, let alone stand on two legs. He screamed and jumped behind his wife and children.

The Beaver, standing six feet tall, was watching the hallway stairs when he opened the door. He turned around when Jim screamed, knocking a lamp off an end table with his tail. A shout came from the top of the stairs, and the Beaver looked back again. Alice Vodwell was charging down the steps, taking them two at a time on shaky legs. The Beaver let out a squawk and shoved past Jim and his family. He dashed into the street, leaping out of the way of a car.

"Stop him!" Alice shouted, dashing out the door.

"Good Lord!" Jim exclaimed, holding Bobby against his body.

"Jim!" Susan shouted.

"What?"

"Aren't you going to help Mother?"

Jim watched Alice and the Beaver disappear around a house. "If your mother wants to chase wild animals in the night, that's her business. I'm staying out of it."

"Did the Beaver eat our dinner?" Tammy asked over the noise of Bobby's giggling.

"No!" Susan shouted. "Jim, you . . . "

"Will Gramma cook the Beaver if she catches it?" Tammy asked.

"Quiet!" Susan yelled, slapping her hand against her own thigh. "Jim, do something!"

"Don't worry," Jim said, putting Bobby down and pointing. "Your mother's coming back now."

Susan turned and saw Alice running back to the house. "Jim what's going on? Motherrr. . ." Alice dashed past them and ran into the house. "Mother!" Susan shouted, following her in with the children. Jim straightened his tie and followed his wife.

Alice, her hair a gray, wiry mess, was on the phone. "It's an emergency," she panted. "Yes, I need help."

Jim stepped forward and raised an eyebrow. "Who are you talking to?" he asked.

"Mother," Susan asked, "what's going on?"

"Hush!" Alice said. She focused on her telephone conversation. "Yes, this is Alice Vodwell at 195 Brewer. My maiden name?"

"Who's she calling?" Jim asked Susan.

Alice listened for a minute, then shook her head. "They put me on hold!" she told Susan. "Can you believe that?"

"Who put you on hold?"

"Mother," Susan said. "What is happening?"

Alice, her eyes watery, looked away. "Your father's gone crazy."

"Crazy?" Susan gasped.

Alice nodded. "He's wearing the Beaver suit!"

Susan glanced at the open front door, then at her mother. "That was Dad?"

Jim stared at Susan. "Your father's a Beaver?"

"Oh, God," Susan gulped.

"Why didn't you stop him?" Jim demanded. "That's all I need is to have the Governor find out that my father-in-law is a Beaver!"

Alice held the receiver to her ear with both hands. "Wait, I think I got through! Hello. . ."

"Are you calling the police?" Jim asked.

"Yes," Alice said. "Hello, I'm . . ."

"No!" Jim shouted. He reached at the phone and pressed the receiver button. "Don't tell the police anything! It would get to the press! I'll lose my job!"

Alice turned on him, her face full of rage. "You idiot!" she yelled, slamming the receiver on the cradle and his finger. "You don't know Frank the way I know him! Once he has the Beaver suit on, it's almost impossible to stop him! It's a sickness with him, an addiction!"

"But I never knew . . ." Susan whispered.

Jim sucked his throbbing finger, then glanced at Alice. "That's the most ridiculous thing I ever heard!" he said. He turned towards his wife. "Susan, if your father does something to embarrass me, I'll . . ."

"You'll what?" Susan snarled, gritting her teeth.

"Quiet! The both of you!" Alice shouted. "Can't you understand? It's not Frank's fault he's this way." Alice removed her apron and set it over a chair. "He's the victim of military medical experiments."

"Mother," Susan said, "what are you talking about?"

Alice glanced at a framed photograph of Frank wearing his youth, along with an army private's uniform. "He suffered shell shock during the war," she said, taking the photo from the mantel. "Army medicine was just beginning experiments on the practical application of Beaver Therapy. They thought a Beaver Suit might help Frank get well. Of course it worked, but they didn't know when to stop the therapy. Soon, Frank was hooked . . ."

Alice coughed into her fist and swallowed before she went on. "He never mentioned it when we got married, but deep down inside I knew something was wrong. At first I couldn't admit it to myself, but after the neighbors' firewood turned to wood chips, and one of our trees, gnawed at the roots, fell onto our house, it was obvious that Frank had a serious problem."

Susan dabbed at a tear with Bobby's sweater. Jim adjusted his tie.

Alice blew her nose and went on. "We tried marriage counseling, group therapy and Beavers Anonymous, but nothing worked. Then Frank put on the Beaver Suit, and all hell broke loose. Once he puts on that suit . . ." Alice stopped talking. Now, she only stared into space, watching far-off events of another time in her life.

"Mother, are you okay?" Susan whispered.

Alice glanced at her daughter, then blinked and shook her head. "We're wasting time," she said. "I think Frank headed west, away from town. Susan, I'll need you to help get some things out of the attic." She faced her son-in-law. "Jim, you take the kids in the car and try to track Frank down."

"Now, wait a minute!" Jim said, shaking his head. "Don't get me involved in all this!"

"Jim!" Susan shouted.

"Susan, I'm not your father's caretaker."

Alice glanced at Jim, knitting her eyebrows together. "I don't know why you married this Bozo, Susan."

"Jim," Susan said, "Daddy helped you finish college. He paid the down payment on our house. How can you talk this way now?"

"Susan . . ." Jim began.

"Let him go," Alice said. "We can't make Jim help if he doesn't want to. The police can take care of it." She put down Frank's army picture and picked up the phone.

"Wait!" Jim said. Alice looked at him, and he looked back. "This is blackmail."

Alice didn't answer his remark, but said, "You'll look for him then."

"Yes, I'll look," Jim huffed.

Alice smiled. "Good. And remember, if you see him, don't do a thing. Just call here and wait for us."

Jim ran his fingers through his hair and shook his head. "I could probably wrestle him to the ground. He's not very young, you know."

"Well, you're not very strong for a young man, you know." Alice said.

Jim's cheeks puffed out, then he sighed. "C'mon, kids," he said, taking their hands and heading for the door.

"That Beaver sure smelled like mothballs," Tammy told Bobby. Then she asked her father, "Do we still get dessert if we don't eat dinner?"

"Oh, shut up," Jim mumbled, and they headed for the car.

Susan shook her head as she closed the front door. "Mom, I never knew . . ."

Alice hugged her daughter. "Susie, just because he's a Beaver doesn't mean he's no longer your father." She let Susan go and turned away. "The last time this happened we tried every trick but one. Maybe tonight's the night for that last trick, and with the element of surprise on our side, maybe we'll end this thing once and for all."

"Mom?" Susan said, subdued, "what if it doesn't work?"

"I don't know," Alice said. "I just don't know." She turned around. "Come with me to the attic. I'll need your help." They headed upstairs together, neither one sure of what the outcome of the evening would be.

*   *   *   *   *

"Now, just what did you say, young man?" the transient asked. He was an old man, with a Santa Claus beard, a toothless smile, and a railroad cap perched on a shaggy, gray head.

Jim looked at the other five transients standing under the sharp glare of the streetlight, then back at the old man again. He was tempted to roll up the car window and drive on. "I wanted to know if you saw a . . . a very large Beaver recently."

"Yeah, but didn't you say this was a six-foot-high Beaver?" the old man asked. He looked like he was about to laugh.

"Thazz what I heard," Bessie, a short, stout bag lady behind him said. "He sez . . . He sez, A Beaver six-foot tall!"

Jim felt his cheeks flush.

A skinny man in dirty overalls and tennis shoes but no shirt or socks stepped forward. "Did this Beaver wear a red tie and patent leather shoes?"

"What?" Jim sputtered. "No! Of course not!"

"Oh," the man replied. "I guess that musta been another six-foot tall Beaver!" The group of transients burst out laughing.

"Look," Jim shouted. "You're being ridiculous!"

Jessie stroked his beard as he turned to the skinny man. "Now, see here, Chubby! This gentleman here says that you're being ridiculous!" They all laughed again. "Now, cut it out afore I slap you up aside o' the head!"

Feeling his cheeks burning, Jim reached for the ignition. Tammy, his daughter, shoved herself past his shoulder and stuck her head out the driver's window. "The Beaver is my grandpa!" she shouted. "Don't laugh at him!"

The laugher died down, and the transients contemplated her words. A man in blue jeans and tattered t-shirt stepped forward. "Just what is she talking about, Mister?"

Jim looked up at him. "My father-in-law is running around, dressed up in a Beaver Suit."

"Well that explains everything," the man said. "You'll find your Beaver down on McKay Street." The other transients looked at him.

"You saw him?" Jim asked.

"Yeah, about ten minutes ago."

"So why didn't you say anything when I first asked?"

The man scratched his belly. "If you saw a giant Beaver running around, would you brag about it?"

"I guess not," Jim said. "Thanks for the information." He started the car, and they drove on. Jim looked in his rearview mirror to make sure that Tammy and Bobby were all right, then turned down McKay Street.

It had turned out to be a most miserable night. His wife, Susan, was at the house with her mother, Alice Vodwell, while her father, Frank Vodwell, was roaming the streets dressed in a realistic Beaver outfit. Whatever was wrong with Jim's father-in-law had something to do with experiments during his stay in the army. Regardless of the reasons, this was no mere Halloween party trick. Frank was going through something, and probably all but believed that he was a real Beaver. And now, Jim Andrews had to find him!

As they drove along McKay Street, Jim spotted the first Beaver Sign: chew marks on the side of an oak. "Keep your eyes open!" he told the kids. Tammy gripped her pony tails with excitement, and Bobby picked his nose.

"Oh, if any of this gets to the Press," Jim muttered, "I'm through!" As a speech writer for the Governor, his work had lately been questioned, especially after the Governor's last speech, when Jim somehow got the pages of the speech mixed up with Susan's letter to Aunt Mildred, and the Governor didn't catch on until he got to the part about Aunt Mildred's hysterectomy.

They drove on, spotting a chewed-up picket fence, a pile of scattered, gnawed-up firewood, and a crudely dammed-up fishpond in someone's suburban lawn. At one house, a carport had toppled onto a car. The support beams had been gnawed in half, and the owner, confused and furious, was stomping around his damaged vehicle.

"Daddy!" Tammy shouted, pointing. "The Beaver! The Beaver!" Jim stopped the car and looked. The Beaver appeared from the shadows between two houses, his great tail pounding the ground as he ran. He was a formidable sight, looking realistic as he charged across the street just in front of them. They heard a shotgun blast, and the Beaver leaped and stumbled on, holding his rump. A man with a shotgun ran out of the shadows, screaming and shaking a fist at the Beaver. He stopped under a streetlight and fired again, but the Beaver had just turned around the corner of another house.

Jim hit his high beams and floored the gas pedal. The car leaped forward as he turned off the road, bumped over the sidewalk and drove across somebody's front lawn and between two houses. He could see the Beaver just ahead, and slowed down to keep some distance between them. The car squeaked and groaned as Jim's shocks crunched in protest. Jim had never driven through rose beds before, and he prayed that nobody could read his license plate. Charging through another backyard, he inadvertently disassembled a swing set with a loud crash and grazed the side of an above-ground swimming pool, effectively emptying it of its water. Jim gritted his teeth but kept going, thinking of how close he was to losing his job, and how, just because his sister was married to the Governor, he wouldn't be forgiven forever.

He bounced through a ditch onto another road, losing his mufflers and hearing a sickening crunch in the back. Sweat froze on his body as he suddenly remembered that the kids were back there. "Bobby!" he screamed. "Tammy!"

"What?" Tammy shouted back.

"Are you guys okay?"

"Yeah, let's do that again!" Tammy giggled.

Jim sighed. "How's Bobby?"

"He's okay, but he needs new pants."

"New pants?"

"And socks," Tammy added. "And a towel to dry the seat."

Bobby and Tammy giggled together. Jim groaned, slowing the car and keeping his eyes on the Beaver, who still gripped his rump. He switched off the headlights, hoping that the Beaver would find a place to stop so he could call his wife and mother-in-law and report that he'd found him. He had no idea what Alice had in mind, but he hoped and prayed that it would work.

*   *   *   *   *

"They found Daddy!" Susan announced.

"Where?" Alice asked, carrying a large, dusty cardboard box into the kitchen.

Susan talked on the telephone again, nodding and glancing at her mother. "He's at the supermarket near the highway. He says Daddy's tired out and resting behind the store. It sounds like he's been very busy."

"Then we'd better make our move!" Alice said. "Tell Jim to stay put. Tell him not to do a thing until we get there!" She set the box down on the kitchen table. The gnawed leg finally snapped, and the table and box went crashing to the floor. "Oh, dear!" Alice said, gathering her skirt together as she knelt to pick up the box. "Sometimes your father is so much trouble I wonder why I never got a divorce!"

"Jim wants to know why he has to stay put." Susan said, covering the mouthpiece. "He thinks he can catch Daddy."

Alice shook her head. "Jim's more useful when he does nothing at all."

"Motherrr . . . "Susan hissed. "At least he found Daddy!"

"Is there anything else?" Alice asked.

"Wait," Susan said, then talked to Jim again. "Yes, dry clothes for Billy."

"I'll get something for him," Alice said as she hauled the bulky box onto the kitchen counter. "Just tell Jim to stay put until we get there."

"I did."

"Tell him again," Alice said as she left the kitchen.

Susan put the phone to her ear. "Take care, and don't do anything until we get there. And don't forget, I love you, and Mom loves you too."

"That's debatable," Alice called from the living room. Susan hung up the phone and folded her arms. She paced the kitchen, then glanced at the box on the table. She ran her finger over the layer of dust, making a design, then noticed the faded emblem of the Beaver standing next to a man with a butterfly net. The initials, B.A. were beneath the picture, and below that, in parentheses, the words, "Beavers Anonymous."

"Mother," Susan whispered as Alice reappeared with a gallon can of gasoline. "Just what it this anyway?"

"This," Alice began, cutting the strings around the box with a paring knife, "is the only way we have of stopping your father by ourselves before we have to call in the SWAT team." She lifted the lid, and Susan glanced inside.

"Mother, you're kidding, aren't you?"

"Drastic times require drastic measures."

"But this . . ." Susan gestured at the box. "If the police catch Daddy, he'll make the front page. If they catch you with this, we'll all be talking to Oprah Winfrey!"

"These are serious times," Alice said. "The last time your father put on the Beaver Suit, I had to dig a ten-foot-deep hole in the backyard to trap him. The neighbors helped get him out and tie him up. I know he won't fall for any Beaver Trap this time. This is our only hope."

"What's this?" Susan asked, holding an old pump-spray bottle.

Alice snatched it out of her hands and put it back in the box. "Don't touch things if you don't know where they came from!"

"Motherrr . . ."

"Now pick up that gas can and follow me," Alice said, carrying the box to the front door. "We've got a Beaver to catch."

    *   *   *   *   *

"Ohhhh . . . " Frank moaned. The buckshot in his buttocks felt like a thousand bee stings. "Ohhhh . . . " he repeated. His body was drenched in sweat, his muscles ached, and his head felt like a drum in a band that had just finished playing a marathon of John Phillip Sousa songs. He considered the pain in his chest, wondering if it was a heart attack getting ready to happen. This wasn't as much fun as it was in his youth.

But the Beaver Suite gave him the power of anonymity, a hiding place in his own body, the way a turtle's shell was its own home. In the army, the Beaver Suite was a crazy replacement for his uniform, and allowed him to break away from the regimentation of his fellow soldiers. The Beavers Suit allowed him to play the animal, to let his imagination go wild. And — he once thought in the army — people shoot people, not Beavers. Tonight he discovered that he was wrong.

"Oh Lord . . ." Frank moaned, leaning against a dumpster and studying his tattered, webbed feet. The Suit was falling apart! The tail was no longer straight and powerful, but bent, tattered and worn. His white chisel teeth were chipped and broken, and his mechanical jaw squeaked and sometimes stuck. The suit was ripping everywhere, not from the running and escaping but simply from old age. Oh, the night was miserable!

And to top it all off, there was that Bozo in the car who chased him for several blocks. Frank thought he'd never lose him. His stomach growled, and he thought about the dinner his family was to have, and he wondered if they ate without him. He couldn't blame them if they did. He felt as though he were the most childish person in the world.

He thought about his daughter and his son-in-law. Then he thought about his grandchildren, and how he hoped they didn't inherit too many genes from Jim. He thought about all the violence on television, and all the stupid sitcoms, and soap operas, and commercials, and talk shows . . . and even that speech the Governor gave about the deficit, more federal spending cuts, higher crime rates, and hysterectomies. With so many problems like that in the world, small wonder he wanted to hide inside a Beaver Suit!

"Ohhhhh . . ." he moaned.

"Ahhhh . . ." somebody answered. He glanced up, turned to the next dumpster, and saw the Skunk. With large bosoms, flashy whiskers, and an exotic black-and-white tail, she was the most attractive Skunk he had ever seen. The oddity of her five-foot-seven height escaped him on a busy night like this.

Frank rubbed his glass-covered eye holes and looked again. The Skunk kept her hands behind her back, but she wiggled her rump and curled her tail. He waved. She winked. He tried to move his tail, but the controlling cables were broken. But perhaps she would overlook his infirmities. He cautiously approached and sniffed. She seductively wiggled her whiskers.

Something wanting, deep inside his soul, made his sore heart beat faster. He stepped closer, and she tilted her head. He blinked; she snickered; he snacked. Then he reached out to touch her glistening fur. He couldn't feel anything through his Beaver Gloves, but he believed that he could live with this Skunk forever. Then he thought about his wife, Alice, back at the reality of his home. He wondered how upset she would be if she found out that he had run off with a Skunk.

In that moment, when Frank, lost in the dizziness of his Beaver Suit, was contemplating interspecies relationship possibilities, Alice, in her Skunk Suit, brought the spray bottle from behind her back and began spraying him.

"What the . . ."

"Frank, you asked for this!" Alice shouted.

"Hey! What's going on?" Frank backed away. "Hey, you're not a real Skunk! Alice, is that you in there? Alice, I wasn't going to run away with any skunk, honest!"

"Frank, you're gonna hate me for this, but I'm doing this for your own good!"

"What are you saying?" Frank demanded. "What are you talking about, Alice?" And then he noticed the horrible odor. "Good Lord!" Frank gasped, still unaware of the spray bottle in Alice's paw. "What's that terrible stink?"

"Essence of Skunk," Alice said.

"Gaaah!" Frank screamed, yanking off the Beaver Head and tossing it aside. The stench enveloped him, burning his nostrils and making his eyes water. He fell onto the ground and rolled back and forth, pulling off the gloves, kicking off the webbed feet, and frantically fumbling at the rusty zipper.

Alice stood back and watched, removing the Skunk Head for a better view. When Frank had the Suit off and backed away, she gave the signal. Susan appeared from the shadows, and before Frank had a chance to react, she doused the Beaver Suit with gasoline. Alice struck a wooden match on the dumpster, and as Frank watched, horrified, she tossed the match. The Suit burst into flame in one air-consuming whoosh, and Frank's jaw dropped open.

"My Suit!" Frank gasped, standing.

"We had to do it, Frank," Alice said.

Frank, shivering in his white boxer shorts, t-shirt, and socks, stepped towards the flames. "My Suit . . ." Susan took his arm and tried to lead him away. "My Suit . . ."

"It's time to go home, Frank," Alice said as Jim drove up and stepped out. The car sounded like a diesel generator without its mufflers, and the paint was scratched and scraped. Jim straightened his tie and opened the door as Alice and Susan guided Frank into the back seat. Tammy and Bobby hugged their grandfather as he sat beside them. The ashen pile of old cloth and burning hairs crackled and gave off a nasty odor as the flames died down.

"My Suit . . . " Frank said as they drove off.

A quiet breeze blew smoke and ashes toward the night sky. At the farthest dumpster, the lid opened a crack. Four eyes peered cautiously at the smoldering pile. "There's a lesson to be learned here, Ed."

"Yeah, Barney."

"It just goes to show you where wild behavior will get you."

"Totally sad. It looks like the old boy got carried away." The dumpster lid was pushed open with a clang, and two large Beaver Heads peered over the side. "You wanna do a few more trees, before we go home, Barney?"

"No can do," Barney said. "My wife thinks I'm bowling tonight. I gotta be home early, you know."

"Yeah, you're right," Ed said. "I'm feeling a little tired tonight myself." The two Beavers climbed carefully out of the dumpster, glanced around, and dashed into the shadows, their massive Beaver Tail's thumping the ground and they ran.

FIVE   1/97   T. NEWTON SCHULTZ

A NEW ORDER

When Tree returned to his room with a mug of red zinger tea, he found a mess. His paints, his poster board, and his son, little Ember, were combined like a bad recipe.

"Oh, shit," Tree groaned, putting his mug on the floor. "CAROLINA, COME HERE!" he shouted. Ember's eyes were crossed as he teetered his oversized head back and forth. He held a paintbrush in his mouth by the bristles, and his face was painted blue and red. Tree shook his head and pulled nervously at his sparse beard. "CAROLINA," he bellowed.

Carolina Angelina, his girlfriend, carrying a dishtowel, rushed into the room with her long, blond braid bouncing behind her. "Tree, what do you . . . oh!"

"Ember got into my room again," Tree growled. "How many times . . ."

"I told you to keep your door closed," Carolina interrupted. She held up her long, Argentinian folk skirt as she knelt toward Ember. "This isn't a lead-based paint, is it?"

"Is that all you care about?" Tree asked. "Tomorrow is our anti-war rally, and I have to have those posters ready by morning. And, besides, the Sunrise Coalition is meeting tonight to plan strategy. It's really going to be embarrassing if I don't have this done. Can't you see how important this is?"

Carolina stood up purposefully and took off her round, wire-rimmed glasses. "Don't go shifting blame!" she shouted. "You had two weeks to work on those posters. And your bike is out of adjustment and I suppose I'll have to do that too."

"Okay, okay," he said. "So I've been procrastinating. But at least I expected cooperation from you. I've been busy . . ."

"Well, so have I," Carolina huffed, kneeling again. She put the dishtowel down, put her glasses back on, and pulled Ember toward her. "There you go, Boo," she said, taking the paintbrush from his mouth. Gently, she touched the two scars from his double-cleft palate. They ran from each of his nostrils to his upper lip. Ember smiled and gurgled. "Momma will have to give you a bath, won't I?"

"That's all nice and well," Tree said, "But what about my poster board?"

Carolina picked up Ember and faced Tree. "Take it out of the grocery money." She gently stroked Ember's head, moving the red hair out of his eyes. Ember grinned and gurgled, pushing against Carolina's hand like a cat. "I'll help you clean up after I bathe Ember." She turned and left.

Dennis Moynihan "Tree" Mitterer almost called her back, but, instead, he watched her walk away. His thoughts turned to Ember as he stooped to pick up the finger painted poster board. After five years, he still hadn't adjusted to his hydrocephalic child. If the truth were told, he didn't like being around Ember at all, and that thought made him feel as guilty as ever. The boy seemed misshapen, his arms and hands uselessly small, contracted, and only movable at the shoulders, his legs and feet also small, and permanently in something like the lotus posture.

As he stood up, he knocked his tea onto one of the few untouched poster boards. "Oh, fucking hell," he groaned through gritted teeth. He picked up the mug and squeezed it. He visualized it smashed against the wall. Instead, he gently placed it onto his loft.

He grabbed his guitar, walked into the living room, and plopped on the giant pillow beside the couch. The pillow was as large as a chair, sat on the wooden floor, something he picked up at the Salvation Army a year ago. He always sat there when he needed to relax and think. He settled in and began strumming the guitar.

A voice interrupted his thoughts: "Hey, Tree, you wanna . . ."

"No!" snapped Tree, opening his eyes. Randy and Travis, Carolina's older children by her last lover, stepped in front of him. "I don't want to play right now," he said. "I need my own space."

"Nowadays, you ALWAYS need your own space," said twelve-year-old Randy. Randy was as blond as his mother and almost as tall.

"Yeah," said Travis, the nine-year-old. "And you're a grouch, too!" The boys stomped out of the room. The wooden beads in the kitchen doorway rattled behind them.

Absentmindedly, Tree strummed his guitar and thought about what Randy had said. Usually, he had time to play with them. He had often put down his work to "rassle" with them or to walk the railroad tracks with them. But, lately, the causes he worked at had become more time-consuming.

He sat brooding about the issues he and his friends were protesting: the debates to keep foreigners, particularly refugees, out of the United States, heightened security because of terrorism, drone strikes in foreign countries, anti-Islamic sentiment, and the resistance to closing Guantanamo Bay.   It was all coming to a head. He just didn't have time for games with kids.

His eyes opened suddenly when he heard Ember screech. Ember sat in front of him, his naked body tapering from his massive, lopsided head to his small rump. He rocked back and forth in perfect time to Tree's playing. Though he could not walk, he shuffled from room to room by pushing himself along waddling on his buttocks.

The sight of Ember rocking tickled Tree, and he laughed in spite of his mood. As irritating as Ember could be, he often had a calming effect on him. Ember gurgled and flapped his arms. Tree sighed and began playing, "Puff, the Magic Dragon." Softly he sang the words for Ember. Both Tree and Ember rocked back and forth as Tree sang. It was their favorite.

"Boo," called Carolina from the kitchen. "Boo! Ember! . . ." She stopped in the doorway and stood smiling at Tree and Ember. When the song ended, Tree and Ember gazed at each other. "O.K., Boo," Carolina said. "Bath."

Ember squawked and pivoted around. Then he waddled toward the bathroom. They heard Ember squawking in the bathroom.

Carolina smiled. "Do you want to bathe him tonight? You haven't bathed him in a while."

Tree was silent for a moment, then he snapped out of it. "No," he said. "No, I can't. I have to finish those posters." He remained seated, making no move toward the posters. Secretly, he was already planning to shift the poster responsibility to the people who came to the eight o'clock meeting.

"I see," said Carolina, icily. She turned and headed toward the bathroom.

Tree watched her go. He didn't like the expression of hurt on her face. Normally, he had bathed Ember whenever she asked, but tonight was different. He knew he should get to the posters. But he resumed strumming his guitar, thinking about all of his commitments and wondering if he would ever be able to work in some time for Ember.

When Carolina was done with Ember's bath, she cleaned up the poster board and went to work on repairing Tree's bike. Tree was still strumming on his guitar.

"You're deep in thought again," Carolina said, adjusting the derailleur with a screwdriver.

"Just thinking about Ember," Tree said.

"It's about time," she replied. "All you ever think about is this anti-Islam thing."

"That's not true," Tree replied. "I also think about wars around the globe, cutbacks in social programs, the deterioration of the middle class, global warming . . ."

"You see what I mean?" said Carolina shaking the screwdriver at him. "You always have your head in the clouds. Wars have been around forever. And global warming has been talked about for decades. You only picked up on it when the Sunrise Coalition did."

"So what's your point?" Tree asked, with exasperation.

"My point is . . ." Carolina started. But she stopped and caught herself. She pushed her glasses up on her nose and changed the subject. 'Pamela Adams called from the Starwolf Collective."

Tree coughed nervously. He was an owner-worker in Starwolf, and he knew what was coming next. "I missed a few days," he said.

"You missed a few meetings, too," Carolina said. "You're just too caught up in your projects. You are part owner of that little business, and even if you aren't there stocking shelves or packaging vegetables, you need to show up and give them your input. Maybe it's not global warming but if others don't show up, the business will collapse."

"Look," Tree said, "I'm just trying to create something better for us, a new order in the world . . ."

"There's no such thing as a perfect government," said Carolina.

Tree could hear Randy and Travis banging away in the kitchen. They were making popcorn. The smell and the popping was working on his appetite. Randy shouted from the kitchen. "Mom! Ember's eating his diaper again!" Ember came waddling from the kitchen. His big grin was like a beacon, and his long, red hair hung down in strands. He gurgled and went to Tree.

"Check his mouth," Carolina said, picking up her mug of lemon-grass tea.

"What?"

"Check his mouth. The inside."

Tree stopped strumming, set his guitar aside, and ran his finger around the inside of Ember's mouth while he held his head with the other hand. He found something soggy. "Yuck." He pulled the wet cotton out. It was part of Ember's Pampers.

"He does that to block the hole in the roof of his mouth," Carolina said. "Maybe I'll go back to using cloth diapers."

With a disgusted expression, Tree put the wet cotton in the wastepaper basket. "I wish we could break him of this habit."

"Well, I've been making some plans," Carolina said. She wiped the bicycle grease from her hands, came over, and picked Ember up. Tree watched Ember tilt his head and giggle. Saliva escaped from his smile onto Carolina's arm, and she patiently wiped it up.

"What are you plans?" Tree asked, strumming again.

"I'm planning to finish the operation on his palate if I can get some financial help from Welfare." Carolina kissed Ember's cheek. "I also found a school for special children that might take him in. He'll be tested next month. And there's a physical therapist who might be able to work on his arms and legs."

Ember rubbed his head with his wrists. Carolina understood and scratched his scalp for him. Ember hummed in satisfaction. He began rocking, and Tree began singing "Puff, the Magic Dragon, lived by the sea, and frolicked in the autumn mist in the land of Hona-Lee...."

"He really likes your music," Carolina said.

"He has good taste," Tree replied. He made a farting sound on Ember's bare belly. Then he caressed his son and brushed his lips against Ember's neck, where he felt it.

Ember's shunt was there, just under the skin. Tree thought of how Ember's life depended on the shunt, that small, plastic tube in his neck that drained fluids from his brain. He remembered the time the doctor told them that Ember's life span wouldn't be long. So far, ember outlasted the doctor's prediction by a year.

He touched Ember's smiling lips. "Eeeee!" the five-year-old chirped, raising his hands to Tree's face. Ember's hands were in one position, looking like the hands of a G. I. Joe doll, able to hold anything you put in them but unable to grasp because his fingers did not work. Tree laughed and nibbled Ember's fingers. Then he held Ember tight. His son, Boo. His son, Ember.

At eight o'clock the members of the Sunrise Coalition arrived. Tree heard a knock at the door and carried Ember with him to the door. A chilling wind entered along with Silverleaf, a large, black-bearded man in a bearskin coat, Silverleaf spotted Ember and laughed. "Yo ho! The Little Buddha! How's Tree been treating you?"

"Why don't you ask him how he's been treating me?" Tree mumbled.

"Tree, you seem a bit unhappy."

Tree sighed. "If your lady took off, sons and all, to go to the movies and stuck you with babysitting . . ."

"Say no more," Silverleaf agreed. He glanced around the living room. "Where's the meeting?"

"My room," Tree said. "Carolina cleaned the house today, and I promised to keep it straight."

They entered Tree's room, which had a loft for a bed. Tree slept there when he wanted to sleep alone, and he wanted to work on is plans for the next protest or meting. It was a large room, large enough for the eight people showing up, with pillows for everybody to sit in a circle, small tables against the wall with burning candles, incense, and anti-war posters on the wall. Though Tree usually slept with Carolina in her bedroom, this was his private place.

Members of the Sunrise Coalition crowded the loft and much of the floor. Conversation, small debates, laughing, and coughing filled the room. Tree's elephant-shaped bong made the rounds. Tree brushed his hair out of his eyes and set Ember down. A large pot of tea passed around, and people filled their mugs.

Ember flapped his arms and screeched. When nobody took notice, he grinned and waddled out the door. The official gavel banged against the loft and talking quickly ceased.

Tree sipped his sassafras tea while talk centered on the world picture. Photos of riots in Greece and Italy circulated about, and suggestions were made about petition drives.

Ember returned with a spoon in his mouth. Silverleaf reached across several people and nudged Tree. "The Buddha wants you," he whispered.

Tree grimaced and then glanced back. "He's hungry." He freed himself from the meeting, picked Ember up, and carried him into the living room.

"Oh, shit," he moaned when he discovered that Ember's diaper was soggy. When he glanced across the living room, he saw the dark spot on his favorite pillow, the big one next to the couch. "Aww, Ember! Ember!" He had to touch the pillow before he actually believed it was wet. "Ember, you God damn little . . ."

Tree held Ember at arm's length, carried him to the kitchen and put him on the table. He glanced back at the open door to his room, thinking about how much he wanted to be there.

He removed the diaper, and was relieved that it was only wet. When he couldn't find the Pampers, he used a dishtowel and made a sloppy loincloth. That done, he found some alfalfa sprouts and sour cream in the refrigerator and spoon fed them to Ember.

"You ought to like this," he said. "It has vitamins and helps you poop. There, take another bite . . ."

Ember smiled and flapped his arms. "Giiiii . . ." Ember squawked.

"Yeah, you think it's funny to make Daddy work, but I'm missing my meeting," Tree growled. "Shame on you! Wetting your pants was probably just a behavioral thing to get my attention, wasn't it? You really didn't have to go to the bathroom, did you?"

When Ember was full, Tree picked him up and rocked him, singing, "Puff, the Magic Drago." At the end of the song, Ember was happily chirping and flapping his arms. Tree glanced at the door to his room. He could hear people embroiled in an interesting discussion about the contributions of Pope Francis to the peace movement. "Shit," he said. He placed Ember on the blankets on the floor in the pantry that served as Ember's bedroom. "Okay, now, go to sleep."

Ember screeched. "You had your song," Tree said. "I don't have time to do a whole opera for you!" Tree ached to get back to his meeting.

Ember frowned. He realized that he was about to be deserted and began moaning.

"That's enough," Tree growled. He felt himself losing control. Suddenly his voice exploded. "Haven't I done enough r you? You're just too much trouble, you know that?" He pounded his fist against the wall.

Ember began crying.

Tree glanced at his hand. He shuddered when he realized that he felt like smacking Ember. He closed his eyes and spent a minute taking deep breaths, his face felt damp and clammy. Finally, he opened his eyes and picked up Ember.

"It's okay," Tree whispered as he rocked him back and forth. "It's okay. Calm down. You have to go to sleep. You have to go nitey-nite. Daddy has to get back to his meeting. We have to look for a new order for our society, a new beginning, a better world, for our society, and for all societies. We don't want hunger in our world, ever again. We don't want suffering, or the threat of war or terrorism or nuclear holocaust. And we're trying to help every person in this world that we can. There's suffering in the Middle East . . ." He stopped when he noticed that Ember was asleep.

He gently placed Ember on the blankets. He sat in the dim light, touched Ember's face and felt his soft breathing. "I don't mean it," he whispered. "I don't mean it when I say you're too much trouble," he whispered. "I was just angry. You're never too much trouble." He kissed his son's forehead, looked at him one more time, and went back to the meeting.

Crawling out of bed the next morning, Tree went to the living room and checked his pillow. It was almost dry, but it smelled of urine. He scooped some lists off the floor, lists of Sunrise Coalition members who volunteered to march against war and the One Percent again next month. Ember had chewed them. Tree sighed and put them on a high shelf. It was time to face Carolina and talk seriously about Ember. He was absolutely sure of that now.

He went to the bathroom and found Carolina and Ember in the tub. He scratched his side and urinated while he watched Ember put his head under water and come up again. "Morning," he said. He wished he could just come right out with it. He bit his lip.

"Good morning," Carolina answered, as she washed her hair.

"Are you planning to teach Ember to swim?" Tree asked, prolonging his real business. He sat on the side of the tub.

Carolina rinsed her hair using a cracked coffee mug. "I plan to teach him at the 'Y' when I get the time."

"You make lots of plans for him," Tree said, drying Ember off. "Do you really think you can handle all this?"

"I don't know," Carolina said, drying under her arms. "Some things you do in this world have to be done as an act of faith." She dried her feet and stepped out. "You can always fail, Tree. Always." She put her wire-rimmed glasses on and left the bathroom. Tree tossed Ember over his shoulder and followed.

"Carolina," he said, setting Ember down near the crackling wood stove.

"Yes?"

Tree worded his next question as well as he could. "What do you think of letting somebody else take care of Ember for a while?"

Carolina glowered at him and adjusted her glasses. "What do you mean?" she challenged.

"I mean," Tree tried again, "just to get him into a different environment while I catch up on some of my important business."

Carolina knitted her eyebrows together. "You can't be serious!"

"Just for a while," Tree said. "A few weeks, a month . . ."

"No!" Carolina snapped. "He's my son! He's your son, for Christ's sake! Be reasonable!" She snatched Ember off the floor and put him on the couch, where she finished dressing him.

"I'm not being unreasonable . . ." Tree began.

"Yes, you are!" Carolina said. "Parents don't give away their children, not even for a week! Catch up on important business? Ember is the most important business you have."

"Look," Tree said, pointing to his bedroom. "Ember has been underfoot for the last few weeks. He's been tearing up important papers, losing phone numbers, getting in my way, and last night . . ." He pointed the other way. "He pissed on my pillow!"

Carolina picked up Ember, who seemed unaware of the fight. "My son stays with me," she said. "It's not his fault that you never close your door or put your files up."

"But he needs so much attention."

"That's right," Carolina said. "But he's staying with me. My doctor tried to talk me into turning him over to an institution. I wouldn't do it. He's my son. My child. Your child. He stays with me."

Tree swallowed. "I didn't mean to get you upset."

"I never knew you felt that way about Ember," Carolina said. "I'll buy you a new pillow out of my next paycheck."

"I don't feel that way," Tree said. "But my work at the Sunrise Coalition is very important. I don't want to lose you, and I don't want to lose Ember. I love my son. Honest I do."

Carolina silently walked off. The discussion was over.

After the rally the next day, Tree, Carolina, Randy, Travis and Ember, along with a few of the protesters, went to the Beanery Restaurant for dinner. Carolina herded Randy and Travis, and Tree carried Ember tossed over his shoulder. Ember chortled as his red braid dangled like a bell cord. He enjoyed the freedom of being upside down, the comfort of his back and neck not having to support the weight of his large head. He slobbered and giggled against Tree's back. Tree gave him pats on his rump.

Some people in the cafe stared, but others knew Ember, and greeted him and his family as they chose a table. "Here you go, Boo," Carolina said, taking Ember from Tree and putting him on her lap. Tree didn't say anything as the boys sat on either side of him. When dinner came, they settled in.

"Carolina," Tree ventured.

"Yes?"

"I didn't mean to cause any hard feelings. I'm sorry."

Carolina smiled cautiously.

"It's just . . . " Tree took another bite and talked on with his mouth full. "Well . . . I feel I need to be active in solving the world's problems." He gestured with his fork. "We live in the richest nation in the world, and we have the resources to make major changes." He took another bite. "But our government is moving toward establishing its own power and ignoring human rights to do it. And what's worse . . ." He shook his fork to keep the emphasis going while he stole a sip of tea. "Most of the people of America aren't concerned."

"Oh, yes they are," Carolina said. "Travis, stop hitting Randy."

"Mom!" Randy mumbled. "We're just playing!"

"You have to understand," Carolina said. "We all have to touch the world's wounds in the best way we know how." She looked at Ember in her lap. "Boo is the piece of the world I take care of." Tree picked at his food, feeling that Carolina was excluding him.

Carolina tried to feed Ember another bite of food, but he was getting stubborn and was not looking happy at all. "I don't have to join your Sunrise Coalition to make your ideas valid. You talk about world hunger, but I see you eat three meals a day." She looked right at Tree.

He felt her gaze. The refried beans he swallowed went down like a large rock. He suddenly lost his appetite.

Carolina smiled sympathetically at his distress. "I understand how you feel. When I see starving children on the news, I feel helpless. When I hear that Congress has put millions into new weapons or sent that money to another country for war, I feel betrayed, because it's my tax money, too."

Tree was just about to take another bite when Ember threw up all over the table.

The next morning, Carolina took Ember to the doctor and returned with several medications. Tree didn't like the way she looked. Her brow was furrowed, and she hurried about nervously.

For the next week, Ember lay on Tree's large pillow in the living room next to the wood stove. For once Tree didn't care if Ember pissed on his pillow or not, Ember was going through something painful and difficult. Tree and Carolina took turns taking Ember's temperature, cleaning the diarrhea, and feeding him chicken broth and Jell-O. When evenings came, Carolina rubbed Ember's body with warm oil while Tree sat and strummed his guitar. The week was a quiet one, with everybody waiting for Ember to get better.

"He'll be back to normal soon," Carolina said.

"I hope so," Tree said. "There's so much I need to do.

It was three-thirty one morning when Tree heard Ember screech for water. Red-eyed and shaggy, Tree had to relieve himself for the third time that night. Otherwise, he might not have bothered moving from his sore-backed, hunched-over position. He was surrounded by folders and an empty, tipped-over teapot at his desk. "Coming," he said.

Carolina was asleep on the couch. The long week caring for Ember made her too tired to hear him now. Tree pulled the blanket over her shoulders and went to the bathroom. He got a glass of water and returned to Ember.

"Here you are, buster," he said. "Sit up."

Ember shook his head, no. "Giiii!"

"C'mon, dammit," Tree said. "Sit up, or I won't give you water."

Ember gurgled, then slowly pushed himself up. His heavy head teetered like a great boulder balanced on a pinnacle. He grasped the glass with both wrists and drank, spilling some water before he was done. Tree felt his diaper; he was dry. He laid Ember down and covered him. He put his hand near Ember's lips, felt the breathing, and kissed his forehead. Then he threw some wood into the stove and walked back to his loft. "God, am I tired," he said. He went to sleep among the files and folders.

The house was silent. The air was fragrant with burning wood and candlewax.

Carolina burst into Tree's room, tearing him from his sleep. He felt Carolina shaking him.

"Your door was closed!" she puffed. "I knocked . . ." Her face was white, her eyes, wide. "Ember . . . Ember's in a coma! He's not waking up!" She ran back to Ember, and time slowed. Tree jumped naked from the loft, his bathrobe in his hand. He floated through the door, wondering why he closed the door, and why he didn't remember doing it. His skin felt like a thousand cockroaches were crawling on it.

A dream about their leaky roof was frozen in his skull. This was a new dream; it had to be. Now he was kneeling beside Ember with no memory of getting there. Carolina was beside him. Ember's blanket was kicked off. He lay on his back. His mouth was open; his eyes half-closed; his large head seemed about to roll away from his body. The shunt still lay under the skin of his neck, like a snake.

He looked at the bluish lips and felt the cold forehead. Now Carolina was at the telephone, looking down at Tree. "Is he all right? They have to know!"

Tree swallowed. He looked at Carolina; her long hair was undone over her bare shoulder and breasts. "The ambulance is coming for Chrissake!" she yelled, "They have to know! How is he?"

Tree snapped awake and looked at Ember. He put a shaking palm against Ember's nose and mouth. It felt like a shallow breath. He touched an artery, and thought he felt a week pulse. "Tell them to hurry!" he shouted. "Tell them he's alive, but they need to get here goddam fast!"

He pulled the blanket up, and Carolina talked on the phone. He could smell coffee in the air, and he heard complaints as Carolina scurried Travis and Randy out the back door, saying something about going to a neighbor's house until it was time for school.

The rain outside pounded the windows. Now Carolina was in the kitchen washing dishes so fast Tree thought they would break.

When the ambulance came, three uniformed paramedics with steel cases entered and surrounded Ember. They talked to each other, leaving the front door open, with the cold coming in and with the ambulance radio outside screeching messages from the road.

Carolina was suddenly by Tree's side. A paramedic approached them. "He's been dead for an hour," he said. Sparing them a concerned glance, he returned to his work.

Carolina removed her glasses and looked at Tree. "I walked right by him this morning," she said. "I walked right by him, and didn't notice!" She ran to their bedroom. Tree felt alone. He went into the kitchen. He didn't know why the paramedics were still working over Ember if he was dead. He wanted them to leave.

He poured himself a cup of coffee and set it down. He smelled dish soap in the air, and he paced the floor. "Jesus fucking Christ," he cried. His eyes felt like they would overflow. He gripped the sink, wanting to hit something. He went to the kitchen doorway, and brushed the beads out of his way. "Can I help?" he asked.

"No," one paramedic said, his back to Tree. "We have it under control."

"He's my son," Tree said, but nobody heard him. Tree returned to the kitchen and pushed his forehead against a wall.

He let himself cry. He didn't care if the paramedics heard him. It felt like a bullrope was wrapped around his chest. He sobbed to release himself. A hand caressed his back. He turned to face Carolina.

"My baby," she said, her eyes red and puffy. "My baby is dead!" They embraced each other, holding each other tight against the darkness that surrounded them.

"I know," Tree said, "I know. My son . . ." They cried together. It felt good, orgasmic, and warm. It was a sinking and a rising. They pulled each other up from the depths. As they embraced, they told each other about their love.

The wake was that night. People brought baskets of homemade bread, vegetarian stew, tofu meatloaf, bottles of wine, whiskey, pot, and mushroom tea, clothing, songs, stories, words, wishes, and hugs. Tree watched, sitting on his pillow as people crowded in, paid their respects, and joined in the grieving.

He had never been so stoned. He'd caught the bong every time it passed. He had sung for a while, but when he played, "Puff, the Magic Dragon," he broke down and cried when he came to the line, "A dragon lives forever, but not so little boys." He didn't try to play the song again.

Carolina, who had been wandering through the house, sat down beside him. "So many people knew him," Tree said. "So many."

"We were lucky that he was ours. Even it if wasn't for long."

Tree looked at her. He knew his own loss was great; he could hardly imagine how much more so hers must be. She had had so many plans . . . Tree took her hand. "I know you're hurting bad," he said. She did not look at him, but squeezed his hand. "I should have done more," he said.

"No," Carolina said, "don't say that."

"But it's true," Tree said. "I had to stick my head in all the world's problems . . ."

"No!" Carolina choked. Her face was puffy from so much crying. "Your ideas are right. Don't surrender them now. When you have one person trying to build a bridge, and the rest of the world keeps knocking it down, you may think you have nothing. But if that one person doesn't give up, you still have one person trying to build a bridge."

Tree was silent. He wasn't really interested in ideas right now.

For a long while he watched the other people in the room. People were hugging and touching each other, paying attention, focusing. He had never quite noticed the importance of that before.

Perhaps, the little Buddha had planted the seeds of a new order in his students. He smiled. He smiled and held on to Carolina.

TEA FOR THE SUNRISE

One day they found the few, fossilized bones of the first woman, and they named her Lucy, and, awed and puzzled, they asked her, "Why did your people die off? Why didn't they survive?" But Lucy asked back, across a bridge of millions of years, "And what makes you think your kind will survive?"

And will I survive? Donna Lane wondered at four in the morning as she crawled from her warm sleeping bag and out of the tent, bare hands on ice and rock until she stood, shivering beneath the inquiring stars. And will the sun last forever? Or will it burn itself out, leaving all life to starve to death?

She fumbled with her flashlight and her portable butane stove, struck a match and got the flame glowing cobalt blue, hissing coldly as she put a camper's pot full of water on it. Then she looked up, cold, her eyes full of the night's gems. And she thought about the pills.

The pills: her answer to what her life had become. She was now trying to be mother and father to her three, small children, still working, a bottle of wine every night to relax against the last few months of loneliness, dinners with canned creamed corn, mundane nights of eleven o'clock news and cigarettes and bills, and she kept telling herself: I'm not going to make it, I'm not going to make it . . .

Now, having had barely two hours of sleep, shivering and scared, she strapped the sharp-toothed steel crampons onto her hiking boots to complete her journey. Her tent was pitched just below Tabletop on Mount Adams in the state of Washington. It was her first, and last, mountain climb, and Mount Adams was, fortunately, not a technical climb that required ropes and pitons, though a rented ice axe and crampons helped. "You got more guts than I do," Maggie Wyles, who was watching her children that week, told her. But Donna knew it had nothing to do with courage. I'm scared, she thought, scared of living, and I'm lonely. So she brought the pills, because she had no intention of climbing back down the mountain.

Her twelve-year marriage with Matt came to mind as she watched the cold blue flame of the stove. A storybook romance, they grew up together, childhood sweethearts thriving symbiotically off each other, always working together, sharing laughs, traveling together, so very seldom apart. He was so kind, so encouraging when she began her career in realty two years ago.

Donna was intensely happy with her husband and her children. Then one night Matt flowered her over with talk of how much he loved her, and how he couldn't live without her, and the next day he went to work, never to return. He called her that evening from another woman's house, talking about separation and the quality of his life.

At the time, she didn't feel anything. She continued working, raising the children, attending those meetings of initials — MADD, NARAL, NOW. As though in a dream, she found herself heading into an affair with Steve Brecht, a songwriter and coworker, and she might have followed through with it had she not listened to three women from the office who casually chatted around a bar table about office affairs they had had with him. She felt even more alone than before.

And now she was on a mountain, wanting to die, the bottle of pills weighing heavily in her pocket. Though she worried about her children, and what effect her death would have on them, she knew her mother would raise them well. Though being on the mountain seemed irrational, she knew she couldn't die like Sylvia Plath, enclosed in a room, suffocated by gas. She needed freedom and a romantic death, because the romance of her life was gone.

It was almost four-thirty when Donna poured the hot, sugarless, lemon-grass tea into the thermos. Surrounded by ice and rock, her tent and the small blue flame from her stove became a sanctuary for her in the darkness. She gazed around, imagining a glacial age of mammoths and timber wolves, and fighting them off, she and the long-dead Australopithecus Lucy, with femur bones and rocks.

Glancing down toward the base of the mountain, she saw a caterpillaring line of lights, two dozen, maybe more, as though some stars had leaked from the sky and were trying to climb back up. They were flashlight-carrying climbers who, like her, were getting as early start. She didn't worry about it; the pills would finish their work long before another hiker would catch up with her.

Sighing, she braced herself against a boulder to urinate one last time, picked up her knapsack and ice axe, and began her ascension. The eastern horizon was already swirling, gray clouds, and soon it would be glowing red. For now, though, she used her flashlight, stepping carefully as a cold wind stabbed at her tear-damp cheeks.

Her breathing quickly became difficult, as though she were inhaling cream-of-mushroom soup, but that was to be expected in the thin air at ten thousand feet. Her crampons gripped ice and stone while her flashlight revealed details of the grayish landscape. Donna had hiked many times before, but she had never trained for a mountain climb. Her calves, still sore from the day before, now screamed with glass-sharp pain, and would be worse by the time she was done. But it didn't matter. Donna was escaping her own helplessness, pain or no pain.

A steep snowfield just east of the Suksdorf Ridge provided the best climbing, so she climbed there, kicking footholds into the snow, sometimes using the ice axe when snow became ice. She was no longer cold but sweating, having to stop every dozen steps to catch her breath. She glanced up at the stars, not so many visible now, as though they were reaching their extinction. The red of morning glowed beyond distant mountains like a swelling artery. Not once did she look back to watch the other climbers' progress.

She kept touching the bulging pocket with the bottle of pills. It both scared her and gave her strength. As she continued her ascent, she thought of the lyrics to one of Steve's songs: "The bear climbed to the top of a mountain . . . To watch a stream run down . . ." She also recalled Ernest Hemingway's story about finding the frozen, preserved carcass of a leopard on Mount Kilimanjaro, and how he wondered what it was doing at such a high altitude.

Donna's lungs now felt like shredded lettuce, and her calves and thighs felt like aching rubber bands, but she went on regardless. Suddenly long shadows leaped like striking snakes across per path. She glanced east, watching the sun peer over the mountains. Turning west, she saw Mount Saint Helens, twenty miles away, still sending up dust plumes a decade after the famous eruption.

Sighing, Donna turned off her flashlight and set it on a small ice ledge while she removed her knapsack to put it away. As she unzipped a pocket on her knapsack, the flashlight suddenly slipped and bounded down the steep slope. Donna pivoted and watched, feeling a sudden wave of vertigo as her new flashlight slid and bounced downhill. Only the lonely sound of each icy impact was audible over the moaning of the wind. Donna almost laughed; she felt deserted again. Watching the flashlight come to a stop a thousand feet downhill, she wondered about the ancient bones of Lucy. Did she die alone? she wondered. Was she a mother? Was she deserted, too? Donna squinted at the rising sun, her only witness. You, too, will make your circuit across the sky and desert me, too, she thought.

Her ascent continued, uneventful and slow. She reached the false summit of Mount Adams, walked the several hundred feet to the real summit, and climbed the last few hundred feet to the top in less than an hour, still gasping but barely aware of the pain in her lungs.

Having reached the top of the mountain, she was ready to take the pills she had planned to use for the last month, when she spotted the cabin. It was an old relic from the turn of the century, she recalled, that was supposed to be buried in snow, but now, most of the roof and part of one wall were visible, reminding Donna of Noah's Ark on Mount Ararat. She walked over to the ancient, cedar-shingled roof and noticed a flat, rectangular aluminum box just inside a window. Pulling it out and opening it, she found a register inside. There were pages and pages filled with names of those who reached the top, and several whittled pencils awaiting more names.

Donna thought of the line of climbers as hour or so behind her. She thought of the pills, knowing they would finish their job before the other climbers reached her. Moving almost mechanically, she unshouldered her knapsack as she recalled the story of the cabin. Two men had constructed it, using mules to haul large logs to the top of the mountain. They were apparently mining sulfur. They are long-dead now, Donna thought, but they didn't climb Mount Adams to die. Neither did the leopard climb Mount Kilimanjaro to die. And Lucy, in her quest for her mountain, wasn't seeking death either.

Donna felt her courage waning. With shaking hands, she unzipped her knapsack and pulled out the thermos. Sitting on the bone-gray shingles of the roof, she unscrewed the plastic cup from the thermos, thinking about her children. She fully realized how selfish her dying was, and what a nightmarish legacy she was leaving behind for them, but her own pain outweighed her maternal instincts. She was not the kind of person who could replace the lifetime love of a spouse with the needful love of her children. She had a void in her life, deep, painful, permanent.

Robot-like, she removed the lid from the thermos and poured out a cupful of brown amber tea, the steam rising in the early morning sunlight, only to be blown away by the icy wind. She knew she would have to work fast, while she had the courage. She removed the pill bottle from her pocket, poured some pills into the palm of her hand, and in one quick motion, her eyes wide, her hands shaking, she dropped them onto the ground, stomping them into the snow with her crampon-wielding boots, pouring the rest of the pills onto those, then scraping snow over them with her ice axe. Until the moment she saw the register, she never realized how much she wanted to survive.

Once again, she recalled the bones; Lucy was dead, and her race of people was gone, but surely they fought hard to survive. Donna glanced east. The sun was high above the mountain, high in a light blue cloudless sky. The sun, always deserting her, but always coming back. And she thought about her children, and how they would have a better chance of survival if she went home.

Having reached the summit of Mount Adams, intending to sign the register, she knew now that she would be surviving, she would go home, pain and all, to overcome other mountains. She lifted her cup, no longer tea of death, but tea for the sunrise, tea for life and a new beginning. She took a sip and thought about a bear that watched a stream run down.

David M. Wood

ELEVEN ROSES

John Martin "Sonny" Preston flattened his large, red, bulbous nose against the Kaufmann's showcase window, watching the mechanical elves inside make toys in a fantasy Santa's shop.

"I just gotta get her something," he told them, his breath fogging the glass. He turned and yanked his thick, dirty blue pullover cap tighter over his long, gray hair. Large snowflakes floated to the streets, slushy from traffic.

Streetlights revealed sooty snow along the sidewalks. It was Christmas Eve, and few pedestrians were left, save for a couple of small lines outside movie theaters. Christmas music reverberated off the walls of old skyscrapers, following Sonny as he hurried on.

A taxi passed, splashing slush onto the icy sidewalk, but Sonny ignored it as he spotted Ginny Anne Marlowe in the line for the Christian Ladies' Shelter. Ginny was massive in her coats, each arm grasping a tattered garbage bag full of all her worldly treasures.

"Ho! Ginny!" Sonny shouted, waving a gloved hand as he rushed up to her.

"Ah, Sonny," she said, laughing through a toothless grin. "Ah, Sonny, I can't talk now, Sonny. I gotta get in here and get my bed, you know."

"Ginny," Sonny said, "Whatcha want for Christmas?"

"Ah, Sonny," she laughed, and Sonny laughed too, her laughter was so infectious. "Ah, Sonny, I want a million bucks and a big car, and a . . ."

"I mean, really," Sonny asked. "For real."

"For real?" Ginny asked, flakes of snow in her brownish-gray hair. "Ah, Sonny, ain'tcha sweet. But Ginny takes care of Ginny, ya know."

"Yeah, well, tomorrow is Christmas," Sonny said, scratching his whiskers, "and . . . well . . ."

"Ah, Sonny, you're so sweet," Ginny said, almost glowing with warmth. The line started moving again, the other women stepping forward passively. Only Ginny, with her garbage bags, was animated. "You know what I'd like?" she shouted at the entrance. "I'd like a big, red, long-stemmed rose." Then she was gone.

"A rose?" Sonny asked. "A rose in winter?" But the door to the Christian Ladies' Shelter was closed.

Sonny got his own bed at the Brother Billy Bob's Soup, Soap and Hope Mission, where the soup was watery, the bread was hard, but the coffee was thick and steamy and ran until bedtime. Brother Bill's sermon about lost sheep was short, followed by plenty of gospel songs from the tattered hymnals. Sonny slept with his socks under one arm and the Ace bandages he used to wrap his stockinged feet under the other arm so they'd be dry by morning. His Christmas Day breakfast consisted of coffee, burned toast and greasy, fried potatoes, another sermon, then back on the street.

The morning light reflected blindingly off the freshly fallen snow. Most stores were closed, but a few would be open until noon. Sonny set off walking, grumbling to himself. "A rose in winter . . ."

He found three flower shops that were open, but none of them had roses. He had been walking for two hours already, and his socks were soaked, and his toes numb with cold. The sky was no longer blue, but overcast, and snow had begun falling again.

"A rose in winter," Sonny growled, his thick, gray eyebrows knitting together like two woolly caterpillars in a *pas-de-deux*. Then he recalled all the times Ginny made him laugh, and he grinned, feeling new energy.

He found roses at Floral Designs — they had a dozen left, but they cost $5 apiece. Sonny rummaged through his pocket and came up with 47 cents. The warmth of the brightly lighted store and the smell of chemical fertilizer and flowers followed him as he went out the door. He wandered, looking at store windows with grates across them to discourage burglary. He saw a pawnshop that was open and recalled the old wedding ring he pawned years ago.

Then, looking across the street at a Gimbels entrance, he saw a thin man in a Santa suit with a fake beard and a real bell. He was standing by a plastic cauldron supported by a tripod advertising some charity. Sonny watched as departing shoppers dropped loose change into the cauldron.

Going into the alleyway, Sonny came up with a Campbell's soup can. He then went to another entrance of the building, where he held the can with both gloved hands, shouting, "Coins for the poor! Coins for the poor!" The passing shoppers wouldn't look at him, but dropped loose change into his can. It was just gaining weight when the Santa's brass bell bounced painfully off his head.

"Git outta here!" Santa yelled, shaking his fist. "This is my territory! Yer messin' with my customers!" Sonny scooped up the dropped coins from the snow and ran off, still hearing Santa's ravings a block away.

He arrived at Floral Designs, walking up to the counter with his change.

"I'd like a red, long-stemmed rose," he said, rubbing his head where the bell hit him, "but I'm a little short."

The woman counted the change he dropped on the counter, then shook her head. "I'm sorry," she said, "but if you would like a chrysanthemum."

"Oh, no," Sonny said, "but maybe I could scape together the money in another hour."

'We close in five minutes," the woman said.

Sonny looked at her with pleading eyes.

The woman shook her head.

Sonny sighed, sliding his coins off the counter into a gloved hand. He went outside and stood in the falling snow. Other stores were closing. It was Christmas Day, after all. A recorded choir sang through outdoor speakers, "Hark! The herald angels sing . . ."

He counted his change again, as though he expected the amount to magically increase. A man stepped out of Floral Design carrying a dozen red roses wrapped in delicate pick tissue paper. *The* dozen roses! Sonny thought to himself in panic.

He walked after the man. "Hey, mister!" The man saw him and started walking faster. "Wait! Please!"

The man stopped and spun around. "What do you want?"

"I'd like to buy one of your roses."

"Do I look like a flower shop to you?" the man snapped. "These are for my wife."

"Sir, listen: I have a friend, and it's Christmas and I already tried to buy her a rose, but I only have three dollars and change."

"And I'm supposed to care?" the man grumbled. Sonny just stared. The man looked away. "Oh, hell," the man grumbled, gently removing one rose from the dozen, a piece of baby's breath hooked to a thorn. "It's Christmas, I guess."

Sonny took it very carefully in dirty-gloved fingers, then handed out the change.

"Keep it," the man said. "I just hope my wife doesn't notice there are only 11 roses."

"Just give her one," Sonny said. "Women think one long-stemmed rose is very romantic."

"And who made you an expert?" the man grumbled.

"Why do you think I only wanted one?" Sonny said. The man tilted his head, then looked at his roses.

Later, on a park bench, Sonny handed Ginny 11 roses. Ginny's toothless grin was never so wide. "But ain't they expensive?" She smelled them. "And so many."

"I would've had 12," Sonny said, "but a man needed one for his wife. And you know how it is — Christmas and all." Ginny crushed him with a hug. "I got some change. Wanna look for a burger?"

"Ah, Sonny," Ginny said. "Ya didn't have to."

"Merry Christmas, Ginny."

"Roses in winter," Ginny said. "It just makes everything so alive." She hugged him again, kissed his bulbous nose. "Ah, Sonny! Merry Christmas!"

The other street people saw them later, Ginny carrying her roses like they were a baby, and Sonny carrying her garbage bags. They were looking for a fast-food place that might be open. The snow fell, and Christmas music flowed through the streets.

FIVE   1/ˈ97   T. NEWTON SCHULTZ

The Language of Bees

"Your cameras talked to me last night," Saul told me as he lit his cigarette off a burning butt. He sat on the linoleum kitchen floor, rocking back and forth. He had five empty soup cans lined up beside him for ashtrays. "They told me to paint the moon black with tar, but I wouldn't do it."

"I promise I won't bring them next time," I told him, but he wouldn't look at me. I couldn't help but notice the blackened callouses between his first and second fingers where he smokes his cigarettes down to the filters. Saul was growing bald, but his beard had grown out bristly and wild. In a gray robe, he could pass for a melancholy monk.

Our mother always had to remind him to bathe, and every time he returned from one of his long wanderings, she took him to Dr. Mahan for a check-up. Although he came home suffering from malnutrition and injuries he had acquired on the road, he was otherwise as healthy and strong as a grizzly. His body was never the problem.

Tomorrow was Thanksgiving Day, a miserable ordeal. Just the three of us would sit around the dining room table with mashed potatoes, corn on the cob, yams, green beans, cranberry sauce, and a stuffed, baked sixteen pound turkey. It was lonely without our aunts, uncles and cousins, who used to come years ago, but I came every year anyway, took photos and put together a couple albums for our mother to put away for some imaginary future generation.

Unlike my brother, I was clean shaven and had all my hair, albeit solid gray. I was forty six and living in New York, divorced, no kids. My brother was forty two and living with our mother in Pittsburgh when he wasn't hitchhiking across the country. For the last two years, I had been trying to persuade Mom to check him into a nursing home where he could get proper care, but she wouldn't do it.

I was thinking about that as I helped my mother was the dishes after lunch. Through the steam-fogged window over the sink, we watched Saul stand in the backyard garden among the dead squash vines and weathered tomato stakes. He was barefoot and wore only a t-shirt and blue jeans, oblivious to the freezing autumn air. He stared at the dried leaves in his hands, sometimes sniffing them and mumbling to himself. Mom told me he might be leaving again soon. This was one of his farewell rituals, gathering smells from home.

Saul left last Thanksgiving after I drove back to New York. It was the first time he ever ventured off in such cold weather. He returned a month later during a blizzard, his finger and toes frostbitten. It was the only time he spent a month in a regular hospital. Now he was thinking of doing it again, and I could tell my mother was just as worried about him as I was.

"He's always happy to see you visit," Mom said, drying a plate. The air smelled of scented dish soap and the grilled cheese sandwiches we'd eaten earlier. "He doesn't know how to say it, but he misses you."

"Maybe that's the way you see it," I said. "I can't tell what he's thinking."

"I still remember when you and Saul hopped that freight train to Akron."

"Mom, why are you bringing that up?"

"You were both so close then," she said. "I remember, I grounded both of you'ns to your bedrooms for a month, I was so furious and scared. But you were both so close."

"We were kids," I said. "Now he's different. We're all different. That was years ago."

"I understand," Mom said. "I just want you'ns to get to know each other better now, while you still can. You know how he is."

I shook my head. "He'll get himself killed someday. He could die of exposure in the woods somewhere a thousand miles away and we'd never know what happened to him. You can't stop him from leaving any time he wants to."

"Maybe he needs to travel," Mom said. "Maybe it would not be right to stop him." She gazed into my eyes, looking for once as unsure as I felt.

Neither one of us knew what Saul did on those long trips. He couldn't concentrate on a conversation for more than a minute; he talked to us seemingly as an afterthought. Yet he could leave the house with nothing more than wearing and survive for months in the wilderness of the highway. Mom sometimes got post cards and letters from as far away as California and Oregon from people who picked him up.

She called me each time he left. Like me, she imagined him standing beside the highway in the rain, hoping for a ride, sleeping under a railroad trestle, drinking muddy water from a culvert, or digging spoiled vegetables from a supermarket dumpster.

She was crying when she called last December. Neither one of us believed he would make it back from tat trip. She told me Saul kept talking about the red pocket knife I had when I was a kid before he left. I remembered reminiscing about it at Thanksgiving dinner. We didn't know how he survived, but somehow he did, and somehow he found his way home, tired, filthy, trembling, with the smell of the road in his beard.

"You know, Seth," Mom said, interrupting my thoughts. "Your brother took care of the garden by himself this year." She was beaming with pride.

"Did he now?" I said, feigning interest.

"We had some nice green peppers, zucchini and pole beans," she went on. ""He wasn't very good at weeding, though, and he seldom mowed the grass."

She chuckled, brushing a few wet strands of white hair off her wrinkled cheek. She was a small woman, five feet tall and thin, bent like a serf hefting a great burden. Then she looked down, her frown and her eyes telling me she was deep in thought.

"He liked playing with the bees," she said, absentmindedly drying the silverware. "He would sit quietly in the flowering clover, and if a bee landed nearby, he would gently coax it into the palm of his hand. He'd watch it crawl back and forth until it flew away."

"But didn't they sting him?"

"Oh, a few times," Mom said. "He didn't mind it, actually, until I told him that bees died after they stung someone and they lost their stingers. He was very careful not to provoke them after that. H didn't want any to die."

I tried to picture my brother sitting in the grass holding a bee. A month before our father died – when Saul was four and I was eight – he took us to a neighbor's farm and showed us the farmer's bee boxes in the apple orchard. The air was full of the humming heartbeat of their activity, the thick smell of honey, apple blossoms and the smoke funnel the farmer carried.

Our father told us about the bees. When a scout bee returns to the hive after locating a good source of nectar, it does an odd dance, shuffling around on the cones in a figure eight and vibrating its wings. This dance conveys the exact location of the flowers, how far away they are, how many, and in what direction in relation to the sun. Other bees gather around the dancer until they understand the dance, then they fly off to find the flowers. The performance is so detailed that, as the sun moves across the sky, precise movement changes by the dancer reflect the changes of the sun. I thought of the bee boxes and wondered what the bees in Saul's palm were telling him.

When we were done with the dishes, my mother picked up her cane and went to her bedroom to give herself an insulin shot. I wandered to Saul's room, still worried about his coming departure. Saul's bedroom was immaculate, a stark contrast to the disordered goings-on inside his mind. His plastic model cars, most of them over thirty years old, were dusted and lined up like moving traffic on two bookshelves. A wooden chair and table was his desk set, and on the table was a stack of typing paper with drawings on each sheet, a porcelain coffee cup with sharpened number two pencils in it, and a clean chrome hubcap he used for an ashtray. I looked at his drawings. Each one was a different tree, and each tree was twisted, deformed and rootless, but finely drawn, finely detailed, from his memory. On his bed was a blue bedspread with steam locomotives chugging through mountain passes and over railroad trestles.

Other shelves held small store boxes, the kinds with clear see through lids, with insects pinned in them like museum exhibits. He never killed any, he found the bugs in the garden, already dead, grasshoppers, crickets, potato bugs, cockroaches, katydids. In an old Nike shoebox, he kept the empty carapaces, hundreds of them, of cicadas, the shells they climbed out of after hibernating underground for seventeen years. Next to the box was a rusted fishing reel, a reminder of what was once his favorite hobby.

When I got my first camera, Saul was ten. In my first photograph, he was smiling and standing barefoot in cut off shorts. He held a fishing rod in one hand and a string of six trout in the other. In the next photo he was fourteen, looking away, angry, tired, already worn down by the lithium the doctor prescribed. He was supposed to get better. In the next photo, Saul was seventeen. He had long, black hair, and the shadow of a moustache as he stared down at the Dairy Queen banana split our mother bought him after his first three month stay in a mental institution. I took the last photo three years ago. Saul refused to let me take any more of him after that. Our mother looked so much older and six inches shorter, but she smoked one of her last cigarettes with defiance as she put an arm around Saul's waist. Saul looked away and up, a sparrow about to take flight.

I was about to leave his room when I noticed the dead bee on an otherwise empty shelf. The bee stood on its mummified legs, the way Saul had placed him there, looking almost alive. Nothing in Saul's room appeared there by accident. I knew he meant for me to see it that way.

My thoughts were interrupted by my mother's panicked shout downstairs and the sound of breaking glass. I flew down the stairs and rushed to the kitchen. My mother sat on the linoleum floor, wrapping her hand with a bloody dishtowel. Saul paced in the dining room, looking away from us, chain smoking and mumbling to himself.

"Help me up, Seth," Mom said, her voice unusually calm. "Saul tried to rinse his milk glass. He dropped it, and when I tried to catch it, I was just a little clumsy."

I knelt and removed the dishtowel. Blood flowed from a deep cut between her finger and thumb. I helped her stand and guided her to the sink, avoiding the broken glass. I held her hand under running water, feeling her wince. "There's no glass in the cut," I said. "But you're going to need stitches." Trembling with anger and fear, I glanced back at Saul.

After Mom explained to Saul where we were going, I drove her to the hospital emergency room. They put her in one of those flimsy gowns and set her on an examination bed. "You're really going to have to put Saul someplace safe," I told her once she saw the doctor and was stitched up. "He's becoming more trouble for you each year."

"If you mean this," she said, raising her gauze bandage-wrapped hand, "it was my fault, an accident, nothing more. And Saul is my son. He's your brother." She held my gaze with her eyes. "You'ns are the two most important people in the world to me, but you don't know him the way I do. You're hardly ever here."

"Mom, you're using a cane," I reminded her. "You're taking blood pressure pills and you're diabetic. You can barely take care of yourself. Let someone else take care of Saul."

"I'm not going to worry beyond today," she snapped.

When Dr. Mahan got back to our room, he suggested keeping Mom overnight for observation because her blood sugar was high. She protested until I said I would watch after Saul and come back early in the morning so she could get a good start on the turkey. I ignored the worried look in her eyes and gave her a kiss on the forehead before I turned and left.

When I got back to the house, I found Saul sitting on the living room rug, rocking as he smoked a cigarette. He didn't look up when I came in. "Mom's okay," I told him, feeling uneasy because she wasn't around. "She had to stay overnight in the hospital, but I'll bring her home tomorrow morning."

"The universe coms from a shoebox," Saul said. "God opened the lid and the big bang rattled the broken teacups inside. I'm hungry."

"I'll scare up a snack, I said.

"Remember the dog wings," Saul said, then roared in laughter. Most of his teeth were missing, a reminder of beatings he got in his travels. Mom said he often returned with bruises on his face, arms and chest. Once he came back with a broken nose, twice, broken fingers. He had scars on his right arm that Dr. Mahan believed were made when he defended himself from a knife-wielding attacker. X-rays showed that his ribs had been broken and healed several times.

He never talked about how he was injured. He never even mentioned that he was hurt. I was angry at him for that, and angry at the slime and scum who would hurt a gentle man like my brother. I wanted to find them, one by one, and do the same to each of them.

In the kitchen, I put a bag of popcorn in the microwave. As I listened to it hum and the first sounds of popping, I glanced around, giving myself a chance to relax. It was only then that I noticed the floor was clean. In my rush to take Mo to the hospital, I forgot about the broken glass. Saul for once had taken the initiative to sweep it up. I bent down and ran my fingers over the linoleum. He got it all.

When I stood up, I saw the red Swiss army knife, rusted and weathered, on the kitchen table. It was my knife. My initials had been engraved in the side b my father before he died. I hadn't seen it in three decades. How long had Saul been keeping it? And why was he showing it to me now?

I remembered, though I didn't want to, how Saul and I held onto a boxcar ladder all night, our pants belts looped to the same rung so we wouldn't fall off. Saul was twelve and I was sixteen, and I should have known better. It was summer, but we were miserable and cold that night, heading for California. I told Saul we could get jobs there, live in the sun and fish off the docks. California had been my dream for a year, and I had hopped a train or two near home and walked back the mile after I hopped off, so I thought I had a good plan. But holding onto the rungs, looking down at the moving ground as the train car rumbled and rocked and trying not to fall asleep, I felt scared and unsure, and I worried about both of us.

Just outside Akron, Saul's belt broke and he tumbled into the darkness. I reached for him, but all I grabbed was air, all I grabbed was the miserable night. Saul was gone. Panicked, I cut my belt with my knife and lowered myself to the gravel bed racing in a blur beneath my sneakers. I pushed off and fell, tumbling, hitting gravel and rolling down a weedy slope.

"Saul!" I screamed, pulling myself back up to the tracks with bloody palms. "Saul!" The ground trembled as the large, dark shapes of speeding boxcars rumbled by. I limped back to where I thought he fell, shouting his name until the train was long gone, the caboose lights disappearing into the night. Finding a break in a fortress of brambles, I slid through the dirt and weeds, my ankle throbbing, and I felt my way through the trees. I found him forty feet down from the tracks. He was sprawled out and unconscious near a large concrete culvert.

"Saul," I whispered, weeping and unable to stop it. I revived him with muddy water, wrapped my jacket around him and held him, both of us shivering in the cold night. I kept talking to him and listened to his ramblings. Heat lightning appeared in the sky through the branches and leaves as crickets surrounded us in their fugue.

"Seth, I hear water," Saul said, just before dawn. "What is it?"

I was staring at the culvert five feet away, though I couldn't see it in the darkness. "It's the source of the ocean," I said, thinking that, in a sense, it really wasn't a lie.

"It sounds nice," he said. "Some day I'm going to see where it goes." He was silent after that, his breathing steady. The wind in the treetops and the sound of water seemed to calm him.

At dawn, I checked him over for broken bones. We shared a Hershey bar for breakfast. His equilibrium was bad that day, but I supported him and guided him through the trees. We followed the tracks the way we had come until we made our way to a highway, and we hitched back to Pittsburgh.

Our mother always remembered our attempt to run away, but she thankfully forgot about the bruises and scratches on our faces, and the dried blood on our tattered, filthy clothes. Memories fade and change with age, but I never forgot how horrible I felt for taking Saul with me on that trip. I never stopped wondering if his injury that day was the catalyst that began the change of his personality.

I looked at my knife, remembering that I had jammed it into a hole in the concrete of the culvert. Saul knew how important that knife was to me. He was crying that day, sick and exhausted, but he didn't want to turn back and head for home. I had promised him California. When I told Saul we would come back to that exact same spot, and we would find my knife someday, and we would start our journey again from that spot, he was finally satisfied and willing to go home, knowing that I would want that knife back.

I looked at the rusty knife again and shook my head. I went back to the living room, knelt and set the hot bag of popcorn beside Saul. He stubbed out his cigarette without looking at me and took a handful.

"How long have you had this?" I asked, holding the knife in my open palm. Saul stopped chewing, his greasy fingers dangling over the popcorn bag. He gazed intently at the floor. "I'm not mad, Saul, I just want to know. How long have you been keeping my knife?"

"It's yours," Saul said.

"I know it's mine," I sighed. "I just want to know how long you had it." I believed that he must have secretly retrieved the knife from its hiding place at the culvert thirty years ago before we headed home. But why?

"The clouds are sheep walking across the sky," Saul said, chuckling and looking at the end table by the couch.

"I heard you tell Mom. The world was white with hurt. Hounds with teeth of ice and stinging saliva, howling, howling. There was no map. I followed the steel paw prints in bloody snow." He was agitated, rocking faster.

"Saul…" I reached for him. He pulled away.

"They bit me. They bit me. The night scratched my cheeks. It is a hungry lion, the cold is, but I walked all the way.

"Saul, it's okay," I whispered. "Where did you go?"

"The source," he said.

He calmed down and lit a cigarette. His breathing eased. I followed his gaze to the end table. On the corner was the mummified bee I saw earlier in his room. It appeared to be watching us, and I knew he put it there just like that for a reason.

"I can take it back," he said. He meant the knife, if I didn't want it.

I sat down on a chair behind him, clasping the knife in both my hands. He hadn't been keeping it all these years. He went back to the culvert last winter because he remembered where I left it. He went because I said I missed it the last time I was in Pittsburgh. He came back from that trip with frostbite, blistered and bloody feet. He didn't hitchhike because he couldn't remember how to find the place by road, so he walked the rails we rode thirty years ago.

This was his figure eight dance. This was his message to me, the directions to the flowers and pollen and nectar I would need, we would need. This was his language. And he gave it to me.

I put my hand on his shoulder. He didn't flinch away this time.

"I'll keep it," I said.

FIVE   1/·97   T·NEWTON SCHULTZ

HUNT

Several years ago, in the dead of winter, a small plane crashed in a wilderness area in Quebec, Canada. The wreck was located by a rescue team a week later. The plane was ripped open and twisted, and the frozen, preserved bodies of the passengers were found strewn within a radius of a hundred feet. All passengers were accounted for except for one three year old boy. The rescue party accounted for the missing corpse by wolf tracks found in the snow, though no traces of bone, blood or clothing were ever found.

■■■

They travelled at a constant rate, forming a single file line through the trees. The snow, freshly fallen the night before, was melting under the noonday sun. The day was growing warmer, though it was still the heart of winter. The wolf pack took no interest in the temperature or snow, pushing through snowdrifts and going forward with a single minded concentration. There were eleven of them in all, each one strong and fast, moving in unison.

The Alpha Male, the One, sometimes took the lead, sometimes hung back and let another push through the snow. He was the largest, the strongest, and the oldest, having seen eight winters. His body was muscular, his fur gray and thick.   Taking the lead again, he led his pack out of the woods, following a new scent he picked up. The others faithfully followed.

From the back of the line, always the last, the Omega, was different from the others. Furless, slower, differently shaped, he ran on two legs, his bare feet kicking up snow as he struggled to keep up.   The boy was not one of them, but he was still part of the pack, still part of the hunt. Naked, he adapted to the cold, like no other human could. His skin was thick, scarred from punishments and play. His hands and feet and knees were calloused, because when he wasn't running on two feet he was walking on all fours like the others. His status was low, he was the bottom, and often took the brunt of another's anger even when he did not deserve it.   More often than not, he looked after the cubs and yearlings when the others could not.

From the back of the line, he spotted the prey upwind the Alpha was leading them to, a large bull moose walking with a limp a hundred feet ahead of them. Four days had passed since the pack had eaten, and though wolves could go a week without eating, the boy could not. He was terribly hungry and growing weaker from the travels, but if he could keep up a little longer, he knew he would eat soon.

At first the moose didn't know the wolves were closing in. Large and muscular, he was crippled by an injury he sustained, a fractured ankle, crossing an icy lake. When he glanced back and saw the wolves, he went faster, galloping away from them.

The Alpha picked up speed, and the pack did the same.   If they could tire the moose, they would be able to bring him down, but they would have to keep up their speed to do so. The boy, already weak from hunger, pushed himself harder, running faster, his toes digging into the snow, his muscular legs pumping. His long, black, matted hair blew behind him as he rushed to keep up, but he was already losing distance as the others pulled away from him.

The Alpha was drawing closer to the moose, his pack just behind him. The moose, limping worse, suddenly stumbled. In one quick motion he quickly pulled himself back up from the snow and faced the charging pack. The wolves stopped, forming a semicircle ten feet from the beast. They already knew from experience that a wolf at bay, especially one in pain, was a dangerous opponent.

The boy slowed down when he caught up to his pack, gasping, and as he pulled up behind the others, he fell to all fours, walking like the others. He could see the moose, watching them back, steamy vapor coming from his nostrils. Some of the wolves snarled and charged and backed off, trying to scare the wolf into running again. If the moose stood his ground, faced them off, there was little chance of bringing him down. The boy was hungry, more so than the rest of the pack, but he had to wait it out like them. He bared his teeth and made his own growl, guttural and deep for a child so young, but he held back. He had neither the teeth nor claws nor strength to do what the others could, so he hung back.

A yearling came around from behind, charging and sinking his teeth into one of the moose's hind legs. The moose bellowed and kicked, catching the yearling in the ribs, and the yearling rolled in the snow, leaping up, running in circles and ki-yii-ing in pain. Fortunately he only sustained a fractured rib, but he managed to panic the moose. The Alpha, seeing his chance, charged, as did the others. The moose, taken by surprise, turned and ran, losing his advantage.

The wolves were again chasing their prey. The boy was again running behind the pack, but hunger spurred him on, and he ran as fast as he could. He could now hear the rumble of hooves, the gasping of the weary moose, as the hunt neared its end. A couple wolves nipped at the side of the moose, avoiding the hooves, coming away with tufts of hair in their teeth. Two wolves slammed his side with their shoulders and the moose, weary and weak fell to the ground. One wolf grabbed a rear leg, keeping him from getting up, and the Alpha went for his throat, tearing it open, the blood pouring onto the snow like a river.

As the life left the moose's eyes, the Alpha and two of his subordinates came around and attacked the belly, tearing it open and feasting on the intestines. Where there was room, another wolf and another approached for his share, but the others held back, waiting their turn. The boy sat beside a yearling, knowing he would eat last, but despite his hunger pangs he was patient. While he waited, he licked a bloody cut on his leg.

After the others ate, they curled up a few feet away and napped, their bellies full. In the end, the boy ate with the two yearlings, biting off pieces of raw meat, chewing them as best as he could with his teeth, and enjoying the taste of fresh blood and flesh. When they were done, the boy curled up with the yearlings, napping between them so that their fur and body heat would keep him warm. As he dozed off, he reached across the chest of one of the yearlings and pulled him closer. The yearling didn't mind, and if he didn't understand why he did it, he understood it was something he needed.

The boy heard sniffing, felt a cold wet nose against his back. He opened one eye and saw the Alpha Female, the Alpha's mate. These were her yearlings, their yearlings, just as two adults napping nearby were also hers. Like her mate, she was also the backbone of the pack. Like the two yearlings surrounding him, the boy was also one of the pack members she raised back when she raised the two who were now adults. As he watched her wander off and he closed his eye, he dreamed about when it began.

■■■

He remembered that day, a very cold day, before he knew the pack or the female wolf he would think of as his mother. Something terrible happened that day, back when he belonged with others, the ones who did not have fur. There was a crash, he was thrown around, and when he landed in the snow, he was bruised and sore and disoriented. He stood, wandered around, saw the dead around him, and he cried, but the tears sealed his eyes shut. Stumbling, shivering, he fell on the snow, the cold sucking his life way as he wept and reached out for someone to take him, to make him warm. Then he passed out.

The rest was a nightmare, waking and blanking out again and again. He remembered being dragged through the snow, sharp teeth digging into his leg, the cold making him all but numb, sounds of snarling, sounds of wind. He was gone again, and then he remembered being dragged into a tunnel, then stopping, then something large, furred, laying on top of him, and the warmth finally reaching through the numbness, and for a while he felt comforted.

The wolf, the Alpha Female, kept him warm inside the den. She was expecting her first cubs, and she sensed the three year old boy was something of a cub himself. She licked him clean, licked where she held is leg in her jaws, where her teeth accidentally cut his skin. At first he was silent. In the dark she could still sense when his eyes opened or shut. He was dreaming. She had to leave and hunt with the pack. Reluctantly she left him alone, hoping he would be safe.

When she returned he was whimpering. He was hungry, that's what the noises meant. She brought home a strip of meat, dropped it near him, but he would not eat. She picked it up in her teeth, rubbed it against his lips, but he pushed it away. She could not understand his refusal, and soon gave up her attempts.

Shortly after that she gave birth to her two cubs. She nosed the cubs to her teats and they began suckling. Then she looked at the boy. The boy was growing weaker from lack of food, and had even stopped weeping because of his hunger. She nosed his head towards her teats, but he couldn't understand. She licked his face and tried again. At first he tried to push away, but he felt terribly tired. Then some milk got on his lips. He licked them, tasted the milk, and sniffed the air for more. Moving his face against her belly he found a teat and began suckling. Content, she lay on her side, listening to their movements in the darkness.

■■■

That was the beginning of the boy's new life. When he and the cubs finally came out of the den together, the rest of the pack were hostile. The Alpha Female took a stand between him and the others, protecting him, knowing one of them might try to kill him if she were not diligent. The boy sensed this too, and, scared and confused, he stayed by her side, knowing he was safest with her. The cubs accepted him completely, and he played with them constantly, often picking one up and standing, or rolling in the grass with them. Their teeth were small and sharp, and he got used to being bitten as part of their play.

He still spoke with the language of his past, the language of his last life. Eventually, though, he forgot the words, and he learned a new language of snarls and facial expressions and body postures. Even pissing was its own language in his newfound society. Though he already knew how to walk upright, he realized the others did not trust him when he did that, and he began to walk on all fours again, as he did as a baby. He developed thick callouses on is hands, knees and the tops of his feet, and he seldom moved upright again, unless he were running with the others, because he could not run like that on all fours.

His senses grew sharper during that summer. He knew that often he had to watch out for danger when he could not be with the Alpha Female. But he also learned to listen more, and use his sense of smell more, because these were essential in the forest. He also had to watch out for the others in the pack. At some point the Alpha Female knew she would not have to protect him from the others, but she also knew he would never have anything but the lowest status of the pack, the Omega. Not only would the other wolves treat him bad, not only would he always eat last, but sometimes he simply took the brunt of a wolf's anger. Even when he was not at fault.

But he had a strong spirit, and though he did not like how the others treated him, he enjoyed playing with the cubs. When the others started teaching the cubs to hunt, they also taught the boy. Despite how different he looked, the others reluctantly accepted him because the Alpha Female and her cubs accepted him. He soon enjoyed the taste of fresh raw meat, and though he could not catch a small animal with his teeth, he had hands with opposable thumbs to catch them. And despite being the Omega, he thrived in the pack that summer.

When autumn came on, the chill air made the boy miserable. When winter began, he suffered horribly. The pack had to band together now. Go on long forays looking for prey. The boy tried to keep up, but at some point, the pack disappeared over the horizon and he was by himself. Barefoot, naked, he headed back to the dens, crawled in, and did his best to stay warm. It wasn't long before he was slowly starving to death.

The wolves never looked back in their travels, so if he did not come along they gave it no thought. Except for the Alpha Female. Eventually she returned with meat, gave it to the boy, and slept with him for a day, giving him her warmth. Despite her efforts the boy grew feverish, weak and sick. But she had to go, she had to join the pack again. She reluctantly left him and returned to the hunt. A week later she returned with her cubs who also brought meat. By the end of the winter, other wolves were bringing meat, and somehow the boy survived the winter despite the cold.

When spring came, he was once again coming out of the den, and by then the last of the cold did not bother him so much. He survived the winter without getting frostbite or starving, and though he was leaner, he felt healthier.

The cubs were now yearlings, and they played rougher than before. The boy sustained scratches and teeth marks all over his body, but by now he stopped crying about the pain. He had suffered during the winter, and his tolerance was growing stronger. He began forgetting about his old life before he was found, and he joined in on the activities of the pack. He ran faster, learned how to hunt, and one day that summer joined the pack when they brought down a deer. He understood that the larger animals were dangerous, that their hooves could break a leg, and a broken leg meant death. He understood there were smaller animals you did not hunt unless you really knew how, like the skunk and the porcupine.

Over the next couple years, he grew muscular, faster, and he tolerated the winters well, though he still had to sleep next to a member or two of the pack because he had no fur. By now his body was heavily scared, though all of his wounds were superficial. And though he was the lowest of the pack, he thrived in belonging to them. And yet, during the last year, he felt the pull to return to his old life, the life he now had no memory of.

■■

The boy was awakened by the sounds of snarling. He woke to find the yearlings fighting. It was only play, of course, but it was also another test of which would be dominant in the end. The boy smiled, something others in the pack could not do, and he rose from the snow and shook himself, then, on all fours, moved away from the others, lifted a leg and urinated.

Then he heard it, a sound he never heard before, a distant drone that sounded hungry and enraged. He looked around, then glanced at the sky. Something was flying towards them, something large, a bird, but not a bird, it didn't have wings. The boy heard snarls around him, and as he looked back, he could see the others also saw it, and sensed its danger. As if in answer to an unseen signal, the pack rose up and started trotting away from the approaching thing, and the boy fell in step, at first walking fast, then standing and running. Now the pack was at a full run in a line through the snow, the flying thing getting closer, wingless, loud, and ominous.

The thing was flying over them now, louder, lower, and then there was an explosion from above, and one of the wolves fell. The others did not stop. As the boy passed the fallen wolf, he could tell it was dead. The flying predator went lower, and there was another explosion, and another. Two more wolves fell, and then the boy saw the Alpha Female fall.

Something inside him curdled, and though he knew he had to run for his life, he also felt that he could not leave her behind. He slowed, went to all fours, and when he reached her body, he fell on her, feeling a deep sadness like he never felt before.

He buried his face in her fur, breathed in her smell, touching all the memories about growing up around her, how she protected him, raised him as one of her own. The sound of the killer flying thing grew louder, but he would not look up. He knew it was very near, landing nearby, and he did not want to see. He knew he would die like the others he saw fall, and he braced himself for it.

But he didn't die. He slowly looked up, seeing the flying thing fifty feet away, a round thing, and he could see through its skin. And climbing out were two creatures carrying long sticks, standing upright as he sometimes did. They walked slowly closer, cautiously moving and watching him and the dead wolf.

Something in his memory clicked. He recognized them, knew they came from where he once came from. He knew he would soon be leaving this place, that his world was about to disappear.

LEGEND

"And these are the Jaws," my dam said, as my siblings and I sat next to her, nuzzling her fur and looking at the Jaws, black and headless and deadly, poking up through the leaves. "They will leap from the ground and grip your leg," she continued. "They will break your bone and tear your flesh, and they will hold you for days until you die of hunger and thirst, or until Twolegs, their master, comes for you. Look closely, my cubs, and fear them."

We looked and I was the first to see it. "They're broken," I said. "They're smashed, aren't they? What did it? What crushed them?"

I saw a sparkle in her eye as she looked down at me. "That was Cloudwalker," she said. "He is protector of the Hunters. He watches us and warns us when danger is near. His scent is on the crushed Jaws. Can you smell it?"

It was there, an odor stronger than all the smells of summer. "But where is he now?" I puled. "Why isn't he here?"

"His den is among the clouds," my dam said. "He comes down by the shadows of moonlight to watch our pack and others like ours. He seeks out the Jaws to close them before they attack a Hunter. He follows behind Twolegs like a breeze to watch them or lead them on false trails. He is the last of his pack, and he knows what it is to be alone. Know his ways and remember his scent, and survive. It is enough, sometimes, to just survive." The lessons began for me that day. I was not yet weaned from my dam's teat when I first heard about the Lone Hunter.

Locked in the whispering of the wind, as old as the spines of the mountains, the legend continued, passed on from each dam to her cubs, and the stories, as numerous as the clouds in the sky, were part of the Hunter's heart and soul. He was known by names other than the Lone Hunter: Cloudwalker, Winddancer, Dogslayer, Thundersnarl, and Snaretripper. He traveled beyond our sight and hearing like a spirit of the trees, but we knew he was out there, somewhere. He hid from Twolegs, too, and as the story went, it was Twolegs who hunted him once before, and Twolegs who killed all the Hunters in his pack.

We knew about the Twolegs. We saw the bodies left behind, stripped of skin and tail and sometimes even paws. They were the masters of dogs and cows and sheep. They set out the Jaws beneath leaves or snow to catch our kind, and they put out tainted meat that killed those who ate it.

Cloudwalker broke the jaws and buried the meat. He left his scent where there might be danger for Hunters. Never seen, never heard, he lived his lonely life for the chance to confuse Twolegs time and time again. He was a mystery. He was our legend. He was the Lone Hunter.

And I wanted to see him someday.

Our pack numbered twelve Hunters in all, myself, my two sisters and two brothers, two yearlings and five adults. Our dam was always with us, but our sire disappeared before we came out of the den. It was said that he was killed by a Twolegs thunderstick, but none of us knew for sure. Still, there was no lack of adults to play with in our younger days, and even the Alpha-Male, our One, joined in our games. Our first summer was a summer of play and heat and fleas, but summer went to autumn and autumn to winter, and food grew scarce and tempers sharp as each of us had to wait our turns to eat whatever was brought down. The snow was blinding and the cold was miserable and we went hungry for days at a time, but we survived that winter, and sometimes it is enough to just survive.

By the next summer we were yearlings, my siblings and I, and we knew how to hunt, catching rabbits and beaver, squirrels and mice. It was our calling to seek out scents, run in the hunt and bring down meat. In the winter, game was scarce, and we had to stay together to bring down the larger beasts, the deer, the moose, and the elk. But the summer changed all that, with the woods and fields overflowing with all kinds of creatures, and our pack split up, some of us heading in one direction and some in another, coming back to the dens as a group only occasionally.

It was one of these times when I wandered by myself at the edge of our territory, wandering back and forth, finding the boundary posts — rocks and roots and tufts of grass — and marking them with my urine scent when I noticed the Twolegs den in the distance, square and jutting from the ground. There was another territory here once, another pack. Their scent markers were once near ours, but the scent vanished during the winter.

I continued along our border, wondering about the pack, when I noticed the meat on the ground, a small pile, and around it the strong urine odor of Cloudwalker. It was a pungent odor, the smell of bitterness and anger. I knew the meat was tainted by the warning, but before I moved on, I saw Cloudwalker's pawprint in the dust. It was a large pawprint, and I could tell that he was larger than any Hunter in our pack. When I continued on, I kept wondering about him, wondering what he looked like.

The next two winters were harsh. During the first, one of my brothers wandered off in a blizzard and was never seen again. The following winter another brother died, kicked in the head by a moose before we brought it down and killed it. Our pack numbered ten now.

It was the following summer that something happened, something that changed me inside. It was a warm afternoon near the dens where I rolled in the dust to keep down the fleas. I had just settled down, about to doze off when something tapped me hard on the head. I leaped up and saw the raven settle on a log near the woods. I charged the raven, and he leaped up, swooping to peck at me again, but I ducked too soon for him. It was our game, and sometimes I'd chase him, and sometimes he'd chase me. Ravens were like Hunters, and formed in packs. They often followed us in a hunt and picked the bones we left behind. And, like us, they liked to play.

It was during our game that one of my sisters raced up to me, chasing off the raven. I could feel her panic, and I knew something was wrong. She rubbed against me and ran off. I followed, not knowing what to expect. We ran a long way until we reached a spot where we found my other sister and our dam. It was only when we got close that I saw what was wrong.

Our dam was trapped. Her left hind paw was gripped tight by the Jaws. Her paw was twisted, the bone was broken, and blood oozed from the wound onto the ground. She was whining and shaking from the pain, standing with the wounded leg lifted to keep the weight off it.

"It hurts," she puled as I approached, rubbing my nose against hers.

"We have to get you out," I growled, looking at her mangled leg.

"You can't," she answered. "You just can't. Once the Jaws bite, they never open to release you. It hurts, but there is nothing I can do, and nothing you can do."

"Then we'll stay with you," I snarled. "We'll bring you food, my sisters and I. We won't let you starve."

Our dam looked at the setting sun. The wind ruffled her pelage. She blinked once, then looked back. "You will leave here," she growled softly. "You will go away before Twolegs comes. They could be here in the next day or in many days, but they'll be here. You cannot change what refuses to be changed. You will leave, now, and survive."

"But . . ." I whined.

"Go!" she snapped, baring her teeth. "Now!"

We stood there for a moment longer, then we turned and left, my sisters and I. We followed a deer trail from the clearing up a hill, trotting quietly as the darkness of night reclaimed the woods. We traveled quietly, but I dropped back and stopped, watching my sisters go on without me. When they were beyond hearing, I turned and headed back, weaving through the forest undergrowth until I reached a hill downwind from my dam. I sat among the ferns, watching as the moon rose. A breeze blew at the treetops, and pine needles sprinkled onto my fur and on the ground around me. I looked up and saw two bats flying their circular patterns above the trees. I stretched out among the ferns, where the moon shadows hid me from view.

I could see my dam in the distance, turning about in the moonlight, occupied with some activity I couldn't see. Sometimes I'd hear her mewling in pain, and she'd stop, rest, and go back to the same activity. When I smelled the odor of blood on the wind, and saw her bare her teeth again, I knew then that she was trying to gnaw through her leg to get free. I wanted to go for her, be beside her, but I knew I wouldn't. I'd wait and watch, and remember her suffering.

The moon made its circuit across the sky, then lowered towards the horizon. My dam was still trying to get free when I closed my eyes for a moment. When I looked again, the sun was rising, and a heavy fog was spreading among the trees. I saw my dam lying calmly in the clearing, her leg still held by the Jaws. She was watching me, her soft, brown eyes telling me not to worry. The snow was stained by her blood, but she didn't seem to be in pain. Above the forest, I could see a blue sky, but I heard thunder in the distance.

No, it wasn't thunder, but a rasping, deep snarl. I looked around, and saw him. He trotted through the woods, his paws hardly touching the snow as he approached her. He was true to his name, Thundersnarl, as his voice ripped the cold air like thunder. He was large, his eyes as black as night, and his fur was well-groomed and whiter than the snow. His muscles were thick, his teeth sharp, and his claws hard as stones.

He stopped by my dam, touching her nose with his, with the greatest tenderness. She nuzzled his fur as he bent closer and licked her wounded leg. Gripping the Jaws in his teeth, he slowly pulled at them, opening them slowly, and my dam pulled her leg free. When she crawled clear, he ripped the Jaws from the ground, chewing them into a mush, and swallowing then whole. I was awed at seeing Cloudwalker, and was about to go to my dam when I heard a sharp crack in the air.

I woke from the dream, hearing a second and third loud crack. It wasn't winter, it was summer, and I could see three Twolegs standing around the body of my dam. Thundersticks were at their sides, and I could smell the burning from where I hid. Before they had a chance to hunt me, I turned and snuck away in the ferns, my body shaking uncontrollably at the sight of my dead dam, and knowing what they would do to her.

I always remembered how she died, but I never dwelled on it long, because time and thought had to be now, when one thought about hunting or resting or playing. Past was past, and now was what really mattered. And so it went, the summer blending into autumn, and then winter, and our pack of nine drew together for survival. The winter was cold, though, colder than normal, and food was very scarce. We went days at a time without eating, and sometimes fights broke out among us over what small portions of meat there were. A day came when we drew together in council, wondering if there was any meat left to be had.

"I know where we can go," our One said, the Alpha-Male, our leader. "I know where there is meat, but we will have to leave our territory, and we will have to be careful."

"If we approach another territory, we could be killed as trespassers," one of my sisters whined.

"We won't be heading for another territory," our One snarled in answer. "But we have to be careful. Remember: we need to eat."

We followed our One by the light of the moon to the edge of our territory, all of us feeling uneasy as we crossed over, none of us ever having been beyond the boundaries before. It wasn't until we saw the squarish Twolegs den that we knew what would be happening. "We're coming to hunt the Twolegs cows," I said to our One. "We can't do that. If we do, Twolegs will hunt us down."

"We'll hunt them in the dark," our One said. "We'll be gone by daylight."

"But there are smells here," one of my sisters said. "Cloudwalker left his scent here to warn us away."

"Cloudwalker doesn't have a pack to feed," our One said. "We will feed and be gone before Twolegs knows it."

We passed the Twolegs den and pushed through the thorned vines that enclosed the group of cows. They were so slow-witted that we dragged one down in a minute. The others tromped off, bellowing and baying, and soon settled down as thought we weren't there. We tore into the meat and ate quickly, not daring to snarl and fight this close to a Twolegs den.

We were almost through when we heard the first blast, and one of our number collapsed dead on the snow. All of us looked up at once. Coming from the Twolegs den was a group of moving shadows, Twolegs with thundersticks, and they stood between us and our territory. We heard more explosions, and in a panic, we dashed in the other direction, heading for the mountains.

It all happened too fast. We kept at a run until we reached the foot of a mountain, ascending its slope as the sun rose over the horizon. We were safe for the moment, but we couldn't go back, not yet. We would wander as far as we could, until we were sure Twolegs wasn't following, and we'd head back by dark. Twolegs couldn't run fast, but they were clever, so we had to be careful if we were to go back to our territory alive.

The sunlight reflected blindingly from the snow, and the icy air blew against our bodies as we climbed higher.

We reached a high pass between two mountains, and followed the trail along a ridge, weaving along with a steep drop on either side. We stopped to rest, seeing the sun at its highest point, and waiting for it to reach the other horizon. We huddled together against the cold, conserving heat and energy for our journey back, when we first heard the noise.

"What is it?" my sister asked.

"I don't know," I growled, "but it's growing louder."

"It sounds like a fast heartbeat," our One said. "Look, there it is, coming around the mountain." We glanced in the same direction and saw it, something huge, flying up in the sky. It looked like a dragonfly, a giant insect, only its body was clear, and inside, as if swallowed by the insect, were the Twolegs. "It's coming this way," our One snarled. "It's coming after us!"

We leaped together from the icy ground and ran along the ridge, all the while the flying insect-thing was coming up behind us, making noise and battering us with the wind of its wings. We ran our fastest, we ran in a straight line, but there was no place to turn, no place to hide. Its shadow was over us now, a predatory thing of noise and wind. One of the Hunters stumbled at the fierce explosion of a thunderstick, but we couldn't stop for him. There were more bursts in the air, and two more tumbled and died, but we didn't stop running. I saw our One ahead of me, stumbling as something hit his leg, wounding him, and he toppled over the edge. There were more explosions, and more deaths, and suddenly I knew I was running alone.

Terrorized, I waited for the explosion that would kill me, but it never came. I kept running, and the giant insect thing flew just at my back, its wind battering me, trying to knock me over the edge of the trail. Just ahead, the ridge came to an end, but there was no way to turn back. As I came to the edge of the cliff, I leaped into the air, seeing only then how far the ground was below me. I toppled through the air, confused and scared and about to die, seeing the ground come up at me, feeling the wind, and then I hit . . . .

The deep snowdrift broke my fall, but the ground slammed the wind out of me. I leaped out of the snowdrift at a run, still unable to breathe, still not sure if any bones were broken, but I kept going until I reached the spruce trees, and I knew Twolegs couldn't see me.

I gagged and gasped, finding my breath, but not sure where I was, I wandered without direction among the trees. I didn't know how to get back to the territory, but there seemed no point to it now, because my pack was gone, all dead, and there didn't seem to be much reason to go back. I was feeling numb, inside and out, empty, and alone. I sat in the snow. It was getting dark. I began wondering when I would eat next, how would I stay warm, and what would happen to me now that the other Hunters were dead. All I could do now was survive, because, sometimes, it is enough just to survive.

I don't know how I survived. I didn't care. I was alone, now. The other Hunters of my pack were all dead, all of them, all but me. It was winter. I was hungry. I was cold. I was lost.

I wandered without direction for a very long time, traveling by night, sleeping under logs and rock overhangs by day, always watching for the giant flying dragonfly that attacked my pack. Time and hunger gnawed at me incessantly until I finally chanced crossing through the mountain pass again by night and finding my way back to the dens. It was a tiring journey, but I was already tired, my paws and legs aching, my body cold. The dens were birthing places, where a dam crawled underground to bear her cubs, but I dug one out wider for my shelter, a place to keep warm against the white coldness of winter.

From the day I was alone, I dreamed about the Hunters in my pack, but being back in the territory and living in a den, I now heard their voices in the wind, whining in pain, howling in fear, haunting me in the shadowless white of winter. I was hungry, I ate snow and chewed dirt, and I wandered from the den area, not too far, looking for food. I could see a moose in the distance, but I couldn't bring it down on my own. There were no scent trails or pawprints of small animals to be seen. I wandered until I picked up a scent. I scratched through the snow and found the remains of a rabbit, mostly bones and skin, but I ate it, all of it.

Once I traveled to the border of the territory, looking for food, when I saw another pack of Hunters in the distance. I didn't belong to them, but loneliness and hunger had clouded my mind, and I crossed my own border and approached them, whining in supplication, crawling across the snow, my ears back, my tail down, as I approached, but they turned on me, hackles up, teeth bared, snarling and charging, chasing me from their territory. I ran until I crossed my scent-markers and I was back in my own territory. I had my life, and that was all I had.

I wandered back to the dens, eating snow along the way. The wind picked up, snow fell, and by the time I was back, it was a blizzard.

My ribs were outlined beneath my skin. My fur was matted. I was growing weaker, and needed food. As I huddled inside the den, I slept fitfully, waiting to die. I dreamed about the Hunters of my pack, and the day they were all killed, and me, leaping off the cliff, and surviving, and once the dream ended, it began again, more real than the den I slept in. Then I dreamed something else. I was climbing a frozen mountain in the blizzard, my claws digging in the ice so I wouldn't slide away. As I neared the top, I saw a giant Hunter standing steady on the ice and rock, his white pelage blowing in the wind. I knew his names, Cloudwalker, Thundersnarl, Dogslayer, Winddancer, Snaretripper, and I knew that, like me, he wandered the wilderness alone. I stood before him, bracing my legs against the wind, and I howled, "There is nothing left! We are alone, you and I, and there is nothing left! What purpose is there for us? What reason is there to go on? What is there left that we can do?"

Cloudwalker looked down at me. His dark eyes showed compassion, but they also held the calm indifference of one who would desert another. He bared his teeth and growled, "Survive!"

I woke shivering, listening to the howl of the blizzard outside the den. The darkness was like a friend, protecting me from the vast whiteness of the winter, but I knew I'd have to face it, search the snow-covered ground again and again until I found meat. I needed to survive. I needed to go on.

The next morning I left the den. The blizzard was over, and I had to hunt. I caught a rabbit that day, and two days later I got a woodchuck. In another three days I got a beaver. I was always hungry, never finding enough to fill myself, but enough to keep going. It went that way all winter, catching enough meat to survive, eating ice and snow to kill the hunger when there was no meat, and going on, hunting the territory when there wasn't anything to hunt. When spring came, then summer, there was more to hunt. Life blossomed, and I ate more. My ribs were no longer visible. I was feeling stronger, and rested.

Alone, I was a pack of one Hunter, wandering my own territory, but I longed for companionship, any companionship. One morning I was awakened by a chirpy woof-woofish sound outside my den. I crawled out of the den and saw a dog, a yearling, darting back and forth in a dusty area of the dens. With all the meat to be caught that summer, he was still ribsy and thin, probably unable to hunt for himself after being fed by Twolegs for so long.

He hadn't seen me yet, and was sniffing the ground, his tail held upright, his ears pointing back and forth. When he saw me, he charged towards me. I rose from the tunnel, my teeth bared, my hackles up, and snarled. The dog stopped and rolled onto his back in submission, exposing his stomach as I stood over him. I sniffed him, picked up his scent. I could still smell Twolegs all over him, but the scent was almost gone. He hadn't been around them for days.

I snorted and turned my back on him, a signal that I would not kill him. As he rose from the dust and romped around, I headed for the den, thinking of a half of a rabbit I could share with him, and wondering if I could teach him to hunt. As I crawled into the dark, I could still hear the dog yipping and yapping outside the den. I wonder if I could teach him to be quiet as well as hunting. Suddenly I heard a thick, grating snarl, and I heard the dog's screeching yelp, then silence. I kept listening, but there was nothing more.

I crawled from the tunnel into the light, watching for any sign of a bear, but all I saw was the mangled body of the dog, stretched across the ground, his throat ripped out. Blood flowed into the dust, and one leg still twitched. I could smell the blood, and with it, a stench of rot and decay. It was a repulsive smell, but there was something about it I recognized.

"Look alive, Rabbit-Turd, look alive!" The voice was a gritty snarl, coming from every angle. I glanced back and forth, trying to locate its source. "Leave you alone I can not, because fraternize with dogs, you do!" The voice boomed and echoed around the clearing, and I braced my legs to fight.

"Who are you?" I growled. "Come on out! I know you're not some forgotten voice from my memory! Not this time! There's spilled blood here to prove it!"

"Be submissive, little Hunter, be submissive! Survived many hardships you did, but still like a twig in the wind you are!" Just as I glanced up the hill, I saw a massive shape, big as a bear, bursting through the blackberry vines like a boulder rolling downhill. He closed the distance between us in a second, knocking me over, rumbling past, then turning and coming back to stand over me, teeth bared and hackles raised. I stayed lowered and submissive, knowing that he would kill me if I moved. The smell was like a dead animal full of maggots in the hot summer sun, so bad I had to hold my breath.

He backed up and sat down, staring into the sun. I raised my head and looked at him. He was a Hunter, but he couldn't be that big, with paws like beaver tails and ears like deer antlers. Despite his size, he was painfully thin, and his ribs were so prominent I wondered if there was any meat at all inside his skin. Each paw missed a toe or two, his tail was bent and ragged, and his pelage was matted and mangy, with large patches of bare, scaly skin on his flanks and shoulders. His teeth were worn and cracked, his black lips tattered, and his head scarred. Fleas infested him so bad he might as well have been their hive.

"Who are you?" I asked.

"Know me not, little Rabbit-Turd?" His eyes stared at me, eyes that looked like they had been through dying and death and come back to see life again. His tattered ears twitched on his head. "Call me not Dogslayer, do you? Have not been wondering about me, have you?"

"Cloudwalker!" I gasped.

"And have I not slayed a dog this day?" he snarled, punctuating it with a yawn. His breath was fiery-hot and putrid, even from that far away. I gagged and stepped back. "Yes, Rabbit-Turd, know me you do, do you not?"

It was him. It was Cloudwalker. In no way did he appear as I thought he would be, but I could feel it in my guts, this was Cloudwalker. Standing at my full height, I still had to look up at him. Even so, he was so thin he had to weigh less than me. He stood before me, this large Hunter, and I could feel his loneliness, his bitterness, and a mischievous power, a fury that took him into danger again and again, and a wit that always brought him out. I recalled my dam's words: "It is enough, sometimes, just to survive." I looked at Cloudwalker, and I wondered if this was what one had to become to survive alone.

I glanced at the dead dog. "Why did you kill him?" I asked. "He was harmless. He was just a dog, almost a Hunter."

"Almost a Hunter?" Cloudwalker snorted. "Almost a Hunter? Hah! And you, Rabbit-Turd, almost a bird, you wanted to be. Leaped off a cliff, you did, and flapped your paws! Hah! And fell like a rock you did! Rabbit-Turd-Bird!"

He was talking about the time I was chased by Twolegs in the flying thing, the thing like a dragonfly, and I leaped off the cliff. It was the time my pack was wiped out. "You saw that?" I asked. "You were there that day?"

"See everything, I do!" he snapped. "And that which I see not, tell me, the wind does, in whispers, in secret, and I know, I know!" He bent towards me and bared his teeth. "Likewise know, I do, when your pack was there. Killed the idiot Twolegs cow for meat you did. Hunt you, Twolegs will, without a reason, but give them a reason you did!"

"We were desperate!" I snarled. "We were starving!"

Cloudwalker scratched behind an ear with a hindpaw. "And was it worth it?" he asked. "Was the meat tasty and warm in the belly after you lost your pack? Missed my warning scent, you did. But hunger . . . If hunger you have, and hunger you fear, then leave my kill, I shall, for you to eat."

My hackles rose. "I would no more eat a dog than I would mate with my own sister!"

Cloudwalker raised his tattered eyebrows in mock surprise. "Mate with your sister I would," he said. "Eat a dog I would. Eat your sister I would. Have not been alone long, have you, Rabbit-Turd? Adapt. Survive. My pack they are, Rabbit-Turd, my pack they are! And you, still a cub you are . . ."

"I am a Hunter!" I growled. "I survived this last winter by myself! The counts for something!"

"Surviving the winter counts for surviving the winter," Cloudwalker said, rising and shaking the dust from his fur. "Many winters to come, there are. Many winters to come." He glanced at the woods up the hill. "Leave you, I will, with this meal, my kill. Feast, Rabbit-Turd, and owe me a kill you will. Be a Hunter, and I'll be watching."

He was leaving! I started after him, but he stopped and looked back, and those eyes, the eyes that must have roamed the bowels of death, stared at me. He would not let me follow, I knew it. "Don't go," I whined. "We can hunt together. Why did you come, if you're going to leave like this?" There was no anger, no pity and no interest at all in those eyes. He turned and walked away, the shadows of the trees swallowing him. Nothing remained but that smell.

Later that day I dragged the dog carcass far away. I felt angry and relieved that Cloudwalker had come and gone as though passing through. But now I knew what he looked like, a twisted, ragged remnant of himself, an ember of something that once flared and burned itself out.

Summer turned into autumn, and autumn turned to winter. The food was scarce again, but I hunted when I could, and when there was nothing to hunt, I went hungry. I knew I'd find food sooner or later, or, if I didn't, I'd just keep chewing on snow and ice until I starved. Once I brought down a deer by myself, one that was weakened by starvation and lost. It was luck more than skill that worked for me, but I didn't care, and I feasted until my fur was completely stained by blood. I slept by the body, and when I woke, I feasted again. I finally walked away, leaving little more than bones.

During the winter, during the times I couldn't find food, I would find bones in my path, ribs, pelvises, legbones, all stripped of meat, and all smelling of

Cloudwalker. He was out there, somewhere, watching me. Survival and life and death were just games to him, and it was nothing to tease another Hunter who might not make it through the winter.

When I returned to the dens, I could smell his scent, though there wasn't a pawprint around. I always looked around, but there wasn't a movement or shape to indicate that he was out there. But he was, and I knew it.

In my dreams, I saw him stalking heads of caribou and buffalo, the Lone Hunter, the last of our kind, bloodthirsty survivor who clung to the land like it was meat itself. In my dreams I saw him running from the Twolegs flying dragonfly, being attached, but not dying, unable to die. And every time I woke from those dreams, I wondered: what did I have to do with him?

When spring came and the snow receded, I felt confidence in surviving my second winter alone. I was getting used to it. I splashed in the overflowing creeks, full of spring runoff, and I basked in the warmth of the spring sun. I ate well, and relaxed, knowing that winter was over.

I spent the spring wandering, traveling the circumference of my territory, and sometimes I would cross over and travel through the territories of other packs, staying downwind of them, watching them from a distance, and wondering what it would be like to be part of their pack. Being alone, I had more freedom of movement, but I had to remain aware at all times. My senses were sharper now, and my skills more refined, but none of it made up for the loneliness.

The summer was hot, and the fleas and mosquitoes were out in force. Even so, problems were few, game was plentiful, and the air was thick with the smells of plants and animals. One afternoon I was resting near the dens with a dead rabbit by my side. I wasn't hungry when I killed it, and brought it back for later. I was dozing in the shade of a small tree when a raven dove down, snatched off a loose flap of skin from the rabbit, and flew away. They watched me, taunting me with that strip of skin that had no meaning to either one of us, so I charged, and as I approached the log, they leaped up and flew off.

As they settled on a rock, I charged them again, and they raised their black wings and flew in different directions, dropping the strip of skin. I snatched it up and charged off, and now they chased me. One was just over my head, flapping frantically, urging me to follow her. The other one dove down, brushing my face with wing feathers as she snatched the flap of skin from my teeth. When I turned to chase her, though, she suddenly veered towards the sky, and was gone, as though something startled her. I was alone again.

Just as I trotted back to resume my nap, I heard the voice: "Tired the Hunter is, eh?" I looked around. "Cannot even catch a mangy raven, he?" Cloudwalker stepped from the shadows of the trees as I watched, big and bulky and deformed, lumbering lazily towards me. "Left for me this rabbit for the meal I left you, have you? A mere rabbit? And no invitation?"

I stepped back, more than willing to let him have the rabbit. He stepped over the carcass, sniffed it once, then scooped it up in his massive jaws, chewed it a couple times, and swallowed it whole. "A mere nibble, Rabbit-Turd, a mere morsel, but good enough."

I approached, humbly and submissively. "Why did you stay away all winter?" I asked. "You could have helped me hunt. We could have helped each other."

"Watching," Cloudwalker said. "Watching I was. Watching to see if survive you could. Watching, watching and waiting."

"Hunters don't hide and watch each other starve," I snarled. "Hunters help each other survive. Hunters band together and share their kill."

Cloudwalker yawned and stared at me. "Maybe," he said. "Maybe." He rose and bared his teeth in a silent grin. "Maybe might not have survived the cold winter, the old Hunter, to help the young Hunter." He stepped backwards and looked at the trees. "Maybe might have killed the young Hunter, the old Hunter, for food." He began walking around the clearing of the dens, urinating in spots as though he was marking his territory. "A lot to learn there is, Rabbit-Turd." He turned, his eyes meeting mine. It was a look of contempt and pity. "A lot to learn you have. Pay attention, Rabbit-Turd, pay attention." He turned and walked into the shadows of the trees, and he was gone. This time I didn't try to stop him.

This was Cloudwalker, but I couldn't imagine him closing the Jaws and tricking Twolegs to help other Hunters. He was nothing like the stories I knew as a cub; I decided I didn't need him for company. I'd survive on my own. It is enough, sometimes, to just survive.

It is enough, sometimes to just survive. But it was my second summer as a lone Hunter, and I had finally met Cloudwalker, the one who was a legend to our kind. He was old, his pelage was matted and mangy, and he carried battle wounds as numerous as pebbles in a brook. The worst thing, though, was his madness, his crazy ideas and impulses, as though his soul had been hollowed out by worms. Yes, he survived, but what had it cost him?

Like Cloudwalker, I survived, and like him, I crossed beyond my territory borders into the territories of other packs. I traveled in secret and I traveled far, for when you cross one border, the next is not so hard to cross. As I traveled I listened to the wind in the trees, because I had no other companion, and sometimes I heard the voices of those from my pack who died, and I felt all that much lonelier.

I found the Jaws everywhere I went, and one day I dared myself to challenge them. Finding a short length of a limb, I picked it up in my teeth and dropped it on the Jaws. They snapped shut with a terrifying clatter that chased me behind a tree. Approaching them again, I sniffed their toothy shape and prepared to run, but they didn't open again, and I wondered if they were dead. "Who are you?" I asked out loud. "What are you? Why do you attack Hunters? What hunger do you have, you with no belly? You certainly have no brains!"

"No brains?" I heard a low, snarling, raspy voice say. "No brains? Stupid, stupid Jaws! But not as stupid as the Rabbit-Turd who talks to them!" I turned and saw Cloudwalker rambling towards me, his cracked, yellowed teeth exposed, his lips drawn back. "No Rabbit-Turd, no, hunger they do not have, but bite your leg they will, and hold you, they will, until Twolegs finds and kills you." His terrible smell preceded him as he approached, his old eyes blazing like the sun. "Bite, they do, and hold, they do, forever. But these Jaws, Rabbit-Turd, will not bite again, they will not . . . until Twolegs opens them . . . and Twolegs will open them."

He bared his teeth, snarling and slathering, and I backed away as he stepped closer, eyeing the Jaws. "Bite you, they do, and sing to you, they do, sing that you will die, sing through the pain . . ." He lunged, his teeth closing with a clatter on the Jaws, and he pulled, but a clackervine held them to a stump in the ground. His paws digging into the dirt, he strained against the ground, pulling and shaking his head, his back arching, his eyes bulging, his teeth chipped and cracking. His neck stretched, his body trembled, saliva and blood dripped from his mouth. When he stopped, letting the mangled mess drop to the ground, he was shaking and gasping for air, as though the sheer effort had taken something out of his total mass.

"Behold, Rabbit-Turd," he gasped, his once-thick voice almost birdlike now. He raised his head, well-pleased with himself, and blood trickled from the corners of his mouth. I looked at the Jaws, awed to see them twisted and mis-shapen, broken, useless. "Do not know how much it hurts, Twolegs do not, but wonder, they do, what killed their precious jaws! That, Rabbit-Turd, makes it all worthwhile, that, and knowing . . . knowing! . . . those Jaws will never bite again!" He sat, closed his eyes, and panted.

I sat facing him. "I've seen the Jaws like this before," I said, "since I was a cub. You've always been a wonder to my pack."

"Wonder, wonder, wonder . . ." Cloudwalker snarled, raising a hindpaw with only two toes to scratch his ear. "Travel far, I do, and other Hunters wonder. But wonder, too, the Twolegs do, about the dead Jaws. Wonder, they do, about you, Rabbit-Turd . . ." He opened his eyes and looked at me. "Wonder how you jumped a cliff and ran off, not dead. And in the telling, leap from a cliff, you do, now leap from a mountain, now leap from a sky . . . Flying Rabbit-Turd Bird!"

"Enough!" I said. "You sound like you are mad!"

Cloudwalker yawned and shook what little fur he had. "Believe you do that lost the soul of a Hunter I have? Do those things taboo, I do, crossing borders, eating the meat of my own kind, living alone, following Twolegs. Mad I am, Rabbit-Turd, and so are you."

I felt my skin crawl. "I don't know what you mean!"

Cloudwalker bared his teeth in a hideous grin. "Crossed the borders you have!" he said. "Watched other Hunters in secret you have! Changing with the season's changes . . . surviving, but adapting to survive, adapting in ways you wish not to adapt . . ."

"No," I snarled. "You are wrong!"

"Am I?" he yawned, rising and walking back into the shadows. I watched him leave, knowing better than to follow him. I was slowly turning into something like him, that's what he was telling me. It was unpleasant to think about.

As summer moved into fall, I saw Cloudwalker more often, meeting him in the woods or walking in the fields. I learned from him, and became more sensitive to the signs of Twolegs, finding tainted meat, snares, or the Jaws in their places under grass or pine needles. When I saw Twolegs, I didn't run but watched them from a distance, learning about them, the way Cloudwalker would.

Food was no longer a problem. I learned to use my eyes and ears better than I ever had before. I always stayed downwind, whether it was because of a deer, a Hunter, or Twolegs. I could tell by the flights of birds disturbed from their perches that Twolegs was approaching, and I was always cautious.

But one morning I wasn't cautious enough. I was sleeping in the crumbling, enlarged den when I was awakened by a distant whine. I crawled from the tunnel and listened: this time it was a Hunter, not a dog. It was a whine of deep pain, and I searched the trees around the clearing until I knew the direction of the sound, and I charged off. Weaving between the trees, running my fastest, I thought of nothing but helping the injured Hunter.

Suddenly I was jerked backwards, pulled to a stop. I collapsed on the ground, feeling the air knocked out of me. The world spun around me, my thoughts were cloudy, and I felt a wave of heat pass over me. I heard the whining again, and I braced my paws on the ground, but even as I raised myself, I felt pain, sharp and furious, gnaw through by body. I collapsed again, suddenly feeling very weak. My left hind leg throbbed painfully, and when I looked back, I felt sickened and defeated. My leg was gripped tight in the teeth of Twolegs Jaws!

The leg throbbed with each beat of my heart. The skin was ripped, muscle was exposed, and blood flowed onto the sand. I stared, not believing. I pulled gently on my leg, and pain shot through by body like wildfire. My dam had died just this way, caught, struggling, suffering. My insides churned with panic of the thing I couldn't tell myself, that I didn't know how to get free.

"Expected better of you, I did, Rabbit-Turd!" I looked up. It was Cloudwalker, trotting through the trees. "Expected better of you, I did. Sadly disappointed, I am. Sadly, sadly disappointed." In the distance, the unseen Hunter whined again. "Came to help the wounded yearling, did we?" he mocked. "Can not even help yourself, now, you can not! A fool, a fool, food-for-Jaws Rabbit-Turd!"

I felt relief, seeing Cloudwalker, but I didn't like what he said. "The Jaws," I whined, "The Jaws . . . they weren't here yesterday!"

"Oh, no, no, no . . ." Cloudwalker snorted. "Not here yesterday . . . Not here yesterday! But put here last night, Twolegs put! Heard you not? Listened not for footsteps? Noisiest creatures of the night, Twolegs are, and did not hear them, you did not?"

"I was tired," I puled. "And the yearling . . . he's in pain, and I wanted to help him!"

"Look where it got you," Cloudwalker growled, baring his teeth. "And here, thought you'd survive, I thought, but no, no . . . Exploded at me, many, many thundersticks did, and many Twolegs pebbles stuck in my muscles and rolling around in my intestines I have, but survive I did, and survive I will! Survive, Rabbit-Turd, survive . . ."

He sat down in front of me, closing his eyes. I raised myself to a sitting position, the pain eating at me. "But aren't you going to do something?" I puled. "I'm trapped. I hurt. I want to get out. Help me."

"Help you?" he said, opening his eyes. "Help you? Close the Jaws I can, close them, and break them, and piss on them . . . but open the Jaws, I can not!" His eyes blazed with unending anger, but for a moment, I thought I saw a sparkle of caring there, too, a sadness that threatened his rock-hard apathy.

"You mangy Hunter!" I growled. "I'm caught! I'm stuck! I'll die if I don't get out! And all you can do is tell me what I already know! Is there no way out? All your learning, all the things you've done, and you can't help me? Cloudwalker, Dogslayer, Thundersnarl, Winddancer, Snaretripper . . . all that mystery about you, and you're nothing more than a weary, worn out beast, losing your teeth and toes and fur, and you stink like a skunk . . ."

Suddenly he growled with all his fierceness and ugliness. His eyes blazed, he bared his teeth, and his hair bristled . . . like the back of a porcupine, his hair bristled! He spoke now from his hollow Hunter soul. "Look at you, you ignorant Rabbit-Turd! Clumsy, you were! Stupid, you were! Hard enough, it is, to survive, without being clumsy! Cannot pull free, I can not, and the yearling, his blood feeding the worms, his guts collecting maggots as he breathes his last breath, cannot stop the bleeding, I can not . . ."

He stood and started walking away. I rose, my leg howling with pain. "Yes! Go! Leave me here to die! You've been watching Twolegs so long you're turning into one yourself!" He didn't stop. The pain chewed at my insides, and imaginary claws tore at my brains and thoughts. "Go away! I'm going to die, but I don't need you to stay and watch! Go!"

In the midst of my raging, I yanked at my leg, feeling the fiery pain leap through my body and gnaw incessantly at my thoughts, and I hated him, Cloudwalker, and all the Twolegs he played his crazy games with. I yanked again, feeling the Jaws bite harder, feeling the clackervine hold me to the ground, and the Jaws sang to me, sang that they had me, sang that I was going to die, and I knew then that I didn't care. I yanked harder, and the pain said something inside my head, echoing through my skull, whispering, whispering, "You have nothing left to use, Lone Hunter! You have no pack, and no purpose, and now you are dying, and you have nothing left to lose!"

I bared my teeth, twisted around, and bit at the Jaws, snarling and pulling, feeling my teeth chip, tasting blood in my mouth from biting my tongue. From the corner of my eye, I saw Cloudwalker stop, turn around, and watch me, but I cared nothing for him now. I turned back and pulled at the leg, straining and pulling, feeling my muscles tighten. The Jaws dug deeper into my flesh, gnawing at the bone as my claws gripped the dirt, my neck stretched, and I pulled even harder, the pain no longer mattering. Something gave, just a little, skin tearing away, something ripping, my ears humming, then giving a little more, and I strained and twisted, snarled, whined, urinated, slathered and bled, and the earth rocked, the ground heaved, the sky blackened, then burned and blinded me, ate my eyes from their sockets, and the pain ripped up through my spine, a fang tearing me, but I pulled, and pulled, until everything went black, and I collapsed.

My thoughts came back with a terrible warmth. My body throbbed. I opened my eyes and saw Cloudwalker sitting in front of me. Rising, dizzy, I glanced back. My leg was bloodied, torn, and swollen, but it was out of the Jaws. I looked back at Cloudwalker again, then remembered the yearling, and started limping in the direction I last heard him. My head buzzed, but I was free. In the shadows of the bare trees I found him, the yearling, dead, his belly ripped open by a Twolegs thunderstick.

"And tell me, Rabbit-Turd," Cloudwalker said, coming up behind me. "Was it worth it? Was it worth it to find a dead yearling?"

I glanced at him once, then turned and limped back to my den. He followed beside me. "Wonder, did you not, why no other Hunter roamed your territory until now?" he asked. "Wonder, did you not, why the yearling was the only Hunter to come this close to your den? Been marking the boundary posts, I have been, and think, the other packs do, that a pack still wanders this territory." I stopped and stared at him. "And how will the Lone Hunter bring down meat with a gimpy leg?" he growled mischievously. I looked back at my leg, torn and gouged, dripping blood, and thought the same thing. Three toes were missing, and much of the skin. "See your toes in the Jaws, Twolegs will," Cloudwalker said. "Ask themselves, they will, 'What sort of Hunter can pull his leg from the Jaws?' And we will know: the same Hunter who can hunt and survive with a gimpy leg!"

When we got back to the den, he walked off while I crawled into my den. I never felt so weary, and the pain in my leg, duller now, seemed to draw my strength from my body. I fell asleep, feeling feverish and old. I wandered through my dreams like a spirit, seeing visions of Jaws piled in mountainous heaps, seeing plains of bodies, dead Hunters, some without their skins, and I wondered if my kind would one day die out. And I saw Cloudwalker, wandering through winter woods, alone, always alone, with just the one purpose, to watch for Twolegs and protect the Hunters from them. In fevered dreams I heard him call for me, howl for me to follow him, not beside him, but alone, and do those things he did, for his kind, for our kind.

Sometimes I woke from the dreams, shivering at times, burning hot at other times, and sometimes I thought Cloudwalker was in the darkness of the den with me, him and his horrible stench, but he was too large, and the den was too small.

When the fever broke, when the dreams were over, I crawled from my den, stiff and weak, into a morning of overcast and cold. It was the first snow, and the light blanket of white changed the landscape. I inspected my blood-crusted leg, licking it clean. In my long sleep, I had soiled myself, and it took some time to clean up. But the swelling was down. The infection was almost gone. I would live after all. Climbing back into the den, I noticed that it had been enlarged, and scraps of meat were scattered around where I slept. I had some help during the fever after all.

I didn't think much about Cloudwalker for a long time. Maybe I knew I'd never see him again. Come spring, I saw three Hunters cross through my territory. I knew for sure he was dead, if he was no longer marking the boundary scent markers. I still had a limp by then, but I made it through the winter, and I knew I'd make it through many winters to come. I was lonely, but now it was a part of me, and I ignored it like it was a growth on my leg, something annoying but inevitable.

I kept closing Jaws, seeking out tainted meat, and watching Twolegs. And I wondered; was this what Cloudwalker had in mind? There was no pack, but now there was a purpose.

One morning I spotted them, four of them, Twolegs, walking through another pack's territory. They were tracking Hunters. By rushing ahead, I gave them different tracks to follow, leading them away. The day wore on, and I thought of losing them once and for all, but something crazy came to mind. I climbed a hill and stopped on a rock outcropping, watching as Twolegs approached. When they saw me, they pointed their thundersticks at me, and I heard them explode. The pebbles flew at me, bouncing off rocks, knocking plumes of dust and rock into the air. A pebble nicked my shoulder, another sank into my leg, stinging, and I knew I might die, but I stood there, and suddenly the noise and the pebbles stopped. Twolegs stared at me from down in the valley. I stared back, feeling my wounds, not caring, not moving. I could feel it from that far away, they were scared, and I felt well-pleased with myself as I turned and walked away.

It is enough, sometimes, to just survive, but sometimes, more is needed. I always knew I would die someday, but I hoped my kind would never die out. And if I had anything to do with it, they never would . . . .

Locked in the whisperings of the wind, as old as the backbone of the mountains, the legend continued, passed on from each dam to her cubs, and the stories, as numerous as the clouds in the sky, were part of the Hunter's heart and soul.

COLD WIND MOUNTAIN

Krash stirred and yawned, flashing his massive yellow canines. The unending hunger twisted in his gut like an impatient worm. He stretched one foreleg until his thick, padded paw and long, black claws hovered and trembled over the trampled snow. Then he rolled over and lumbered onto all fours. The hunger burned itself into his brain, and he ominously bared his teeth.

"Ah, the little ones," he muttered, smacking his massive, bristly lips. "The little tasty morsels!" They were easy to catch and carry off, and their pack was no match for him. He could pick up their trail and find them by nightfall. As he wandered off, licking his lips in anticipation, he muttered, "Little crunchy ones!" Drool dropped off his hairy chin.

* * * * * * * * * *

"He's out there somewhere," Old Log whined to himself. "I can feel it!" He conversed with himself a lot these days because there was no one there to walk with him through the trees. His joints creaked as he followed the trail cut through the snow by his pack hours before.

He was old and tattered and walked with a palsied limp. His gray fur was thin around his hips and shoulder blades, and his brows and muzzle were turning white. Cataracts blurred his vision, but he could still make out shadows, and his sense of smell and hearing were still acute.

But it was the endless, biting cold of the White Death — winter — that crippled him worst of all. It gnawed on him incessantly, left him weary and worn out but unable to sleep, caused him to throb in every arthritic joint. He was afraid of the cold, as he was every winter, but this time more so than before, because he was not sure he would live to see the next warm summer.

The pack had left him behind because he could no longer hunt, so he followed at a distance, seeking out the bones they left behind. He ate snow to fill his empty stomach, but he needed meat to sustain his strength.

The one thing he feared worse than the cold, though, was Krash the bear; not for fear of his own life but for the lives of the Hunters in his pack. "He'll come again tonight," Old Log growled. "I know it!" Earlier that morning he strayed from the trail and found Sharptooth, the yearling. Or, rather, he found his head and part of his spine. Krash had claimed another meal during the night. And he would do it again. And again.

Log stared at the blurred face of what had once been Sharptooth, and he knew something had to be done. He was slow and weak, but his jaws were still powerful — he could crush thick bones the others of his pack could not. If only he could face Krash, just one, he though. As he continued limping through the snowy woods, he hoped he would be able to stop the killing once and for all.

* * * * * * * * *

They called every winter the White Death, and this one was viciously cold and brutal. The Hunters of the Thundertooth Pack were struggling to find food. Just that day they brought down an old, crippled moose, but too many days had passed since the last time they had meat, and none of them knew when they would eat again.

Thundertooth looked up from his resting place in the snow. There was hardly any meat left on the carcass, though one flank was still covered with muscle and tendon. Wind blew dry snowflakes through the ribs and backbone. The other Hunters, their fur stained by blood, slept fitfully, scattered around the skeleton.

Thundertooth was their leader, the Alpha-male, the One. As he gazed through the trees in the waning afternoon light, he felt the responsibility for their survival weigh him down. The search for food was a constant worry, but he was also afraid of another attack from Krash, the large black bear who had been following his pack for days.

Larger than any bear he had ever seen before, Krash always came at night. Three times in as many nights he had killed a yearling, carrying its body off in his massive jaws despite the pack's efforts to protect their young.

Krash the Devourer, Krash the Vicious, Krash the Cruel, hungry like fire burning through dry autumn grass. Other bears slept in their caves during the White Death, but Krash was not normal. Something was wrong in that oversized, deformed head of his. And it was costing Thundertooth his pack, one Hunter at a time.

He lowered his muzzle onto his forepaws, about the doze off himself, when he saw the slow, limping figure of Old Loghead coming through the trees. Log was an outcast, and Thundertooth was sure he would be dead long before winter was over. His ribs and pelvis bones were prominent beneath his matted fur, and he moved a little slower each day. He scavenged what they left behind to stay alive.

But now he was limping toward the pack's carcass, and they hadn't moved on yet. "Stay back!" Thundertooth snarled, his hackles up and his teeth bared. "Go away or

I'll rip your throat out!" Several Hunters woke from their naps, growling when they spotted Old Log.

"I'm hungry," Log snarled back, gazing at nothing but the last meaty flank of the carcass. Thundertooth gazed back in astonishment. The old Hunter was not pleading but demanding.

"Go away while I still let you live!" Thundertooth growled as his Hunters rose and gathered behind him.

"After I eat," Log growled back, almost to the carcass.

Thundertooth charged, his paws kicking up snow as he rammed the old Hunter with his shoulder, knocking him down. He snarled as he attacked, biting and tearing, but to his surprise Log was fighting back, his nubby, cracked teeth drawing blood. Thundertooth gripped the old Hunter's belly skin in his teeth when he felt an unbearable pain in his left rear ankle. Log gripped the bone tight in his jaws.

"Let go or I break it," the old Hunter growled through his teeth.

Thundertooth knew he could kill Log, but not before he lost the use of that leg. He'd be crippled and useless to the pack. He reluctantly released his grip, and Log released his, rising and shaking snow from his fur.

"Allow me this one last good meal," Log puled, now submissive, his ears back, his head held low, his tail down. "There is only enough meat left for one Hunter, and you are all full. What is that meat to you? You will all just fight over it again."

Thundertooth eyed him with suspicion. He was right, of course, and yet there was a feeling he had, looking at the old Hunter, that it would be his last meal.

He turned and started walking off, but the other Hunters blocked his way. "What are you doing?" Moonwater, his mate, growled. "You're giving Loghead food he did not even hunt! And we're barely alive as it is! We cannot spare meat to the weak and useless!"

"I say leave him be!" Thundertooth snarled. "And that settles it. You want to attack Old Loghead, you'll have to fight me first. Now, what's it going to be?"

The other Hunters backed off, knowing their leader's temper. Loghead limped up to the carcass. He held the leg bone down with an arthritic forepaw and tore off a strip of meat with his teeth. It was cold and half-frozen, but he could still taste the blood, and for a moment he felt warmth radiating from inside.

As Log ate, Thundertooth led the others away, hoping to find a sheltered place to sleep. Log watched them disappear into the trees, thinking to himself that he just might have one good hunt left in him. Despite his infirmities, he still had some strength left. He could run faster than he let on, and he had a plan, if only he could keep himself going a little longer.

* * * * * * * * * *

The Thundertooth Pack traveled well into the night before settling down in a copse of tall pine trees. As a light snow started drifting down through the branches, each Hunter dug a hollow in the ice, then curled up with his thick-plumed tail covering his nose and paws.

The wind picked up as they slept, bending the tops of the trees. The snow was falling thicker when Creekdrinker woke and raised her head, sensing something. She sniffed the air and listened intently. Recognizing the faint smell, she snarled long and hard, giving a warning to the others — Krash, the bear, was heading their way.

The other Hunters looked up from their resting places, rising as they sensed the encroaching danger. Moonwater roused the four yearlings from their sleep and herded them together, getting them ready to run if they had to. The others formed a loose barrier between them and the deadly Krash.

Despite the wind they could hear the huge bear huffing and clumsily kicking up snow, and then they saw the massive, dark shape barreling through the trees towards them.

Thundertooth attacked first, charging ahead to meet the malicious enemy, but Krash swatted him aside in one blow, hurling him into a snowdrift. Thundertooth lay stunned, two of his ribs fractured, four bloody furrows cut shallowly through his skin.

Krash picked up speed like a roiling avalanche, charging into the blockade of Hunters who now attacked from all sides, leaping and snarling. Their teeth barely penetrated his thick fur and skin, and one by one they were shaken off, slapped aside, until none of them were left to stand between him and his goal. The yearlings stood paralyzed by fear as Krash bared his teeth and closed the distance.

Suddenly a dark shape charged from the low boughs of a pine tree, closing in from behind the bear. Thundertooth rose on shaky legs and stumbled toward them, too slow but still trying to catch up when he saw the shadowy figure, smelled the familiar odor. "Loghead!" he puled to himself, watching the old Hunter chasing Krash.

The pack had never seen him run so fast, but Log was feeling stronger after his meal of fresh meat. Though he could not see the giant bear in the near-darkness, his nose and ears guided him, and he quickly closed the gap. His hunting instincts came back to him, and he made one last leap, his teeth clamping hard onto the bear's left hind ankle.

Krash stopped and roared in pain, twisting around in circles, trying to shake the Hunter off. He rolled in the snow, kicked and swatted, but Old Log held on, his teeth gripping harder as he twisted back and forth, trying to avoid the deadly claws he could not see. Suddenly the loud crack of hard bone echoed through the woods, and every Hunter gazed in awe at the battling pair.

Krash bellowed in pain, rolling and arching his back, leaping up and limping in circles, dragging Log through the snow behind him until the Hunter let go and dropped off, exhausted and battered. As the yearlings finally scattered and the snarling pack of Hunters closed in, Krash charged off, limping and keeping his wounded leg off the snow.

Log groggily lifted himself up. Clumps of snow stuck to his fur. The others approached him cautiously awed at what they had just seen him do. Only Thundertooth, his ribs aching, stepped close enough to touch noses with him. "He's gone," he said. "You drove him away."

"So I did," Log grunted, still gasping for breath. "And now I'm going after him."

The other Hunters stepped closer, surrounding him. "You can't go after him," Moonwater said. "You're tried, and he's so much stronger."

"And mad," Creekdrinker added. "And wounded. He was vicious before. He's even more so now."

"Don't go!" Thundertooth snarled. "You're old. You're tired."

"Krash is hurt for now," Log said, his cataract-clouded eyes following the voices. "But if he recovers he'll be back. He's hungry, and he likes the taste of our flesh. Somebody has to find him and kill him while he's still weak, and if not me, than who?"

"You can't even bring down a deer," Moonwater puled. "How could you kill Krash?"

Log gazed at her as though he could see. "And who wounded Krash?" he snarled. "I did. I started this, and I intend to finish it. I have one hunt left in me, and this will be it."

"How can you hunt?" Thundertooth asked. "You can't even run."

"I'm in no hurry." Log said. "I can't go fast, but neither can Krash. I will catch up. I'm patient." He snorted, turned and followed the deep trail Krash kicked through the snow. Thundertooth watched him disappear through the trees, swallowed up by the falling snowflakes, and he knew Old Loghead wasn't coming back.

* * * * * * * * * *

The snow fell heavier, the wind blew stronger, until Old Log found himself traveling through a relentless blizzard. He was buffeted back and forth, his weary body barely able to stand up against the blowing snow, let alone push forward through the rocking trees. Cold gnawed at him, made his joints and bones ache, and his own weariness weighed down against the last of his strength. Trickles of tears froze against the sides of his face. He was afraid of freezing, of dying cold and alone, but he was even more afraid of losing the giant bear's trail.

He caught an occasional whiff of Krash's odor, but more often than not he moved by blind feel, sliding through the cut snowdrift, or stepping into deep pockets crushed through the ice by massive paws. Occasionally he heard a growl up ahead in the blurred darkness, and he gratefully knew that, if he wasn't closing in on him, at least he wasn't falling farther behind.

The cold mercilessly drained his strength. He was too tired to shake the clots of snow off his fur, but he had to continuously stop and pluck the ice forming between his toes with his teeth. He was slowing down as the trail moved upwards along the ridge of a mountain. Where was Krash going? he wondered. Did he know he was being pursued? Why didn't he stop to rest?

"You can't lose me that easily," Log mumbled. "I may be old, but I'm the one that wounded you, now, didn't I?"

But his confidence was waning. He was shivering now, and the long ascent was tiring him out.

His weary mind could not focus on the task of travel, and he remembered summer days when he was a club, play-fighting with his siblings near their den as flies hummed over a dead rabbit nearby. He was young and growing and felt as strong as the sun. Suddenly he turned and spotted his dam and sire, Skylark and Digger. They stood in the shadow of trees. He felt a pang deep inside, longing to be with them, to run to them.

"No!" he growled, shaking his head, trying to knock out the painful dreams. A gust of wind toppled him into a snowdrift, and it took all his strength to rise on his shaking legs. Gasping for breath, he glanced around.

It was still night, but light reflected off the snowdrifts. There were no trees to shadow the snow; he was above the timberline, vulnerable more than before to the wind and cold. He could not smell Krash, could not feel his trail beneath his paws, but something in his guts told him he was still on the right track.

Panicked, he rushed up the steep slope, only to stop, gasping for breath as wind whipped at his fur. The air was thin, and his lungs were burning. He splayed his legs to keep from being knocked down again. He could hear his heart pounding in his ears, and he thought of going back. But Krash was still ascending the mountain, he was sure of it. The image of Sharptooth, the yearling came to mind, the remains of a mangled, tortured body. Stealing a deep breath from the wind, he moved on.

The mountainside grew brighter — the sun was rising somewhere beyond the thick, gray clouds — and Old Loghead saw a large, dark shape moving ahead in the distance. Not even his cataract-shrouded eyes could hide so large a bulk from him, limping wearily. The ground had leveled, and Krash was heading to a rock overhang to protect himself from the wind.

Log pushed on, his body shivering uncontrollably, his breath coming out of him in painful wheezes. Krash, now at the cliff, quickly turned around, spotting the old Hunter.

"You!" he growled, baring his teeth. "You're the one that broke my leg! And now you've followed me all this way so I can kill you for what you've done! Fool!"

"No fool," Log gasped. "I've come . . . to finish the hunt."

Krash stepped closer, snarling. "I could crush your head in my jaws! But why should I bother? The air is thin, and I am used to it, but you're suffocating! And the cold! It will kill you, but I'll survive to gnaw your bones clean!"

"No matter," Log growled, his hackles rising. "I'll kill you first."

Krash roared in outrage and charged, running on three legs as his broken foot dragged behind. Log raced toward him, the last reserves of his strength quickly dwindling. He didn't see the large paw swing, hurtling him through the air to slam into the rock wall. Ribs snapped like twigs before he slid down, gasping, blood oozing out of his nostrils and freezing.

He rose up just long enough to feel the searing pain of a broken rear leg, then collapsed, gulping as the cold slowly blanketed his consciousness. His disappointment hurt worst of all, coming so far, only to fail.

The cold shadow of Krash loomed over him.

"Sniveling, huddling little annoying creature," he growled. Log sensed the giant jaws, just over his head, and his rage burned against the cold.

"You will never kill another yearling," Log snarled, raising his head and snapping onto the thick, muscular throat.

Krash rose up in excruciating pain, dragging the Hunter into the air. He rolled, kicked, and thrashed, but Log would not let go. The raging went on, and large claws raked at Log's back, leaving bleeding welts. Then he slowed, his movements deteriorating to trembling, then twitching. Soon he wasn't moving at all. Krash, the bear, was dead.

Several minutes passed before Old Log realized that he had won the battle, his mind was so fogged with pain and cold. He couldn't move at first, couldn't even unlock his jaws from the massive throat without working his teeth left and right until the muscles relaxed.

He gasped for breath as he slowly raised his shoulders from the snow. The wind had finally died, and large snowflakes drifted down around him. Vapor crystallized on his nose and whiskers.

Fighting to keep from blacking out, he gazed at the large, blurred shape before him, well-pleased with himself and satisfied the bear would kill no more yearlings. He ignored the painful throb in his ribs, and he was unaware that one of his rear legs was twisted at an odd angle beneath him. Thick snowflakes clung to the fur on his back, but he was beginning to feel a flowing warmth. Thundertooth and the others would be glad to hear that Krash was dead. He closed his eyes for a moment and took a deep breath.

＊ ＊ ＊ ＊ ＊ ＊ ＊ ＊ ＊ ＊

"Look! You can see Mount Saint Helens now!" Gail Dowling said, adjusting her binoculars.

"Same as always," Bruce, her husband, muttered, adjust the focus on his Nikon before pressing the shutter button. "It still looks like a snow-covered dump."

"Okay, okay," Gail snapped, lowering the binoculars and glancing at him. "So maybe you've seen it from up here two dozen times, but I haven't."

"You can still get St. Helens post cards up and down the West Coast," Bruce said. "It will save us time."

"Don't patronize me, Bruce," Gail said. "We didn't argue all the way up here. Let's act like we can keep the peace until we at least get home. Humor me on this."

"Okay, Gail," he sighed, checking his light meter and taking a few more photos. He pulled his gloves back on and gazed at her through his mirror shades. "Truce." He smiled.

Gail glanced at him one more time before turning back. He still looked handsome in his tan parka, a contrast to her blue one. Their marriage had started out wonderfully, but over the last ten years he had grown distant, they had grown distant, homogenized, and now communication between them was strained at best.

They had just signed the register at the summit of Mount Adams, twelve thousand three hundred feet above sea level, in the state of Washington. The register was kept in an aluminum box chained to a log of the century-old cabin atop the mountain.

It was January 1st, the worst part of winter, but Gail and Bruce wanted to celebrate the New Year in ad adventurous way, and perhaps heal some of the scars covering their relationship. In the last few years every small problem became a contentious sore spot of epic proportions between them. Their marriage, which had begun as a forest paradise, had decayed into a brutal wilderness where every day was an act of emotional survival.

Mount Adams was Bruce's idea. It was not a technical climb, which meant that all they needed were ice axes and crampons strapped onto their boots to make the ascent. They had completed the climb that morning from their campsite at Tabletop, a few thousand feet below. Bruce was impressed that Gail had not complained about the thin atmosphere or the steep climb along the Suksdorf Ridge, and Gail was secretly glad that Bruce knew his way around the mountain.

Even so, the windstorm that hit on New Year's Eve and continued into the early hours of New Year's Day left them both tired and irritable. Several times during the night, Bruce had to climb out of his tent in his long underwear and pound the stakes back into the frozen ground while Gail straightened the tent poles inside.

By dawn the wind had died down, but the dark clouds were a harbinger of a heavy snowstorm to come. At first Gail wanted to pack the tent, head back down the mountain, find the car and drive home, until Bruce casually made the remark that he should have climbed the mountain himself. It was a cheap shot, a dare, and the kind of manipulation she knew they used a lot on each other these days, but she changed her mind and they began the last ascent. It was only then that she sensed he didn't want to go to the top either.

Now at the top of the mountain as they had coffee and granola for breakfast, sitting on rocks, they pointed out bare spots on the mountain to each other, where snowfields once hid the stone. The wind had blown whole snowdrifts away overnight, exposing icefields and crags they hadn't seen before.

When Bruce finished the roll of film and put in another, they gathered their knapsacks and ice axes and began their descent, planning to pick up their tent, supplies and backpacks when they reached camp and continue on to their Jeep Cherokee at the trail head. They hoped to reach White Salmon before nightfall and have a quiet dinner at the tavern they passed on the drive up.

Snowflakes were already drifting down as they began their descent. Hoping to get back faster, Bruce led Gail along a different route. She was having trouble breathing in the thin atmosphere, and though she wouldn't admit it, he could tell she was miserably tired.

Distant mountains were fading in the fog of falling snow, and Bruce was feeling apprehensive at how quickly the weather was changing. A winter storm could trap them, confuse their sense of direction, turn their vacation trip into a rescue mission. He had been through worse before on higher, more dangerous peaks, but not with Gail to worry about.

As they edged around a rock outcropping, using their ice axes as canes, Gail grabbed her husband's arm. "Bruce. Look!"

He removed his mirror shades and glanced at the flat area ahead of them, sheltered by a wall of rock and ice. "Holy cow," he muttered as Gail leaned against him.

Not twenty yards away were two large animals. A black bear larger than any he had ever seen before lay on its side, obviously dead. A gray wolf, emaciated and mangy, sat upright near it, its eyes closed, its stature noble and serene.

"Bruce!" Gail whispered, trembling. "Let's get out of here!"

"No, wait," Bruce said, cautiously disengaging his arm and moving closer to the animals. "They're dead, Gail. They're both dead."

He approached them slowly, holding his ice axe like a weapon, just in case. Gail followed close behind, gripping the tail of his fiberfill parka.

"Gail, they're mummified," he said. "They're frozen to the ice, but if they weren't we could probably carry them home. They're that light."

Gail reached past him and stoked the wolf. Even through her gloves she could feel the parchment-thin skin beneath the fur. She could sense the emptiness of a body that had been frozen and dried by the cold of a brutal mountain. "How did the wolf die like this?" she asked. "Sitting up?"

"It must have frozen to death that way," Bruce said, stroking his beard. "Or maybe a snowdrift formed around it before it could collapse on its side. Can you imagine how long these animals have been here? Probably hundreds of years. Thousands, maybe."

Gail glanced at the bear, awed by its size, wondering about the grimace of pain still on its face. "But why didn't anybody else ever find them?" she asked.

"I'm not sure," Bruce said. He looked up at the bleak clouds, almost low enough that he could reach up and touch them. He knew that they should move on, but not yet, he thought. Not yet.

"They must have been buried in the snow," he said. "Had to be. I've been here before, and I've never seen them, or these rocks. The windstorm last night must have uncovered them. Can you imagine that? But . . . ."

"But what?"

"Something I can't understand." Bruce glanced at his wife. "I can't help but wonder: What were they doing this far up the mountain?"

"Can't you tell?" Gail whispered, her eyes seeing something no longer there. "For them it was a fight to the death. The wolf killed the bear — He had to. I couldn't tell you why, I just feel it. And he had to know that if he followed the bear this high, he was never coming down again."

"Gail," Bruce signed, shaking his head. "They're only animals. You can't project heroic fantasies on them just because you've got a romantic imagination."

"Bruce — please don't." Gain's voice was trembling. She reached out and took his hand. "We don't need to argue or throw insults. We aren't battling for mortal survival."

Bruce squeezed her hand, smiling to himself. "You're right. But if we don't get off this mountain soon, it'll sure feel like a battle for survival. The snow's coming down harder."

"Just one more minute. I want to remember this."

Bruce nodded. He reached for his camera and removed the lens cap. Gail glanced at him. "What are you doing?"

"I'm going to take a few photos."

She shook her head. "Please don't."

"Why not?" Bruce asked, checking his light meter. "The way the snow is coming down, they'll be buried by tomorrow, and nobody'll believe our story if we don't have a few photos."

"Let's keep the story to ourselves," Gail said, looking at him. "Let's make it our secret — our story." She smiled. "Like you said, they'll probably be buried again by tomorrow, probably for another thousand years. Whatever happened here was probably very important in a way we'll never understand. Maybe we were chosen to be the only humans to see them. Maybe we should keep it that way."

Bruce was about to argue the point but caught himself just in time. He remembered other arguments they had, all of them over small, insignificant things. None of them were ever important. He smiled back. "Yeah, you're right. Even if they were buried again, if I told someone he'd probably hike up here with a shovel to dig them up. Take 'em home and make coffee tables out of 'em."

Gail laughed. "Or lamps."

Bruce kissed her on the lips. "Our secret," he said. And he thought to himself it would be a chance for them to make a new start without angry debates, and the memory of the animals would be theirs alone.

Together they glanced one more time at the wolf and bear before they started back down the mountain. A thin film of snowflakes were already adhering to their fur, gently hiding the lonely sentinels one last time

CHOWHALL BLUES

DRAMATIS PERSONAE:

Charles "Mac" DeLeon
Jack Hall
Freddie Faircloth
Inmate #1
Inmate #2
Correctional Officer

SETTING: Prison chowhall. The only props on the set are (1) a prison chowhall stainless steel table with four stainless steel seats attached to the table at the base. (The table will be situated so that the actor sitting at the farthest seat will directly face the audience.) And (2) a large (or "over-large") sign behind the table reading: "NO YELLING! NO FIGHTING! NO FOOD FIGHTS! NO DISORDERLY CONDUCT! NO SMOKING! ANYTHING NOT FORBIDDEN IS MANDATORY! HAVE A NICE MEAL!" The sign has these words in the form of a list. Background noise (taped) is made up of chowhall sounds: many voices talking, the clanking of utensils and dishes, etc. Noise begins loud and volume drops off as Charles "Mac" DeLeon enters, stage right, carrying a tray of food, eating utensils, paper towels, and a plastic glass of red juice. He sits in the seat to the right. He wears a blue prison suit, which contrasts with the white kitchen prison outfit Inmate #1 wears as he enters, stage right, looking over his shoulder as he approaches the table and takes the left seat.

INMATE #1:   Hey, DeLeon! I got chicken sandwiches for tonight! Whaddaya say?

CHARLES "MAC" DELEON: So that's why the chicken-a-la-king is so thin this afternoon! Mostly gravy and peas over rice, with a little bit of chicken — mostly skin and pieces of cartilage. Did all you kitchen peons make sandwiches out of my lunch? Sheesh!

INMATE #1:   Hey, a man's gotta have a hustle to get cigarettes, you know. Only fifty cents. Whaddaya say?

MAC: That's my cigarette money you're asking for, buster!

INMATE #1:   Oh, well, hay, maybe another time, huh? Tomorrow I'll have cheese and ham omelette sandwiches. You liked 'em last time I made 'em.

MAC: The last sandwich I bought offa you had pubic hairs on it from you stuffing it down your pants to sneak it out of the kitchen.

INMATE #1:   Yeah, but, hey, I use baggies now. Whaddaya want? A New York deli? Didja hear about Freddie Faircloth? You'd better stay away from him.

((((Correctional Officer in official brown uniform enters, stage left, and stands behind Inmate #1.
     Mac takes a bite of his meal and speaks.)))

MAC: You'd better save it. Tell me later.

INMATE #1:   Yeah, but . . .

CORRECTIONAL OFFICER: On our break, are we?

INMATE #1 (LEAPING UP): Oh, hey, I was just showing this gentleman the wine list!

CORRECTIONAL OFFICER: I'm glad you reminded me. I've been meaning to shake down the kitchen for the longest time. It smells like someone's been making buck out of the canned peaches again.

INMATE #1:   Nah, you shouldn't waste your time, Sir. I think we drank it all last night. (EXIT, STAGE RIGHT.)

CORRECTION OFFICER: I wouldn't want to bet on it. (EXITS, STAGE LEFT.)

(((JACK HALL ENTERS, STAGE RIGHT, DRESSED IN PRISON BLUES. HE CARRIES TRAY OF FOOD, EATING UTENSILS, AND A GLASS OF RED JUICE. HE SITS AT THE TABLE IN THE SEAT VACATED BY INMATE #1.)))

JACK HALL: This stuff looks like puke. What is it?

MAC: Roadkill.

HALL: Don't play with me, Mac. This shit's gross enough to be roadkill. What is it really?

MAC: Chicken-a-la-king. It reminds me of when I was a child, Jack.

HALL: Your mother used to serve this shit?

MAC: My foster mother. I was raised by wolves, you know. After the hunt, all the wolves would come back to the den and regurgitate the partially digested deer meat for me. It looked just like this.

HALL (DROPS HIS FORK ON THE TABLE): You're sick, Mac.

MAC: Of course, the stuff back then was much better than the roadkill the inmate cooks regurgitate here. Look at this mess.

HALL: Put a cork in it, Mac. I invited Freddie to sit with us.

MAC (LOOKING UP): Freddie Faircloth?

HALL: He's been depressed all morning.

MAC: Small wonder. I've been hearing about him all morning.

(((FREDDIE FAIRCLOTH ENTERS, STAGE RIGHT, WEARING PRISON BLUES,

CARRYING A TRAY OF FOOD, UTENSILS, AND A GLASS OF RED JUICE. HE REMAINS "OUT OF EARSHOT" UNTIL JACK HALL SPEAKS.)))

MAC: The dude is trouble, Jack. Now, I don't care if he sits here, but you better be careful about getting too involved in his problems. Some people have a natural inclination to fuck up their lives . . .

HALL: (LOUD, IN AN ATTEMPT TO WARN MAC, AND CLUE HIM IN TO FAIRCLOTH'S APPROACH.) Hey, there Freddy!

MAC: Like I said, Jack, some people have a natural inclination to fuck up their lives, and it's a good thing we don't know any, right, Freddie?

FAIRCLOTH: Hello, Charles. Thanks for inviting me to sit with you, Jack.

HALL: No problem, Freddie. Eat up.

FAIRCLOTH: The food doesn't look too good.

MAC: No, it isn't, but look what they give you to wash it down with. (HE HOLDS UP HIS GLASS.) Bug juice! Or is it red tide? Or maybe a urine sample from someone whose kidneys are dying?

FAIRCLOTH (TO HALL): Does he always act this way?

HALL: Only when he's awake.

MAC: You need to get a sense of humor around here, Homeboy, or you'll be singing the chowhall blues.

FAIRCLOTH (TO MAC): Charles . . .

MAC: Don't start this "Charles" shit. I'm Mac around here.

FAIRCLOTH: Mac, I have a problem.

MAC: We all do, Bucko.

FAIRCLOTH: Hall here said you could help me.

MAC: Oh, hell, here it comes. Jack, you're putting me on the spot again! Freddie, I probably can't do shit for you. I can hardly do for me sometimes.

HALL: Hey, hear him out, Mac!

FAIRCLOTH: I borrowed some money . . . .

MAC: Yeah, I heard you did! In eleven weeks, you borrowed about one hundred twenty-four dollars and fifty cents!

FAIRCLOTH: (HE IS SILENT AT FIRST, SURPRISED. THEN HE SPEAKS.) How did you know?

MAC: A person's business gets around if he isn't careful.

FAIRCLOTH: So, can you help me?

MAC: Better eat, Freddie. Your lunch is getting cold.

FAIRCLOTH (TO HALL): I don't think he wants to help me.

MAC: What do you want me to do? Give you money?

FREDDIE: Well, it's a little more than what you mentioned . . . .

MAC: A little more?

FAIRCLOTH: Something over two hundred and fifty . . . .

MAC: Over two hundred and fifty, Jack, I never knew anybody who racked up over two hundred and fifty! Freddie, didn't you figure on the interest? How could you be that stupid? What were you buying? Crack? Dope? Where'd the money go?

FAIRCLOTH: No, I don't do that stuff. It was just cigarettes and snacks from the canteen.

MAC: What the hell did you eat? I didn't know they sold caviar on this compound! I don't believe you smoked and ate your way into this mess!

FAIRCLOTH: Well, I got it all in the canteen in the dorm.

MAC (PAUSE): Okay, homey, let's figure this out. You borrowed money at a hundred percent interest to buy Twinkies and cigs at price and a half the legal canteen price from an inmate's canteen. Okay, Yeah. That makes perfect sense now.

HALL: Mac, this is no time to joke. Freddie here is in trouble. They want their money back. Today. Now.

MAC: I'm sure they do. And you need my help now? What exactly am I supposed to do?

(((INMATE #2 ENTERS STAGE RIGHT, DRESSED IN BLUES, CARRYING TRAY, UTENSILS, AND GLASS OF RED JUICE.)))

HALL: Look, Mac, what it come down to is . . .
.

INMATE #2:   (HE PAUSES WHILE PASSING BEHIND THE TABLE AND FAIRCLOTH. HE PLACES HIS FREE HAND, BUDDY-LIKE, ON FAIRCLOTH'S SHOULDER.) Hey, old buddy, you'd better eat up. You don't want to miss the fun, huh?

(((HALL AND MAC GAZE AT THEIR TRAYS AND EAT, PRETENDING TO IGNORE THE

EXCHANGE. FAIRCLOTH IS VISIBLY SHAKEN, NOT SURE HOW TO REACT TO THE STRANGER.)))

FAIRCLOTH: Can we talk later?

INMATE #2:   Of course we can talk later. That's what friends are for, right buddy? (SMILES, THEN EXITS, STAGE LEFT.)

HALL: Mac, you gotta do something.

MAC: Like what, tell me!

HALL: I don't know. I was hoping you'd know.

FAIRCLOTH (SIGHING): Well, it's my problem. I'll have to handle it.

MAC: That sounds fucking brave. We'll put it on your tombstone.

HALL: Mac, I thought you had a little more heart than that.

FAIRCLOTH: You guys can have this tray. I can't eat. (RISES.)

MAC: Look, Freddie, sit down. You acted real stupid, getting a debt like that, and it's about time you acted smart for a change.

FAIRCLOTH: But there isn't anything you can do.

MAC: No, I can't. But you can! Go to that officer and tell him you're in trouble. He'll put you into protective custody. They'll ship you to another camp.

FAIRCLOTH: But that's snitching.

(((MAC SLOWLY RISES FROM THE TABLE, HIS EYES RIVETED TO FAIRCLOTH'S.)))

HALL: Mac, what are you doing? Sit down!

MAC: Snitching? You got guys you owe money to, guys who'd gladly make hamburger out of you, waiting just outside the chowhall door, and all you can worry about is snitching? (VOICE LOWERS, NOT IN CONFIDENCE BUT ANGER.) These guys'll put a second smile on your neck, or they'll rape you and take it out in trade . . . and you can't go to P.C. because it's snitching!

HALL: Mac, leave him alone! He's depressed!

MAC (SITTING): Freddie, how long you been doing time?

FREDDY (CONFUSED): A year, year and a half.

MAC: I've done ten years. And tell me, Freddy, how often have you worried about snitching on the streets?

FAIRCLOTH: I guess I never thought of it. I never heard of snitching until I came here.

MAC: Let me tell you something, honey. There's snitches and there's snitches. The asshole who snitches out a card game or a little sack of weed isn't worth a shit, but if your life is at stake, that's a different matter. It's common sense, homey!

FAIRCLOTH: But . . .

MAC: I've been here for ten years, and if I got myself in a fix where I didn't have a fair fight, hell, yeah, you'd bet I'd snitch to save my life!

FAIRCLOTH: But . . .

MAC: But then again, I wouldn't get myself that deep in debt. Do what you want, homey, but give it some thought. You don't want to be a stupid asshole all your life, do you?

(((A SILENCE ENSUES. HALL PICKS AT HIS FOOD WITHOUT EATING IT. MAC EATS
     HIS LAST ROLL. FAIRCLOTH IS STILL STANDING. ALL THREE ARE
          UNCOMFORTABLE.)))

FAIRCLOTH: Anybody want anything off my tray before I go?

HALL: Freddy . . . .

MAC:Nobody likes sharing the last meal of the condemned, Bucko.

FAIRCLOTH: I got an extra helping of Jell-O for dessert.

MAC (AFTER A PAUSE): Never let it be said I refused an extra helping of horse's hooves! (HE SCOOPS THE JELL-O ONTO HIS TRAY.)

HALL: Mac, I don't believe you! This guy is in deep trouble, and all you can do is eat the food off his tray.

MAC: He offered.

HALL: Hell, man, I thought you were the one person on this compound who had heart!

MAC: Hey, I told the man what to do, Jack.

FAIRCLOTH: Don't bug him, Hall. I'm giving him the Jell-O.

(((AS FAIRCLOTH TALKS, THE OFFICER IS LEADING INMATE #1 THROUGH THE
CHOWHALL THEY ENTER, STAGE LEFT. AS THEY PASS THE TABLE, MAC STOPS
EATING THE JELL-O AND WATCHES THEM INTENTLY.)))

CORRECTIONAL OFFICER: If you sneak out of the back door one more time, I'm transferring you to the laundry. I don't see how you do any work in the kitchen with all the breaks you take!

INMATE #1:   Hey, you don't have to work back there! It's a sauna, man! We could salt the food with our own sweat.

FAIRCLOTH (TO HALL): I gotta talk to these guys anyhow. I'll just tell them that my brother promised to send money and changed his mind. They'll understand.

(((MAC TURNS COMPLETELY AROUND TO WATCH THE OFFICER AND INMATE #1
     EXIT, STAGE RIGHT. THEN HE GLANCES BACK AT FAIRCLOTH, WHO HAS PICKED
     UP HIS TRAY TO LEAVE.)))

MAC: Don't go yet.

FAIRCLOTH: I got to.

MAC: No, you don't. Sit down. We'll discuss this some more. Eat something.

FAIRCLOTH: I'm too nervous to eat.

HALL: Leave him alone, Mac. You don't want to help him anyhow.

MAC: Shut up, Jack, you're filling me with self-pity. Just sit down for a minute, Freddy.

FAIRCLOTH (NUMB): I'll see you guys later.

(((FAIRCLOTH EXITS, STAGE LEFT, AS MAC
WATCHES HIM GO, AND HALL LEANS
OVER THE TABLE TO TALK TO MAC.)))

HALL: Mac, you could have done something,
talked to those guys, something. All you ever do is crack
jokes. Freddie is a good dude, and . . . .

(((NOISE OFFSTAGE: CRASHING, YELLING.
THE BUZZ OF CONVERSATION THAT
HAS BEEN THE BACKGROUND NOISE SINCE
THE BEGINNING RISES IN A
CRESCENDO OF SHOUTS AND YELLS.)))

HALL: What's that?

(((BOTH MAC AND HALL STAND AND GAZE
OFF STAGE LEFT AS SOUNDS OF
FIGHTING CONTINUES AND RISE. THEY
REMAIN STANDING AND STILL AS THE
OFFICER ENTERS, STAGE RIGHT, DASHES
ACROSS THE STAGE, AND EXITS STAGE
LEFT. AMONG THE SOUNDS IS AN
UNFAMILIAR VOICE YELLING: "ALL THAT
BLOOD! ALL THAT BLOOD!" FINALLY,
NOISES SETTLE, RETURNING TO
CHOWHALL SOUNDS, AND BACKGROUND
NOISES.)))

MAC: All the damn budget cuts they make,
and now we only have one officer in here! Damn!

HALL (SHOCKED): Is he dead?

MAC: They carried him out too fast. I couldn't tell. We'll know in an hour, though. It'll be all over the compound.

(((HALL AND MAC SIT DOWN. HALL CONTINUES PICKING AT HIS FOOD. MAC EATS THE LAST OF THE JELL-O.)))

HALL: You could have done something for him.

MAC: Yeah, last rites. You know, you keep saying that, but you don't say what I could have done. Besides, the guy was suicidal.

HALL: Suicidal? Man, you're just saying that.

MAC: Shit, Jack, look at how much money the man borrowed. To buy Twinkies, potato chips and smokes, no less. I told him a way out, protective custody, but he refused. What am I supposed to do, take his hand and lead him there? He says he doesn't want to snitch, a fake sense of honor, but if he had that honor before, he wouldn't be in this fix now. I mean, come on, Jack. Borrowing one hundred and twenty-four dollars. In ten years in the chaingang, I never met anyone who borrowed that much. I shoulda shook Freddie's hand and told him it was an honor. (PAUSE) Jack, you're not talking.

HALL: I feel sick.

MAC: So barf it up. Chicken-a-la-king looks the same coming up as it does going in.

HALL: That's not funny.

MAC: No, but this is.

(((MAC REACHES ACROSS THE TABLE, SNATCHES HALL'S GLASS, AND POURS IT OVER MAC'S NEAR-EMPTY TRAY. MAC GRINS AT HALL.)))

HALL: Hey!

MAC (STILL GRINNING): Don't you fucking get it? You need to have a sense of humor around here, homey, or you'll be singing the chowhall blues.

HALL: Mac, a man just got stabbed a minute after we talked to him! He may be dead!

MAC: Yeah, and we're still alive, Jack. Go back to your rack, homey, and after you're done feeling miserable, we'll walk the compound and talk a little. (PAUSE) Survival is going on, Jack. Life is happening. Let's not miss out.

HALL: Yeah, yeah, let's get outta here.

(((MAC AND HALL RISE WITH TRAYS, AND EXIT STAGE LEFT. CHOWHALL NOISES RISE. CURTAIN.)))

LISTEN TO THE RIVER

The stage is bare, except for a stationary prison cell door facing the audience. The actual cell of the play will have no walls but will be marked by duct tape, eight feet wide and twelve feet long. The only other two props will be a toilet near the door, with a roll of toilet paper at the foot of the toilet, and a single bunk and bare mattress at back. The bunk and toilet both face the audience sideways. The lighting will either focus on the cell area or light the entire stage during the performance to reflect moods, times of day and Duncan's fantasies.

DRAMATIS PERSONAE:

TWO OFFICERS (NON-SPEAKING ROLES)

"THE PUNK" (NEVER SEEN, IN THE DIRECTION OF THE AUDIENCE)

DUNCAN SIMMONS (AGE THIRTY-FIVE, A LIFER IN A FLORIDA PRISON)
(HE HAS JUST BEEN TAKEN TO LOCKUP. HIS CELL FACES ANOTHER CELL, AND THAT IS THE ONLY PERSON HE CAN SEE, THOUGH HE CAN HEAR THE NOISE OF OTHER INMATES DOWN THE HALL. HE HAS CLAUSTROPHOBIA AT FIRST, THEN RELAXES AS THE DAYS GO ON.)

ACT I

<u>SCENE ONE</u>

(((THE SCENE OPENS WHEN ALL THE LIGHTS COME ON OVER THE STAGE. DUNCAN SIMMONS IS HEARD OFFSTAGE. BEHIND THE AUDIENCE, YELLING.)))

<u>DUNCAN SIMMONS:</u> Get the fuck offa me! Stop pushing, I don't want to go! Let me talk to the Superintendent! I can straighten this out with him! Hey! Hey! Goddamn it all to fuck! Man, c'mon, you're hurting me! All right! All right! I'm going, okay? Stop pushing, goddammit!
(((DUNCAN IS HANDCUFFED IN BACK, BEING LED BY TWO OFFICERS IN UNIFORM.
THE OFFICERS NEVER SPEAK. DUNCAN IS LED, SOMEWHAT FORCIBLY, TO THE
CELL AREA, WHERE HE IS PUT ON THE OTHER SIDE OF THE STATIONARY CELL
DOOR AND REMOVE HIS HANDCUFFS THROUGH THE BARS, STANDARD
OPERATING PROCEDURE.)))

<u>DUNCAN:</u> About time you got those fucking things off! How would you like to be wearing them?

(((DUNCAN IS RUBBING HIS WRISTS. AS THE TWO OFFICERS WALK OFF,
APPARENTLY UNAFFECTED BY HIS WORDS. DUNCAN RAISES HIS VOICE AFTER
THEM.)))

DUNCAN: Someday all this will come back on your heads! The way you treat people like that, you shiteaters! What goes around comes around! You hear me! You think I'm afraid of you! Suck my cock!

(((DUNCAN STOPS AS THOUGH SUDDENLY AWARE OF THE FOOL HE IS MAKING
     OF HIMSELF. HE IS SILENT AS HE LOOKS AROUND HIS CELL. HE TOUCHES THE
     INVISIBLE WALLS AS HE INSPECTS HIS NEW ENVIRONMENT. MEANWHILE, THE
     LIGHTS DIM, FROM THE OUTSIDE OF THE STAGE IN, SYMBOLIZING DUNCAN'S
     CLAUSTROPHOBIA.)))

DUNCAN: Why do they make these cells so small? It's like a broom closet. Nothing here. (((TOUCHES WALLS))) I feel like these walls are going to close in on me. Yuk! (((PULLS HAND AWAY))) Slimy! Nobody's cleaned anything in here in years! Goddamn, I hate it here. I don't even have my smokes. I'm nicking already. Shit!

(((DUNCAN STARTS NOTICING GRAFFITI ON THE WALLS. HE READS SILENTLY
     AT FIRST, THEN OUT LOUD.)))

DUNCAN: "Carpe Diem!" What the fuck does that mean? It's Latin, I think. (((GAZES AT WALL ACROSS FROM THE TOILET))) Here I sit, so lonely hearted, came to sit and only farted." Christ, that's old. (((LOOKS BACK AND FORTH))) That's how you keep yourself busy around here, writing all over the walls. Hell, don't they ever paint the cells? I need a cigarette. And a cup of coffee. Man, this is a fucked-up situation."

(((DUNCAN GLANCES OUT HIS CELL DOOR, NOTICING THE MAN ACROSS THE
        HALL FOR THE FIRST TIME, "THE PUNK" AS DUNCAN WILL REFER TO HIM. THE
        AUDIENCE NEVER SEES HIM, BUT DUNCAN LOOKS AT HIM IN AN IMAGINARY
        CELL THAT ONLY HE, AND NOT THE AUDIENCE, CAN SEE. HIS GAZE MUST BE
        INTENSE SO THEY CAN IMAGINE THE OTHER INMATE IN LOCKUP. DUNCAN
        COMES TO HIS DOOR, GRIPS THE BARS, AND SHOUTS.)))

DUNCAN: Hey, you! What the fuck are you staring at? Didn't your mother teach you any fucking manners, or were you too busy sucking your thumb? Don't look at me. (((PAUSE — OTHER INMATE APPARENTLY STOPS LOOKING AT HIM))) Fucking asshole. Gets himself locked up and decides I'm his television.

(((HE STEPS BACK AND NOTICES SOMETHING WRITTEN OVER THE DOOR. HE
        STEPS BACK AND READS IT SEVERAL TIMES.)))

DUNCAN: "Listen to the river!" Now, who wrote that up there? (((FOLDS ARMS AGAINST HIS CHEST))) "Listen to the river!" What's that mean? And why put it over the door? (((LAUGHS))) There are no rivers here. Hell . . . .

(((DUNCAN BEGINS TO RELAX, HANDS AT HIS SIDE, MOVING ABOUT AS HE
        TALKS. LIGHTS COME ON ACROSS THE STAGE FROM THE CENTER LIGHTS OVER
        THE CELL, SLOWLY, UNTIL THE ENTIRE STAGE IS ALIGHT.)))

DUNCAN: I remember when I was a kid and swam rivers and streams around my home in Pittsburgh — the Monongahela, the Allegheny, polluted down to their river bottoms with who knows what and tires and old shopping carts and whatnot . . .

(((DUNCAN BEGINS WALKING IN CIRCLES THAT WIDEN AND BRING HIM OUT OF
        HIS CELL, THROUGH THE IMAGINARY WALLS. IT IS NOW THE LIGHTS SPREAD
        OUT ALONG THE STAGE, FOLLOWING HIS PROGRESS.)))

DUNCAN: Sometimes I'd skip school, and go fishing along the bank. Sometimes I'd go with the other boys where this long bullrope was hung on a big oak limb way out over the river, and we'd swing out, and for just one minute, we were airborne, flying. .

(((DUNCAN IS NOW WALKING AN ELLIPSIS FROM ONE END OF THE STAGE TO
        ANOTHER. HE IS HAPPY, SUCKED INTO HIS MEMORY.)))

DUNCAN: I had a dog until I was twelve, and he and I would swim in the water together. (((GOES BACKWARD, PRETENDING TO DO THE BACKSTROKE))) He was a good swimmer . . . (((GOES FORWARD, DOING BUTTERFLY STROKE))) And I missed him when he was gone . . . (((DUNCAN'S STROLLING CLOSING IN AGAIN ON HIS CELL, THE ELLIPSIS IS GROWING SMALLER))) My dad took him away, back then, just before things changed . . .

(((BY NOW, DUNCAN IS BACK IN HIS CELL, HE IS NO LONGER ACTING OUT
     SWIMMING. HIS ARMS ARE AT HIS SIDES, AS THOUGH HE IS TIRED. HE IS
     CAUGHT IN SOME SAD MEMORY. THEN HE LOOKS ACROSS THE HALL AT THE
     OTHER CELL.)))

DUNCAN: Hey!

(((THE LIGHTS ALL SHUT DOWN INSTANTLY, AS THOUGH IN RESPONSE TO
     DUNCAN'S QUICK CHANGE OF EMOTION. DUNCAN APPEARS TO BE ENRAGED.)))

DUNCAN: What the fuck are you looking at, punk? What the fuck are you looking at? Goddamn you! Now I recognize you! You're the guy who got caught sucking that black guy's dick. Hah! You really are a punk, aren't you? (((LAUGHS, MEAN-TEMPERED))) Got busted servicing your daddy! Yeah, I know you. You're also in prison for child molesting, chasing after little boys. (((LOUDER))) You had to get those Vienna Sausages, didn't you? You're goddamn lucky we got bars between us, bitch! I'd smear your face on the cement, babyraper! Go ahead, lay down on your rack, face the wall! You still can hear me! I can't see any other lockdowns but you, so you'd better keep quiet over there! You hear me? (((BY NOW, DUNCAN IS HYSTERICAL, BUT SUDDENLY SHUTS UP))) (((LONG PAUSE))) Jesus Christ. I wish I had a cigarette and a cup of coffee! The walls are closing in. The walls are closing in.

(((ALL LIGHTS GO OFF.)))

ACT I

SCENE TWO

(((LIGHTS COME ON OVER CELL, THEN SLOWLY SPREADS AROUND THE
     PERIMETER, SIGNIFYING SUNRISE.
DUNCAN IS ASLEEP, SLOWLY STIRS AND SITS
     UP, PICKING THE SLEEP OUT OF HIS EYES.
HE STANDS AND GOES TO THE TOILET,
     WHERE FACING AWAY FROM THE
AUDIENCE, HE URINATES. SOUND FX CREATES
     A SOUND OF WATER IN WATER
(URINATING). HE ADJUSTS HIMSELF AND LOOKS
     AROUND.)))

DUNCAN: I must have missed breakfast. Hell, I'm not hungry. (((GLANCES AT WALL))) "I once knew a pretty young lass/who had such a marvelous ass/but it wasn't round and pink/as you may well think/but had ears and a tail and ate grass." words to live by. (((LOOKS AT GRAFFITI ON ANOTHER WALL))) "Jesus is Lord." And here's some more classic stuff: "Vox populi, Vox dei." Great. (((LOOKS OVER THE DOOR AGAIN))) "Listen to the river." That's all there is to it. Just "Listen to the river." Yeah, that reminds me . . . .

(((HE FLUSHES THE TOILET — SOUND FX. AS HE STANDS, HE LOOKS AT THE
     WALL BEHIND THE TOILET. HE MIMICS PLACING HIS HAND ON THE WALL,
     BENDING OVER TO GET A BETTER LOOK.)))

DUNCAN: What have we here? (((WHISTLES)))
Somebody was a real artist. This is a great big pussy, with
all the details included . . . Good shading, nice the way the
flesh rolls around the clitoris. Somebody must have been a
gynecologist.

(((HE TURNS AND SITS DOWN ON THE
TOILET, LOOKING OVER THE SHOULDER AT
THE DRAWING. HE SIGHS.)))

DUNCAN: Good drawing, but he put it on the
wrong wall. I could have some real fun with that.

(((HE CONSIDERS HIS POSSIBILITIES, THEN
RISES AND STRADDLES THE TOILET
BACKWARDS. IT WORKS. HE SMILES TO
HIMSELF, HUMMING, AND BEGINS TO RUB HIS
CROTCH.)))

DUNCAN: Damn this looks good. I haven't had
any fun for so long I could fuck the crack of dawn.

(((HE GLANCES ACROSS THE HALL AT THE
OTHER CELL. HE IS STILL RUBBING
HIS CROTCH, HUMMING TO HIMSELF.)))

DUNCAN: Old dickbreath is still asleep. Hmmmm
. . . .

(((HE FOCUSES BACK ON THE PICTURE. HE
STOPS HUMMING AND STARTS

FUMBLING WITH HIS PANTS. THE
AUDIENCE CANNOT SEE WHAT HE IS UP TO
    BUT THEY CAN PRETTY MUCH GUESS. HIS
RIGHT ARM BEGINS MOVING IN THE
    ACT OF MASTURBATION. AT FIRST,
DUNCAN IS HUNCHED FORWARD, BUT THEN
    LEANS BACK, HIS BREATHING DEEP, HIS
CONCENTRATION FOCUSED, UNTIL
    HIS BODY JERKS IN SPASMS AND HE
GRUNTS IN HIS ORGASM. WHEN HE IS
    THROUGH, HE LEANS FORWARD, HIS HEAD
AGAINST THE IMAGINARY WALL.)))

    DUNCAN: Great! (((SIGHS))) Just great!

    (((HE OPENS HIS EYES — THEY WERE
CLOSED DURING HIS ORGASM — AND
    LOOKS DOWN, GRIMACING AT THE MESS IN
HIS RIGHT HAND. HE REACHES
    FOR THE TOILET PAPER ROLL WITH HIS
LEFT HAND, AND UNWRAPS TOILET
    PAPER ONE-HANDED, SETTING TO
CLEANING HIMSELF UP. WHEN CLEAN, HE
    REFASTENS HIS PANTS, AND AS HE PUTS
THE TOILET PAPER BACK ON THE
    FLOOR, HE LOOKS ACROSS AT THE OTHER
CELL. HE FREEZES. THE AUDIENCE
    CAN TELL BY HIS EXPRESSION THAT
"PUNK" IS AWAKE AND WATCHING HIM.
    HE QUICKLY STANDS, FACING AWAY, AND
FINISHES FASTENING HIMSELF
    UP.)))

DUNCAN: Goddammit! Once a fucking fag, always a fucking fag! (((TURNS, FACES "PUNK"))) So you wanted to see a real man in action, hunh? I guess your days of sucking boys' dicks are over, so you want to see what else is hot, right? (((SCREAMING))) You fucking stupid asshole bitch! Fuck you! Fuck you! (((PACES, LIMITED TO THE IMAGINARY BOUNDARIES OF HIS CELL))) If these bars weren't here I'd go over there and kill you! What kind of asshole are you, watching a man jerk his dick!

(((HE PAUSES, LOOKS AWAY, RUNS HIS FINGERS THROUGH HIS HAIR. THEN HE TURNS BACK AND LOOKS INTO THE OTHER CELL.)))

DUNCAN: Stop looking at me! Stop looking at me, dammit! (((LOOKS BACK AND FORTH))) Goddam, I hate enclosed spaces! I wish I could get out of here! You! (((LOOKS AT "PUNK" AGAIN))) What are you doing over there, looking at me like that? (((PAUSES, SLOWS DOWN, BREATHING HEAVY A LITTLE FROM HIS OWN EXCITEMENT AND ANGER))) What's a matter with you? You crying? (((PAUSE))) Hey, man, I'm sorry. You shouldn't have looked at me when you did.

(((PACES CELL AGAIN, LOOKS BACK AT "PUNK". PACES YET AGAIN. AS HE CONTINUES TALKING, HE CONTINUES PACING.)))

DUNCAN: Goddamn, man, you don't have to cry. Christ, it's not like I hit you or anything! Look, my old man used to beat the shit out of me, but I didn't cry. (((PAUSE))) Maybe once or twice. Aw, man, look at you, you're blubbering again. C'mon, calm down, will you? Here, let me read you some of the good shit graffiti on the wall here!

((((DUNCAN WALKS BACK AND FORTH, FINDING GRAFFITI AND READING IT,
      SHOUTING IT ACROSS THE HALLWAY. HE IS LESS ANGRY THAN CONCERNED
      NOW.)))

DUNCAN: Look, two guys wrote this. One guy says: "My mother made me a homosexual!" And the other guy wrote this: "If I get her the wool, will she made me one, too?" (((LAUGHS NERVOUSLY)))

(((DUNCAN GAZES CAUTIOUSLY OUT HIS BARRED DOOR. HE IS CLEARLY UPSET
      THAT THE OTHER MAN IS CRYING. FINALLY, HE WALKS SLOWLY OVER TO THE
      BARS, GRIPS THEM, AND STARES. SADNESS SHOWS IN HIS FACE.)))

DUNCAN: Look, man, I'm sorry I got you all upset. Look, I can't make you happy, you gotta do that yourself, okay? Hey, homeboy, why don't you speak? Can you speak? (((PAUSE))) Hah! You nodded yes. So why don't you? (((PAUSE))) Shit, you're playing games or something, but I don't care. Make faces if you wanna, okay? (((PAUSE))) Hey, hey, look here. You looked this way while I was jerking my dick, you can look now. That's it. Hey, did you hear that Mickey Mouse was divorcing Minnie? You see, and Mickey's lawyer says: "You can't divorce Minnie on the grounds that she is going insane." And Mickey says: "I didn't say she was going insane, I said she was fucking goofy!" Hah-hah! (((LAUGHS, THEN SETTLES DOWN))) See, you laughed. That's good.

(((LONG PAUSE. DUNCAN RUBS HIS CHIN. HE PRESSES HIS FOREHEAD AGAINST
THE BARS. HE SEEMS DRAINED FOR THE MOMENT, THEN HE SNAPS OUT OF IT.)))

DUNCAN: Hey man, you're okay. (((STEPS BACK, LOOKS OVER HIS DOOR))) Look, there's something written over my door. It says, "Listen to the river," and I was thinking to myself, maybe you are the river. (((LOOKS ACROSS HALL AGAIN))) You're sure quiet as a river. Hey, man. Lighten up. Everything will be all right.

(((DUNCAN RUBS HIS FACE, PACES HIS CELL, THEN BEGINS PACING OUTSIDE THE
LINES, GOING THROUGH THE "WALLS". HE KEEPS MUMBLING THAT
"EVERYTHING WILL BE ALL RIGHT." AS HE HEADS BACK WITHIN THE WALL OF
HIS CELL, THE LIGHTS GO OFF, SO THEY ARE ONLY REFLECTING INSIDE THE
CELL. THERE IS A FEELING OF CLAUSTROPHOBIA.)))

DUNCAN: I'm not too crazy about any of this either. To tell you the truth, I don't like being enclosed. It makes me feel like I'm being crushed like a cockroach. The only thing that bothers me more is heights. Once my mother took me to New York, and she took me up into the Statue of Liberty. I was okay until we got to the top and she got me near a window. I puked up all the footlong I ate for lunch that day. You shoulda seen it. What a mess! But being locked up, I can't stand that too much. (((LONG PAUSE))) Hey, look at the poem over here. Somebody must have been feeling romantic. (((HE READS)))

"With all my love, my woman sweet,
I think of you every time I hold a rose.
My precious darling, faraway and neat,
Lying on my bed in full repose.

(((PAUSE. DUNCAN GLANCES THROUGH HIS DOOR.)))

DUNCAN: Damn. He fell asleep.

(((LIGHTS FADE OUT.)))

ACT I

SCENE THREE

(((LIGHTS COME UP OVER CELL AND SPREAD OVER ENTIRE STAGE. DUNCAN IS DOING PUSHUPS, HIS TOES ON HIS BUNK, HE WEARS NOTHING BUT BOXER SHORTS. TIME HAS PASSED, AND HE IS IN GOOD SPIRITS.)))

DUNCAN   Forty-seven! (((GRUNTING AT EVERY SHOUTED NUMBER))) Forty-eight! Forty-nine! Fifty!

(((HE FINISHES COUNTING PUSHUPS, AND STANDS. HIS CHEST AND FOREHEAD ARE COVERED WITH PERSPIRATION. HE WIPES HIMSELF WITH HIS T-SHIRT, AND THROWS IT ON THE BED. HE PACES, CATCHING HIS BREATH, THEN LOOKS THROUGH DOOR AT "PUNK")))

DUNCAN   Hells Bells! Looks who's up! (((SMILES))) You see what I've been doing? I haven't been interested in exercise since I was in high school. Now look at me. It's so boring here that pushups are like tickets to a Grateful Dead concert with free pot. (((GRINS))) See, I made you laugh.

(((FLEXES MUSCLES, PACES, YAWNS, THEN LOOKS AT WALLS.)))

DUNCAN   By the way, you ready for the quotes of the days? Listen to this one, Punk: "Quid pro quo." That's Latin for tit for tat. I read it when I read <u>Silence of the Lambs</u>. Jodie Foster was in the movie, but the book was good. Anyhow, this young lady F.B.I. agent, Clarice Starling, was trading information with this psycho killer in a prison cell named Dr. Hannibal Lecter, and at each exchange, one of them would shout, "Quid Pro Quo!" In other words, I gave you something, give me something back. That Hannibal Lecter, or Hannibal the Cannibal, was something else. He knew what was going on in the streets, even though he was in a prison cell in a psycho prison. I'm in here, and I don't know shit.

(((DUNCAN THROWS A FEW PUNCHES INTO THE AIR, MAKING "TISH" SOUNDS
WITH EACH PUNCH. HE DANCES ON HIS FEET LIKE A BOXER.)))

DUNCAN   I don't even know what goes on down the hall. Last night two guys in a cell tore into each other. I guess they have two-man cells down the hall. Anyhow, I couldn't see shit from here, all I can see is you, and you slept through it. At least I think you did. Were you asleep? Yeah? Well, anyway, it sounded like some bone crushing going on, with lots of yelling. By the time the cops finally showed up, one was passed out, or just silent, and the other was still kicking on him, still cussing him out.

(((DUNCAN PAUSES AND REVIEWS THE WALLS AGAIN. HE GLANCES ACROSS THE

HALL AT "PUNK", SMILES AND WINKS
WHILE POINTING.)))

DUNCAN   Here's a good one for you, Punk:
"He who writes on prison walls
Rolls shit into little balls.
He who reads these words of wit
Eats those little balls of shit."

A good one. I knew you'd like it. I laughed at it
too.

(((HE GAZES AT ANOTHER WALL, RUBBING
HIS CHIN. HIS FACE TURNS
      SERIOUS.)))

DUNCAN   Okay, here's another one. I saw it
yesterday. Here it is. "Stupidity got us into this mess.
Why can't it get us out?" I think it was Mark Twain who
said that. (((STARES AT "PUNK" FOR HIS
REACTION))) Or Will Rodgers.

(((DUNCAN PACES HIS CELL, VERY SERIOUS
NOW. HE PICKS UP T-SHIRT AND
      ROLLS IT INTO A BALL AND TOSSES IT
BACK ONTO THE BED.)))

DUNCAN   It's true, though, stupidity and all that.
I mean, here I am, two weeks in lockup, allover stupidity.
I've been here five years with a clean record, no
paperwork, nothing, then one day I score some pot and get
royally stoned. I'm feeling so good I get a couple coffee
cups of buck from a friend down the hall. Next thing I

know, I'm skimming up and down the hall, making a lot of noise, when I knew I should've stayed in my room and gone to sleep or something. A guy comes out of his room and cusses me out, I cuss him out, and next thing you know, we're pounding on each other like punching bags. His face looked like bruised oatmeal. I didn't get hit once, not because of skill but luck. I was so drunk I couldn't hold still long enough to get hit. Then the officers come out, and what did I do? I cuss them out, let them know I think their parents were a subspecies of garbage can rodents. I was so fucked up they kept me overnight in a medical cell before bringing me here. Shit!

(((DUNCAN SITS ON HIS BED, AS THOUGH TELLING HIS STORY HAS EXHAUSTED
HIM. HE RUNS HIS FINGERS THROUGH HIS HAIR.)))
DUNCAN   Anyhow, you know those words written over my door? "Listen to the river?" They do more for me than if someone threw in a bible. I don't go for that church stuff any way. But I keep thinking, "Listen to the river." What does a river do but take its time going downhill, taking the easiest course, and I think that is what I need to learn. (((HE GRINS AGAIN))) I'm thirty-five, and still banging my head against the walls. I need to learn to go with the flow.

(((DUNCAN GETS UP AND STANDS AT HIS DOOR, NOT TOUCHING THE BARS.)))

DUNCAN   I didn't tell you why I came to prison, did I? Yeah, I know what you're in here for, diddling little boys, but I'm not going to pick on you for that. You're all the company I got. The officers don't even stop for a chat, just walk by once an hour every hour to make sure I'm still breathing. Anyhow . . .

(((DUNCAN STARTS PACING. LIGHTS ABRUPTLY GO OFF EXCEPT FOR THE ONE
        OVER THE CELL. DUNCAN IS FULL OF ANXIETY AT THIS POINT.)))

DUNCAN   I had a friend named Joe, my fall partner. He's at another prison now, but we were good friends at one time. Besides getting drunk and picking up women, we robbed gas stations.

(((ONE LIGHT AT EACH END OF THE STAGE GOES ON, SO THERE ARE THREE LIT
        AREAS ON THE STAGE, SURROUNDED BY DARKNESS. DUNCAN PACES OFF, LEFT,
        INTO THE DARKNESS. EVENTUALLY ENDING UP STANDING UNDER THE LEFT
        LIGHT.)))

DUNCAN   We'd pull up, me driving a '62 Ford Galaxy 500 in light blue with rust spots, and Joe would get out and head into the office with his gun, robs the store, and we take off. (((PRETENDS TO HOLD A GUN. THEN BLOWS AWAY SMOKE FROM GUN BARREL.))) Good situation, only one day he kills two people.

(((DUNCAN STEPS OUT OF THE LIGHT. THE LIGHT OVER THE CELL GOES OFF AND

HE WALKS THROUGH THE DARKNESS
UNTIL HE REACHES THE OTHER LIGHT AT
THE OTHER END OF THE STAGE.)))

DUNCAN   He hops in the car. He screams that he killed two people and off we go. You see, what he doesn't tell me is that the gun accidentally goes off, and he shoots the man — there's a man and a woman behind this counter. They sell sandwiches and stuff besides gasoline, you know how these places are now. He shoots the man . . . . (((MIMICS GUN GOING OFF IN HIS HAND))) . . . by accident. The man falls, the woman is screaming. So what does the asshole do? He shoots her, too, through the head, brains against the meatball sandwiches and the slushee machine! (((HE STANDS LIKE JAMES BOND, BOTH HANDS HOLDING GUN AT THE READY))) Two killings, and he hops in the car and I drive him off. Only one thing . . . .

(((LIGHT COMES BACK ON OVER CELL, DUNCAN HEADS FOR IT.)))

DUNCAN   (((BACK AT CELL))) Only one thing. The man he accidentally shot in the face lived, and became a witness against us. Had Joe let the girl live, we'd be out of here by now, no murder, just an armed robbery. But because Joe thought he killed someone, he had to go and kill someone for real. (((SIDE LIGHTS GO OUT.))) So, Punk. (((LOOKS OUT CELL DOOR AGAIN))) You see where panic gets you. Go with the flow. Listen to the river.

(((DUNCAN GOES BACK TO DOING PUSHUPS, COUNTING, "ONE, TWO, THREE . . ." LIGHTS FADE TO DARK.)))

ACT II

SCENE ONE

(((LIGHTS STAY OFF AT FIRST. DUNCAN IS SITTING IN THE DARK ON HIS BUNK,
   DEEP IN THOUGHT. DUNCAN HAS A BLUE HANDBALL, WHICH HE BOUNCES IN
   THE DARK, SO THE SLOW THUNK . . . THUNK . . . THUNK IS HEARD IN THE
   DARKNESS. THERE ARE LONG PAUSES BETWEEN HIS WORDS, EMPHASIZING HIS
   REFLECTIVE DEMEANOR.)))

DUNCAN   (((IN THE DARK))) Harry S. Truman once said, "If you can't convince them, confuse them." I know, it's written on the wall of my cell. (((LONG PAUSE. THUNK . . . THUNK . . . THUNK OF HANDBALL))) Give them hell, Harry. God, he was so far before my time . . . but I remember Woodstock as a kid, John F. Kennedy dying, Bobby Kennedy and Martin Luther King being shot, John Lennon being shot. Disco, rap, punk rock, reggae, MTV, Bill Clinton and his wife President Hillary Clinton, the Gulf war, Woodstock II brought to you by Pepsi Cola, O.J. Simpson being chased in his white Ford Bronco on national TV . . . (((LONG PAUSE. THUNK . . .THUNK . . . THUNK.))) But Harry, you were before my time. Fuck history. Napoleon Bonaparte once said, "What is history but a fable agreed upon?" He was before my time, too, but his words are on my walls. (((LONG PAUSE. THUNK . . . THUNK . . . THUNK))) And over my door. It says, "Listen to the river." Wasn't there a door somewhere that says, "Abandon hope, all ye who enter'? Maybe I'll write that up there, too.

(((LIGHTS RISE OVER THE CELL ONLY, AT FIRST CREATING DEEP SHADOWY
EFFECTS SO THAT THE AUDIENCE CANNOT SEE DUNCAN'S FACE, BUT THEY CAN
SEE HIM MOROSELY BOUNCING THE HANDBALL.)))

DUNCAN   I've been here a month now, feel like I'm suffocating every day. The walls are always trying to crush me, but I'm like a flea, maybe nobody loves me, but it's hell trying to crush me. (((LONG PAUSE. THUNK . . . THUNK . . . THUNK))) When I was a kid, I used to pick fleas off the belly of my dog, we didn't have any flea collars for the dog. They were around, just couldn't afford it, or so my dad said. (((LONG PAUSE. THUNK . . . THUNK . . . THUNK))) But I'd pick the fleas off the dog, then try to squish them between my fingers. You couldn't do it. They were flat critters, and you could bust their tiny bodies up if you roll them back and forth between your fingers, but you just couldn't crush them between your fingers. (((LONG PAUSE. THINK . . . THUNK . . . THUNK))) I guess I'm a flea. I'm not crushed yet.
(((LIGHTS OVER THE CELL ARE ON FULLY NOW. DUNCAN STANDS AND WALKS
OVER TO THE BARS OF HIS DOOR. HIS EYES ARE RED. HE HAS BEEN CRYING. HE
IS GAZING ACROSS THE HALL.)))

DUNCAN   Hey, Punk! Are you awake? Yeah, I thought you were. Look, the lights are on. They'll be bringing breakfast in an hour. It's probably five in the morning now. C'mon, rouse yourself up. You look like you're down because there are no dicks to suck. (((LAUGHS))) Hey man, don't look pissed off, I know why you're in lockup, and you do too. I'm not putting you down. There's a trusty here, I heard, who goes around, and anyone in lockup can stick their pecker out and get it sucked. The officers look the other way, so if you want to get your whanger whooped, hang it through the bars. I'm not kidding, but make sure you get the right trusty. The other guy ain't about that shit. You see this handball, a trusty gave it to me. (((HOLDS BALL UP))) He owes me money. He said he might get me coffee and smokes, but I don't know about the smokes. I've gone without for so long I might as well try quitting. What do you think? I've been smoking since I was twelve.

     (((HE STARTS PACING THE CELL, AS LIGHTS COME ON OVER THE STAGE. SOON
     HE WILL BE PACING UP AND DOWN THE ENTIRE STAGE.)))

     DUNCAN   When I was twelve, that's when I started having troubles. It was the first time I got caught shoplifting. Then again, it was about then that my mother got into the habit of slapping the shit outta me and my father took to using his belt on my ass. School was still a shelter for me back then. You wouldn't know it to look at me, but I played the trumpet in the school band and I was popular with the other kids. Of course, I smoked to keep my popularity, too, but that wasn't a big deal. In junior high school, it was pot and booze, and half the time I was lifting the booze from my parents. In high school I got a girl pregnant, but I had enough money to get her an abortion. Now I wish I hadn't. I wish now I had a kid out there somewhere, but that's the way it bounces sometimes. (((HE BOUNCES HANDBALL))). And after all that, would you believe I still graduated from high school with honors and started college.

(((DUNCAN IS NOW AT THE EXTREME END OF THE STAGE, STARING OFFSTAGE.
HE IS GRIPPING THE BALL WITH BOTH HANDS NOW. TENSE.)))

DUNCAN   Anyhow, I dropped out of college. But I wanted to tell you about the things when I was twelve. It wasn't shoplifting it was something else. Me and two friends were stealing Coca Cola bottles. Cases of them, for the ten cents deposits. Can you believe that? Anyhow, all we had to do was pick up the cases, two at a time, and carry them from a fenced-in area behind the store to a place about a hundred feet away, behind some trees and bushes. It was night. The lock on the fence gate was busted. I did it. And we were carrying these cases . . . .

(((DURING THIS TIME, DUNCAN MIMICS CARRYING CASES OF EMPTY COKE
BOTTLES FROM ONE SIDE OF THE STAGE TO THE OTHER. AS HE DESCRIBES THE
ACTION, HE ACTS IT OUT.)))

DUNCAN   So any way, there I was, halfway between the back of the store and the trees, (((HE IS

HALFWAY ON THE STAGE)))   when I saw George and Paul drop their cases and run off. They were almost at the trees. I thought they were nuts until I saw the flashing red and blue lights on the trees. I turned around, and there is a cop car. Right behind me. At that point, I knew I couldn't run, so I set the bottles down, and they put me in the back of the car.

(((DUNCAN RETURNS TO HIS CELL, SITTING ON HIS BED, HOLDING HIS HANDS IN
    FRONT OF HIM, AS THOUGH HE WERE HANDCUFFED.)))

DUNCAN   But the worst wasn't the arrest. There I was, a twelve-year-old kid, handcuffed and in the back of the squad car. And how did I get off? I snitched out my friends who got away. They always said, both of them that I'd snitch them out someday, and I always said I wouldn't, but in the end it did. They both went to juvenile detention, and I got off scott free — the cops thought I was just under a bad influence. They were right, but it was my parents, not my friends. Little did they know.

(((DUNCAN STANDS, GOES TO HIS DOOR. HE HANGS HIS FOREARMS THROUGH
    THE BARS. HE LOOKS LIKE HE IS ABOUT TO CRY.)))

DUNCAN   There's a saying on my wall, by Isaac Bashevis Singer: "When you betray someone else, you betray yourself." Well, I felt like Judas that time around, and it still sticks with me today. (((STEPS BACK,

BOUNCES HANDBALL))) Shit. I'd better put this away. It's almost breakfast time.

(((LIGHTS GO OFF. THE SOUND OF THE BALL IS THE LAST WE HEAR.)))

ACT II

SCENE TWO

(((A SINGLE LIGHT COMES ON IN THE FRONT OF THE CELL ONLY. DUNCAN IS AT THE BACK, SITTING ON HIS BUNK, HEAD BENT DOWN. THERE ARE THREE STYROFOAM CUPS BALANCED ON THE TOILET ON THE DOOR, ONE ON THE ROLL OF TOILET PAPER, TWO BY THE BEDSIDE, ONE IN HIS HAND. DUNCAN LOOKS UP, HIS FACE HARDLY VISIBLE.)))

DUNCAN   I can feel the walls close in.

(((HE RISES, WALKS TO THE BARS OF HIS DOOR, STUMBLING. HE IS OBVIOUSLY DRUNK, HIS EYES ARE REDDISH, AND HIS WORDS ARE SLURRED.)))

DUNCAN   (((HOLDING STYROFOAM CUP)))
The walls are closing in. I can feel them almost against my skin. I remember once when I was five, I broke a gravy boat. Mom was pissed as hell, screaming and hollering, like I'd spoiled a national treasure. I was bawling my eyes out . . . (((SIPS FROM CUP))) and she kept telling me to shut up. I couldn't, I just couldn't. So she throws me in the pantry with the canned goods and closed the door. I was bawling, finally shut up, and waited to her to open the door. She never did. I waited, and

waited, and I began suffocating. I had to piss, but the door never opened. The only light was a crack between the bottom of the door and the floor. I put my head down in the dust and looked. I saw linoleum but nothing else, it wasn't much of a crack. I didn't hear anything out there. I thought she left the kitchen. I thought she left the house for good. And that's when the walls, full of canned goods, creamed corn, string beans, Campbell's chicken noddle soup, I couldn't see them but I knew they were there, but that's when those walls began to close in for good and I knew I was gonna die. (((TAKES ANOTHER SIP))) Christ, I need a cigarette!

(((DUNCAN PACES THE CELL, THEN COMES BACK TO THE FRONT. HE STANDS AT
        THE TOILET, BACK TO THE AUDIENCE, ONE HAND STILL HOLDING THE
        STYROFOAM CUP, THE OTHER FUMBLING WITH HIS PANTS FRONT. THERE IS THE
        SOUND OF URINATING)))

DUNCAN   Goddamn, I need a smoke! (((TURNS AROUND, STILL FUMBLING TO CLOSE UP HIS PANTS))) Hey, look who's awake this late at night. Hey Punk, you dreaming about sugarplums and giving candy to little boys? (((LAUGHS))) Hey, I heard a joke before I got in here. A man just finished his meal, and the waiter wants to know if he wants . . . goddamn, now I can't remember the punch line. (((TAKES ANOTHER SIP))) Oh, this stuff here. (((HOLDS UP CUP))) You're probably wondering where I got this. That friend of mine who owes me money, the trusty, well, he makes buck, good stuff, too, and since he didn't have the money to get me tobacco, he got me this instead. (((LAUGHS))) And you know, I still want a smoke! I don't think I'll ever quit. (((LAUGHS)))

(((LIGHTS ON EITHER SIDE OF THE STAGE FLASH ON AND OFF QUICKLY, AND
 DUNCAN LOOKS UP, THEN DRAINS THE CUP AND SETS IT DOWN BY THE BARS.)))

DUNCAN   Hear that? Thunder. Rain. It's a helluva night, isn't it? That trusty I told you about, he can't figure out the saying over the door that says to listen to the river, but he knows the Latin phrases. Like, "Carpe diem!" means seize the day. And I found other ones in here. "Sumus quod sumus" means we are what we are. "Cogito ergo sum" means I think, therefore I am. It turns out that he was in this cell, and he wrote down the Latin shit years ago. He also knew the artist . . . (((POINTS TO SPOT ABOVE THE TOILET))) who drew the giant pussy over there.

(((LIGHTS ON EITHER SIDE OF THE STAGE FLASH AGAIN. DUNCAN LOOKS UP AT
 THE UNHEARD THUNDER, THEN ACROSS THE AISLE.)))

DUNCAN   Look here, Punk, look here. I've been talking to you for over a month and a half, and you haven't answered me yet. So what's up? What is there about me that you don't like. You suck boys' dicks, you suck niggers' dicks, and do I hold it against you? No. So why don't you talk to me? What's wrong with me that you won't say a fucking . . . thing! Like Hannibal the Cannibal said, "Quid pro quo!" I did the talking for a long time, now you do the talking! What's the matter with you? Fucking Punk! Fucking Punk!

(((DUNCAN PACES HIS CELL, STEPPING PURPOSELY ON HIS CUP, ONE OF THEM,
 AND KICKING ANOTHER OUT OF THE WAY. HE IS VERY AGITATED, THE
 PRESSURES OF HIS TIME IN LOCKUP ARE GETTING TO HIM.)))

DUNCAN   The only human voice I hear are my trusty friend once a day and the officers announcing chow three times a day. (((STOPS AT BARS))) Look, man, I need to hear you say something. You are all I got. Don't you understand that? Look, I never told anybody this. The reason I was so angry about you diddling little boys was that my dad molested me when I was twelve. You know, that's probably why most people don't like child molesters like you any way, they've been molested or their conscience is killing them. Look, I don't hold it against you. (((PAUSE))) Look man, I'm lonely. I'm drunk, and I need to hear someone's voice. You hear that snoring down the hall? They're all asleep. It must be three a.m., and it's only you and me. Why don't you say something?

(((DUNCAN WATCHES. FLASHES ON EITHER SIDE OF THE STAGE. DUNCAN STEPS
 BACK FROM BARS FOR A MOMENT, THEN RETURNS.)))

DUNCAN   What the hell's the matter with you? Jumping up and down and waving your arms at me like that. Banging your head against the bars! You're gonna bring the guards. You fucking asshole! You fucking babyraper! I opened up to you since the day I got here, and you never said anything to me. Fuck you! Fuck you! (((PAUSE))) You know something else, I hope you die! I hope you fucking die!

(((LIGHTS FLASH AT EITHER SIDE OF THE STAGE. DUNCAN PACES BACK AND
FORTH. HE LAYS DOWN ON HIS COT. HE STIRS AROUND SEVERAL TIMES, THEN
SETTLES DOWN. LIGHT GOES OUT OVER CELL. LIGHTS ON EITHER SIDE OF
STAGE FLASH SEVERAL TIMES, THEN GO OUT.)))

ACT II

SCENE THREE

(((LIGHTS COME ON, FIRST OVER THE CELL,
THEN ACROSS THE STAGE FROM THE
    CENTER OUT. DUNCAN IS IN HIS BUNK IN
THE SAME POSITION AS HE WAS AT
    THE END OF THE LAST SCENE. THE
STYROFOAM CUPS ARE STILL SCATTERED
    ABOUT. NOTHING HAS CHANGED FROM
THE LAST TIME WE HAVE SEEN HIM.
    DUNCAN STIRS AND MOANS, SLOWLY, LIKE
A CRIPPLE, RISING FROM HIS BED.
    HE FINALLY FACES THE AUDIENCE, BUT HIS
HEAD IS DOWN, HELD IN HIS HANDS.
    THEN HIS HEAD RISES, AND HE LOOKS
ACROSS THE HALL. HIS EYES OPEN WIDE
    IN HORROR.)))

    <u>DUNCAN</u>   (((WHISPERS))) He hung himself.
(((SHOUTS))) He hung himself, Goddam! He hung
himself!

    (((DUNCAN LEAPS FROM HIS BUNK AND
GRABS THE BARS. HE STARES, AT FIRST
DUMBFOUNDED, SILENT. THEN HE SCREAMS,
LOUD AND LONG, FERAL, HIS EYES OPEN WIDE.
HE HAS THE LOOK OF A CAGED ANIMAL ABOUT
TO DIE. HE STOPS SCREAMING, GOES INTO
SHOUTING AND WAVING HIS ARMS BEYOND THE

BARS SO THE OFFICERS DOWN THE HALL CAN
SEE THEM.)))

DUNCAN   Hey! Hey! Somebody! Get down
here! This man's hung himself! Hey! We need some help
down here! Goddamn, help me, help him! Don't leave us
here by ourselves! We aren't just pieces of meat! This
man needs to live. Help him. Goddam! Goddamn.

(((FROM THIS POINT ON, DUNCAN
NARRATES EVENTS TO THE AUDIENCE,
        MOSTLY NOT LOOKING DIRECTLY AT
THEM, BUT TELLING THEM WHAT IS GOING
        ON. HE GOES FROM A STATE OF EXCITED
HYSTERIA TO EXHAUSTED
        RESIGNATION. HIS ARMS DANGLE OUT THE
BARS, THEN HE PULLS THEM IN AND
        HOLDS THE BARS AS THOUGH FOR
SAFETY.)))

DUNCAN   The officers finally came. They ran
down the hall and flung open the punk's cell door. They
rushed to get his body down. He was hanging by a sheet
around his neck. They had to cut it, it was so tight and so
deep into his flesh. Medical showed up, but they couldn't
revive him. When I saw them slow down their efforts, I
knew it was over.
        (((DUNCAN STEPS AROUND HIS BAR DOOR,
STANDS IN FRONT WITH ARMS
        DANGLING AT FIRST. HE IS AT A LOSS.)))

DUNCAN   All I could think of was when I said last
might that I hoped he died. Why did I say that? I didn't

want him to die. He was the only person I had to talk to. (((GRIPS HEAD))) My head hurt from the buck last night, but there was a deeper pain. (((HUGS SELF AS THOUGH COLD))) I found out days later from the trusty that he had no tongue. The punk really was a child molester, and an angry parent cut out his tongue before he was turned in to the police. I just kept thinking about that . . . and how I told him I wish he were dead. I didn't know he wished the same thing.

(((DUNCAN GOES BACK INTO HIS CELL. HE STANDS THERE, RUBBING HIS ARMS,
        LOOKING THROUGH HIS BARS UNCERTAINLY.)))

DUNCAN   I listen to the river now. (((PAUSE))) The river talks in trickles. Nobody else was put in the other cell for the rest of my stay here. So I listened to the trickles, telling me there is no going back the way you came, you can only go forward, and when there is something solid in your way, you can't knock it out of your way, you have to go around, and you take the path of least resistance, because any other way is too frustrating. You accept what is there, because things won't change just because you want them to. And the only way out is through. (((RELAXES))) I'm still listening, still learning, and I wish the punk had listened too. I miss him. It's not easy. Sometimes I feel the walls closing in. (((SIGHS))) God, I wish I had a smoke.

(((DURING THIS LAST SPEECH, THE LIGHTS FADE TOWARDS THE CENTER. AFTER

DUNCAN'S LAST LINE, THE LIGHT GOES
OUT COMPLETELY.)))

<u>THE END</u>

<u>THE END</u>

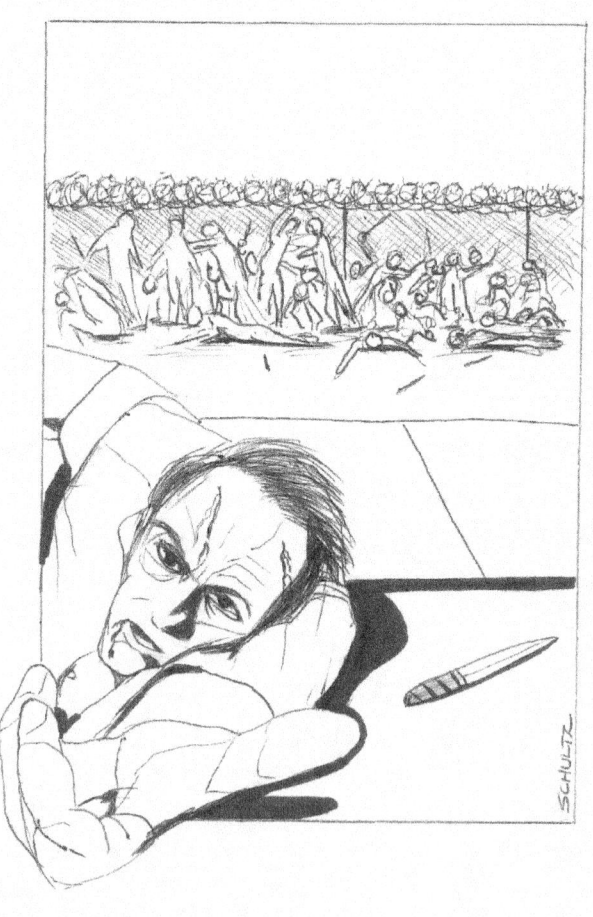

SIRENS

Almost six years as an inmate at Baker Correctional Institution in Olustee, Florida, and I'd never seen a prison riot until Friday, June 3, 1994. I heard days later that it all started with a fight between two men from two different Florida cities and escalated as other men joined in, a few at a time, as though called by Sirens. Maybe it was a territorial thing; maybe it was the heat and humidity; but the pull was real; and the crowd grew.

I was one of the last few inmates in the chowhall finishing my lunch that day when the officers slammed and locked both chowhall doors. Through a window I watched them charge off towards the east end of the compound. Something was up. A kitchen officer came out of the kitchen, unlocked a door and gazed out. I took my cue and squeezed by, knowing he'd be too intent in seeing what was going on to notice me. I rushed back towards my dorm, curious and apprehensive about what I might see. Ahead, I saw clusters of inmates staring in the same direction, and I hurried around the Education Building to get a look myself.

It was there in the field, not four or five or ten men fighting, but well over a hundred, a large mass of bodies twisting and turning in upon itself, slowly moving back and forth across the field like a giant amoeba or a tide of men. It was a choreographed chaos, tangled bodies kicking and punching at each other, torn shirts, shouts, constant swarming so that you didn't really see individual men, just the mass. A few inmates broke from the circle only to return a minute later with broken mop handles for weapons.

Three workers from Medical, wearing their blue-green uniforms, worked over a seriously injured inmate, oblivious to the fighting uncomfortably close to them. Officers in brown uniforms charge into the melee from every angle, trying to separate men from each other. They were outnumbered, but a few of them, sweating and disheveled, were already marching handcuffed inmates back to lockup as other officers rushed in to replace them.

It was a far cry from the infamous Attica riot, but watching its progress, one could feel the tension, the anger, the buildup of pressure. It was the blind rage of men who were hot and frustrated by problems compounding themselves, men who would take their frustrations out on anybody at hand. Fists slammed into heads and stomachs as men grappled with each other. Officers continued to pull men from the roiling crowd, but it was like trying to block the overflow of a broken dam with your bare hands.

I was about fifty feet from the fighting now, and walking closer, lulled into a false sense of security by my own fascination. It was like seeing a grizzly bear in the woods and walking towards it, and thinking it was perfectly safe; it would never attack. I wasn't into violence; I didn't know how to fight; but the Sirens were calling me too, and like others around me, I was being pulled into the human maelstrom.

The steam whistle over the boiler room signaled recall, a strident whine that drew everyone's attention. Classification officers from the Administration Building, out of place in their suits and ties, came into the compound and began directing inmates back to their dorms. For me, it was a moment of confusion and resentment, stuck between the draw of the riot and the annoying regimentation so common to prison life; but common sense got the better of me, and I started for my dorm. The spell of the Sirens was broken.

After the whistle sounded, the riot broke up faster than it had formed. The compound was cleared; the inmates sat quietly on their racks, waiting to be counted. The Riot Squad, with shotguns and Plexiglas shields, came in through the front gate to make sure the compound was secure. Torn and bloody shirts and T-shirts littered the field like remnants of a carnival. The wind hummed through the razor wire and fences, but the Sirens were now silent. They'd had their fill.

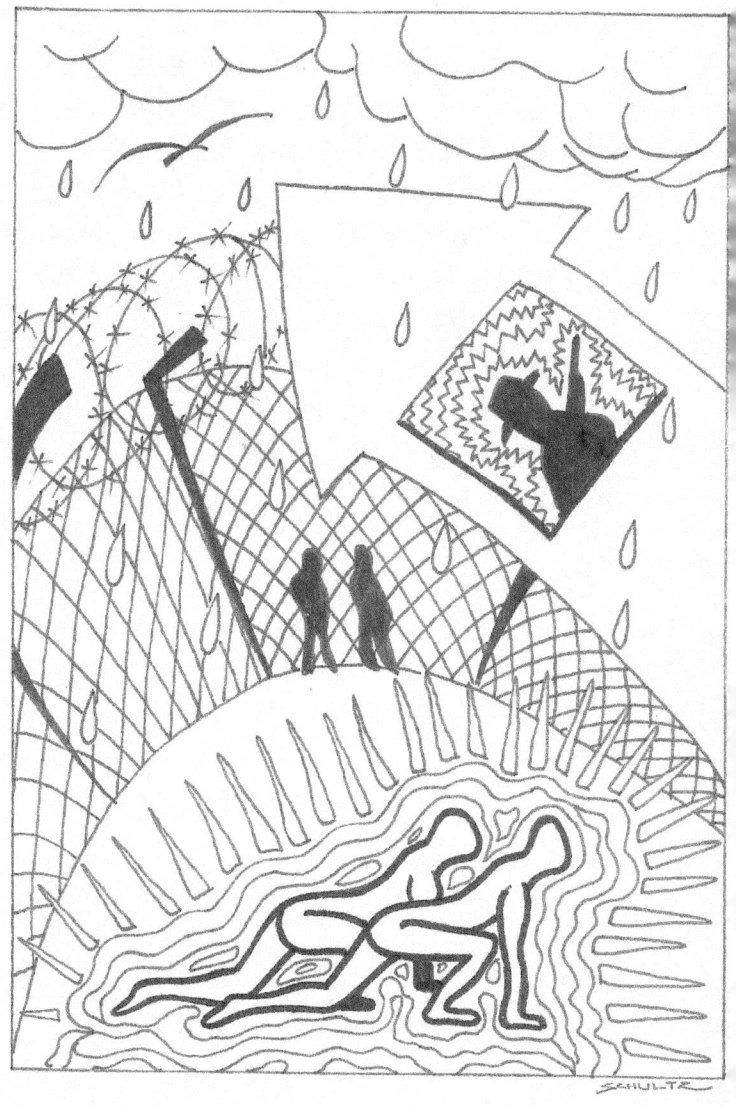

David M. Wood

ASANAS

The Punk Angels and their Daddies stay inside today and watch wrestling. Harold, Mark and I are on the Yard, moving through Surya Namaskar, Salute to the Sun, beneath the overcast sky. No sun to salute today.

I gaze beyond the fence, razorwire and gun towers at the fir trees, watching a hawk spread its wings against the gray. We hold our palms together in the Namaskar position before we begin again. There are twelve positions, one for every month. Each round becomes a year of our sentences. We've gone through five so far, but we've still got a lot to go.

The wind picks up, humming through the razor wire as the gun tower guards hum along. The rain begins to fall, our baptism. The inmates walking the track stare at us as we go on, in unison, into the Cobra Pose, Bhujangasana. One shouts at us: "Hi-ya-hi-ya" in a mock Eastern chant. "Fuck off," I mutter, my mantra.

We move fluidly through the Asanas, the rain falling harder now. I shiver and recall telling Donna about the last time this happened. "How spiritual," she said. "Practicing Yoga in the rain on a prison compound."

"Getting stoned at a Grateful Dead concert," I answered before hanging up. "Now that's spiritual." I call my cell my Ashram, but it is all bullshit. Mark and Harold stretch before finishing. The prison cat purrs at our feet. I sneeze and say, "Wanna go one more round?"

FIVE   1/197   T. NEWTON SCHULTZ

SYMBIOSIS

Das dass uns nicht totet macht uns schwerer.

— Nietzsche

("That which does not kill us will make us stronger.")

The first day:

Duncan John Lee arrived on Fresh Fish Friday, carrying his box of possessions off the armor-welded bus and through the razorwire-lined fences and rusted gates to the Orientation Room. With streaks of gray in his close-cropped brown hair and a glint of apprehension in his blue eyes, he tried to ignore the stares of the crowd of hungry inmates on the other side of the fences, sizing him up, sniffing him out, holding him against their plumlines.

He felt queasy and out of sync as he sat on a folding chair with the other new arrivals in a brightly lit room with bulletin boards cluttered by memos and a wall of trophies recalling the past victories of the prison's softball and basketball teams. He gained twenty pounds during his stay in the county jail from the fatty foods and his own lethargy, and now his prison blues felt a little too snug. The Department of Corrections sergeant paced before them in a crisp, brown uniform, reading from a clipboard about personal hygiene, drug testing, orderly conduct and the risks of HIV and tuberculosis. "Why don't this shiteater mention shankings and rapes while he's at it?" the inmate next to him whispered.

Duncan's thoughts drifted back to when they woke him at two a.m. days ago at the county jail, loaded him on the bus and shipped him to the Reception and Medical Center — the hospital prison — where he was probed and poked and questioned and siphoned of blood and urine before he was bussed to his permanent camp. Those days were now a blur, and the fog showed no promise of lifting any time soon.

At the end of the orientation session, he and six other white inmates carried their boxes across the compound to D-Dormitory, an open-bay dorm with seventy bunks in one large room. He made up his assigned rack and locked his few belongings inside his locker, recalling the last time he talked to Old Gus, the scarred, knotty-armed Black man in the county jail. "Jes' keep your head up," Gus told him. "Look every man square in the eye and let him know you'll fight back. You don't have to win a fight, just hurt the other guy bad enough so he won't want to scrap with you again. Prison ain't so bad you can't earn a little respect. You c'n live there in a sorta symbiosis, you give a little to the place and it gives something back. And look every man square in the eye."

But Duncan hung his head, sitting on his rack, his Bible open on his knees as he pretended to read, ignoring the prying eyes. It was going to be a lot harder than he thought.

The first dream:

He wandered through his mother's house, the bare rooms lit by moonlight through the curtainless windows. His footsteps echoed on the polished wooden floors. He felt his chest constricting as a heavy, invisible blanket of loneliness weighed him down. He looked into his bedroom, his brother's bedroom, searched for familiar smells but there were none. He wandered down the hall, through the living room, dining room, kitchen, glanced down the cellar stairs, but nobody was there, they were gone without a trace. He was alone. And then he turned and looked out a window, and he knew they were out there, not his family but — them — hidden in the shadows, breathing, watching, waiting . . . .

The first week:
He placed a collect phone call to his wife, Amanda Lee, on the dormitory phone, skipping dinner to do it because it was the only time other inmates weren't fighting over it. He also didn't want anybody around when he brought that subject up again.

"But Duncan," he heard Amanda say, "I love you, Duncan. I told you I'd stay with you forever."

"I know, Amanda, I know," he answered, feeling small. "I love you too, but I got a mandatory quarter, Amanda. You can't wait twenty-five years, Hon, you gotta get on with your life. It's not fair I hold you to an unhappy marriage . . . ."

"I don't want a divorce, Duncan!" Amanda whimpered. "I'll wait for you, I promise! I said I'd love you forever, and I meant it!"

"But Amanda, I . . . ."

"Duncan, no!"

"Amanda, listen!" he said, trying to remain calm. "It would be cruel of me to expect you to wait that long. You'll meet someone else . . . ."

"Duncan, I'm not going to do it! I've got a good job and . . . ."

"But . . . ."

"Duncan, no, I won't talk about it anymore! Please!"

He could see her tears in his mind, he knew her voice when she was crying, and in the end, he gave in before he hung up. Later, as he sat on his rack reading an Agatha Christie novel, he began to have hope. But what kind of job could he get, coming out of prison an old man? It didn't matter, he thought, as long as his wife stood beside him.

The sixth dream:

He was lost in a giant boiler room, wandering among massive, rusty furnaces that rumbled like the dormitory fans in the summer heat. He was trying to get out, but he couldn't remember which way he came in. The maze of pipes, gauges, valves and grates left him disoriented, walking on a concrete floor slick with greasy water. The brick walls were slimy with mold and fungus and patterned by red bars of light blazing through the furnace grates.

"Duncan, I told you . . . ." he heard, and his head snapped around. He went to the large, rusty grate in the cinder block wall and peered into the darkness, and then he heard his grandmother's voice again. "When I was a child . . . . The church, Duncan, I always sang . . . ." Her voice grew faint over the throbbing rumble, but he couldn't answer her, afraid to go near the old iron grate, but wanting her to come back, and then he remembered his grandmother died while he was in the county jail . . . .

The first month:

He was sitting on one of the eight dormitory toilets, each separated from the other by a short wall for semi-privacy, when the dark figure stepped in front of him. "Suck my dick, white boy!"

Duncan looked up into the angry black face, a black, muscular body covered only by boxer shorts and sweat in front of him. "Look, I'm not that way . . . ."

"You look like you that way to me, punk," the man, called Deathrow Dog, said. "Maybe if I bitch-slap you . . . ."

"Hey, man, I'm taking a shit!"

"Your shit stinks too, punk," Dog said, his white eyes blazing, muscles flexing. "You'd better flush the shit jacket, and after you're done you can douche, too. I want you to be ready."

Duncan returned his gaze, it took all his will, and he remembered Old Gus's words, "Watch your back, Dunc, and don't take a shit without pulling one leg outta your pants so you can stand like you ain't shackled if you gotta fight." He wished now he'd taken that advice more seriously.

"Look, man," Duncan grumbled, trying to sound tough though his voice was cracking. "I'm not a fucking queer. Why don't you go to the T.V. room and watch cartoons? I just wanna be left alone."

"So stroke my cock a few times and I'll leave you alone." Dog smiled ominously.

Duncan wanted to glance toward the officers' booth, but he could already imagine the brownshirt leafing through a People magazine, oblivious to the world beyond the Plexiglas. "Why don't you fuck off?" he growled, his words lame and impotent.

"I'll fuck you before the week is up."

"I can't tell!" Duncan shouted, his eyes blazing. "All I hear is words, and I'm getting tired of talking to you."

"Well, you don't have to talk," Dog snarled. "But I'll talk to you later, hear?" He walked away, and Duncan stared after him, his bowels unable to work, his legs falling asleep, his hands shaking, but he didn't dare move.

"Fucking nigger," he mumbled. Then he spotted Big Blue, the Black man who always watched him, never spoke, and he raged inside at his own fears and weaknesses, wondering if they were working together to scare him. "Fucking nigger!"

The twenty-fifth dream:

It was like a 1950's sci-fi B movie, a McCarthy-era cold-war cheap double-feature film, a city, the remains of a holocaust in black and white, crumbling buildings, and as he ran down empty streets he saw nuclear missiles sail across the horizon, not the sleek, straight vehicles he'd seen in photos and documentaries but the rounded rockets with tailfins and flames from old Buck Rogers films, rising overhead in apocalyptic splendor, and he knew he had to get out of the fallout, so he rushed down the broken stairs into the empty basement, only then realizing that the ceiling was shattered, open to the sky, and the fallout was coming and there was no place to run . . . .

The first year:

It had been a truly rotten day. He asked the Housing Officer if he could be transferred to the T-Building, F-Dormitory, the dorm made up of two floors, three wings each, forming a "t" if seen from the sky. Six wings altogether of two-man cells, with steel doors that could be closed. He wanted to get out of the noise and pandemonium of the open-bay dorm, but for the twelfth time he was told there were still other inmates on the waiting list ahead of him, he'd have to wait, and he was losing patience.

And then there were the tennis shoes. Someone had cut up the high-tops he'd worn since his arrival, razor-bladed them to shreds one night while he was sleeping. He asked his mother to mail him another pair on his package permit. They arrived yesterday, and today at noon when he returned from his work on Inside Grounds he found his locker open, his combination lock smashed and useless, and his new Reeboks gone. He'd have to wear his brogans for another six months until his next scheduled package permit.

During lunch he called Amanda. The dorm was empty except for an old white man asleep and buzzsawing on his rack. Amanda answered and accepted the charges on the sixth ring. "Oh, Duncan!" she whined when she heard his voice.

"Amanda, Hon, I've had such a fucked-up week . . . ."

"Duncan, I'm so sorry, I didn't mean to do it!"

"Do what?" Duncan asked, thinking of the Mazda he bought second hand months before he was arrested. An accident? The car totaled?

"I'm sorry, Duncan! I was tired from work, and Bruce said he'd drive me home because the Mazda was in the shop, and I didn't want to take a cab, so I cooked him dinner, and we talked later, drinking wine . . . ."

"Yeah!" Duncan said calmly, neck hairs bristling.

"And, Duncan, I felt so lonely, and I'm sorry, but . . . ." Amanda was blubbering now, barely understandable, but Duncan got every word. "I didn't mean to, you know, let him spend the night . . . ."

"On the couch?" he asked, trying to be optimistic.

"Oh, Duncan, we slept together, I'm so sorry, but I was so lonely, and I hadn't been touched by a man in so long . . . ."

Duncan felt his chest constrict, his skin prickle as Amanda began crying in earnest. "You goddam fucking bitch! You fucking slut! I knew you'd sleep around sooner or later! Damn you! Don't you know I'm suffering in here? Don't you know I'm fighting for my life? And you have to spread your legs like a common whore, like a dog in heat . . . ."

Instead he said, "I understand," lied through his teeth and hated himself for it. Hated her for it.

"Always watch out for thieves," Old Gus told him in the county jail. "Inside the fence they'll steal your shoes, and outside they'll steal your girl."

"I understand," Duncan said through her whimpering, though he really didn't, and six months later they were divorced when Amanda announced she wanted to marry him. "Bruce," he muttered to himself later. "Bruce."

The three hundred thirty seventh dream:

He walked through bare autumn trees, the leaves crunching beneath his sneakers as he searched for a way out of the woods. Nothing looked familiar, but he felt like he'd been here before. Dark clouds roiled above the naked branches over his head, snow clouds, he recalled from his childhood in Pennsylvania.

He thought he saw a house ahead, but as he looked closer he could tell it was more than that. Giant gray stones and lichen-covered mortar towered a hundred feet up, the wall stretching in both directions beyond his vision. A large arch revealed what looked like the entrance of a railroad tunnel but without the tracks or a distant light at the other end to indicate the tunnel's exit. He eyed the cavernous trail as far as the light let him see, but the darkness beyond that was threatening. It scared him to know he'd be walking blind, but he took the first step . . . .

The second year:
Duncan sat in the bleachers, sweating and watching Blue at the pitcher's mound coaching the batters of his new softball team, the Jawbreakers, during their Sunday afternoon practice. Blue had moved into the T-Building a month after Duncan, and the two had taken an instant dislike to each other.

"Dunc, why don't you try a few swings?" Jerry Parks, a heavily-tattooed white beanpole, shouted from his position as catcher at home plate.

"Another time," Duncan shouted back.

"We need a couple good hitters, Dunc!"

"Jerry, stop bein' a fool!" Blue shouted from the pitcher's mound. "Jesus Christ, that stupid cracker there couldn't hit a dustball with a broom!"

Duncan gazed angrily at Blue, then hopped off the bleachers and walked toward Jerry. The catcher smiled and handed him the aluminum bat.

"Ah, shit!" Blue fumed. "This silly cracker wants to clown around while we got serious practice to attend to!" He took a stance and prepared to pitch. "Okay, Joe DiMaggio, take a few swings and go back to your seat!" He nodded at the catcher, then pitched.

Duncan swung, missed, almost lost his balance, while Blue and the other players laughed. Jerry tossed the softball back to Blue and patted Duncan's shoulder. "Don't choke it, Duncan," he whispered. "Easy on the grip, and watch the ball, not the pitcher."

"I know what I'm doing, dammit," Duncan whispered back. "I played this game before." He adjusted his stance and nodded. Blue went into the windup, pitched, and Duncan heard a hissing in his ears, timed the trajectory, then swung. The bat made contact with an angry thok and the ball arched into the sky. "Gotcha!" he hissed through clenched teeth. The softball kept going, then sailed over the fence and razorwire, just missing the Plexiglas windows of the gun tower. The officer slid the window open and gazed out, his mirror shades gleaming. "Oh, shit," Duncan whispered, sweat pouring off his forehead. "Now I've gone and done it!"

A grim silence hung over the field, the players glancing at the fence, then at Duncan. Then each man pulled off his glove and applauded. Jerry patted his back as catcalls and laugher came from the outfield, and the gun tower officer smiled and gave the thumbs up signal. "Shit!" he gasped, and then he was laughing, too.

That night, after count, he was walking to the water fountain for a drink when a Black inmate cut in front of him. "Hey, man!"

"What?" The muscular man turned around, and Duncan recognized Deathrow Dog. "You trying to cut in front of me, cracker? You want trouble?"

"You cut in front of me!" Duncan shouted.

"You calling me a liar, white boy?"

"No, but . . . ."

"Leave the man alone, Dog."

"Who says?"

"I do." Blue stepped closer. "You're fucking with the star hitter of my softball team, Dog. I'm his manager, and if you got some shit with him, bring your team on the field and we'll play it out."

"You're fuckin' crazy!" Dog huffed, then stormed away. Blue glanced at Duncan, nodded, and wandered back to watch the television. Duncan stared after him, surprised that they were now on the same side.

The seven hundredth dream:

He was lost in an open bay dormitory as large as a factory warehouse, the racks stacked six bunks high, rows and rows of them lined up in every direction. The dorm lights had been out for hours, but the red ceiling night lights glowed far overhead, giving the bunk bed labyrinth an eerie aura. Men slept in shadowy blanket-covered mounds. Nobody snored, no radios played, and there wasn't an unused rack in sight. He was tired, and he had to find his own worn-out mattress before the officers came by for count.

As he walked around another stack of racks, he spotted Amanda in a black gown, her long, red hair spilling over her shoulders. At first he was afraid the men would wake, see her, but she seemed uncharacteristically calm and confident, gesturing for him to follow. He trailed behind her until she located his rack. Then she turned back the sheets, in one graceful motion. He glanced at her, and she smiled the way he remembered. Then, without a word, she turned and walked away.

Duncan felt an immense longing as she disappeared in the shadows. He wanted her to come back, stay. He glanced at his pillow. A bright, red rose was set across it, and seeing it, he felt a momentary warmth, as though everything was still okay . . . .

The fifth year:

Duncan found out later that it wasn't just the water rationing that caused the fiasco but that the sewer pipes under the dorms were four-inch pipes instead of the eight-inch pipes required by the state building code. When the prison water tower was damaged by lightning, the dorm water ran twice a day, at noon before lunch and at nine after evening count. Toilets held turds and piss until then, covered by pieces of cardboard, old magazines or empty pillow cases, but when the water finally came on and everybody in the dorm flushed their shitjackets, there just wasn't enough water pressure to turn them off.

Duncan figured he'd laugh about it twenty years later.

His cell was on the bottom floor, and he was reclining on his rack reading Anne Rice and listening to his toilet rage like Niagara Falls the first time it happened. Leon from across the hall shouted, "Ho-lee Moses! We're getting a flood in here!"

Duncan leaped off his bunk and peered out the door. The drain lids on the hall floor were rising up as water gushed into the hallway like the great oil strike. Large turds and tattered toilet paper came out of the drains. "Christ, I'm gonna puke!" Duncan shouted, glancing down the hall. "Rick, run down to the station and tell them brownshirts to open the fire doors! And Pimp! Hey, man, hand me that broom!"

As an officer ran outside to unlock the emergency exit door, Duncan, wearing nothing but his boxers, stepped into the rising brown water and began shoving waves down the hall with the push broom. The officer leaped back as effluvium poured off the outside stoop and into the grass. "Willie! Jack!" Duncan shouted. "Lend a hand! There's other brooms!"

"I'm not stepping in shitwater!" Jack yelled.

"Then don't, pussy boy!" Duncan shouted angrily. "Ajax, c'mon man! Pete! This is your hallway too! I can't do this by myself."

Several men reluctantly stepped into the water and picked up pushbrooms as others threw blankets down in their doorways, keeping the water off their cell floors. Forming something of a bucket brigade, they created a river flowing outside. "All right, buckaroos!" Duncan shouted, never losing his rhythm. "Welcome to the holy healing waters of the Muddy Mississippi, where you can cure your own ugliness and stupidity and still get ringworm and sewermouth!"

The men laughed as he broke into song, first "Black Water," then "Old Man River." He kept up a constant chatter as other men stepped up to take their turns. Three Black men did a rap song about life in the sewers, and Duncan held his post, sweat pouring down his bare chest, sewer water up to his ankles, until ten minutes before the water shut off, long enough to catch a quick shower.

It was to become the routine for the rest of the week, until the water tower was finally fixed. Duncan, who before that time was referred to as "the silent monk" or "that quiet cracker," was nicknamed Noah for years afterwards for how he survived the flood.

The seventeen-hundredth and second dream:

He walked around the outside of his grandmother's house, stopping when he saw the two white-furred bulldogs standing in the front yard, one about thirty pounds, the other as big as a St. Bernard, both of them heavenly creatures with pupil-less eyes like solid white granite. Feeling the urgency of something left undone, he quickly went around the house again. Stopping near the front, he noticed the large bulldog was gone. The small one lay on its side, dead, its white coat torn and stained by blood, a sticky puddle forming around its body. He felt rooted to the spot by fear.

"It's a dangerous world," his grandmother said. He looked back at her — she wore her apron, her thick Hungarian skirt and her babushka. She stared through thick bifocals past him, unaware of him. "You must always stay in the house."

"Maybe I will," he said, feeling an unexplainable rage. "Then again, maybe I won't!" He looked back. Both dogs stood on the lawn, pure white, absolutely still. They were porcelain statues . . . .

The tenth year:

"You had this cell to yourself for a month now, man, you need a new roommate," Blue told him, his hair half-gray these days. "What do you say, Dunc? You sleep on the upper rack anyway, and Shawn has a lower bunk pass."

"Man, Shawn's a kid, just twenty years old," Duncan said, thinking of his own gray hair. "What's he need a low bunk pass for?"

"Weak arms and shoulders," Blue said.

"So take him to the weight pile."

"You take 'im, cracker," Blue growled. "You been doin' a lot of workin' out lately, your old carcass getting big." Duncan rubbed his hands together, feeling the horn-hard callouses on his palms from not using gloves when he lifted weights. "So?" Blue continued. "You want a new roommate or what, man?"

"Why are you begging me, man?" Duncan snapped, looking up and feigning anger. "If the jit wants to move in, I don't give a shit."

"He's being pressured for his ass," Blue said. "He could use a friend."

"So if I take him in, the other daddies leave him alone and you get him for yourself."

"Hey, man, you playin' me close!" Blue snarled. "I don't go out like that, and you know it! I'm tryin' to help the kid!"

Duncan laughed, letting Blue know he just pulled his string. "Good thing Deathrow Dog ain't here these days, he'd gnaw the kid like a bone."

"Deathrow Dog's buried, bro," Blue said. "Caught the ninja big time."

"Yeah?" Duncan muttered, surprised. For a moment he almost missed Dog.

"So will you help the kid?"

"He can cell with me, bro, but I can't help him much, I'm just an old inmate."

"You ain't no inmate, Duncan," Blue growled indignantly. "You're a convict. You got sense, man. Show the ropes to this white rugrat before his mouth writes a check his ass can't pay."

"Allright, allright, I'll be his fuckin' nanny, okay, homeboy?"

"Show you right, roaddog!" Blue said, smiling, and Duncan couldn't help but smile back, both of them with a few less teeth than when they first met.

"Goddam, Blue, you sure getting soft in your old age."

"I think it's a virus, man," Blue joked before he left. "It'll pass. See ya tomorrow at practice, bro!"

Duncan watched him go, then climbed back on his rack and reread the letter he got from the nineteen-year-old Filipino girl. He began to write: "Dear Maria — I want to thank you for the photo you sent. Your long, black hair is beautiful. In your last letter, you asked what it's like living in prison. First, the food stinks . . . ."

The three thousand six hundred fifteenth dream:

They picnicked on a prairie that stretched as far as the eye could see, with a bright, cloud-dappled sky that flowed over them like a great dome. He ate a sandwich as Gus sat beside him and explained the Yin-Yang symbol: "What goes around comes around, man, like Karma, 'cause everything must have its opposite . . . ." Blue got most of them on the field, trying to start a softball game, Paul, Shawn, Willie, Pete, Ajax, Rick and Pimp, but Duncan sat under the tree with Old Gus, admiring the view. "There's only fences and gun towers and razorwire around you if you think there are, man. Life is a symbiosis, give and take, man, with everybody . . . ." Amanda served him lemonade, and he was surprised to see Deathrow Dog bring the picnic baskets, but Gus nudged him and pointed at the distant buffalo herd. "The Sioux Nation respected the wolf and the hawk, and they knew your roaddog was your partner who walked the long, lonely road with you . . . ." And Duncan nodded his thanks, picked up his bat and glove, and headed for the game . . . .

THE THEORY OF FLIGHT

They said he discovered the theory of flight. They said he was crazy, even before the three black guys raped him on his rack and everyone started calling him "that punk" and he started walking the compound like a dazed rabbit left wounded and vulnerable for the predator's return. They said he was hurting so bad he was going to try and soar over the fences, gun towers and razorwire to get away from the pain. And in all the times I saw him walking the inner perimeter track, alone, that lost look in his eyes, I wanted to help.

But I was afraid.

After five years of prison, at Whitebury C. I. in the Florida panhandle, I knew better than to interfere in anything that was not my business, especially something that was about sex or rape or property or anything between two inmates that had nothing to do with me. My first year here, I had to go through the boogames and sex games one inmate forces on another through coercion and threats and false friendships and promises of protection. And if I could survive with my ass, literally, intact, I figured anybody else could. But even after five years, I was still naïve, and maybe, just maybe, I had more to learn.

He was a kid in his twenties, nicknamed "Shorty" because he stood about five feet tall. He was quiet and timid, with blue eyes, blond hair, and a dimpled smile on the rare occasions he smiled. Someone told me he'd been in prison since he was fifteen, but he didn't carry himself like a convict familiar with the chaingang façade of callous indifference. With small, gentle hands, a hairless chest and curved shoulders, he appeared almost feminine, though not effeminate, and I could almost understand what the other guys saw in him, and why it all went down the way it did.

It rained hard that night. I was thankful I was a heavy sleeper. I lived in the same open bay dorm as Shorty, a hundred men on double bunks sharing a dozen toilets and sinks and one television room smelling of cigarette smoke and piss. The next morning, I heard the whispers about the rape in the dorm on the way to the chowhall with the morning crowd. When I got back, I could see the shape of Shorty's body curled up under his flannel blanket, his head buried. He stayed hidden under his bedding all day, didn't even come out for chow call that first day. Something was twisted in the pit of my stomach every time I saw him across the dorm. Of course nobody snitched, so the guards didn't do anything, and the rest of us went about our business as though nothing happened.

From that day on, Shorty walked the compound, usually alone, sometimes followed by the guys who raped him who laughed and shoved him and grabbed his ass a few times before wandering off to find something else to do. And sometimes Shorty would force a smile, but you could tell it was fake, like plastic flowers at a funeral.

A month passed like that, me watching him when I wasn't working in the vocational automotive shop and when he wasn't making another trip to the infirmary for another blood test or whatever. A few times he disappeared off the compound for a day, handcuffed and shackled in the prison van with others taken to the Reception and Medical Center – RMC – the closest prison hospital to our camp. At first, rumors spread that Shorty caught the Ninja – AIDS – but one of the infirmary trustees said it was just something normal, like anemia.

Still, I didn't worry about any sickness of the body Shorty was going through but the sickness of the soul, because it seemed that he had given up, and he was dying from something that had nothing to do with anemia or anything else.

One day I saw him walking by himself when he suddenly stopped and picked something off the ground. He held it up and stared at it, as though checking for imperfections. I was walking towards him on the track, and as I walked past, I saw that he was holding a shiny, black feather. I almost stopped, but he glanced at me, so I looked away and kept going.

As the summer days dragged on, I continued to see him walk the compound and pick up more feathers. I tried not to watch, I tried to isolate myself from him the way I isolated myself from other inmates who were hurting on the compound for one reason or another. But I wondered, what was he doing with all the feathers? He always carried the feathers in his hands, each fist full of what looked like a dozen feathers, pigeon, sparrow, raven, swallow, seagull, and he did nothing but walk the track searching for more.

Other inmates noticed too. "He's trying to put together a bird!" I heard, or, "Shorty got a bird brain now!" I felt sorry for him, locked in his loneliness, and me, knowing what loneliness was about, and wondering how much more he felt it on his lone walk. And still I wouldn't talk to him. Not in this place. And I wasn't about to cry over his problems if I wasn't going to cry over mine. And that was the hardest part, because sometimes I need to cry so much my chest hurt, but I couldn't, not any more, not after five years.

And how much worse did Shorty feel, with the rapists trailing him like hungry hyenas? I'd look at my wrists, seeing a sharp, white scar across each one from when I was in the county jail awaiting sentencing, and then I'd look at him, walking, picking up feathers, two dozen in each fist now, and I wondered, with a great deal of awe, if I could handle all his pain.

Then one day Shorty did something different. As though he got an invisible cosmic signal, he extended his arms to the sides of his body, and as he walked, he began raising and lowering his arms like a bird flapping its wings. He did this all day, his arms never tiring. Other inmates shouted bird calls at him or ran past him, trying to snatch his feathers, but he gripped them tight, and if he dropped a few, he patiently stopped and picked them up, then walked on, flapping his arms.

Days later I was walking the track, deep in thought, when I found myself in step beside Shorty, almost bumping into one of his flapping arms. I would have walked on had I not glanced at him, noticing the sadness radiating from his face. I could tell he didn't want to be hurt any more, and I felt sad myself.

"Hello." I said, staying beside him just beyond his flapping arms. His features never changed, he was ignoring me. "I've been watching you," I went on. "I see you doing this every day, and I hear the other guys talk. They think you're crazy. They all think you're crazy." His arms raised and lowered over invisible winds. "It's none of my business, I know, but I don't think you're crazy. So I want to know, why ar3 you doing this? What are you trying to prove?"

"I want to go home," he said without looking at me. His voice was like a mummy's, dusty, a million years old.

"Yeah, we all want to go home," I said. "Who doesn't? But you won't get home by acting nuts. This won't get you home. They'll know you aren't crazy, and even if they thought you were, they'd keep you any way. So how will this get you home?"

"Fly," he said.

I walked silently for a moment, wanting to walk away and forget him, but, despite his words, his actions, and everything else about him, I just couldn't believe he was nuts. "We both know you're talking crap," I said. "Why are you playing this game?"

Shorty stopped and turned towards me, gripping his feathers against his chest, his blue eyes bitter and desperate, his shoulders shaking. "I want to go home!" he rasped. "I want to see my Ma and Pa! And I really am going home! I'm gonna fly home!" He raised his feathers between us, his eyes wide and all-seeing. "I'm gonna fly. I'm gonna do it. I've been watching the birds, studying how they do it. I discovered the theory of flight."

"Oh, for Chrissake!" I mumbled. "So you're gonna grab a bunch of feathers and fly away."

"The feathers," he whispered, gazing at his fists as though he noticed what they held for the first time. "Yeah, the feathers. That's where it started. One day I saw a feather. It was just lying there, and I picked it up, and I heard a voice. 'You can do it,' the voice said. 'You can fly home. If only you try, you can do it.' All I had to do was watch and learn, and someday I'd be flying. I wouldn't even need the feathers. I could leave them behind."

He glanced at me one more time, then he walked off, flapping his arms in slow-motion flight. I watched for a minute before turning and walking away.

He told the same story to everybody who asked. He was flying home. He discovered Shorty's version of the theory of flight. "But he doesn't have a home!" some of the guys said. "This is his home for the rest of his life. And his mother and father are dead. He has nobody out there for him. Nobody."

Hearing them talk, I could almost feel my tears welling up, not for myself, but for Shorty in his futile quest, and for all the Shortys always being hurt somewhere, living their own desperate lives, with no way out but their own theories of flight. I'd watch him walking the compound perimeter trail and look up at the razorwire atop the fences, and deep down inside, I really wanted him to fly.

One day I was walking on the yard when I saw five guys surrounding Shorty like a trap closing on its victim. For once, Shorty could not ignore his environment and the people around him. His wings lowered as he gazed from face to face. The men started yelling and shoving him back and forth. He was in trouble, and he knew he couldn't fly out of this one.

One of them slapped him, and feathers fluttered to the ground as Shorty raised his arms against the blows to his face and head. I saw him double over from a punch to the gut, and something inside me snapped. I ran towards them, shouting, "Stop it! That's enough!" When I reached them, I shoved one of them down. The others, stopped hitting Shorty, threw him on the ground, and turned to me, one of them grabbing my t-shirt in two meaty fists and shaking me.

"This has nothing to do with you," he said, pulling me closer to his face. For a moment, Shorty looked up from the ground at me, blood streaming from his lips, his eyes wide. One of the men turned back to him, kicked the air out of him. "Walk away," the inmate said. "Get out of here.'

"No,' I said. "He's my friend."

"He's nobody's friend. He's nobody." And as he held me, too strong for me to get away, the others kept kicking Shorty.

It was over in a minute that seemed like forever. The meaty fists released my t-shirt, and they walked off in different directions like nothing happened. I knelt, took off my t-shirt, and dabbed at Shorty's bloody face. He gazed questioningly at me through swollen eyelids. "You gotta stop this craziness," I told him as I helped him stand.

"It's not crazy," he said, wiping a wrist against a swollen lip.

"Yes, it is," I said. "It's crazy. But you aren't. And it won't help you to play crazy. Look what just happened."

Shorty stared at me, his eyes full of anger. He knelt and started picking up the feathers, some of them trampled into the dirt. I sighed and knelt to help him. "No, I'm not crazy," he said, straightening the shaft of a feather. "And I will fly home." He looked at me with complete confidence.

I watched him stand and walk away, and, in another minute, he was flapping his arms again. I saw a feather in the grass, and was about to pick it up, but it seemed like a futile thing to do. I stood and went back to the dorm.

Shorty was still out there when autumn arrived. I could still see the bruises on his arms and face from that day, and sometimes it seemed as though the bruises refused to go away, they were still there weeks later. It rained, and Shorty kept walking, flapping his arms, both fists full of bouquets of feathers. Nobody really watched him much anymore, the novelty had worn off, but once in a while I would see an inmate look up from a card game and watch Shorty pass a dorm window and say, "He says, pretty soon, pretty soon, he says." And in the sun, or the rain, or the coldest days, Shorty was out there, flapping his arms, never giving up on the theory of flight.

It was about that time that I had an infectious boil that would not go away no matter what they did at the infirmary, and I had to go to RMC for a checkup, blood tests and treatment. They woke me around three in the morning, took me to the holding area and handcuffed and shackled me, then put me on the prison van. I would be gone all day, and the way they worked things, nobody would know I was gone except for administration, who always corrected the counts.

Another man, handcuffed and shackled like me, climbed into the van and took the bench across from me. Normally a dozen men went to RMC each day, but today it was just the two of us. It was dark and I was too tired to start a conversation. I dozed sitting up, something you learn in prison, and I dreamed of places I had never been, or never would see, mountains, trees, oceans, deserts. I was groggy and disoriented when the morning was beginning to turn bright. My ass and back were sore and my legs numb. I shifted around and stretched as best as I could. The van's engine droned on, and the two guards in front, a cage between us, were not talking. Fumes seeped through the rusty floor.

When I looked at the other man's hands for the first time, I saw two handcuffed fists, both of them full of feathers, robin, hawk, pigeon, dove, raven. I looked up. Shorty was watching me, smiling, a real smile this time.

I still felt a profound sadness come over me. "They hurt you pretty bad," I said. "Didn't they?"

"You mean the rapes?" he asked. His frankness shocked me, And I was embarrassed, because that wasn't what I meant, but then again, I thought, maybe it was. Shorty frowned and shook his head. "They been raping me for ten years, from prison to prison. Once they make a punk outta you, your reputation goes ahead of you, and it never stops."

"I'm sorry," I said. "Ten years is a long time."

"I got a life sentence when I was fourteen," he sighed. "I ran away from home and ended up hitchhiking with a man who made me his partner. We robbed a few gas stations and liquor stores. He had a gun. I was with him when the robbery went south. He killed a cop, and when we were arrested, I kept my mouth shut, like he told me, but he turned state's evidence, testified against me. He later got a note to me. He said he figured they wouldn't give me the death sentence because I was so young. Somehow he got five years.

"When I finally got to prison, I didn't last twenty-four hours before I was turned out like a whore. Back then I was scared, horrified, in shock, in pain. Nowadays I don't feel nothing. When I transferred here, I thought things would be different."

I lowered my gaze to avoid his eyes, thinking that maybe I shouldn't be hearing this, and then I noticed his arms for the first time. I had a scar on each wrist. He had over a dozen scars on each forearm, with one long scar from bicep to wrist, probably the closest one to death. You could see the dots where the thread went through, where they saved him again and again. His arms were healed hamburger.

Shorty noticed my gaze. "All of that for nothing," he said, raising his arms. "They just kept sewing me up and putting me back on the compound. But now I'm flying home."

I looked back into his eyes. "Don't start that shit again," I whispered. "Not now."

He stared at me, and his smile faded. His fingers untensed, and feathers dropped from his hands like autumn leaves. Tears welled up and streamed down his cheeks. "I'm glad you were there," he said. "I'm glad you were there. You know, I got knocked down a lot of times. But nobody ever helped me stand again. Nobody until you came."

"It's okay," I said. "I just wish I coulda stopped them."

Shorty glanced at his empty hands. "I figured if I started acting crazy, they'd leave me alone. And you know?" He looked up at me. I was mostly right. Mostly." He cleared his throat as though trying to get rid of his raspy voice. "I had to do something. This would be the last time I would be on any compound."

"What are you talking about?" I asked.

"I got leukemia."

"What?"

"Leukemia. Cancer of the bone marrow and blood. I was diagnosed that way a while back. Now I'm going to the hospital to stay. To stay and…"

"Die?" I asked. "But couldn't you get treatment for it?"

"Yeah, I coulda," he said. "They coulda started treatment on me a long time ago, after the first diagnosis, but I said no. They can sew me up without my permission, but if I don't sign their papers, they can't treat me for this.

They can't force me. Not this time. So now I'm flying home to see my Ma and Pa."

He grinned, tears running down his cheeks, and then I was crying, too. We sat there, feeling the sorrow between us, and I reached out and gripped his hands in mine. And just for a little while, neither of us was lonely.

Later that day, I rode back from RMC in the prison van by myself. It was only then that I realized that I didn't know Shorty's real name. When I glanced at the floor of the van, I saw the feathers, and I knew I would never forget him.

It was dark when I finally got back. An officer opened the van door and unlocked my handcuffs and shackles. "Where did you get all the feathers?" he asked.

"I found them," I muttered.

"You inmates are all crazy," he said.

He guided me through the gates. Both of us were glancing at the stars as he escorted me back to my dorm, and as we walked, he never noticed when I droped the feathers on the ground in a pile.

Tomorrow, someone on his way to breakfast would find them, and he would remember Shorty, and he would wonder if he really did discover the theory of flight.

And who knows?

Maybe he did.

FIVE   1/'97   T. NEWTON SCHULTZ

FEATHERS ON THE SOLAR WIND

A heavy winter rainstorm drummed the buildings of Hesiod Correctional Institution the night Daniel Martin Pinkston finally died in the AIDS dormitory. It was two a.m. when four corrections officers in protective clothing wheeled him on a gurney out of the iron door for the last time. Kenneth "South Philly" Johnson and Willie Norton looked up from their card game. John Mohammed "Deathrow" Rollins spared one glance at the closing door before he began his cleanup duties.

"That's two we lost since midnight," Willie said as he began shuffling cards. "First Parker Calloway, now Pinkston. You know when it goes like this there'll be a third."

"Third time's a charm," Johnson said. "I'll put up a pack of Lucky Strikes that Morgan will go next."

"Be quiet, man," Deathrow snarled. "You don't respect death and you don't respect God." He was stripping off Pinkston's soiled sheets and double-bagged them in red contagious bags. "And keep it down! These sick men are trying to sleep!"

"Sorry, man," Willis said. "We just can't sleep."

Deathrow looked up as he scrubbed the waterproof mattress with bleach. "I can get you some sleeping pills if you want."

"No need, brother," Willie said. "I'll just play with South Philly here and let him tell me his life story. I'll be asleep in fifteen minutes." He nodded at Johnson, who'd spent most of his life in South Philadelphia before coming to Florida and landing a bid for armed robbery and kidnaping. Now in his mid-forties, he was an animate human skeleton, his neon-white skin spotted by Kaposi's sarcoma. Willie, at fifty, was just as thin, his black skin dry and flaky, most of his graying hair gone.

"But if you need something, you tell me," Deathrow said, pointing his thumb at his chest. "You got a problem, I'll take care of it."

He returned to his duties, and the older men watched him for a moment. Like them, Deathrow had HIV, but he was still big and muscular, his voice deep like James Earl Jones's, his energy and patience endless. At nineteen he had killed two police officers, and he'd spent twelve years shooting one writ after another into the courts from death row, doing all he could to keep from making that last walk to Old Sparky, Florida's electric chair. He'd finally got his sentence changed to life, but one year later he had the virus.

After six months of bitter denial he converted to Islam, and though he could have spent years on the compound until full-blown AIDS set in, he volunteered to live in the AIDS dorm to work as a nurse's aide. He humbly performed all the duties shunned by the officers and the doctors and nurses, who visited the dorm as little as possible. He emptied the catheter bags, changed soiled linen, and gave bed baths to men too weak to bathe themselves. He held men up and fed them, checked them for bedsores, and his muscular killer's hands massaged sore spots to keep them from becoming bedsores. His prison job required him to work eight hours a day, five days a week, but he never stopped working as long as he wasn't asleep.

"I wish I had that kind of energy," South Philly said, watching Deathrow carry the contagion bags to the laundry.

"You got plenty of energy," Willie said as he dealt the cards. He noticed Jimmy Long across the dorm climbing out of bed into his wheelchair. "Look at you, up all night partying and playing cards. You're as lively as a feather on the wind."

"Give me three cards," answered South Philly. "And hold your sarcasm. You're full of shit and bad jokes, and your farts stink like roadkill when they float over to my bunk." He examined his cards and bet two tailor-mades - Lucky Strikes - while he puffed a cigarette he'd rolled himself. "Deathrow had to slide my locker between our bunks so we could play. My strength is draining."

"At least you don't have to wear adult diapers." Willie reached for his Chesterfields. "I'll see your two and raise you three. Now when you ask me if I'm going to wear briefs or boxer shorts tomorrow, I answer, 'Depends.' Jimmie's coming for a visit."

"What got you up?" South Philly nodded at Jimmie. "You're usually sawing logs about now."

"Can't sleep," Jimmie mumbled.

"Deal you in?" Willie asked.

"I'll watch," Jimmie said. Though he looked healthier than the two older men, his legs were quickly growing weak. The doctors couldn't figure out why. Under the red ceiling lights, his face looked as if he had a rash.

"I call." South Philly set his cards down, two queens, ace high. Willie showed him three deuces before scooping up his cigarettes. "Damn."

"You never traveled enough to play against good players," Willie said.

"Well, I won't get a chance to travel now."

"Oh, you are, in a way," Willie said. "The earth is twenty-four thousand miles around, and it spins like a sonovabitch. You're going about a thousand miles an hour and don't even know it."

"Who give a shit," Jimmie growled.

South Philly looked at him. "Homey, you in a bad moon or something?"

"I know what it is," Willie said, putting on his state-issued glasses and gazing at Jimmie. "Pinkston died tonight, and he's the one who gave you AIDS, isn't he?"

"Man, I'm no fag!"

"You two were cellmates," Willie went on. "You can't tell me you didn't get some mud on your turtle."

"Man, just shut your fuckin' mouth!" Jimmie yelled, his cheeks redder than normal.

"Watch your mouth, bro," South Philly said, scooping up the cards. "We didn't invite you over here, so if you want to cop an attitude, take it back to bed."

"And don't get defensive," Willie added. "None of us got in this dorm by sharing a needle or getting a blood transfusion."

"Man," Jimmie shook his head. "I just don't want to die like him. This place stinks like a busted meat locker, people dying every other day, we're fenced off from the rest of the compound, and all we can do is wait to die. I don't want to die like this, I want to die like a man!"

"Shut up, punk," South Philly hissed, rising up on bony legs hidden in nylon pajama bottoms. "This *is* how a man dies. Look at me. My mother writes me every week, but here I am, I got myself locked away from her and dying. You think she's proud of me? You think I'm proud of myself? My father has Alzheimer's and she's trying to take care of him, and she probably wonders every day who's going to die first, me or my father. But this is how a man dies, with the Ninja or Alzheimer's or cancer. If you wanted to throw yourself on a grenade and save your buddies and die a hero's death, you should've joined the Marines."

"South Philly, stop running your jaw," Wyman Reed said, walking through the maze of bunks toward them. "If Deathrow comes back and catches you waking up his patients, he'll gag you and tie you to your bed."

"You guys are waking the dead over here," Carl "Smokey" Dukes said. "Can't you keep your voices down?" Wyman and Smokey wore their blankets over their shoulders. Like Jimmie, who had a sweatshirt over his pajama top, they couldn't put up with the cold air in the dorm. The heaters were in the ceiling instead of the floor, and the slow-turning ceiling fans couldn't quite get the warm air down. Willie and South Philly both had fevers that night, and sat on their bunks shirtless, their ribsy chests like washboards.

"I'm sorry, Smokey," Willie said. "We won't holler and hoot again. This was supposed to be a quiet party. Go ahead back to sleep."

"Hell with that," Wyman said. "Deal me in." He held up a pack of generic cigarettes.

"You up to a game this late?" South Philly asked, shuffling the cards. Wyman nodded. "Smokey?"

"I'm all out, homey. I'll just watch," Smokey pulled an empty wheelchair closer as Wyman sat on the bed next to South Philly. Wyman was a tall black man who hadn't yet shown signs of the virus, but three long bouts of pneumonia had weakened him. He couldn't live in open population anymore. Sometimes he'd go outside and stand by the fence, watching inmates play basketball in the distance. He never stayed out long, because it was only a matter of time before he'd be noticed and become the target of insults and catcalls. This irritated him no end: at least a third of the others were also infected, though outwardly healthy, and they, too, would be landing in the AIDS dorm.

"You know they took Pinkston and Calloway out tonight." Willie said, rolling a cigarette.

"Hospital?" Smokey asked.

"Morgue," replied Willie.

"Two?" Wyman whispered. South Philly nudged him to cut the cards. "Jesus Christ, that's not good."

"Don't take the Lord's name in vain, man," Smokey told him.

"Save your church for Sunday," South Philly snapped.

"Philly thinks someone else will go before the dawn comes up," Willie said.

"This is too morbid," Jimmie whispered.

"Why three?" Wyman said.

South Philly began dealing. "It goes in threes, Wyman. If two die during the week, it's a sure bet a third will go before that week is up. Just listen." He held up his hand for silence. The sounds of snoring men mixed with the whirring of the fans and the steady tattoo of rain on the roof, but behind this was the rattling, deep breath of several men struggling through pneumonia. "You hear that? We got Death waiting in the wings. It's that kind of night."

"Man, you're getting a bad attitude," Smokey said. He was feeling uneasy, as were Wyman and Jimmie. "You're not psychic."

"I don't know," South Philly said. "But that's the way it goes, people die in threes. I used to work in a nursing home in Pennsylvania. Weeks would go by, and then three old people would go in one week. It was strange, no reason for it, but there you are."

"C'mon, man, let's play cards," said Wyman. "Your talk's getting too creepy. And I don't believe it anyway."

"What?" Smokey whispered. "That someone else will die tonight?"

"Far as I'm concerned, that's a given," South Philly replied. "I propose we each bet on *who* will die."

"Man, you're sick," Smokey growled.

"Ashes to ashes, dustballs to dustballs," Willie said. "Even the Bible admits that, Smokey. I read my King James daily, too, you know."

"So we pick someone in the dorm?" asked Wyman. "One of our sick patients?"

South Philly set his cards down, his face serious. "No, that's too easy. Way too easy. I predict it will be one of us here." The other men gazed at him in silence. Even Willie looked shaken. "I say we bet one pack of tailor-mades each, we each choose a different one among us, place our bets, and wait for the dawn."

A dreadful silence fell over them, a silence like an arctic night. Smells of the dorm wrapped around them, smells of sickness and sweat. "It's sinful," Smokey said.

"Sin got us here thus far," Willie mimicked, "and sin will lead us home."

"Don't try me, Willie!"

"You fucked a punk like the rest of us," Willie said. "Don't give me any of your self-righteous crap, Smokey.

South Philly has hit on something. I don't know what, but I'm game."

"You want to die?" Smokey asked. "Is that it?"

"No, it's not," Willie said. "But I'm going to die anyway, whether I like it or not. And if I gotta die, I might as well play one last game with Death himself."

Wyman nodded. "Yeah, maybe. But I don't think no one's gonna kick off in our little circle. What if it happens, Philly, and it's not one of us?"

"Then nobody wins, and we all keep our cigarettes, and die of lung cancer instead." South Philly looked from man to man. "In fact, the way I see it, winning and losing are both desirable. You win, you get the cigarettes. You lose, you get out of the goddamn dorm."

This time Smokey didn't complain. Jimmie was staring into his lap, gripping his wheels. At twenty-five, he resembled a little boy awaiting the whipping of his life. Wyman looked intrigued but scared, as though he had just been invited to play a game of Russian roulette and knew he was too tempted to refuse. "All right," he said. "Let's go for it."

"It's not right!" cried Smokey.

"Shut the fuck up!" someone yelled from across the dorm. "I'm sleeping!"

"You're all a bunch of fools!" Smokey whispered. "No wonder you're in this mess."

"You're in the same predicament, my man," Willie answered. "And you fall as short of the pearly gates as the rest of us. I know more about you than you might think."

"And what's that supposed to mean!"

"It means you don't have much leeway to complain about anybody else," Willie took off his glasses and stared at him. "Now, if you don't like what we're doing here, go back to bed. I'm tired of your mouth."

Smokey was silent, but he stared back until Willie looked at the others.

"Boys, I don't know how real this all is, but I swear I feel spirits in the air. I've been scared of dying since I popped out of my momma's womb, but just tonight I'd like to look Death in the eye and prove I'm a good sport."

He put his glasses back on. "Now there's science and there's the spirit world. According to science, we are mostly made up of water, but we are what's known as a carbon-based life form. Carbon is that black stuff left over after we burn something, and a friend once told me that no planet naturally has carbon on it anywhere. Carbon comes from the sun and other stars."

"So what's your point?" Wyman asked, still holding his cards.

"My point," Willie said, examining his hand, "is that we are made of stardust. And when we are dead, out carbon molecules go into the soil and become part of other life forms. So you see, part of us goes on, just like how the carbon molecules of other living things are in us now, and how all of it comes from the big burning stars in the sky."

"So there's bits and pieces of dinosaurs in us, too," South Philly said.

"Something like that. But now we're heading slowly back to our old carbon selves. I like to think we're heading back to the sun myself, we're going back to be cremated into nonexistence, nothing but that damn stardust. And if I go, I might as well play over the sunspots, and this little bet is how we can do it, how we can be feathers on the solar wind for a while, floating and dancing on the music of the cosmos before the final incineration."

"Willie, you sure know a lot of big words and ideas for a black man," South Philly snorted.

Willie grinned at his old friend. "If it makes you too uncomfortable, Philly, I could talk like Aunt Jemima for a while."

"It's all still a lot of bunk," Smokey said.

"If you think so," Wyman answered, "then you make the first bet."

Smokey opened his mouth, about to refuse, but then he looked around. "A pack of smokes, you said?"

"Exactly," South Philly told him. "But you got to pick one of us."

Smokey stoked his chin. "Okay, I bet a pack of rip that old Willie here will die first."

The other men looked at each other.

"Man, that's slimy," South Philly said. "Just because he told you about your ass . . ."

"He done right," said Willie. "And he chose well. I look like I'm halfway to the crypt, the way I see it."

"And who do you choose?" South Philly asked.

"I place my bet on Wyman," Willie said. "No offense."

"None taken," Wyman looked a bit shaken. The game was too real to him.

"Wyman's the healthiest one here, and I got a feeling too much health is not always a good thing," Willie explained.

"That's crazy," Smokey said.

"Yeah, it sounds sorta crazy, but I figure I'll go against the odds."

"And you, Wyman?" South Philly asked.

Wyman looked around from face to face. "I don't think any of us are going to die, leastways not for tonight. And I'd hate to name someone and actually have them die and me win cigarettes on their body. I just don't know."

"Yeah, it feels a little dirty, I admit," Willie said. "But I feel the spirits kicking tonight, and me, I gotta dance with Death, just one slow dance. If you don't feel up to it . . ."

Wyman shook his head. "Philly, I put my pack on you. God knows, I hope I lose, but I'm gonna play this game."

South Philly smiled at him. "No hard feelings, brother. Tonight I don't feel afraid. I don't even care. But I put my smokes on Jimmie."

"Oh no, man," Jimmie gasped. "Hell no, man! I'm not gonna die tonight!"

"Well, if you don't, then I lose. You got nothing to worry about."

"Change your bet, Philly. Change it!"

"You're my pick, bro. Now your turn."

"I'm not gonna."

"Smokey's left," South Philly said. "Though he looks like he'll live a good long time, but you can never tell."

"Back off, man," Smokey said. "The boy doesn't need any help."

"Man, I'm through with this shit," Jimmie said, and wheeled off.

"We scared him," Wyman said. "Maybe we shouldn't have done this."

"It's done," South Philly replied. "The boy needs to cope with what's happening."

Jimmie's wheelchair clipped a steel bunk as he turned and headed for the shower room. They watched him disappear through the door.

"Sirius is high in the sky tonight," Willie mumbled, "and the natives are restless."

"Sirius?" South Philly asked. "What's that?"

"Sirius, the Dog Star, the harbinger of death. The brightest spot in the sky, if the moon isn't out."

"Putting out carbon molecules," Wyman said, picking up his cards. "Maybe if we get enough carbon molecules, we can all be made whole again."

The shower room was a long hallway illuminated by filthy neon lights. The walls and floor were covered by worn white and tan tiles. A chest-high wall ran along the middle, with sinks and mirrors on both sides. To the right were a dozen stainless-steel toilets, and an equal number of metal urinals. To the left were a dozen showerheads, with two specially built showers to accommodate the handicapped.

Jimmie rolled his wheelchair through the meat locker-cold room to the farthest sink. He looked into his haunted eyes in the bent steel mirror, his rash-covered cheeks. He turned on the cold water and let it run while he reached beneath his sweatshirt and pulled out two bottles of pills - Pinkston's pain pills, which he'd stolen before the officers had come to take Pinkston away. When he heard somebody come in, he quickly stuffed the bottles out of sight between his legs.

One of the showers came on. Someone couldn't sleep, he thought. He was shivering from the cold, but he got one of the plastic bottles open and poured six pills into his palm, tossed them into his mouth and leaned over the sink, scooping water into his mouth. He had dumped six more pills into his hand when he noticed steam filling the room.

Something seemed out of kilter. He gripped the pills in one hand and with the other pulled himself up to a standing position. He gazed at the naked figure under the spray of hot water, and his weak legs nearly gave out. "Oh my God," he whispered.

"Give me two cards," Wyman said, setting two cards on the locker. "I know what you're talking about, us under the influence of that star."

"Sirius," Willie said, "*Canis Major.*"

"Just a star," Smokey said.

"With stardust," South Philly added.

Smokey pulled his blanket closer around him, glancing at Deathrow, who was going from bed to bed emptying catheter bags into a plastic urinal bottle, writing down the amount, then pouring it into a bucket before moving to the next bag.

"We'd be in a bad fix without Deathrow," Wyman said. "That man's a saint. If I could choose one person to survive this dorm, it would be him."

"Maybe in the parallel world, he's out free and clear of the virus," Willie said. "Erwin Schrödinger once mentioned that there might be a whole series of different dimensions where the same people were living different lives."

"That doesn't help me none now, does it?" South Philly said. "Maybe next time I'll try a different dimension."

Wyman looked over his shoulder. "Jimmie must be off beating his meat, he ain't come back yet."

"He's just taking a dump," South Philly said.

"He could've passed out," Smokey said. "Let me check on him." He rose from the wheelchair and stalked off, his blanket dragging the floor.

"He needs to deal with things," South Philly said. "Maybe we all do. I'll see your two cigarettes and raise you two, Willie."

In the shower room, Jimmie stared over the wall at the naked inmate in the steam. The two bottles dropped on the floor. Pills fell from his sweaty palm. He was staring at Daniel Pinkston, very much alive, young and muscular as he was when they'd first met, not in his later, emaciated state. Jimmie felt he was hallucinating, but Daniel stared right at him, smiling. The tiny metal ring pierced his left nipple, and over that was the emblem of the Florida State Seminoles, tattooed where it always had been.

"But you're dead," he whispered.

"What does a small thing like that matter to anyone?" It was Daniel's voice.

His mannerisms, his movements, everything; Jimmie felt sick. "I never even tried to say good-bye."

"I never did like that word," Daniel said.

"My God, Dan, do you forgive me?"

"For what?"

"For every way I wronged you. For ignoring you in this dorm while you were lying there, dying and pissing your bed, and you wanted to talk, I could see it in your eyes . . ."

"There's nothing for me to forgive," Daniel said. "It's you who must forgive yourself." He turned, and Jimmie followed his gaze. Smokey stood in the doorway, his mouth open, his eyes wide. Steam filled the room in billowing clouds. "Only you can forgive yourself. Nobody else." He said this while staring at Smokey.

South Philly picked up the cigarettes, his winnings. Wyman shuffled the cards. They turned their heads when Deathrow gave a yell, stepping out of Jimmie's way as he wheeled into the room. "Next time you run over my foot, I'll pour this bucket of piss on your damn head!" he shouted before continuing to the shower room.

"I saw him," Jimmie banged against the bunk, gripping Wyman's arm. The cards fluttered to the floor. "I saw Danny's ghost! Danny Pinkston."

"Brother, what got into you?" Willie asked.

"Danny didn't give me AIDS, I gave it to him!" Jimmie cried. "I swear! It wasn't his fault! I was punked out when I first came to prison. When I started doing Danny, I didn't even know I had the virus! I should've died first, I had the virus first."

"The truth comes out," South Philly mumbled.

"Easy on the boy, Philly," Willie said. "I believe he really did see a ghost. I told you the spirits were restless tonight."

"I asked him to forgive me," Jimmie gasped, his voice trailing. "But he said I had to forgive myself."

"That's the first thing you said tonight that makes sense," South Philly said.

"Wyman, I need your help."

Deathrow stood silhouetted in the doorway. His voice was soft, almost a whisper, but the authority in it carried over the roomful of snoring men. "After I tell the bosses." He nodded at the two officers sleeping on chairs in the Plexiglas-enclosed officers' station. "After I tell them, I'll need you to help me with the body."

"Body?"

"Smokey — he cut his throat with a razor blade," Deathrow said.

Jimmie stared after him, dumbstruck, as he went to wake the officers. Wyman gazed sadly at the empty shower room doorway. South Philly angrily picked up his cards. "Third time's a charm."

"Why?" Jimmie whispered.

"He had a dirty little secret," Willie said. "Parker Calloway told me before he died. Smokey turned state's evidence on his brother, got his brother the chair, when it was him who did the killing. When you saw Daniel Pinkston's ghost, he probably saw his brother's ghost. Only he wasn't capable of forgiving himself."

"You should've took that bet," Wyman said bitterly. "You'd have scored a few packs of cigarettes." He rose and headed off to help Deathrow.

"That could've been me," Jimmie said, feeling tears well up, remembering Daniel when he first met him. He leaned over, weary. Willie, suddenly cold, pulled his blanket over his bare shoulders. South Philly shuffled the cards.

FIVE   1/ '97   T. NEWTON SCHULTZ

KADDISH

PEN America Fielding Dawson Citation
for a Body of Work 2003

Blackbird singing in the dead of night,
Take these broken wings and learn to fly,
All your life…
You were only waiting for this moment to arrive.
> **---Blackbird**
> **---John Lennon and Paul McCartney**

For last year's words belong to last year's language,
And next year's words await another voice.
> **---Little Gidding**
> **---T. S. Eliot**

He stood by his cell window in his boxers, feeling the damp morning air against his chest as he inhaled the scent of orange blossoms.   It was March, and he was a little more than twenty-four hours away from walking out the gates of Baker Correctional Institution, the prison near Olustee, Florida, that he knew like his own skin.

At times like this, Jared Aesop Martin remembered working on his uncle's Pennsylvania farm picking tomatoes in the morning fog, the plant juices staining his hands black where he touched the vines, and the smells of the rich humus, the rotten tomatoes that had fallen on the ground, the hay under the plants used for mulching, and the sounds of morning birds. During his fifteen years of prison, when the television noise, fights and shakedowns all threatened to crush him, he brought up those memories to help him cope. Now he wondered what kinds of difficulties he would face in the freeworld as an ex-felon, and if he would recall the memories of prison to get through them. He smiled at the absurdity.

The screeching of Sergeant White's static-distorted voice over the P. A. speakers in the hallway interrupted his thoughts. "Work call! Work call! Make sure your cells are clean! Inspection today! Work call!" Jared quickly pulled on his prison blues and brogans, ran his fingers through his close-cropped gray hair, and locked his locker, then checked to make sure his cellie's bunk and locker were okay. Charles "C. J." Jackson was a blond-haired old con, a good cellmate who often went to work early as Coach Denver's clerk.

Jared stepped out of his cell and locked the door, then headed down the wing. He lived at the end of the second floor north wing in F-Dormitory, a two-story T-shaped building with three wings going north, south and east. As he pushed through the fire doors and moved into the flow of inmates through the dayroom, he spotted Samuel "Stormie" Lawson just heading down the stairwell. He hung back, feeling a sudden jolt of hatred as he watched the old con disappear with the crowd down the stairs. Jared had avoided him successfully for three years, even after Stormie had moved into his dorm. Stormie had killed two inmates early on during his twenty-six years of prison, and despite his age, he was still strong enough and mean-spirited enough to hurt someone. Even so, Jared could see that he was beginning to show his age. He walked slower, hunched over more, talked less, and lately he seemed withdrawn, deep in thought.

When enough time had passed, Jared headed downstairs past the officer's Plexiglas-enclosed wicker and out the door, nursing a core of relief in his chest. He felt the last day of his incarceration like a distant thunderhead coming his way. Working at his assigned job one last time, he raked and picked up litter around the handball courts, but the day was going way too fast. After work and dinner, he soaked and scrubbed in the shower, then walked back to his cell.

He didn't see his attackers. They were too fast, jumping him from behind as he pushed through his door. He was shoved to the floor, his towel thrown over his head as his wrists were pulled painfully behind his back. A dozen fists pounded his ribs and back.

"We don't like faggots like you!"

"You're gonna remember us, Cracker!"

"When you hit the streets, you can sell your ass and send us cigarette money!"

"Don't go telling the womenfolk out there you're straight, punk! You might as well go back to your favorite leather bar and put on your old dress!"

"Don't come back here, asshole!"

"Don't ever come back!"

Jared tried to break free, but he was laughing too hard, as were his opponents. When they let him up, he gripped his sore ribs and looked in the mirror. "You sons-a-bitches!" he growled, then laughed again. They had rouged his cheeks with contraband lipstick stolen from a female guard. "You girls are just mad because a real man is goin' home!" he snorted, wiping his cheeks with the back of his hand.

Although the bruises and pain were real, the mock beating was Jared's going-away gift, his friends' way to tell him not to return to prison. Jared looked from face to face---Luis "Buzzard" Gonzalez, Robert "Gonzo" Gordon, Theo Spencer, and Sammy Logan---already feeling the loss of leaving his friends behind. His cellie, C. J., pushed into the cell carrying two large brown bags. "Your sendoff wouldn't be complete without a Last Supper, Homeboy!"

As Logan, the only Black man in the group, urged Jared to the cell window, the others set clean towels on the two foootlockers and began laying out the food. C. J. ran his out-of-the-locker canteen by buying food and supplies from the prison canteen, then selling them at a fifty percent profit to inmates in the dorm who would be getting money soon. Despite a number of deadbeats, he still made a handsome profit and was able to finance his tobacco and coffee habits.

"So what's the first thing you're gonna do when you get your goat-smelling ass outta here?" Gonzo asked as he and Theo sorted cans of lukewarm sodas, packs of cookies, potato chips, crackers, and icing-coated packaged honeybuns called "six-fifties".

Jared sipped a soda. "Oh, I don't know. Maybe get a double-thick deep-dish pizza with everything, a pitcher of beer, and a little pussy on the side."

"Goddam!" Buzzard, the old gray-haired Mexican, snorted. "I been down so long I didn't even know they moved that thing!" He brought out the peanuts, candy bars, and a large, brown, greasy paper bag full of Chaingang Goulash---a specialty made of Ramen oriental noodles, mayonnaise, packaged tuna, chunks of cheese, crushed Cheetos, and other odds and ends stolen from Food Service.

"Did you ever say anything to Stormie about your going?" Gonzo asked cautiously, rubbing his bald scalp.

A shadow fell over Jared's face. "Why would I want to do that?" His light blue eyes narrowed. They all felt his mood change.

"Yeah, after the way Stormie betrayed him, why would he?" Buzzard explained. He rolled a cigarette and lit it. Jared quit smoking three years ago, but he never complained when someone else lit up.

"What betrayal?" Theo asked.

"Stormie and Jared were solid once," Buzzard explained. "Good amigos. Real tight. Until three years ago, when Stormie put down on him, started a fight, just about beat the shit out of him. And when the guards showed up, Stormie rolled, got them both locked up for a month."

"Jared was having a rough time back then," Logan added, taking the cigarette C. J. offered him and lighting up. "Good looking out, Bro. Anyhow, Jared fell off the wagon, stopped going to A. A., got back into weed, and when Stormie started the fight, Jared was too strung out to defend himself properly."

"I doubt I could've beat him on a good day," Jared mumbled.

"Point is," Logan went on, "they wouldn't have been locked up in the first place if Stormie hadn't run his mouth to the Captain. They both got a month in Confinement. Stormie had hit the hole a dozen times over the years, but it was the first time for ol' Jared here. Not only was he claustrophobic, he was also going cold turkey in a cell by himself."

"Poor ol' boy was bawlin' all night long for his momma, keeping all the other Confinement boys awake," Buzzard taunted.

"Fuck you, Buzzard!" Jared snapped, tossing the empty soda can at him. He laughed too, but he could still remember how bad it was, huddling on his rack in the confinement cell, trembling and sweating like an oversaturated mop, feeling his breath being crushed from his body. Even three years later, he felt the raw terror like it had been branded into his flesh.

"Stupid marecon!" Buzzard grumbled. "Pulling shit like that!"

"But Confinement broke you of your addiction," Theo said.

"I slipped one last time after that," Jared said. "Did a little joint, but I learned my lesson."

"Jared really impressed the guards!" C. J. said. "A couple days after he smoked the weed, the brownshirts woke him at one A. M. for a piss test. By the next morning, everybody on the Yard knew."

"You tested positive?" Theo asked.

"Nah," Jared said. "I tested negative. I 'studied' for the test."

"He drank a lot of water," C. J. explained. "He had fifteen minutes before the guards escorted him to Medical to piss in the cup. He gulped down cup after cup of water to dilute his urine and any traces of THC. And it worked. His test came out negative, and he didn't get locked up. Just one problem. He pissed his pants on the way to Medical!" They all laughed. "He never touched anything stronger than a Tylenol after that!"

Conversation waned as the men finished off the goulash and other snacks. Jared felt morose as he watched his friends. Gonzo and Buzzard were lifers. C. J., Logan, and Theo had years to go before they got out. His eyes felt watery. "You guys are really important to me," he said.

"Yeah," Theo grunted. "Let's just see you send just one fuckin' post card when you get out!"

"I'm serious," Jared said. "I coulda made it through this bid on my own, but I had a lot of help, and that made things easier. I can't leave without sayin..."

"Hold on, Homeboy," Gonzo said. "You're way too sentimental for me right now. Kick my ass or steal my shit, but don't you say goodbye!"

"I wouldn't do that, Bro," Jared smirked, covering his tracks. "I was just gonna tell you I was gonna send you all T-Backs when I write so you fags can get more money for your fat asses!"

"You pinga!" Buzzard shouted as the others laughed. "You faggot! First girl you meet on the streets, you'll want to share recipes and decorating tips!"

"The important thing is you're getting out," Theo said.

A pall settled over the crowded cell. For the first time in three years Jared wanted a cigarette. "You know," Gonzo said, staring at the floor, "Stormie finally saw the Parole Man about six months ago."

"Fuck Stormie!" Buzzard snorted.

Jared felt a twinge. Stormie had a life with a quarter, a life sentence with twenty-five years mandatory time. Supposedly an inmate could see the Parole Man after the mandatory for a release date, say, five years down the road, but it usually didn't work that way. C. J. asked the question Jared was afraid to ask: "So what did he get?"

"He walked out of the interview like nothing happened," Gonzo went on. "Like nothing was wrong. But you could tell that something had whipped him real bad. Turns out they gave him a Buck Rogers date, 2095. You ask him about it, all he'll say is, you gotta die somewhere. But you can tell it's gnawing at him. He's looking at the fences these days the way he did in his first years. He's waiting."

"Waiting for what?" Theo asked.

"For the Parole Man," Gonzo answered. They all knew what he meant. When the fog rolled in--- the "Parole Man"---it provided the best conditions for a man to get over the fences and razorwire and escape.

"So what's the deal with this betrayal you all talk about, and what's so wrong with Stormie?" Theo asked.

They all glanced at Jared. It was his story, after all. He glanced around, then shrugged. "He's an old con," Jared said. "About fifty-five or so, a decade older than me. About ten years ago, he moved into my cell. Right from the get-go he hated my guts because I was only a 'newcock'--- I had five years in to his fifteen."

Jared slowly related the story of how Stormie started up like a rabid, menacing wolverine. He remembered it clearly. Stormie's gray hair was combed back with pomade, and his light blue eyes were predatory and watchful. When he took off his shirt, Jared saw that his muscled body was covered with images of Confederate flags, Rebel soldiers, naked women, skulls, demons and dragons. His chest and biceps were cut and thick. The long, gray scar that ran from throat to belly across his sternum was a memento of a triple bypass five years earlier. He was truly an old soldier.

From that first day they argued. When they weren't yelling, the silence was as thick as smoke. Often they threatened each other back and forth, but as long as Jared didn't throw the first punch, Stormie wouldn't fight. And Jared wouldn't throw the first punch; he knew he wouldn't have a chance against the old con. Even at his age, Stormie was a scrapper.

On three occasions, Stormie brought another inmate back to the cell and threw Jared out so they could throw fists to settle a dispute. All it took was an insult or comment directed at him. Stormie always won.

One day Stormie got into it with another old con named Mong. The fight started before Jared could get off his rack and out the door, and when it was over, Mong had a split lip and bruises all over, and once again, Stormie, sporting his own bruises, was victorious. But this time, someone didn't like it.

Two days later the three of them were handcuffed and taken to Captain Stark's office. Someone had sent him an unsigned note about the fight. Even though Mong and Stormie claimed they got their bruises playing a rough game of basketball, Stark wasn't buying it. He had his officers lead Stormie and Mong out so he could talk to Jared alone. "No sense worrying now," Stormie hissed at Mong, meaning he expected his roommate to run his mouth.

When they were gone, Captain Stark leaned over his desk. "I know everything," he said. "But I can't lock them up without a witness. An unsigned note just won't cut it. And if I can lock them up, they'll get a month in Confinement for fighting. But you were a witness to the fight---the note said so. I also know that you and Inmate Lawson don't get along, and you'd like to be rid of him." Jared stared at the paperweight on the desk, a black, shiny scorpion in a half-sphere of glass on a stack of interoffice memos. "You don't have to worry about Lawson getting back at you," Stark went on. "One more lock-up for fighting, and he gets a year in Close Management. He's had that coming. What do you say?"

Jared swallowed. "I don't know about any fight."

"Inmate Martin," Stark went on, his smile radiating hostility. "Maybe I forgot to mention I could lock you up for a six-month investigation. I know you're claustrophobic, and time in the Hole could really drive you nuts."

"You mean," Jared said, "you could lock a guy up for a month for fighting, but you can also lock him up six months for an investigation, for not doing nothing? That's fucking nuts!"

"So, do you have something to tell me?"

Jared stared back at him. He was trembling, sweating, just thinking about Confinement. As far as he was concerned, he didn't care one way or another what happened to Stormie, and he'd be glad to get him out of his cell. But even so, the fight between him and Mong was over, and none of the Captain's business. It didn't seem right to him.

"Yeah, I have something to tell you," Jared said. "That was one hell of a rough basketball game I saw them playing." He held eye contact with the Captain, smiling as sweat trickled down his back.

"You're full of shit, Martin," the Captain said. "A confinement cell is a miserable fucking place to spend your time."

Jared held his gaze steady. "Do what you gotta do, Captain."

In the end, they were all let free.

Later, back at his cell, Jared unlatched his locker to get out a library book when Stormie stepped through the door. "Martin. Look here." Jared stood up. They locked eyes. "I was wrong about you. I apologize. I misjudged you from day one. You did good telling the Captain it was a basketball game, even though he was threatening you with lockup."

"How'd you find out?" Jared asked.

"First off, I'm not in Confinement," Stormie said, smiling. His grill was worse than Ernest Borgnine's. "And second---Jack, the inmate orderly, had his ear on the Captain's door."

That was the day their friendship began, and it grew from that point on, even though in time they moved to different cells. When Jared began encouraging him, Stormie reluctantly went with him to the AA meetings. And Jared began working out with Stormie three days a week on the Weight Pile. For seven years they looked out for each other, worked with each other, watched each other's back, and usually where one went, the other eventually showed up.

Until Jared met Bobby "T-Bone" Webber. T-Bone was a good-ole-boy from Alabama who got caught running drugs in Florida. He was a fast talker and a willing listener, and he helped Jared get the job he wanted as head trustee in the Visiting Park. The job was a lot of work, but it had its perks, too. When the Foodservice Rep came in to restock the vending machines every Thursday, he gave Jared all the expired packaged sandwiches and junk food.

Jared's friendship with T-Bone drove a wedge between him and Stormie. Three months after Jared met T-Bone, he and Stormie got into the scrap that ended their friendship forever.

"And it burns me that he's in this dorm!" Jared finished. "I have to see him every fuckin' day, and it gnaws at me! I don't need him around! He had no business moving in here, the sonovabitch!"

"Seems to me he snitched on himself, too," Gonzo reflected. "Seems to me he made a helluva lot more trouble for himself. You both pulled box time, but you got out. They put Stormie on Close Management for a year. Now, why would Stormie tear his own ass like that?"

"Because he was a slimeball who went and showed his true colors!" Jared snapped, angry that his own integrity was being questioned. When he finally was released back into open population, he heard that Stormie got one year in C. M. With his ex-roommate off the compound, Jared called him everything from a punk and a jeffer to a brownnoser and a snitch.

A year later, when Stormie finally got out, his pasty-pale "confinement tan" made him look like a walking corpse. The first thing he heard on the Compound was how Jared had talked cash shit about him. By that time, all their mutual friends had polarized, half taking up for Stormie, half for Jared, and for a week they waited tensely to see if Stormie would dig up a knife and get some straightening. Jared, hearing the rumors, began worrying.

But Stormie didn't do a thing. He didn't even try to explain himself. To Jared, it was a nonverbal confirmation of what he said about the old con, but he was still gravely uneasy, always aware of Stormie's angry eyes watching him.

"Look here, Bro," Gonzo said. "I think you got him all wrong. Stormie's a good dude. You two are a lot alike. You both got heart and live by the old code. Sure, Stormie's a bug, and he gets into all sorts of fights, but if he thought he'd wronged you, he'd make it right somehow, no matter what it cost him."

Jared snorted and shook his head. "The man started a fight with me, and I don't know why!"

"Did you ask?" Gonzo said. "You were strung out. You and him both had the monkey, only he's the one who stayed clean since the first time you dragged him to his first twelve-step. You're the one who fell, Homey."

"The fucker got me locked up!" Jared shouted. "I coulda got off! We both coulda got off had he kept his fuckin' mouth shut! Sonovabitch was jealous I was hangin' with T-Bone!"

"T-Bone bumped you off the wagon, Bro," Gonzo continued. "What kind of friend is that? You're lucky the bastard transferred while you were locked up."

"So maybe I misjudged him, but I'm right about Stormie."

"I'm not gonna argue about it, Bro," Gonzo sighed. "But if Stormie was such a prick, why didn't he do something to you for all the times you badmouthed his rep?"

"Whose side are you on?" Jared snapped. "The dude got me locked up and cost me a primo job in the Visiting Park!"

"All right, that's enough!" C. J. growled, rolling another cigarette. "Jared's going back to the freeworld tomorrow, and all you're doing is getting him into a fighting mood." He gave a meaningful glance at Gonzo. "We want our boy in a good state of mind when he hits the streets."

The others nodded as they thoughtfully lit up. "You say you worked in the Vee-Pee for a while?" Logan asked Jared.

"Yeah. Why?"

"I was just thinking---after you got locked up, a guy named "Carp" got that job. The man was a really fast worker; he set up a source in no time. Two weeks after he got the job, he and Sergeant Bromide got busted for a pound of hash." Logan took a deep drag. "Bromide got a clipped sentence just to keep the story out of the papers. But Carp got an outside rap for fifteen years. Sad thing is, he only had two years left on his bid. Why would a guy go and do a fucked-up thing like that?"

Buzzard guffawed, staring at Jared. "And you thought you had drug problems when you pissed your pants!" The others laughed, but Jared just stared at the wall, thinking, desperately wanting a cigarette.

Later they left, one by one, promising Jared they'd see him off at breakfast, exchanging hugs, not a convict thing to do, but they hugged any way, awkwardly, cautiously. At ten o'clock, all the cell lights in the dorm went off as they always did. C. J. turned in, and in a few minutes, he was snoring.

Jared could hear the television down the hall, another Jerry Springer trashtalkfest. He sat on his bunk in the dark, staring at his laundry bag bulging with his property. Freedom, like a waiting predator, was just hours away. At eleven, all the cell doors in the dormitory would be locked for good for the night and not reopened until 5:30 A. M., breakfast wakeup. Maybe there was still time.

Jared had unfinished business he had to take care of before locking down for the night. It haunted him like a red-hot ball of lead stuck in his craw that he could neither swallow nor vomit up. He pulled on his socks, then his brogans, lacing them up tight. It was called "strapping up," for times when traction was essential. He didn't want to do this, not with the freeworld and frightening changes just hours away. But there was still time, maybe.

He gently pulled his door shut without locking it, then headed down his wing, through the television room, and up the south wing. Stormie's cell was the last one to the left. A couple inmates in another cell were shouting at each other. The air stank of years of sweaty men and chemical cleaner. The cell door was wide open so both men could read by the light of the hallway---Stormie on the lower rack reading a *Hustler,* while his cellie on the upper rack, Art Smalley, read his Bible. Jared stepped up to the cell door, blocking the light. Both men looked up. At first, Stormie's face registered surprise, giving way to a quiet, seething rage. "What do you want, Martin?"

"I want to talk," Jared said.

"So talk."

"Alone."

Stormie glanced down, noticing that Jared was wearing his brogans. He reached for his own. "Art, we need the room."

"But it's almost lockdown!" Art whined.

"Art," Stormie growled, "I'm not fucking telling you twice!" He finished tying his shoelaces. Art put down his Bible, crawled off his rack, and quickly went out the door. Jared stepped in as Stormie reached over to push the door shut. The cell door window---a one-foot square opening---allowed a little light in from the hallway.

Stormie drew a weary breath. "Talk to me, Martin, I'm all ears."

"I've come to apologize," Jared said.

Stormie stared at him, his face barely visible. His arms looked smaller, the tattoos faded. The scar on his chest looked ripped open and rehealed, a thick discolored river through a forest of white chest hairs.

"Look," Jared went on. "I was wrong. I didn't understand, three years ago, when you started that fight with me. I didn't understand it when you told the Captain about it and got me locked up. I'm really sorry I turned my back on you. I'm sorry about everything."

Stormie glanced away, his face now completely in shadows. "Enlighten me, Martin. What are you talking about?"

Jared drew a breath. "I don't know why things happened the way they did. But you were looking out for me. I know that now."

"Was I?"

"I was really strung out that day. I had been for over a week."

Stormie snorted. "Imagine that," he said, bowing his shaggy head to the task of rolling a cigarette.

"The only asshole in creation who could talk me into going to an Alcoholics Anonymous meeting and giving up getting drunk on buck, and he is the one to fall off the wagon."

"I went back after I came out of the hole."

Stormie licked the cigarette paper and sealed it, then lit it and sucked in smoke. "You wouldn't listen to reason. You couldn't see that that punk was toxic. Pure shit. When I saw he was using you, I should have beat his ass, but you wouldn't have understood why. So I tried to talk with you. That was a mistake, too." He took another drag.

Jared shook his head. "By then, I wasn't just doing weed, but horse and coke as well. When I fall, I fall big time."

"All you did," Stormie said, "when I tried to talk to you, was run your mouth, rant and rave that I was jealous that you had a new friend. And, yeah, I guess I was, a little, but I couldn't talk any sense through that thick drug haze of yours. I got tired of arguing, just started swinging. Every bit of rage I was feeling for T-Bone got directed at you for all your stupidity. And then the fuckin' guards came. Didn't see us, but cuffed us up any way, took us to the Captain.

"But that was an opportunity for me. I knew I couldn't beat any sense into you, so when Stark pulled us in, I told him, yeah, we were fighting. If I got us locked up, if I got you locked up, you wouldn't be in the Visiting Park to make that drug sting with Sergeant Bromide that T-Bone had set you up for."

"But you knew you'd get that year in C. M. if we got locked up," Jared said. Stormie nodded. "Why risk it?"

Stormie shook his head. "There was nothing else I could do," he said. "There was no other way. I knew it was a setup, and I wasn't about to let T-Bone fuck over my Roaddog. That punk just wanted something to tell the Warden as leverage for a transfer. Had you got busted in that deal, you wouldn't get thirty days in the hole like you did. You would've gotten an outside charge, and another fifteen-year bid. I wasn't about to see that happen to you. I couldn't let that happen. I just couldn't"

Jared drew a deep breath. "I just tonight heard about the Parole Man, Stormie. I know he must've aggravated your date because of the fight that day and your C. M. time."

"Don't flatter yourself," Stormie grumbled. He finished the cigarette and tossed the butt in the toilet. "You forgot the two dudes I killed after I first fell and all the fights in between. But the Parole Board don't need a fuckin' reason. They were gonna slam me either way. Keep me and other old cons still in the old parole system in, so they could keep their goddamn jobs longer. Job security, you know. I don't blame you for their bullshit."

"I'm really sorry," Jared said. "I'm sorry about everything."

Stormie took a deep drag, then blew the smoke towards the floor. He looked away, scratching the back of his head. "Okay, Martin. You had your say. Don't let me keep you from wandering back to your cell."

"I just apologized," Jared said.

"So what do you want? A medal?"

"But I thought….."

"You thought what?" Stormie snapped around. "You thought that we'd maybe kiss and make up? That I'd clear your conscience before you went home tomorrow? I don't begrudge no man his freedom, Martin, even if I myself have to leave this shithole someday in a body bag. But you called me a snitch! A snitch!" Stormie glared at him, his face in shadows. "You rolled on me like I was slime. You never once came to me to hear my side, just decided I was a rat! You treated me like goddamn motherfucking puke!"

The finality of Stormie's words stung bitterly. "But I didn't know," Jared said. "Things were confusing for me back then."

"Don't give me that whiny shit. You coulda found out easy."

"C'mon, Stormie, all I'm askin' for is to make peace."

"You don't get it, do you, Martin?" Stormie snapped, pointing with the red tip of his cigarette. "I've been beat and kicked down and bruised and stabbed a lot more times than I care to remember, but nobody tore up my guts as bad as you did when you called me a fuckin' snitch! You were supposed to be my goddamn friend! I had to make myself not do anything about it!" Stormie's shoulders trembled in the shadows. He shook his head and looked away. "Now, take your almost-free punk ass outta my cell. You gave your apology, now get the fuck out."

Jared looked down. "I need to settle this."

Stormie took one last drag and tossed the butt in the toilet. "I thought you were claustrophobic, Punk."

"A month of Confinement broke me of that."

"Get out, Jared," Stormie whispered. "Get out now. There was a time I'd batter a fool like you into a coma, smash his nose, smear him, but I'm holding back now because we were once friends."

"Don't let me stop you," Jared growled.

"I got no more rap for you, Martin! Get the fuck out!"

"No!"

"Get out!" Stormie stood and shoved Jared backwards. Jared caught himself and shoved Stormie back, surprised that the old warrior almost lost his balance. At one time he was like a boulder, unbudgeable.

"Fucking bastard!" Stormie growled. His fist caught the side of Jared's head. Jared shook it off and swung back, his knuckles glancing off Stormie's chin, though it didn't seem to faze him. Even so, Stormie was surprised and angered, and began fighting in earnest. He caught Jared in the ribs and bloodied his nose, slamming his body into the door, locking it shut.

"Goddamn you, Jared!" Stormie screamed, pounding his stomach, his arms, his chest, his head. Jared realized too late that he started something he could not control. Each punch brought new levels of pain and dizziness. He couldn't even raise his arms to block them. Blood and saliva sprayed from his mouth. Two ribs cracked. His consciousness flickered as he slid to the floor. He tried to curl into the fetal position, but there seemed no defense against the violent barrage. Stormie was punching, kicking, spitting words Jared could no longer make out, yelling, yelling, yelling. Then he stopped.

Jared choked out a moan. He could hear the old con wheezing over his body. He couldn't bring himself to move. Each breath hurt his chest. Suddenly he felt himself gripped unceremoniously under the armpits, dragged deeper into the cell, and dropped onto the concrete floor. He opened his one good eye. Stormie was sticking his head out the cell door window. "Hey! Mack!" he yelled. "Mack! Yeah, my door accidentally locked. Get the brownshirt to click my button. Yeah, thanks!"

He stood by and waited, and when the door lock popped open electronically, he pulled his door partially open, then sat on the toilet. Opening a new bag of rip, he rolled two cigarettes, lighting one and dropping the other and his lighter on Jared's chest.

Jared hadn't smoked in three years, but he heaved himself up on one elbow, put the cigarette between his lips, and lit it with a shaking hand. He went into a racking cough after the first drag, then took another.

"You were nothing but a fucking punching bag," Stormie growled. "I said for years I shoulda taught you how to fight." As he took another drag, the glowing ember lit his face in red light. Jared could see how much he had aged. "You came here to my cell tonight with your boots strapped on," Stormie continued. "Like you were ready to get it on tonight. But all you wanted to do was to get me to whip your ass so I'd maybe have a change of heart. Well, that was really petty, especially from you. How could you be so fucking stupid?"

"I don't know what the hell I was thinking," Jared groaned. He wiped his mouth with the back of his hand and looked at the smeared blood. "Maybe I was trying to make amends."

"Amends!" Stormie grunted. "Was that the sixth or seventh step? I can't remember, it's been awhile." He laughed dryly. "Once I thought you were the smartest shit I ever met. When I moved into your cell, I didn't have a real problem with you being puny, but I was jealous of your thinker. Sure, you were low on street smarts, but you learned fast. You stood up to me, even though you knew I could whip you, even though you were trembling inside. I tried, I tried hard, but I couldn't break you. I was getting to really hate you for that. But when you took a stand against the Captain to save my ass, sticking your own neck out for an asshole like me, well, that's when I knew you had heart."

Stormie rolled two more cigarettes and tossed one to Jared. "Nobody but you coulda gotten me into A. A. Nobody but you coulda talked about Mozart and Debussy and Satchmo and Bird and kept my attention like I was listening to an Atlanta Falcons game. I thought you were Mensa Mike. But then you got stupid and got back into drugs and believing T-Bone's bullshit."

He sighed, almost choked. "Don't think I didn't feel bad about getting us locked up. I never forgot your fear of closed spaces. I knew it would eat into you after a day or so, and what with you going cold turkey… I was right down the hall. I heard you screaming your fucking guts out. T-Bone got you hooked worse than I thought. I hated him for what he did to you, almost hated myself for what I had to do." Stormie drew slowly on his cigarette. "But nobody twisted your arm to take that first hit. You chose that road, even if somebody did give you a nudge. You chose to be stupid."

"I'm sorry I put you through that shit."

"What shit?" Stormie glanced at him. "A year in confinement? When you stuck your neck out for me, I couldn't understand why. We hated each other, I treated you like garbage, and yet you pulled the line for me. And all this time I wondered why. Well, now I know, now I know. You did it because it was the right thing to do. You did it because it was personal, no matter what."

"Stormie…"

"Count time!" the hallway P. A. system blared. "Eleven O'clock Count! All inmates back to your cells and lock your doors!"

"Go," Stormie said. "The time for talk is over. I don't care how bad I beat you. I'm not your fucking priest."

"But..."

"Fuck the words, Jared. You can't ever make it right, no more than any of us can go back and undo our crimes, put back the stolen property, un-rape that woman, bring the murdered back to life." Stormie coughed into his fist. "You can't go back in time, and you can't expect me to, either. You're getting out. You can't come back here. There's nothing here for you. Nothing."

"But Stormie…"

"Jared, shut up and get out!" Stormie didn't look up. For the first time since he came into the room, Jared knew that his old friend truly hated him. It gnawed at him worse than anything ever had. He slowly rose from the floor, wincing at the pain.

Art pushed open the cell door, then stepped back, startled at Jared's bruised face. Jared took the handful of toilet paper Stormie handed him and dabbed at his bleeding nose and split lip. He would have to keep his head down when he went out the gate, maybe have a story ready, maybe say it was a really rough basketball game.

He stopped at the door and glanced back, but Stormie would not look at him. It hurt him, but not half as much as knowing what he had done to his friend, and what he could never take back. As he walked down the hall, trying to not think about tomorrow or the thing he would carry out the gate with him, he heard Art go into the room and lock the cell door.　　The click of old steel followed him back to his cell.

CREDITS

Artwork by T. Newton Schultz

Boots' Story about Princess - **Phoenix Rising
(May, 1995)**

The Night of Menapede - **The Endeavour
(February, 1993)
The Pillar (1989)**

The Gift - The Obelisk (1977)

Bicycle Ride in the Sky - The Obelisk (1984)

**The Boy who Was and Would Be - Poetic Space
(December, 1992)**

Grandfather Carp - Puck and Pluck (1991)

Listing - Experiments In Words (1991)

Calling - Cerberus (Autumn, 1997)

Planting - Phoenix Rising (November, 1995)

**Mustard Seed - Tribute: A Collection Of Poetry
And Short Stories (1999)**

**Tuesday's Scenario - Writers Open Forum
(January, 1993)**

The Man who Lived in the Cellar - The Endeavour
(January, 1993)
Popular Fiction
By Oregon
Authors
(Fiction anthology
- 1986)

Beaver Attack - The Endeavour (April, 1995)

A New Order - Popular Fiction by Oregon Authors
(Fiction anthology - 1986)

Tea for the Sunrise - Renegade (1994)

Eleven Roses - The Florida Times-Union
(December 23, 1989)
(2nd place, Christmas Story Contest,
By The Florida Times-Union)

The Language of Bees – Corrections (Fall 2001)
(Volume I Number 1)

Hunt - The Raconteur (January, 1979,
Volume 1, Number 1)
(ATHENIAN LITERARY SOCIETY)

Legend - The Endeavour (December, 1992)

Cold Wind Mountain - ????

Chowhall Blues (One act play) - (Performed
                                                July 14, 1993
                                                At Baker C.I.)
                                        (Honorable Mention,
                                        Drama category,
                                        1991 PEN Writing Awards
                                        for Prisoners)

Listen to the River - Fortune News (December, 1996)
                                (A Monologue, Three Acts)
                                (1st place, Drama category,
                                1994 PEN Writing Awards
                                        for Prisoners)

Asanas - Sun Dog (1993)

Sirens - Cerberus (May, 1995)

Symbiosis - Black Ice (1998)
                Fortune News (1998)
                (1st place, Fiction category,
                1997 PEN Writing Awards for Prisoners)

The Theory of Flight - State Street Review (1995)
                                (2nd Place, Fiction category
                                1991 PEN Writing Awards
                                        for Prisoners)

Feathers on the Solar Wind - 1998 PEN 25th
                                  Anniversary Booklet
                                  (1st Place, Fiction
                                  category)1998 PEN Writing
                                  Awards for Prisoners)

Kaddish - PEN America Center Website
                           PEN America Fielding Dawson
                           Citation for a Body of Work 2003

FIVE   1/97   T. NEWTON SCHULTZ

ASANAS
AND OTHER STORIES
By
David Martin Wood

www.ingramcontent.com/pod-product-compliance
Lightning Source LLC
Chambersburg PA
CBHW060151260626
47160CB00001B/222